Milly Johnson is a joke-writer, greetings card copywriter, newspaper columnist, after-dinner speaker, poet, winner of *Come Dine With Me*, *Sunday Times* Top Five author and winner of the RNA Romantic Comedy of the Year award both in 2014 and 2016.

She is half-Barnsley, half-Glaswegian so 1) don't mess with her and 2) don't expect her to buy the first round.

She likes cruising on big ships, owls, browsing in antiques shops, sighing at houses on Rightmove and is obsessed by stationery. She hates marzipan.

She is proud patron of Yorkshire Cat Rescue (www.yorkshirecatrescue.org), the Well – a complementary therapy centre for cancer patients allied to Barnsley Hospital, and the Barnsley Youth Choir (www.barnsleyyouthchoir.org.uk).

She lives happily in Barnsley with her fiancé Pete, her teenage lads Tez and George, a spoilt trio of cats and Alan the rabbit. Her mam and dad live in t'next street.

*The Queen of Wishful Thinking* is her thirteenth book.

Find out more at www.millyjohnson.co.uk or follow Milly on Twitter @millyjohnson

# milly
# johnson

## The Queen of
## Wishful Thinking

**SIMON &
SCHUSTER**

London · New York · Sydney · Toronto · New Delhi

A CBS COMPANY

First published by Simon & Schuster UK Ltd 2017
A CBS COMPANY

5 7 9 10 8 6

Simon & Schuster UK Ltd
1st Floor
222 Gray's Inn Road
London WC1X 8HB

www.simonandschuster.co.uk

Simon & Schuster Australia, Sydney
Simon & Schuster India, New Delhi

A CIP catalogue record for this book
is available from the British Library

Library Hardback Royal: 978-1-4711-6379-1
Trade paperback Royal: 978-1-4711-6175-9
B format paperback: 978-1-4711-6173-5
eBook: 978-1-4711-6174-2
eAudio: 978-1-4711-6243-5

This book is a work of fiction. Names, characters, places
and incidents are either a product of the author's imagination or are
used fictitiously. Any resemblance to actual people living or
dead, events or locales is entirely coincidental.

Typeset in Bembo by M Rules
Printed and bound by CPI Group (UK) Ltd, Croydon, CR0 4YY

MIX
Paper from
responsible sources
FSC® C020471

Simon & Schuster UK Ltd are committed to sourcing paper
that is made from wood grown in sustainable forests and support the Forest
Stewardship Council, the leading international forest certification organisation.
Our books displaying the FSC logo are printed on FSC certified paper.

This book is dedicated to my dog. Teddy was my darling 'bear'. He sat behind my chair when I wrote so I couldn't move, he sat on my feet when I watched TV, he even followed me into the loo to check I didn't need a bodyguard to protect me from any harmful toilet rolls. We were together all the time and I feel his loss tremendously because he took a part of me with him when he died. No one in my house now looks at me as if I am an international catwalk model and nothing rushes at me in a red blur of excitement when I walk into the house as if I have been gone for months, when in reality, I've just nipped to the garage to get fish fingers out of the freezer. The space at the side of my desk is cold and empty because he was my writing buddy, a patient, loving, huge, warm presence.

If you're an animal person you'll 'get it', if you're not then your heart will be less broken in life but you'll miss out on so much. I wouldn't swap with you.

*Teddy Johnson, Eurasier,*
*11.11.2008–11.10.2016*

*First wish it.*
*Then think of yourself doing it.*
*Then do it.*

THE QUEEN OF WISHFUL THINKING

# Prologue

All Lewis Harley could really remember about that night was thinking, *Is this how it ends?* His body was in chaos but his brain was running along a parallel track of clarity calmly observing what was going on across the way, deeply regretting that he had not had the chance to retire from the rat race and open up the antiques shop which had been in his plans since . . . well, since forever. All those years with his delicious secret ambition tucked up inside him and he'd been cut off at the pass. He'd been an idiot, presuming he'd never be the recipient of such a cruel curveball. And now it was too late.

The pain was in his shoulders, his arms, his back – everywhere but in his chest strangely enough, the place he would have imagined a heart attack would choose as its centre. But still he knew he was having one, and that any moment now, he would be heading towards the famous tunnel of bright light on a one way ticket.

So when Lewis Harley woke up in hospital to a trio of smiling medical faces, he resolved that he would take the gift of this second chance and live the life he had wished for himself.

There will be a report from the *Trumpet* FM roving reporter Ailsa Shaw from the Plot of Gold Antiques, Summer Hill this Saturday. Proprietor Leslie Harley is providing a buffet to celebrate the first six months of being open and all are welcome. After having had a heart attack, Leslie had a total carrier change from investment bonking to antique dealing. There will also be a full written report in the *Daily Trumpet* in our Shop-till-you-Drop supplement next Wednesday.

# Chapter 1

Bonnie Brookland tried to concentrate on polishing the smears out of the cabinet door and block out the nasal voice of her boss Ken Grimshaw spouting the biggest load of bull she'd heard all year, but he was nigh on impossible to ignore at that volume.

'You see, it's just a lot of old junk really, love, so twenty-five quid would be my final offer,' he was saying to the little old lady who had just handed him a box full of what she'd hoped were treasures. People did it so often. They came through the doors hoping they'd leave ten minutes later as millionaires after watching a couple of *Antiques Roadshow*s and *Cash in the Attic*s. They presumed every decorated egg was a Fabergé, every cracked blue and white vase was a Ming. And even if they were, asking Ken Grimshaw to value them was a huge mistake because, Rolex or rubbish, he'd automatically say they were junk so he could offer peanuts. Bonnie couldn't see all of what was in the old lady's cache, but she did spot a white Holmegaard Gulvase vase on top which was quite rare and alone worth more than the twenty-five pounds which Grimshaw was offering her for everything. He didn't know as much as he purported to about antiques, but he'd definitely identified that piece correctly because it had set off his facial tic, which is what usually happened when he recognised something of value and knew he was going to get it for a song.

Bonnie had worked at Grimshaw's since she was a schoolgirl, first just weekends then full-time after leaving school. Once upon a time it had been Sherman and Grimshaw's because her dad, Brian Sherman, and Ken's father Harry had been in partnership, but when Brian became ill, Harry had bought him out, though, as a mark of the respect in which he held his friend, he kept the Sherman name above the door alongside his own. Harry had been very good to Bonnie and she'd loved working for him and had learned a lot from him over the years. He'd been a fair man, a respected man and the shop had been beautiful. Then he'd died suddenly two years ago and his revolting son had taken over the business and it had gone downhill faster than an overweight bull on a bobsleigh. It was full of junk now, car boot stuff, give or take a few lovely but ridiculously overpriced bits of jewellery in cabinets. Bonnie knew that many of the gemstones in them were fake. People automatically presumed if a stone was set in gold, it was the real McCoy, even if the 'ruby' had scratch marks on it or there were tiny bubbles in a 'sapphire', but Ken had advertised them all as if they were. He was prepared to take a risk that he wouldn't be found out. So far, he was winning.

Harry Grimshaw had valued Bonnie's extensive knowledge, her intuition and her wonderful way with people. Ken Grimshaw treated her like something nasty that he'd stood in. As far as he was concerned, she was there to sell things, clean up, make the tea and occasionally, when his cronies were in, to leer at. They'd make under-the-breath smutty comments about her as if they were all in a seventies sitcom. Bonnie hated the days when they came in, but she needed the job so she put up with them.

Ken reached in his pocket and pulled out a creased tenner and when he went into the back room for the rest, Bonnie reckoned she had a window of thirty seconds tops. She darted over to the old lady and spoke rapidly to her in a low voice.

'Don't take his money. Go to another antique shop. That vase alone is worth much more than he's offering.'

'Really?' came the reply, along with a plume of warm breath which showed up in the cold air because Ken didn't waste money on heating.

Bonnie raised her finger to her lips. 'Shh. Don't say I said anything.'

She managed to be back into glass-cleaning position by the time Ken reappeared to see the old lady replacing her things in the box.

'I think I'll see if another shop is interested,' she said. 'You're not paying me enough.'

Ken shrugged. 'Of course you're at liberty to do that but I could have saved you some shoe leather. What about thirty quid then?'

The old lady stole a glance over Ken's shoulder at Bonnie who was shaking her head.

'Thank you but there's a nice antiques shop in Spring Hill Square,' said the old lady. 'I'll try there.'

Ken laughed. 'You'll get even less there, love. He's only been in the game five minutes. Wouldn't know a Vincent Van Gogh from a Dick Van Dyke.'

The old lady pointed at Bonnie. 'She said that vase was worth a lot by itself.'

Ken Grimshaw's head twisted sharply to Bonnie and she felt an instant stun of embarrassment. She knew that she was in for it as soon as they were alone. And she was right.

Ken Grimshaw started shouting the moment the door had closed on the old lady.

'You snidey bitch. You've got a nerve, haven't you? If you think I'm paying you for sending people away to rivals you've got another pissing think com—' He snapped off his rant as if he had just realised something. 'You've done this before, haven't you? No wonder I've got no frigging customers left.'

'No I have not, though I admit I don't know how I've stopped myself, but this was one step too far. You could have given that woman a fair price and still made a decent enough profit. Your dad would be disgusted if he were here, Ken Grimshaw.'

'Well he's not here, is he, he's dead,' said Ken, spittle spraying from his mouth. 'He and that stupid bastard of a father of yours might have been soft, but I'm not and I'm not paying you to send people to other fucking dealers. You should be working over there, love,' and he stabbed his finger at the window towards the Hospice charity shop across the street. 'In fact you can piss off and ask them for a job. Go on.' He stomped into the small, scruffy office at the back of the shop and returned with Bonnie's handbag which he threw on the floor at her feet. 'Now fuck off and don't come back, you cheeky cow.'

Anger pulsed through Bonnie's whole body. As much as she needed this job, she couldn't work for this vile human being one more minute but she bit down on what she would have liked to have thrown at him because she needed her wage. It would be bad enough going home and telling

Stephen she was now unemployed without having to add that she'd worked nearly a month for nothing.

'You owe me three and a half weeks' money please,' she said, her voice riding a tremble. 'I'll take that, then I'll go.' She held out her hand, reading from his expression that she had about as much chance of getting it as Oliver Twist had of getting a second bowl of gruel.

He pushed his face into hers and let loose a loud 'Ha', his breath rank from the cigarettes he chain-smoked. 'You're sacked, love. Gross misconduct. Here, that's all you're getting because it's all you're frigging worth.' He picked up a two pence piece from the counter and tossed it at her. 'You can whistle for the rest. Take me to fucking court, I dare you.'

If only her dad or Joel had still been around. They'd have flown up here for her as soon as she told them about this and not only would she have had her wages but Ken Grimshaw would be missing his front teeth. But her dad was gone and so was Joel and the man she was now married to would equate such confrontation with Neanderthals.

Bonnie bent down to pick up her things. She was aware that Ken was watching, enjoying the sight of her bending in front of him, scooping up the items that had spilled from her bag when he'd thrown it. She walked as steadily to the door as her shaky limbs would let her, feeling his eyes burn holes in her back. It was of small consolation that he'd have no one to manage the shop whilst he was on a stag week in Benidorm at the end of the month. He'd be furious later on, when he thought of that.

# Chapter 2

Bonnie was too shaken to go straight home, plus Stephen was on an afternoon off and would be no doubt playing Wagner at full blast in the lounge, which was not conducive to unwinding. She unlocked her car door, belted herself in and set off in her ancient Vauxhall. It had been a faithful old rust-bucket, but it was nearing the end of its days and she doubted very much it would get through its next MOT in August without a small fortune being spent on it. The thought of having to ask Stephen for things she needed always filled her with dread. He made it into such an ordeal, she felt like Bob Cratchit asking Scrooge for a day off at Christmas. The last time she'd needed a front tyre, she'd had to 'apply' for the money as if he were a bank. He had made her shop around for prices and list them and then, after all that, he'd taken the car to a garage and had a part-worn one fitted. It was Stephen who put the most money into their joint savings account, therefore he was in charge of it, he said.

Bonnie knew her dad would be spinning in his grave about her situation. He'd saved all his life hoping to leave her enough money to be comfortable, only for most of it to be spent on his nursing home costs. Bonnie could have found a cheaper home but her dad deserved the best and she made sure he had it. He'd been so strong, the illness which crippled his brain so quickly had taken years to kill his body. The little that hadn't been absorbed, Stephen had taken care of for her, adding it to the joint savings that she wasn't allowed to touch.

She drove away from town and found herself on the Penistone road where Spring Hill was situated. She hadn't heard of it before and was pleasantly surprised to find a square of shops around a pretty central garden area. There was a florist, an old-fashioned toyshop, a gift shop and next to a quaint-looking teashop in the corner, an antiques shop. So the old lady had been right then. The Pot of Gold, it was called. It had a painted wooden sign hanging from elaborately scrolled metalwork. There was a rainbow arcing over the lettering and adjacent to the last 'd', a small golden pot complete with radiating lines of shimmer. Bonnie had nothing to lose and everything to gain by going in and asking if they had a job, but the way her luck had been going the last few years, she expected an instant rebuff.

As she passed by the window, she noticed there were a couple of customers in so she went into the teashop instead to wait until they had gone, plus it would calm her down having a breather and a coffee. Her nerves were pulled to the tautness of harp strings. She was forty-two and had never had to apply for a job in her life until now.

The teashop was pretty from the outside with its hanging baskets full of pink and cream scented flowers, but inside it was even lovelier. The pink and cream theme was repeated on the painted walls and there were standing cabinets full of gorgeous book-themed gifts: handbags, journals, scarves, quills. Behind the teashop counter was a slim, smiling lady in an apron and a reed-thin boy scratching his chin and hiding a grin. A tall, handsome man with a twinkle in his eye was standing cross-armed and teasing the lad about his stubble.

'Ah, you don't need a razor for that. You could wipe it off with a cloth.' The man was laughing, his accent strong Northern Irish.

'You take no notice of him, Ryan. He's just jealous of your youthful charm ... Hello,' the lady with the apron called to Bonnie. 'Please take a seat, I'll be over in a minute.'

There was just one table empty, next to a wall covered in postcards from all over the world. Bonnie sat down on the heart-backed iron chair at the side of a large ginger cat in a basket which she thought was a stuffed toy, until it yawned and then settled its great head back down onto its paws. She picked up a menu. *Charlotte Brontë Brandy Snap Basket*, she noticed. That sounded lovely, maybe one day she'd come back and treat herself. But for now a coffee would suffice.

Bonnie let the calm air of the teashop work its magic on her frazzled nerves. She realised she'd left a cardigan and the book she read in her lunch hours back at Ken Grimshaw's shop. Well, they'd have to stay put because she would never set foot in there again. She felt sick about not getting her wage, although the loss of the money was secondary to the prospect of the lecture she'd get from Stephen about it. She wished she didn't have to go home today. Or ever. Her dad had told her many times that her mum said if you could imagine doing something in your head, you could do it in real life. She'd been wrong though. Bonnie had been pic-turing herself leaving Stephen and his house for years, yet she was still there.

She finished her coffee and waved a thank you at the lady with the apron and crossed her fingers that the antiques shop was empty now. It was. She tried to will some steel into her backbone by reciting a precis of her mother's favourite saying. *Come on, Bonnie. Wish. Think. Do.* Her whole body felt as if it were shaking when she opened the door of the Pot of Gold.

# Chapter 3

The Pot of Gold antiques shop in Spring Hill Square belonged to Lewis Harley and it was everything he had planned it to be during his months of recuperation. He had created a bygone haven of tranquillity with his choice of decor. The walls were painted in period colours of smoky green, creamy ivory, bronze red, muted gold; the solid display cabinets were predominately dark wood. Clocks charmed the walls, their chimes aged and mellow, bright but gentle lighting complimented everything it touched and the perfume of polish and old books pervaded the air. More than once Lew had been told by customers that they felt as if they had gone back in time when they had crossed over his threshold.

Footfall was building but much more slowly than he had hoped for. It wasn't viable for the large L-shaped shop to be filled with Lew's finds alone so he rented out space for traders to sell their goods. Some only leased a single cabinet, a few wanted larger chunks of floor space to display furniture but so far the fees collected didn't cover the rent that Lew paid out to the landlord Mr McCarthy. Too many units were empty for any profit to be made. He needed customers to attract dealers, he needed dealers to attract customers and he hadn't worked out yet how best to break the cycle. But he would, because Lew was determined to make it work. The Pot of Gold was a dream come true for him. He loved walking in through the doors every morning to the sight of all the beautiful old treasures, he loved the smell, the noise, the peace of his new world after his fraught, pressured past world of investment banking. There was just the one major fly in the ointment: his sales assistant Vanda Clegg.

It was a very different Vanda Clegg who came in for the interview last year to the one who now worked in the shop. 'Interview Vanda' was smiling and genteel, professional and knowledgeable. 'Shop Vanda' was moody, moany, lazy and didn't seem to know her arts from her nouveau. Thinking back to that interview, Vanda had steered the ship of their conversation to waters in which she was obviously safe, sailing in between familiar islands of Clarice Cliff, Cranberry glass and Cloisonné. He'd been too easily impressed by what, he now suspected, was a scripted performance. And, on second reading, her carefully written references looked a little suspect too. 'Vanda would suit *many* work environments,' said one, as if Vanda would suit many – but not theirs. The references supplied were all written with a cold pen, he now felt, filled with telling phrases such as: '*generally* pleasant', and Vanda apparently had 'a *considerable effect* on workplace morale' in her two months working at Hobbyworld. It didn't say that effect was a positive one. He also wondered if the same author who wrote 'full of chatter' really wanted to write 'could talk a glass eye to sleep'.

He'd presumed that Vanda, at forty-four – the same age

as himself – would have a seasoned work ethic, be reliable, responsible and honest. He had no proof that she was on the fiddle, but a couple of times he hadn't been able to balance the takings against the ledger and a few items had disappeared without trace, coincidentally from the blind spot area which the security camera didn't cover, and only the electrician, Lew and Vanda knew that.

The grandfather clock behind the counter, which was the only one in the shop that was set to the exact time, tolled a deep bass note to mark the half-hour which meant that Vanda was over twenty minutes late back from her lunch. Again. Lew had never been a hardline boss; he found that most of his staff respected the leeway he gave them and the ones that took advantage of his good nature didn't last long. Vanda wasn't doing his blood pressure any good and he wondered if that might be a sackable offence. He had just stepped into the office to switch on the kettle when he heard the tinkle of the bell above the front door. He doubled back expecting to see Vanda huffing and puffing and apologising for her tardiness because there was a five-mile tailback of traffic/road-block/alien invasion, but instead he found a woman considerably more attractive than the stout, blubbery Vanda. She was of average height, average build with dark-brown hair tied in a ponytail behind her but there was nothing ordinary or average about her eyes which were large, hazel and beautiful.

'Hello,' she said, smiling nervously. 'I'm looking for the owner, would that be you?'

'Yes that's me,' said Lew. 'How can I help you?'

'My name is Bonnie Brookland, I'm local and I know it's a long shot but I wondered if you had an assistant's job going.'

Oh if only, thought Lew. His face creased up with regret. 'I'm sorry, I don't.'

'Like I say, it was a long shot,' said Bonnie, shrugging her shoulders. 'Oh well. Thank you.' Her eye caught a painting on the wall as she turned to go which stopped her in her tracks. She leaned over to study it.

'It's not an original, hence the price,' said Lew.

'Some of the copies can cost a bob or two though,' smiled Bonnie. 'You'll have heard of Percy Lake, of course?'

'Oh yes.' Lew nodded, impressed that she mentioned him. There had been a resurgence of interest in old Percy following the unearthing of some of his work in the area. He'd been a genius art forger, as good as the grand masters whose work he copied. 'This was done by a local artist. Student. She's very good. She takes famous paintings and gives them her own twist, hence the London skyline under the Starry Night. I said I'd try and sell a few of her paintings to help pay off her accumulating university debt.'

He smiled and Bonnie noticed his even square teeth, his strong chin, the sunray wrinkles spanning out from the corners of his eyes. This was a man who had smiled a lot in his life, she thought. Stephen owned no such marks.

There was a rack of old pipes on the table underneath the picture.

'You obviously haven't had the Pied Piper in here then?' Bonnie said. 'You wouldn't still have those Petersons if he'd seen them.'

'Sorry?' said Lew. He was aware that some of the dealers had nicknames – Starstruck, the autograph seller, for instance – but he hadn't come across the Pied Piper.

'The Pied Piper. He collects pipes and especially likes Petersons. I'll send him your way the next time . . .' Bonnie's voice trailed off. She was going to say that she'd send him this way the next time he came into the shop, except that she didn't work there any more and so she probably wouldn't see him again. She sighed and Lew heard it and wondered why the sound was so deep and sad.

Curious of the depth of her knowledge he picked up one of the other pipes from the rack.

'What about this one? Any good, do you think?'

Bonnie took it from him and immediately raised her eyebrows. 'Very nice,' she said. 'A Dunhill Bruyere. Early 1970s. You've priced it too low at seventy-five pounds. If the Pied Piper came in here, he'd offer you one hundred and fifty pounds for that but he'd pay two hundred and ten, maybe twenty, depending on how desperate he was to own it.'

'Really?' said Lew. Pipes weren't his speciality. He'd been sold a job lot of them and he knew that he would have made a profit at seventy-five pounds for the Dunhill, but maybe he should have gone back and done his research properly.

He noticed the ring that Bonnie was wearing on her middle finger when she passed the pipe back to him. An eye-shaped piece of amethyst mounted on a gold twist. It looked identical to one which he'd had in the jewellery cabinet a couple of months ago, until it disappeared into the ether.

'I see Stickalampinit Stuart is renting some space from you.' Bonnie pointed to a large cabinet where various lamps were displayed.

'Is that what he's known as?' grinned Lew.

'Stickalampinit for short,' Bonnie grinned back. 'Although it's not that much shorter, is it? Anything he can find to make into a lamp and he will do: telephones, bottles, radios, pigeon clocks, even an old mannequin torso once. It was the ugliest thing I've ever seen. Not surprisingly it didn't sell and it took up a ridiculous amount of space.'

'Quite a character, isn't he?'

That was one way of putting it. Stickalampinit was like Tigger on Prozac. Lew had never met anyone as full of beans.

'He's convinced that one day he'll win the Turner prize,' chuckled Bonnie. 'And, of course, if he's displaying here, you'll have had his friend in – Butterfly Barry. He doesn't sell but he buys anything with butterflies on. He's obsessed by them.'

'Velvet jacket, quiff?'

'That's him.'

'Yes, he has been in and bought a few things.'

Bonnie flicked at a stray hair that had fallen over her face. The ring caught his eye again. 'That's pretty,' he said.

Bonnie spread her fingers and looked at it. She'd fallen in love with it as soon as it had come in to the shop. Ken said she could have it instead of a wage if she came in on her weekend off so he could go to the races with his cronies. 'I thought so too,' she smiled. 'I got it from the place where I work.' *Used to work,* her brain reminded her.

'Oh, where's that?' asked Lew.

'Grimshaw's Antiques,' replied Bonnie.

'Oh, you work there, do you?' Lew had paid it a visit once, eyeing up the competition, but found only badly displayed rubbish in a freezing environment. He hadn't seen the woman in front of him in there though, just a swarthy, miserable-looking man reading a newspaper which was laid flat out on the counter.

'My dad used to be the joint-owner. I've worked there

since I could reach the till. It was very different back then, of course.'

Lew did a quick calculation of how many years that could be. He thought she might be late thirties, so quite a few then. Plenty of time to build up considerable knowledge. He nodded, impressed.

'I didn't even know this place existed until today,' said Bonnie. 'Have you been here long?'

'We had our six-month anniversary a couple of weeks ago,' replied Lew. 'I took an ad out in the *Daily Trumpet* to invite people along for a celebration but they printed the wrong date, the wrong place and the wrong everything else. They promised to send a "roving reporter" for their radio station, but she never turned up so the article she was going to write for their supplement the following week didn't appear either.'

'The *Daily Trumpet* are useless,' said Bonnie.

'You're telling me. They printed that I was once an investment bonker.'

'Oh no,' returned Bonnie, covering her mouth and once again showing Lew that unusual ring. 'I hope you got your money back for the advert.'

'Oh yes.'

'And are you busy?' Bonnie asked. This shop deserved to be. It had that indefinable feeling of a place that could attract treasure, plus it was warm and browse-friendly.

Lew bobbed his head from side to side in a 'so-so' gesture. 'Not as much as I'd like, but I suppose it takes time to build up a new business. I gave the present dealers a rate they couldn't refuse for six months to bring them in. But I know I'll lose them very soon if we don't get more customers.'

'Do you—'

Then the bell above the door gave a mad jangle, cutting off Bonnie's question and in thundered Vanda, wheezing like an asthmatic steam engine. Lew prepared himself for the words, 'Sorry I'm late because . . .' but instead it was Bonnie who spoke next, and to Vanda.

'Hello there. I nearly didn't recognise you. You've changed your hair.' Bonnie smiled, not having the slightest clue of the impact her words would have on the woman she had just addressed.

Vanda momentarily froze, then she dropped her head and scurried quickly into the back room without saying anything in reply, leaving Bonnie looking slightly confused and Lew smelling a very large rat.

'You know my assistant?' he asked Bonnie.

Bonnie appeared slightly embarrassed. 'I thought I did, but . . .' she shook her head then looked down at the ring on her finger as if seeking an answer to the puzzle there.

With a low voice, Lew asked, 'Did she, by any chance, sell that ring to Grimshaw's?'

Bonnie was totally convinced it was the same woman who had sold a few things to Ken Grimshaw, including her lovely ring. But from the way the owner of the Pot of Gold was looking at her, there was more than met the eye to those transactions. She nodded slowly and felt the weight of a responsibility she wished she hadn't been lumbered with.

'You don't happen to have had anyone sell you a Bionic Man, still boxed, in the last month, do you?' he asked her. 'And a stylophone, a Game Boy, an old Acorn Electron computer maybe?'

Bonnie knew that these were all things that the portly woman with long jet-black hair had sold to Ken. Plus some jewellery – her dead aunt's, she said; the toys she'd found in the loft of a house she'd recently bought. Even with her short blonde hair, rather than the shoulder-length black, Bonnie would have recognised her face, especially with the protruding brown mole near her upper lip.

'I ought to go,' said Bonnie, feeling that she'd inadvertently kicked a hornet's nest. The day was just getting better and better. 'Thanks anyway.'

As she turned, Lew touched her arm to halt her. 'Please, leave me your name and number. Just in case something turns up.'

'Certainly,' said Bonnie and scrabbled around inside her bag for a pen. Lew picked up a pad from the counter. He had a feeling something might be turning up sooner rather than later now. Bonnie wrote down her details.

He hadn't caught her name when she'd first introduced herself. Bonnie Brookland, Lew read. Bonnie suited her.

'Bye then.' Bonnie flashed a strained smile, hoping she hadn't caused as much trouble as she thought she might have. She would have liked to have stayed and wandered around the shop but thought it best to leave – and quickly. She'd visit the supermarket before going home so she could delay telling Stephen that she'd lost her job. He wouldn't be very pleased. But then, was he ever?

Vanda had clearly been waiting until Bonnie had gone before emerging from the back room. She didn't seek eye contact from Lew but went straight into work mode, and if that wasn't cause for suspicion, nothing was. Lew didn't say a word at first, but made sure that she saw him take the book out of the drawer where he recorded any losses. He could feel her glancing at him, wondering when he was going to mention something. He let her sweat for a full ten minutes and didn't look up when he eventually addressed her but kept his eyes down on the pages of the book.

'Vanda, quite a few things have gone missing over the past months, wouldn't you agree?'

Vanda mumbled something under her breath by way of an answer.

'I hear that some of them have found their way to Grimshaw's. Imagine that. Someone stealing and selling them stupidly on their own doorstep.'

There was no comment, even though Vanda was listening to his every word as she adjusted pieces on display.

Lew went on, his voice calm, controlled, masking the anger. 'I think that if that person were so brainless not to realise they could be traced very easily, then she would be as well getting out of the way before the police were called in. Wouldn't it be a wise move on her part if that person got their coat and left instead, knowing that nothing more would be said about it if she did?'

Out of the corner of his eye, Lew noticed that Vanda had gone into the back room. He opened the drawer and replaced the book. By the time he had closed it again, Vanda Clegg had swept past him with her bag and her coat as speedily as her dumpy little legs could carry her. The bell above the door signified her exit and Lew knew that she wouldn't be returning. The mystery thief had vacated the premises.

# Chapter 4

Bonnie pulled up outside 39 Greenwood Crescent with a boulder-like heaviness in her stomach. Her mother's philosophy didn't work so well for her. She unclipped her seat belt slowly, anything to delay walking into the house. It had never felt like her home, not the way the house she grew up in had done. That house had closed its arms around her when she walked through the front door and she felt safe and calm there; this one was just bricks held together with mortar that she slept in, ate in and cleaned. She and Stephen hadn't chosen it together: he was already living there when she moved into it thirteen years ago and his personality was already firmly stamped upon it. It was a nice enough mid-sized detached house in the bowl of a cul-de-sac with neat front and back gardens. It had three bedrooms, one with an ensuite, and a house bathroom upstairs, a long lounge and dining kitchen downstairs and a rectangular conservatory at the back where Bonnie liked to sit and read when Stephen was playing opera on his ancient CD player tower system or watching highbrow programmes on the TV. There was a single garage where he parked his Mondeo; Bonnie always used the drive. The garden was devoid of a single dandelion, the edges precise, the square of lawn spirit-level flat. The borders were full of run-of-the-mill bedding plants: Lobelia, Busy Lizzie, Dianthus. Everything was trim and ordered and balanced ... and totally without character. Bonnie played a game with herself when she switched off the light at nights and settled down to sleep. She used to plan her dream house, right down to the contents of the cupboards. She had a few of these houses, depending on how she was influenced by *Grand Designs* that week but she wished herself into them all with the same kind man and the same large red dog. One of them was a mansion with secret passages and a lake, one was a cosy canal boat. Another was a small cottage covered in ivy with a wild garden at the back which attracted all sorts of butterflies, all very different but what they shared was that they screamed out colour and individuality. And all of them were free of the great dark cloud that hung above Greenwood Crescent.

Stephen would be furious that she was out of a job. He wouldn't shout, because he rarely shouted but he would convey his displeasure with a series of sighs and lifts and drops of his shoulders as if she were a child in whom he was dreadfully disappointed. As for why she lost her job, well, he wouldn't see it that she was trying to stop an old lady from being ripped off, he would view her intervention as poor business sense, idiocy, treason. He would tut and shake his head quite a few times over the next couple of days, reminding her that her 'disloyalty' was still playing in his brain. Oh, the irony that he could think of her as disloyal.

As she opened the car door, her mobile phone rang in her bag. She didn't recognise the number that came up on the screen.

'Hello,' she said, answering it tentatively.

'Hi, it's Lewis Harley. From Pot of Gold.'

It took Bonnie a couple of beats to realise that this was the nice man from the antiques shop. Taking her details was the equivalent of 'keeping her name on file' which is what Ken Grimshaw used to say when anyone came in looking for a job, then he'd slam-dunk those details in the bin behind his counter.

'I'd like you to come in and see me if you would. It's about a job. I have an unexpected vacancy.'

Bonnie gulped before answering him. 'Really?'

'Erm, yes, really.' He seemed amused by her tone.

'I'm free now,' blurted Bonnie. 'If that's not too soon.' Anything not to have to confess to Stephen that she was unemployed.

'If that's convenient for you, then it's convenient for me.'

'I'll be there in twenty minutes.'

Such was Bonnie's enthusiasm that she was there in fifteen.

\*

Bonnie had to stop herself from racing to Spring Hill Square. She had to get this job. Surely life wouldn't be so cruel as to present her with this quirk of fate only to snatch it back from her.

Lew smiled as she opened the door. That was the second time she had been in his shop and the second time he felt as if she brought something in with her that whipped up the air, adding a sprinkle of lightness to it. Vanda weighed it down with her presence, and her industrial-strength perfume that smelled like fly spray.

'Hello there,' he called and lifted his hand in a wave.

'Hi,' said Bonnie, feeling breathless with nerves. The Pot of Gold was so much nicer than Grimshaw's, at least as it was now, but it reminded her very much of how Grimshaw's used to be when her dad and Harry styled it. A step over the threshold and you were in a different world, an older, calmer place. People used to say that it was better than therapy going into the shop, soothing and relaxing.

'I'm so glad you could come back,' said Lew, going to the door and locking it. He hung a sign in the window which had a clock with adjustable hands. The shop would open again at three, it read. 'We won't be disturbed if I close for twenty minutes,' he said. 'Would you like a coffee?'

'I'm fine, thanks.'

'Well I'm having one,' said Lew. 'Have a look around whilst the kettle is boiling.'

'Oh,' Bonnie shrugged. 'Okay. A coffee would be nice then. Just a dash of milk for me, please.' She took herself on a quick tour of the shop whilst she waited for him to return and thought it was a shame that so many of the units were empty. She would bet that her friend Valerie, who dealt in quality vintage clothes, didn't know about this place, and if Valerie didn't know about it then Jackpot and the dealers they hung around with wouldn't know either. She recognised the long display cabinets of Thimble Simon, and a small bay in which the walls were covered in framed signed photos. The unit was called 'Autograph Hunters' and she knew that the seller was called Starstruck, because many of the autographs were ones he'd collected himself over many years and had provenance for. She could see a sign with the name 'Mart Deco' on it. Martin dealt with fabulous antiques from the Deco era: 1925–1939. But there were many familiar traders' names missing who would help to draw in custom.

Lew returned with two mugs and set them on top of the huge central counter which had once graced a gentleman's outfitters.

'You've got some good dealers in here,' said Bonnie. 'I recognise most of them. You did well to get Uncle Funky and his toys because last I heard he was giving it up. He's particularly bonkers, isn't he?' She laughed and Lew thought what a nice sound it was. Vanda had a shriek of a cackle which he was always afraid would start cracking all the glass.

'Oh yes, Uncle Funky. I'm presuming that isn't his real name,' grinned Lew, picturing the wild-haired tall thin gent, always in a suit complete with waistcoat and novelty bow tie.

'I have no idea what his real name is. I'm not sure he does any more,' replied Bonnie. He had stopped renting a unit from Grimshaw's months ago. He'd been the first person to ever rent a cabinet from Harry and yet Ken hadn't even bothered to try and persuade him to stay.

'They're quite an eclectic bunch of people, aren't they?' smiled Lew. Which was a polite way of saying that a lot of them were absolute nutters.

'I was only a little girl when I first met most of them,' said Bonnie, sipping her coffee. 'Billy Boombox must be eighty-five if he's a day. He deals in ghetto blasters and Walkmans, radios, that kind of stuff. If you haven't heard of him, you soon will because he's not selling anything at Grimshaw's. But then, no one is.' Bonnie sighed then thought she'd better add some sort of an explanation to that. 'It's not my sales technique that's at fault, just in case you're wondering. Ken Grimshaw would be better running one of those bargain bin shops. He doesn't have the passion for antiques that his dad had and he's not big on fairness or goodwill. And his accounts are a mess which doesn't help and the dealers expect you to be dead straight with money . . . ' She realised she was talking too much and apologised. 'Sorry. I'd better let you get a word in, hadn't I?'

Lew liked her. He wasn't the sort of man who would use phrases such as 'he got a good vibe from someone' but today he would have broken a rule and said that. He got a very good vibe from Bonnie Brookland.

'I'm looking for someone full-time,' he said, putting his professional cards on the table. 'Someone that I can trust to leave in charge, someone who knows their onions. Nine to four-thirty, Tuesday to Saturday, Sundays ten till two and I shut Mondays, though that might change. I'm pretty easy going if you have a doctor's or dentist's appointment or anything like that. Coffee-making duties are split fifty-fifty between us.' He grinned, a lopsided, lazy and genuine grin that any male Hollywood star would be proud to own, thought Bonnie. He went on, 'You'll know lots more about the business than I do, so I'll be happy for any tips. Seven pounds fifty an hour is what I was thinking as a starting wage. Is . . . does that sound all right to you?'

He knew it wasn't a lot for her expertise at thirty pence per hour above the minimum wage and he fully expected her to pick up her handbag and say they were both wasting their time, but she didn't. Bonnie nodded approvingly.

'That sounds fine,' she said. She would be up on what she earned at Grimshaw's by over a pound an hour – Ken didn't acknowledge the minimum wage – and this looked an infinitely nicer place to work.

Lew knew that he shouldn't offer her the job straightaway.

He should ask for a reference, quiz a few of the dealers who might know her. Acting impetuously had gained him Vanda Clegg, but he found himself sealing the deal without heeding his own warnings, thanks to that ridiculous 'good vibe'.

'So, when could you start?'

'Tomorrow,' Bonnie replied, barely leaving a beat after his question.

'You don't need to work any notice?'

'No.' Bonnie shook her head and saw his tilt slightly, the way her dog's used to when he was trying to make sense of something. Maybe he was thinking that she was walking out of her job and leaving Grimshaw's in the lurch, not exactly loyal. Oh, that word again.

'I left Grimshaw's today,' said Bonnie and a voice in her head warned her to stop at that. *But what if he rang Ken asking for a reference*, asked another voice. *Tell him the truth*. She dropped a heavy sigh, 'Look, Ken Grimshaw caught me telling an old lady to go somewhere else to sell a big box of items that she'd brought in. He was going to rip her off. She had a white Gulvase in there and he was only going to offer her a pittance for the lot. I couldn't let him do it. He threw me out on the spot.'

Lew looked back into her large hazel eyes, widened in anticipation of his opinion on that. She was wondering if she'd told him too much, he knew. But he respected her honesty. In comparison to Vanda Clegg, she was like a breath of fresh air in more ways than one.

Lew held out his hand to seal the deal. 'So I'll see you tomorrow at nine, Mrs Brookland. Welcome to the Pot of Gold.'

# Chapter 5

Lew was just turning off the lights in preparation for closing up for the evening when the doorbell tinkled and a customer walked in. An old lady holding a box.

'Oh are you shut?' she said.

'No, no, you're fine, come in,' said Lew, with a smile. 'I'll put the lights back on if you want to have a browse. No rush. I never turn a possible sale down.'

'I've not come to buy, I've come to sell. I'll be quick because I've got a taxi waiting.'

'Okay then,' said Lew, stepping forwards to take the box from her because she appeared to be struggling with it. She gave her arms a grateful shake when the weight was transferred.

Lew put the box down on the counter and carefully took out the most prominent piece, sticking out of the box, wrapped clumsily in newspaper. It was a white Gulvase. This had to be the lady Bonnie Brookland had told him about. He lifted it up to the light, checked it carefully for nibbles and cracks, but it was perfect. And the weight felt right for it to be a genuine piece. It still had the original Holmegaard sticker on it, bearing the Danish flag.

'Very nice,' he said. 'Very nice indeed.'

'Is it really?' asked the old lady. 'I went to another shop earlier on but the woman in there told me to go somewhere else to sell it.' She leaned over as if about to impart an onerous secret and was scared of being overheard. 'I think I dropped her in it. I feel awful because that bloke Grimshaw was only going to give me a few pounds for everything and she said it would be worth a bit more than that. Look at this.' And the garrulous old lady plunged her hand into the box and brought out a medal. 'That's got to be worth summat, 'an't it?'

Lew could see instantly that it was a fake. There was no age to it at all. The market was overrun with fakes, some of them clever ones too. The 'ancient' Chinese vase in the box which the old lady lifted out was a fake as well but the pot with the chipped top that she almost dropped onto the counter had interesting character marks. People presumed because there was damage to pieces that they were worthless, and Lew didn't like to think of how many treasures had ended up in the bin because of that misconception. Also in the old lady's stash was a coloured Chinese saucer, terribly cracked and repaired with iron staples. He guessed the saucer started off with a plain blue pattern in the 1600s, but then was painted over and repaired in the 1700s. Those staples were part of its history too.

'There's the matching cup in there,' said the old lady. 'It's knackered an' all.'

Lew felt prickles of excitement creep over his scalp. If this two-piece was genuine, it could be worth a small fortune. It was so hard to tell because there were whole streets in China filled with artisans producing plates complete with

overglaze and rivets, ageing them to look like ancient treasures. He'd need to take some time over making a decision
whether or not to buy them.

'And there's this, look.' It was a mug commemorating the
coronation of Edward VIII. 'They made these but he was
never crowned. That's got to be rare.'

Funny how people judged what was valuable, thought
Lew. You could pick them up for fifteen pounds on markets
everywhere yet an unused Nazi toilet roll could fetch eight
times that. Wrapped in newspaper in the bottom of the box
was a collection of carvings in white stone: a hand, a crab,
a disc, a hook. Lew felt the hairs on the back of his neck
stand up and a renewed wave of scalp-pricking ensued.

'I think these might be jade.'

'Give over, jade's green,' laughed the old lady. 'You trying
to pull the wool over my eyes?'

'No, I mean white jade. Where on earth did you get these
pieces from?'

'My husband's dad was a sailor,' she answered. 'When he
died the family went through his stuff like locusts. This box
was all that was left and so they gave it to us. We had it in
the cellar for years. I'd forgotten about it but I've just moved
into a maisonette and had to empty the house.'

'You do have a couple of nice pieces in here, but I'll need
to have a really good look at them. Do you want to leave
them with me? I promise I'll give you a fair price.'

The old lady narrowed her eyes. 'Aye, I'm full of them
tricks.'

He knew that if she took away her box, he wasn't likely
to see her again. He decided to take the chance that she had
something very special. He was absolutely sure the Gulvase
was genuine, even if nothing else was.

'What if I said a hundred and fifty pounds?'

The old lady spasmed so violently that her glasses nearly fell off. She clearly hadn't been expecting that much.

'Or, as I say, you can leave them with me for a few days and I'll—'

'I'll take the money,' said the old lady. 'That'll do nicely. I'm going on one of them coach holidays in Italy with my sister in September and that'll do towards my spend.'

'Would you like to give me your name and address,' said Lew. He knew that if the carvings and the cup and saucer were what he thought they might be, he wouldn't have slept easily in his bed knowing he'd paid so little for them.

'My name is Pauline Twist.' She started to recite her details before Lew had picked up a pen, so he had to ask her to repeat them. He sent her away with a hundred and fifty pounds and a big smile on her face. It seemed that Bonnie Brookland might have been a good luck charm to him today.

# Chapter 6

Just before Bonnie pulled into the estate, she rang Valerie's home on her mobile. Valerie was the only person she socialised with these days. One by one, over the years, all the girls who had been her friends had fallen away from her life for various reasons, but Valerie remained firm. It wasn't the deep sort of friendship where each was laid open to the other. Valerie had always played her cards close to her chest and Bonnie had never told her how unhappy she was in her marriage, though she suspected that Valerie had picked up on that. Theirs was a friendship based on cups of tea and a slice of cake or a scone and nice banter, a respite from whatever problems were demanding their attentions in the background. It was the pleasant froth that rode above the cold, dark waters below. Valerie was the same age that her mother would have been had she not been felled by a ninety-year-old driver who should never have been on the road.

'Bonnie, how good to hear from you,' said Valerie in her lovely, rich, plummy voice. 'How are you, dear?'

'I'm fine. But I rang to tell you that I'm not working for Ken Grimshaw any more.'

There was a telling sniff on the other end of the line. 'I've seen that coming for some time. Did you walk out or did he find some way to sack you?'

'He sacked me,' said Bonnie, adding quickly, 'but I walked straight into another job. Do you know there's a new shop up Spring Hill? The Pot of Gold?'

Valerie was disappointingly nonchalant in her response. 'I'd heard, yes. It's on the square that the Irish guy built, isn't it? Jack went up to do a recce a few weeks ago but he said that the shop was dead and wouldn't last the year out.'

'Stickalampinit and Starstruck are in there. Oh, Valerie it's the most beautiful place and yes, it is a lot emptier than it should be, but it won't be if a few more dealers move in and take a chance. There's nowhere as good for miles.'

'Are you asking me to go up and have a look for myself?' asked Valerie, with amusement dancing in her voice.

'You wouldn't want to see me out of a job, would you?' replied Bonnie, smiling.

'Okay, I'll go and get a feel for the place,' Valerie said.

'There's a lovely little tearoom next door as well – we could pop in for a cake,' said Bonnie.

'I'll have a look tomorrow. When do you start working there?'

'Tomorrow.'

'Perfect. Well, I'll see you then,' said Valerie.

Bonnie clicked off the phone and wished she could fast-forward to the morning. In fact she had wished for years that she could fast-forward at the end of every working day to the beginning of the next.

\*

Stephen was in the front room reading a broadsheet when Bonnie walked into the house with a bag of shopping. His eyes instinctively dropped to what she was carrying, as she knew they would.

'Did we need any comestibles?' he asked, though it was a rhetorical question. He had an inbuilt detector for knowing exactly when they'd run out of milk or sugar or flour.

'No, we didn't. I just felt like getting a few extra bits,' she said and steeled herself for his reaction to her next words. 'To celebrate my new job.'

Stephen's eyebrows lifted so high that they almost got entangled in his still-thick, steel-grey hairline.

'New job? What new job? What are you talking about, Bonita?'

It wasn't necessary to give him all the details, so she left out what he didn't need to hear, and added a few small fibs.

'I've not been happy at Grimshaw's since Harry died, you know that.'

'Yes, you have commented upon it on more than one occasion . . .'

'So when I heard that a new antiques centre had opened up, I wrote to them and asked if there were any positions available. There weren't but they kept my letter on file and rang me today. They wanted someone to start immediately.'

'Don't you have a notice period to work?'

'As soon as I said I was leaving, Ken told me to go.'

She waited for the money question to raise its ugly head, which of course it did.

'I presume he paid you severance pay then.'

'Ken Grimshaw? I think I might have to write that off.'

Stephen rattled his paper, as a display of his outrage.

'Then I expect you're going to see the small claims court about that.'

'No, Stephen,' she replied. 'I would really rather just forget the whole thing. It would be more trouble than it was worth because he will lie and I'll end up with nothing.'

Stephen humphed. 'Money does not grow on trees, Bonita.'

'I'm well aware it doesn't grow on trees, Stephen.' Bonnie tried to keep the annoyance out of her voice but traces of it seeped out in hissing sibilance. 'I don't think Ken will be in business for much longer anyway, so I think all things considered, I've made a wise move.'

He sighed impatiently. 'Well, we'll have to economise for a month or so, I suppose,' he said, returning to the business page. 'I just hope you appreciate the tolerance with which I am viewing your rashness, Bonita.'

Bonnie didn't know if she wanted to scream more than she wanted to laugh. They had no mortgage on the house, Stephen had a good salary from his job in the council, with the prospect of a huge pension to come. They didn't go out for meals – or anywhere else for that matter, they didn't drive around in his and hers Ferraris or blow a fortune on drugs, drink and gambling. Plus his mother had left them a considerable sum, she supposed. Bonnie had no idea how much they had in their savings account because Stephen said she didn't need to know. Expenditure such as new white goods or furnishings, or car repairs, came from the fund, after a lot of deliberation and price-haggling on Stephen's part, but Bonnie had no direct access to it. Stephen held the purse-strings, and he held them with an iron fist with a five-lever mortice lock on them.

What she did know was that there must have been

enough funds in there to keep them both comfortable for the rest of their lives even if neither of them worked again. The real problem was that Stephen did not adjust to any sort of change very well. And he was getting worse with every passing year. God forbid that she brought in Heinz beans instead of the shop-brand ones or the velvety loo rolls of Labrador puppies instead of the cheaper variety. Such subversion could cause Stephen to have an aneurysm.

'I'll get on with tea,' said Bonnie. They had pasta on Thursdays. Pasta Bolognese. They always had bloody, sodding pasta on Thursdays.

# Chapter 7

After Lew had locked up for the evening, he didn't know why he felt so compelled to swing a left instead of the right turn that would have taken him straight home to Oxworth. He just wanted to see what was happening with his old house. He had rented it out for a couple of years because a part of him didn't want to sell it, but he had two months ago and the family who had bought it moved in last weekend. He didn't know why he needed to see it, but he went with the feeling. It was the right thing to do to sell The Beeches because it was far too big for just Charlotte and himself and it cost a fortune to heat, not to mention the gardening costs; not that he would have cared about any of that had his wishes come true. He'd bought The Beeches for a snip just after they were married, hoping to fill it with children. As soon as he walked into it, he'd visualised kids skidding down the long wooden hallways, sliding down the polished banister of the great staircase. He'd imagined them splashing in a pool outside, climbing on frames, holding secret meetings in the treehouse he intended to build for them, but his dream of a large family had withered and died.

Charlotte had never got over the miscarriage she'd had eight years ago. She had blocked him every time he'd broached the subject of trying again; she wouldn't even talk about adoption because she'd wanted her own too much. Being near children upset her and reminded her of the one she lost, so they'd decided they'd have to accept their status as a childless couple. It made it slightly easier on them that their friends were childless too.

Lew's heart attack, which had happened just after they'd moved out of The Beeches, had thrown all the cards up in the air. He'd taken the very generous redundancy package the company had offered him, he cashed in his shares when they were cresting and only sold The Beeches when the property market peaked. He invested in safe and riskier markets and had a golden touch with both to the extent that he was a very wealthy man. He could afford to run the Pot of Gold at a loss, view it as an expensive hobby, but he didn't want to. Lew poured his soul into that shop because it was within his capabilities to make it a success and he wasn't such a fool that he didn't realise he was over-compensating for his dashed hopes of being a father.

Woodlea, the house he and Charlotte now lived in was a fresh space for their new life going forwards, not one full of ghosts of children who never were and un-lived dreams but a place where they could start making new ones. Charlotte found the four-bedroomed new build with a lantern-roofed conservatory – the biggest one on an estate of fifteen exclusive builds. It was still too big for them, but she refused to move to a box, and it was well within their budget.

There were lots of cars parked outside The Beeches and fastened to the front gate with ribbon, bunches of pink balloons. A woman with two small girls, one dressed as a fairy, one as a Disney princess had just got out of a people carrier. The woman was carrying a tower of sparkly boxes. Lew pulled into the side of the road, just for a minute or two because he didn't want to be spotted and mistaken for a paedophile.

The new occupants had twin six-year-old girls, a four-year-old boy and the mother was newly pregnant. The Beeches would be a house they would all grow up in, cherish and remember all their lives. It had everything a child could love: a secret room, a huge attic, the perfect slope in the garden for sledging down on winter snow. Lew felt the slightest prickle behind his eyes as if emotion were sharp and he twisted the key in the ignition after silently wishing the Orton family everything he had wanted for himself and Charlotte in that perfect family home.

# Chapter 8

Charlotte was on the phone when Lew walked in. She had such a strange telephone voice it always made him want to laugh, though he didn't. Her vowels rounded and she developed a silky purr worthy of Fenella Fielding. He wasn't even sure she was aware that she sounded as if she had just quit sixth form at Roedean.

'It *has* been too long, Gem, you're right ... yar ... totally ...'

*Yar ... totally.* She was even starting to employ that ridiculous pretentious tone with her best friend.

'Seven ... or when you're ready. I'll do steak ... haven't made my special sauce for ages.'

She indicated to Lew that she'd only be two seconds.

'Okay ... see you Saturday. Great stuff. Ciao Gem ... yep, hope you get on all right.' Charlotte pressed the end call button with a very long silver-tipped nail then turned to Lew. 'Hi darling, good day at the emporium?'

Charlotte never referred to it as a shop because it would sound too downmarket. She hadn't said as much, but Lew knew. She'd always enjoyed the kudos that came with being able to brag, 'My husband is an investment banker in the City' but it wasn't so palatable to admit that he now rented a shop dealing in old things, so in her head the Pot of Gold was a high-end 'emporium' full of things that Sotheby's might covet.

'Wonderful,' he smiled and meant it.

'That was a very enthusiastic answer,' trilled Charlotte. 'What's happened?'

'I've managed to get rid of Vanda Clegg,' grinned Lew. 'I never thought it was possible to be so happy about being ripped off.'

'Ripped off? What do you mean "ripped off"?' Charlotte's newly microbladed left eyebrow rose a full Roger Moore inch.

'To cut a long story short,' began Lew, pulling the glass top from the decanter on the work surface and pouring himself a finger of malt, 'she's been stealing from me and then selling the merchandise on in another antiques centre virtually on the doorstep. Arrogance or idiocy, I have no idea which.' Charlotte opened her mouth to speak, but Lew pre-empted the question. 'If you're going to ask how I found out, freakishly a woman who worked in the other shop came into mine asking for a job and recognised her. I gave Vanda the option to take her bag, leave and never darken my door-step again or I'd let the police handle it. Not surprisingly she took me up on the offer.'

'Oh my God, the cheeky cow,' gasped Charlotte.

'And what's more I set on the woman who recognised Vanda. She's worked in the antiques trade for years and really knows her stuff.'

He noticed that Charlotte stiffened slightly.

'That was a bit quick. What does she look like?'

'Mila Kunis,' said Lew, feeling the whisky hit the back of his throat with a satisfying burn.

'Really?' Charlotte's eyes widened.

'No, not really,' chuckled Lew. Mila Kunis was his favourite. But even if it had been Mila Kunis herself who had turned up looking for a job, Charlotte would have had no worries. Lew was married and that was it as far as he was concerned. He'd never strayed and he never would. If he ever fell out of love with Charlotte, he'd end it and then move on, not try the waters beforehand. And he'd seen very up close and personal recently, the full effect of an extra-marital affair, and didn't want any of it.

'Well then? What is she like?'

'I don't know,' shrugged Lew, 'Average, I suppose. Brown hair, medium height, quiet. I was more interested in the fact that she appeared so knowledgeable than what dress size she was.'

Charlotte, quickly bored with shop talk, moved on to another subject. 'Gemma and Jason are coming up for supper on Saturday night.'

'I thought that's what you might have been arranging when I walked in.'

'And Patrick and Regina. We haven't seen any of them for weeks and it's our turn to host.'

Lew liked Gemma and Jason a lot, he could relax with them, less so with Patrick and Regina, especially at the moment. He tried not to sigh but failed.

'Oh, don't react like that, Lewis, everything is back to normal now,' huffed Charlotte.

Lew nearly spat out his whisky. 'Are you joking?'

'Well, it is until Regina has too much to drink. So we'll just make sure she doesn't.'

'Okay,' said Lew, blowing out two large lungfuls of air which made his lips vibrate in a judder.

'Oh, Lewis, don't look like that.'

'Like what?'

'They've put it all behind them. Nothing has happened since they renewed their vows.'

'Oh yeah,' said Lew, with sarcasm. 'How much did all that cost? Three weeks in the Maldives, not to mention Regina's dress and the diamond eternity ring and all the other things he bought her. And remind me what happened two weeks after they came home, when we all went to the Koh-i-Noor on Regina's birthday.'

'Ah, I'd forgotten about that,' said Charlotte with a grimace, recalling a very drunk Regina lobbing a party-sized mixed platter of starters at her errant husband, Indian snowball-style.

'How can you forget about it, Charlotte? I didn't think it was possible to get a suspected detached retina from having an onion bhajee land in your eye. She nearly blinded her own husband.'

'She was off her face. She couldn't remember anything about it afterwards.'

'Oh well, that makes it okay then.' Lew shook his head in exasperation. 'She got all six of us banned, five of us who remember it in glorious technicolour. This, my darling Charlotte, will not go away for years, trust me. If ever. I don't have Regina down as the forgiving sort, even with a diamond the size of one of Nanny McPhee's warts.'

'Oh, gross, Lewis.' Charlotte gave a shudder.

Thirteen months ago, news of Patrick's affair had rocked their little group of six. Regina was beautiful, clever, scary and the only child of a very rich daddy and Patrick had always known on what side his bread was best buttered: the look but don't touch side. Not surprisingly the object of his affection, Marlene, had been a blue-eyed blonde. Surprisingly, she was not a delicious young floozy with fake boobs and inflated lips, the type Patrick usually ogled, but a plain, gentle, homely-looking woman older than his wife. And if THAT wasn't enough, the smart, preened, savvy Patrick had got himself caught out with the stupidest of mistakes: sending a Valentine's card meant for his mistress to his wife. Needless to say, Patrick cut off the affair before he was cut off from Regina, her daddy's money and his bollocks. Patrick had done whatever he could to mend the damage, but Regina's forgiveness ran only surface deep because there was a lake of magma that surged up as soon as she had reached a certain level of inebriation, which always led to a spoil of festering sarcasm and bilious, excruciating, bitterness.

'So, talking of affairs, do I need to check this . . . what's her name . . . out then?' asked Charlotte.

'Bonnie,' returned Lew. 'And no, don't be silly.'

'Bonnie?' Charlotte quirked both eyebrows this time. 'Nice.'

'Yes she is,' said Lew, stepping towards his wife, looping his arms around her, refusing to play any jealousy games. He gave her a big kiss on the cheek. 'But she's not as nice as you. How do you fancy going out for tea tonight instead of cooking? Pasta Papa. To celebrate the fact that I never have to walk in and see Vanda Clegg again.'

'Oh, that would be good,' said Charlotte, though her voice carried a note that suggested otherwise.

'What's the matter?' asked Lew, pulling her to arm's length.

'Well . . .' Charlotte sighed, 'Pasta Papa is okay but . . . couldn't we go to Firenze instead?'

Lew pulled a face of gentle protest. Firenze was a wonderful place to dine, but more for a grand occasion. Pasta Papa was cheap and cheerful and around the corner and he wouldn't have to dress smart for it or get a taxi. A bowl of Tagliatelle Papa-style, their thin garlic and mozzarella bread and an ice-cold Peroni was all he wanted, not the full posh and pernickity shebang. He would need to have a word with Charlotte about her spending habits anyway after taking a very close look at their accounts recently. She was going through money as if it were loo paper.

Charlotte was now pushing out her bottom lip. 'Oh, please. You did say it was a celebration and we haven't been for ages. We don't have to have every course.'

Lew conceded. Anything to make her happy. 'Oh, go on then,' he relented.

Charlotte giddily clapped her hands. 'I'll change into my new dress.'

She scurried up the stairs and Lew watched her. Charlotte didn't like to do cheap and cheerful any more, she'd been spoilt. Lew picked up the phone to ring Firenze and book a table, but he would still have preferred Pasta Papa.

# Chapter 9

Stephen went to bed early that night with a headache brought on by the stress of Bonnie's news, so he said, so she claimed the front room and flicked to the news, but it was all doom and gloom. CCTV footage of a student raped on a street, a bomb blast in a holiday resort in Egypt and yet another death of a small child who had slipped through the net of social services. The image of the little boy's face remained in her brain long after the point where she turned over. He was smiling, despite a split lip, looking up at whoever was taking the photo with big blue eyes full of light which would be extinguished just a few days later. Bonnie gulped down a throatful of tears. How could someone who had carried such a beautiful little boy for nine months treat him so cruelly? There were too many people in the world who shouldn't have children but did, and too many who should but couldn't. It was an imbalance that Mother Nature hadn't managed to rectify yet.

There was no gynaecological reason why Bonnie couldn't have children. She'd always wanted them. She hadn't had them with her first love Joel, because he was a metronome that swung wildly between two versions of himself: a balloon that sailed high and carelessly with the clouds and a dragging dead weight that couldn't lift its head from the ground. The *High Joel,* the exhausting, full of life, happy, funny Joel would have made a wonderful dad. That Joel loved everyone and everything, he was a Red Setter pup in a beautiful man's body. *Low Joel* couldn't see beyond himself. A dark half of paranoia, sadness and self-loathing who tried to alienate Bonnie, pushing her buttons to prove the self-fulfilling prophecy that he was unlovable, but she had stuck firm to him whatever he threw at her, always hoping the doctors would find the combination of medicines that would allow them to be a normal couple, doing normal coupley things like socialising, holidaying, having a child. But no amount of wishful thinking had helped defeat the black forces at work in his head. He had bailed out of his white-knuckle roller-coaster life and left her crushed.

As for Stephen, the subject of starting a family hadn't risen up in conversation before they were married. Not much had, she'd realised with hindsight. She'd been lost, disorientated, struggling under the weight of her failure to help Joel or her father and he'd been on the scene, a self-imposed guide-rope through the confusion, patching up her broken heart with kind words and patience and she'd married him through gratitude masquerading as love. She had thought he would lead her into the light, but instead he had pushed her into the dark.

They hadn't slept together after the first few weeks of their marriage. They'd tried to have sex just a couple of times and it was awkward and cold and it was obvious that Stephen had no interest in that side of marriage at all. He had suggested that Bonnie might want to move into the bedroom across the landing, the larger one with its own ensuite and Bonnie, hurt but stoical, had complied. They had quickly settled into a sexless companionship of a relationship, with not much companionship.

It was half-past eleven when Bonnie turned all the lights off, checked that the doors were locked and went upstairs. She read in bed for another half hour until she felt her eyelids dropping. She liked Midnight Moon romances, where heroes were strong and handsome and heroines feisty and beautiful and passion flared between them like a factory-full of fireworks. Stephen frowned on them because he said they were 'lesser books' and Bonnie didn't disagree with him, not because she thought he was right, but because he would never accept he was wrong. Her books were her escapism, they gave her hope that there was a strong, handsome hero out there with her name on his heart. She knew she was too young to settle for the life she had, but she had been forced to accept this quagmire of complacency because she had nowhere to go, no money to go with, and she was scared to make the break.

She used to feel sorry for Stephen. He had no friends, nor family since his mother had died – just her. She gathered he wasn't a popular person at work; one of the grey people who came in, did their job efficiently, needled a few people by being a Norman-know-it-all and went home. He'd promised to look after her, keep her safe and he had. Safe from everyone but himself. She lived in a nice house with him, they had no debts or pressures and he wasn't bad to her, but neither was he good to her. They went abroad once a year on holiday for seven days, always to the same quiet Spanish place. Bonnie read a lot in the sun, Stephen walked and took photos of buildings and try as she might, Bonnie could not recall any of the conversations they must have had over dinner at the hotel before retiring to their twin beds in any of those years. He had tricked her into believing she was loved. He needed her, but not for love. She used to feel sorry for him, but she didn't any more.

She had recurring dreams in which she was eighty years old and she was still in this house, married to him, and she would wake from them feeling as if all the air had been stolen from the room. She was bored beyond belief by her life.

But tonight, for once, she was going to bed with wishes and hopes in her heart that tomorrow was not going to be just another same-old, same-old day. She could have kissed the old lady with the Gulvase for dropping her in it with Ken Grimshaw.

The *Daily Trumpet* would like to apologise to the Nobb family for the unfortunate wording under their photograph in a feature on them last week. It should have read: *Five generations of the Nobb family*, not *Five generations of Nobbs*. We apologise for any offence incurred by any of the Nobbs.

# Chapter 10

Lew's eyes opened slowly and took moments to focus on the time showing on the bedside alarm clock. When they did, he had leapt out of bed as if it were on fire. It was quarter to nine. He had never once been late for work. He had either slept through his alarm or not set it, neither of which seemed possible for someone like him. Charlotte was awoken by his racing around getting dressed. She propped herself up on her pillow and asked why he was tearing about like a loon.

'I've overslept,' he explained. 'When do I ever do that? And I've got the new sales assistant starting this morning. She'll probably be there now. Great start.'

'Oh don't worry about her, she's nobody. She can wait,' said Charlotte, flapping her hand.

That little show of snobbery needled Lew. Charlotte had been a sales assistant herself once upon a time. Lew hated money snobs. Top of that list was Regina Sheffield. She came from stock that thought cash could buy class and taste, the sort who thought it was okay to treat waiters like crap if they threw a twenty-pound tip at them or bought three-hundred-pound bottles of wine at dinner tables merely to show off when really they couldn't tell a Lafite Rothschild from a Lambrini.

Lew raced into the bathroom. It wasn't that he'd drunk a lot the night before, but that red wine he'd had with his meal didn't sit well with the large whisky he'd had at home. It could have been much worse because as soon as they walked in, lo and behold, they found their ex-neighbour Tony and his equally boozy wife Liz looking at menus. 'Come and join us,' they'd called and though Lew had been about to decline on the grounds of not intruding, Charlotte had heartily accepted the offer on their behalf.

'What are you doing today then?' Lew asked her, hopping into his trousers.

'I'm going to the gym,' Charlotte replied. 'For lunch.'

'There's a shocker.' She had platinum plus membership to the most exclusive gym in town, allowing her full access at any time to any of the facilities, fresh towels and a discount in the spa and yet she only ever went there to socialise in the restaurant.

'That reminds me, I'll need to renew my subscription next month.'

'Maybe you shouldn't,' Lew said, expecting exactly the reaction he got. Rushing around like this, the timing was off for this conversation, but he could at least prepare her for a much more detailed conversation to come.

'Whaaat?' Charlotte froze, iPhone in hand, ready to record her voice memo.

'Maybe you shouldn't. It's a total waste of money. You don't even need to be a member to eat in the restaurant. And if you remember we converted one of the bedrooms to a gym. Is it only me that ever uses it?'

'I use it of course but we don't have the machines that they do there,' protested Charlotte.

'Like what?' quizzed Lew, because he knew she didn't use any of the equipment either upstairs or at the gym.

'The ... thingys with ... the weights on ... I don't know the names.'

'Charlotte, the overspending has to stop. I'll talk to you when I get home about it, but I've been looking at the visa bills and the direct debits and something is going to have to give, my love.'

'But I like being a member.'

She liked boasting that she had platinum plus membership, is what she meant.

'Well, I no longer work in the City pulling in a six-figure salary, Charlotte, if you haven't noticed.' He hadn't told her that the shop wasn't making any profit. Not yet.

Charlotte's lip began to do its characteristic little-girl-tantrum curl.

'I'm not exactly suggesting we live off value beans, Charlotte, but I want to ensure that we have enough money to be able to live comfortably for the rest of our hopefully long lives; and we won't if you continue to throw money away on unnecessary things like luxury gym memberships that you don't use and whatever "shrink-wraps" are costing four hundred pounds in the spa.'

Charlotte's lip was now so curled that it annoyed him to look at it. He wasn't a mean man, but it had come as a complete shock to see how much she had been frittering away over the years. And he was equally annoyed at himself that he'd let her. He'd felt guilty that she was up in Yorkshire all week, whilst he was down in London for most of it and let her spend, spend, spend to compensate. But he was at home every night now. There was no need to dull any ache of boredom by buying Jimmy Choos and a full range of Crème de la Mer. They were wealthy, but he was hardly in the Getty family league.

'Well, I won't renew it then,' said Charlotte with a familiar passive-aggressive sigh, which he wasn't going to cave in to.

'Good,' he said, leaned over and gave her a kiss on the cheek. 'I'll see you later.'

The rain was just starting when he shut the back door behind him. By the time he had driven out of the road, the skies were squeezing the saturated clouds and it was pouring down. He had an image of Bonnie standing outside the shop, drenched to the skin, and nudged the speed limit with his car, anxiety claiming his heartbeat which flagged up as an instant warning. He'd been a hard taskmaster on himself over the years: lots of commuting, early mornings, late nights, figures, targets, responsibilities. Stress had nearly killed him and he'd escaped its grasp once; he might not be so lucky next time. He hated being late for anything and prepared to apologise profusely to Bonnie and then get on with the day.

As he sat in a very long queue of traffic waiting for some temporary lights to change, his thoughts wandered back to the previous evening. It had been a lovely surprise to see his old neighbours Tony and Liz. They were full of gossip about the Ortons who had bought The Beeches. Apparently they were wasting no time applying for planning permission for all sorts of things including a swimming pool and a third-storey playroom for the children. The kids were gorgeous, Liz said. Well-behaved and just on the right side of mischievous.

When they got home, Lew had wanted to make love to his wife. The good company of Tony and Liz had chilled him out, but unfortunately it'd had the opposite effect on Charlotte. She hadn't needed all those details about children rampaging over The Beeches, she said; it had upset her, although she hadn't looked very traumatised in the restaurant when she was downing all that Prosecco, thought Lew. Still he didn't push it and anyway, by the time he had come out of the shower, Charlotte was making snuffly snoring noises into her pillow.

Eventually the traffic lights changed and Lew rinsed the events of the previous night out of his head and concentrated on getting to the Pot of Gold as quickly as possible. Bonnie was standing hunched under the narrow eave outside the shop which afforded the barest protection from the elements. She had a bright sunshiney-yellow mac on and blue suede ankle boots which had darkened with the rain.

'I am so sorry I'm late,' Lew said, jogging over. 'Come on in, quickly.' He hurriedly opened up the shop door then tapped in the numbers which would deactivate the burglar alarm.

Bonnie pulled the sodden bottom of her dress away from her legs. 'The forecast said it would be dry today,' she said. 'I think it lied.' She'd deliberately dressed in the brightest colours that the contents of her wardrobe offered up: the thin yellow mac, her favourite blue boots, her turquoise pinafore dress. She felt bright, excited by the prospect of a new job away from the revolting Ken Grimshaw and being able to see old friends again.

'Anyway, good morning. A belated good morning. Hardly the best indication of a reliable organised boss but I promise you, I slept through my alarm clock for the first time in my life.'

THE QUEEN OF WISHFUL THINKING

Bonnie laughed. 'Ah, no worries,' she said. The shop was warm and she'd dry out in no time. Ken was too tight to switch on any heating and she was surprised she hadn't lost the tops of her fingers to frostbite by now.

Lew shook the wet drops off the dark waves of his hair as he turned on the lights.

'Would you like me to make you a coffee?' asked Bonnie.

'That would be lovely,' said Lew. His throat was parched. Thank goodness he'd refused the brandy that Tony was trying to press on to him, otherwise he would have still been in bed now. 'Here, let me show you the back office-cum-kitchen-cum-storeroom-cum-staffroom.'

He pointed out where she could leave her coat and bag securely and where the kettle, cups and fridge were, and the compact washroom. Then he left her to make the coffees whilst he went through the post.

'I've been thinking,' said Bonnie, as she arrived at the counter with two mugs of coffee, 'Would you like me to make some calls to some of the old dealers who might be interested in those empty units? Goldfinger, he's from Doncaster so probably he hasn't heard about you. Gary Glass is based in York and he's got some beautiful stuff, and then there's the Watchman . . .'

'Does everyone in this game have a nickname?' asked Lew, taking his mug with a thank you.

'More or less,' grinned Bonnie. 'And the ones that don't think they do, do.'

'What's yours, then?'

'I'm not aware of one,' she said.

'Make one up in that case,' urged Lew.

What would have been hers? Bonnie mused. Unthinking Idiot, probably. Blind Betty, stumbling from one dark place to another, frying pan to fire. One name came to her louder than the others though.

'Bonita Banana, that's what my dad used to call me. Mum saw the name Bonita on a crate years before I was born and thought it was lovely so she saved it in case she ever had a daughter. She didn't realise until someone mentioned it at my christening that she'd named me after a firm who exported bananas.' She smiled.

'And here's me thinking you were named after Bonnie Langford,' chuckled Lew.

'Nope, a crate of foreign bananas. Apparently she never called me Bonita again after she found out.'

'Apparently?' Lew questioned the word.

'Mum died when I was two so I couldn't ask her about it first hand,' said Bonnie. 'Dad brought me up by himself. I can't remember her.'

'Oh, I'm sorry,' said Lew.

Bonnie shrugged. 'She was knocked over by an old man who shouldn't have been driving.' She stopped herself, not wanting to drag down the mood. 'I've asked a friend of mine to come in and look around. She deals in vintage clothing and goes by the name of Vintage Valerie. If she moves in, lots of other dealers will follow because they tend to gravitate towards each other, like a pack.'

'Spread the word as far as you like and invite them all in to check out the place,' said Lew. 'The more the merrier.'

'Just let me know what you charge so I can go to them with all the information. I've left an envelope on the desk in the back room with my bank details and info you might need,' Bonnie said.

'Thank you,' said Lew. 'I can pay you cash if you'd prefer.'

'I would if that's possible,' said Bonnie, nodding her head

keenly. That way Stephen wouldn't know what she earned and she could siphon off a few more pounds for things she needed so she wouldn't have to go to him cap in hand.

'Then shall I do a bit of dusting?' she asked.

'Er ... yeah ... please.'

Lew wasn't used to such efficiency. Vanda might have mooched around with a duster sometimes, but she didn't make much impact with it. He warned himself not to be taken in so easily though. Bonnie Brookland was a new broom, and he shouldn't expect any initial level of enthusiasm to last. Then again, Vanda Clegg had been a knackered old brush from the off.

*

Vintage Valerie needed no introduction. She swept regally into the Pot of Gold in a long honey-coloured maxi dress with a peacock blue shawl draped beautifully over her shoulders, and a scarlet Gloria Swanson turban on her head complete with feathery plumes. She looked as if she had just walked off a Cecil B. DeMille film set.

'That's Valerie,' Bonnie whispered to Lew, out of the corner of her mouth.

'I figured,' he replied.

As he was about to walk towards her, Bonnie caught his arm. 'Just let her have a wander first and get a feel for the place by herself.' She knew that way, Valerie would recognise the same potential she had seen. Valerie wouldn't be pushed into making up her mind by anyone.

After fifteen minutes, Lew's nerves were jangling as he watched Valerie end her slow and silent circuit of his shop. Then she approached the counter and smiled first at Bonnie,

then at Lew. She held out a long slim pale hand towards him
and introduced herself.

'Vintage Valerie,' she drawled.

Lew gave his own hand a drying slide down his trouser
leg because he realised it was slightly damp with ridiculous
nerves.

'Lewis Harley,' he replied. 'Lovely to meet you.'

Valerie's head swivelled round to Bonnie. 'Yes, you're
right,' she said. 'It has appeal. I'll make a few calls.'

'I thought you'd say that,' said Bonnie with a satisfied
grin.

'Expect some visitors, Mr Harley,' said Valerie over her
shoulder as she glided towards the door like a multi-
coloured swan.

'Result.' Bonnie clicked her tongue and winked at Lew,
as the doorbell made a cheerful sound like the bell equivalent of a 'hurray'.

Bonnie passed a very pleasant and productive first morning
in her new job. She'd managed to get in touch with Gary
Glass and the Watchman and they promised to come over
when they could find a moment to check the place out.
They'd both been very grateful for the heads-up and said
they'd spread the word. Grimshaw's was a mess, they'd both
said. Gary would be seeing Goldfinger the following morning at the twice-yearly Ribury Fayre and he'd mention it
to him as well. They all worked the markets and the car
boots and they'd collectively do a better job in advertising
than anything the *Daily Trumpet* could herald. Which,
admittedly, wasn't that hard. Then Bonnie took a call from
Valerie who wanted to talk rates with Lew. Then Jackpot
rang to ask the same thing and Bonnie knew that if those

two were on board, the others would come flocking too –
and soon.

Clock Robin and Starstruck both came in to replenish
their stock mid-afternoon and Lew was alerted to how
warmly they greeted Bonnie. Starstruck in particular.

'Hello lass,' he said, enveloping her in his noticeably long,
weathered arms. 'You've left that shit'ole, have you? What
a disgrace. Old Harry will be spinning in his grave.'

'I have, Starstruck,' said Bonnie. 'Though my hand was
forced, if I'm honest.'

'Nasty bastard that Ken,' snarled Clock Robin, who was
a very tall, skinny angular man with a huge hook nose. He
reminded Lew of a crow.

'Never liked him,' agreed Starstruck, hanging a signed
photo of Diana Dors up on the wall. 'What a lovely woman
she was. She used to live next door to my granny in
Swindon, you know. Ooh, she wor a warm 'un.' He chuckled affectionately. 'She signed this for me just before she tried
to crack America. "Starstruck," she said, "they're trying to
market me as the English Marilyn Monroe." I said, "Di,
you're far bonnier than her, lass." She gave me a right big
kiss ... here.' He touched his lips and his bright grey eyes
had a faraway look in them.

There didn't seem to be anyone that Starstruck hadn't
met. He always seemed to be in the right place at the right
time or was connected to the rich and famous in some way.
His mum was born on the same street at the Krays, he'd
worked as a cameraman in Pinewood studios, his sister had
married a top showbiz agent, he'd been on holiday with
Roger Moore. It was as if he'd known that one day his profession would be selling memorabilia and he'd been storing
it up for decades like a squirrel. And he could spot a

counterfeit from five hundred yards, though goodness knows how. Autographs had been his life, his thing. He was the expert's expert on signatures; some of the big auction houses even employed his services. It was as if he could psychically identify a person from their writing.

'Nice little spot this,' said Starstruck, looking around him and waving over at another trader, John Lemon, a man with disproportionately short legs who dealt in silver and was therefore affectionately labelled Long John, though his unit was called 'Silver Service'. He was adding some more precious pieces to his cabinet. His specialty was exquisite silver trinkets such as pepperettes, sugar shakers, snuff boxes and spoons. 'All right, John?' Starstruck called.

'Not bad lad, and yourself?'

'Aye, not bad either.'

Then Starstruck turned back to Bonnie and leaned in close for confidentiality. 'I like this bloke,' he said, cocking his head in Lew's direction. 'He's straight down the line. Like your dad and Harry Grimshaw.' He dropped his head reverently at the mention of the two men before continuing. 'It's got a lovely feel to it, this place, but it could do with a few more people coming through that door, Bon, do you know what I mean? I'm giving it a chance, but . . .' The word hung ominously in the air.

'Of course,' said Bonnie, adding in a conspiratorial tone, 'It's not my business to say, but I think you're about to be working alongside some familiar faces, very soon.'

Starstruck gave a little delighted gasp but before he could follow that up with any questions, Lew's cough interrupted them.

'Bonnie, could I borrow you for a moment?' Bonnie hoped she hadn't been talking too much and was about to get a telling off. Ken didn't like her chatting to the dealers. He was paranoid that they were slagging him off, though was it really paranoia when they were?

'The old lady with the white Gulvase came in last night just before I closed up,' said Lew.

'Oh good.' Bonnie was glad she had.

'She brought in the full box of stuff. Look at this.' He unwrapped the Chinese cup and saucer from the protection of the bubble wrap he'd placed around it. 'I found this incredibly interesting and I'd like to hear what you think.'

Bonnie took the saucer from him. 'Blimey. I'm surprised this hasn't ended up in a bin. Someone must have known what it's worth to have hung on to it. Oh my . . . it's got the matching cup too.' She blew upwards and ruffled the stray hairs which had worked themselves loose from her hairband. 'You should show these to Jackpot when he comes in to set up. He'll say the same as me though, that you should send photos of this pair to Christie's. There are some clever fakes out there but I have a feeling these could be very special.'

'I thought so.' A thrill tripped down Lew's spine that she agreed with his assessment. It was wonderful to share such a moment with someone who *got* that excitement that discovered treasures brought.

'What Jack doesn't know about ceramics you could write on a postage stamp.'

'He's coming in on Tuesday,' said Lew. 'I'll ask him then.'

Bonnie whistled as a thought came to her. 'It's a good job that Ken didn't see this in the old lady's haul. Good grief, I hope he never finds out what I might have cost him.'

'His loss is my gain,' said Lew. It would have sounded flirty to say it so he stopped himself, but he didn't only mean the old lady's treasures. He watched Bonnie turn the saucer over in her hands. Her hazel eyes were shining with fasci-nation. He was aware that he was staring and forced himself to shift his focus before she caught him. He wondered what Mr Brookland was like.

There was only a trickle of customers in the afternoon, people who had been to the teashop next door and decided to have a poke around, but one of them had bought a silver toothpick from Long John's cabinet along with a gorgeous Asprey cigarette case.

The clock wound around to closing time surprisingly quickly; Bonnie couldn't remember when she'd had such a pleasant day at work. Mr Harley seemed like a good man to work for, but she hadn't to rule out that this was a new broom situation and he might turn out to be another Ken Grimshaw. But, even after only one day in the job, somehow she didn't think so. As she bade Lew good night and walked out of the door towards her car, she wondered if there was a Mrs Harley and what she was like.

# Chapter 11

When Bonnie woke up the next morning, she thought her alarm clock had gone off too early because the sky was charcoal and lumpy with grubby dumplings of cloud. The rain was lashing against her window, distorting the view of the fields beyond and giving them the appearance of an Impressionist painting. Angry March winds with ADHD were pushing and pulling at everything they could find in their stream. It was one of those mornings where a bed might have called in a silky purr, 'come back to me', except her mattress had been chosen by Stephen for its sensible orthopaedic qualities and going in to the Pot of Gold was a far nicer prospect. On Saturdays the dealers who didn't go to the huge fayres searching for stock used the day for replenishing their cabinets, so they could hang around talking to customers and fish for sales. There was always an extra pleasant feeling about Saturdays which made them her favourite working days.

As she walked downstairs, she could hear Stephen on the telephone saying goodbye and thank you to whoever it was he was talking to. He was wearing his best self-righteous smile when Bonnie entered the kitchen. It was the only sort of smile he was capable of. He momentarily flicked his eyes towards her but he didn't greet her with a 'good morning'. He never did, and she wondered again if other couples behaved like this towards each other, co-existing rather than *living* together. They never did anything as a couple except eat or watch 'intellectual TV' occasionally. They had no common interests: she didn't even know what he thought about her, or if he had ever loved her, especially in the beginning when he acted as if he did, even if he had never said the actual words. She didn't love him. She hadn't loved him for many years but she didn't know how to change things. Wishing and thinking about herself being away from him certainly hadn't worked.

She picked up her handbag and knew that Stephen had been snooping inside it, because she never zipped it up more than three quarters of the way and now it was fully closed. She should have been used to it, because it wasn't the first time it had happened. She had no idea what he thought he might find and a flare of anger made her ask on this occasion.

'Why have you been in my bag?'

'I've just had a very interesting conversation with your boss,' he replied, avoiding the question.

Bonnie looked at him, puzzled. 'What?'

'You're to go back, apologise and he'll say no more about it.'

Bonnie was just about to ask what on earth he was talking about, when she realised he wasn't talking about Lew Harley, but Ken Grimshaw.

'I beg your pardon?'

'I've negotiated a way out of your problem for you. There

will be no more nonsense about going to work for someone who won't be in business this time next month, so Mr Grimshaw says.' That supercilious smile on Stephen's lips stretched into a self-congratulatory arc. 'So you can ring the new place and tell them you won't be returning. I was just about to do it for you, but if you'd prefer to tell them your-self, that might be courteous.' He held the house phone out for her to take and use. She stared at it in his hand but made no move to relieve him of it.

'I wouldn't go back and work for that creep if he dou-bled . . . trebled my wage.'

The smile shrank. 'You will, Bonita. Mr Grimshaw has a long establish—'

'No I won't.' Bonnie cut off his words and snatched up her bag. 'You had no right to—'

It was Stephen's turn to interrupt now. 'You're lucky he was so amenable after your disloyalty.'

'He's *amenable* because he's off to Spain soon and there is no one to look after the shop, so no, I won't go back.' Bonnie made to step past him but Stephen caught hold of her hand and forced her fingers around the phone.

'You will and you will apologise.'

As soon as he let go, she dropped the phone onto the kitchen table and it bounced onto the floor. The back flew off and the batteries spilled out. 'No I wo—'

When the slap landed on her cheek, Stephen looked more stunned than Bonnie did. It all happened so quickly that it took Bonnie a few seconds to realise that he had, for the first ever time, hit her. It wasn't a hard slap, her cheek might have pulsed with the contact but the real impact was in her brain where the shock pealed like a church bell.

'You silly girl,' yelled Stephen at volume. 'That was all

your fault.' And with that, he strode out of the kitchen towards the lounge, chuntering to an invisible audience about lies, deceit and betrayal.

But Bonnie couldn't move. Her legs felt numb whilst pins and needles prickled her arms. Her dad's voice was loud and clear in her head. *If a man ever hits you, just once, you walk out of the door and you keep walking because if he's done it once, it'll happen again. And then you tell me and he'll never hit another woman as long as he lives because I'll chop his bloody arms off.*

But her dad wasn't here to tell. And leaving was easier said than done when you didn't have anywhere to go.

Bonnie arrived at the Pot of Gold wet and wild-haired; her yellow mac was only shower-proof and the elements laughed at it. Even in the short walk from her car to the shop, the material had plastered itself to her skin. But once she had opened the door, her spirits instantly soared in relief both for the respite from the icy downpour and for reaching a place that felt a million miles away from Greenwood Crescent.

'Good morning, Bonnie,' Lew greeted her. 'I'm gathering that it hasn't stopped raining.' And he smiled a welcome and Bonnie thought that he must be the sort of man who kissed his wife goodbye that morning and told her to have a nice day. A man who didn't slap his wife when she didn't do as she was told.

'I bet I look like something out of a Tim Burton film.'

'Not at all.' And even if she did, it would still have been a thousand-times improvement on Vanda Clegg.

Bonnie disappeared into the back room to get herself tidy and ready for duty. There was no evidence on her cheek of the scene that had happened at home. The scene that was

replaying itself on a constant loop in her head. Stephen had
never hit her before, but then they'd never had a stand-up
argument where she had dug in her heels and defied him
before. *You have to leave him* said a voice in her head, a deep
man's voice that sounded a lot like her father's and she knew
it was right. But where would she start the process of untan-
gling her life from his? And would she ever really be able to
cut *all* the threads?

'I imagine the weather will put a lot of people off ven-
turing out,' sighed Lew, walking into the back room and
interrupting her thoughts.

'Have faith,' replied Bonnie, switching into shop-assistant
mode. 'People will have paid off their Christmas bills so
they'll have a bit of spare money in their pockets again, plus
it's officially spring next week. They'll defy the weather and
come flocking.'

'I hope so,' said Lew, reaching into his jacket. 'I think
your first official duty of Saturday should always be to go
next door and buy a couple of their very excellent toasted
teacakes. Heavily buttered. Leni knows just how I like
them.'

Bonnie thought he was joking until he handed her a ten
pound note.

'Really?'

'Yes,' he said. 'Really.'

It hadn't been a tradition he had practised with Vanda but
then she had never walked into the shop in the morning
bringing the sunshine in with her, even on a day such as
this, giving him faith that he hadn't been mad to gamble on
opening up his business. Then the doorbell tinkled and a
couple of people in waxed coats wandered in and asked if
the shop was open because they'd been in the mood for

checking the place out and were determined not to let the weather put them off.

The Pot of Gold was busier that afternoon than it had been on any other Saturday before and Lew was gobsmacked. He sold a space-consuming mahogany table and six chairs that he never thought he'd shift and had been about to slash the price on it. He threw in free delivery and was so giddy he had to stop himself throwing in the dinner service that was displayed on it as well. Then two dealers called in to size up the shop after bumping into Gary Glass at the Ribury Fayre: the rough and ready Stantiques, who dealt in Victoriana and the very dapper Goldfinger whose speciality was old gold and precious gems. Lew couldn't help but be impressed by how the faces of the two dour-looking men were split by smiles when they saw his new assistant. Lew left Bonnie to work her magic and persuade them to come on board. Within the half hour they had asked if it was all right to move their stock into a couple of spare units on Tuesday.

Starstruck made an appearance with a framed, signed Evel Knievel T-shirt along with his handwritten message, 'Follow your dreams'. It was accompanied by a photograph of him wearing it as provenance. 'He died that same year,' Starstruck sniffed. 'What a man. Reminded me of your dad in the face when he was younger, Bon.'

Bonnie tilted her head one way then the other and yes, she could see what he meant. Her dad was a big, strapping handsome man with a thick head of hair of which he was very proud. Before. His illness had even taken that away from him.

'Hey, Bon, you don't know anyone looking for a house to rent, do you?' asked Starstruck. 'Our Alison has moved in with her fella but she's not selling up in case he turns out to be a plonker like the other one, so she's letting her house out in Dodley Bottom. It's a lovely little place, two-up, two-down, not furnished, mind, but I think it's got a fridge and a hob. Number 1 Rainbow Lane, tagged onto the side of the old Duck Street chapel that they turned into offices, do you know where I mean?'

'I think so, Starstruck,' Bonnie said. 'But I don't know anyone who might want it, sorry.'

'Never mind, I thought I'd ask. She'll end up selling, I think, because this bloke's a good lad but she's erring on the side of caution. Once bitten, twice shy. She's not greedy. Seventy quid a week she wants, just to cover her mortgage and a bit extra.'

'Seventy pounds?'

Bonnie's heart gave a leap like a racehorse over a fence. That was very cheap. Was it doable? One side of her brain started doing manic calculations in her head whilst the other seemed to be nudging up its bosom and warning, 'Calm down, dear.'

'She'd like a six-month lease on it,' said Starstruck.

Oh goodness, thought Bonnie. The timing on this couldn't have been better. Dodley Bottom was near to the shop too and there was a direct bus from there to Penistone which stopped at Spring Hill, should her car ever play up.

'I'll let you know straightaway if I hear of anyone who might be interested,' she said.

'Thanks, lass.'

The last customers left just after five, half an hour after the official closing time. Lew apologised profusely to Bonnie and couldn't understand why her eyebrows rose when he said he'd make sure he paid her for the extra time, but then he had never worked for Ken Grimshaw. He cashed up quickly, having something worthwhile to bank for once, knowing that Charlotte would be annoyed that he was late. He headed back to his car with the rain pelting him from one side and the sun shining on him from the other. He drove out of the car park towards the brightest rainbow that he had ever seen in his life, with a fainter duplicate printed above it. He wondered if it was a sign. Double rainbows meant serendipitous magic was on its way: he was sure he'd read that somewhere once.

Bonnie saw the rainbows too. The inner one was rich with colour as if it had been painted on the sky with an artist's heavy hand and it was especially vivid being set against such dark, blue-smoke clouds. She stopped the car at the top of Half Moon Hill in order to look at it properly and wished the camera on her ancient phone still worked.

She'd had a lovely day at work after such an awful start at home and, though she had only completed two days at the Pot of Gold, she felt as if colour was returning to her life again, warmth . . . *hope*. Hope that there was something bright waiting for her behind the clouds . . . and maybe she would find it on Rainbow Lane. It was a sign, it had to be.

# Chapter 12

Charlotte was busy preparing for her dinner party when Lew got home. Prawns in coconut panko crumb to start with, fillet steak with her special secret-recipe sauce for main and strawberries in Pernod and black pepper for dessert. The breadmaker on the work surface was busy baking a parmesan and olive loaf and Astrid, their cleaner, was sprinkling confetti stars on the beautifully laid table in the middle of their cavernous open-plan dining kitchen.

Charlotte, as expected, was pulsing out vibes of annoyance when he kissed her on the cheek. She merely replied to his 'sorry I'm late' with the brusque words, 'Lewis, get a shower, they'll be here in just over an hour.'

'Hello to you too,' tutted Lew, but good humouredly. 'And hello, Astrid. I see my wife has roped you into helping with arrangements?'

'Yes. I dun't mind though. I could alvays do viz the over-time,' Astrid replied in her strange hybrid broad Barnsley-German accent.

Lew went upstairs and sighed, a little crossly. They were only having their friends round, it didn't merit bringing in their cleaner to help throw a meal together. The stair carpet had tell-tale vacuum tool marks on it, so Astrid had obviously given the place a once-over before she started in the kitchen. He was pretty sure it wouldn't have been Charlotte. As Lew walked into the main house bathroom, a hoot of laughter escaped him at the sight of the huge swan fashioned out of a towel perched on the side of the bath and then the towel elephant with mini soaps for eyes which was sitting on the toilet lid. Also the edges of the toilet roll were creased into a V and a tiny paper fan sat in the fold.

Charlotte's voice barked up the staircase.

'Lewis, use the ensuite and NOT the towels and toilet roll out on display in the main bathroom, please.'

'Aye aye captain,' he shouted back.

On his bed was a giant moth with a bath towel for the body and two hand towels for the wings. Astrid was very clever at those finishing touches though he seemed to remember that a couple of weeks ago he had walked into the house and found her purple-faced with rage as Charlotte was telling her that it might be better if she concentrated on things like skirting board dusting rather than creating such fripperies. Astrid had pulled herself up to her full height of six foot four and responded that the skirting boards were dust-free, *danke schön*, and that she had made those in her own time as a friendly gesture but that 'She vud not be doing zem *ag-ean* so *madam* vud have *nowt* to worry *abart*.' Astrid had stormed out of the house, mortified at the merest suggestion that she'd been slacking and Charlotte hadn't been best pleased that Lew was taking the cleaner's side on this; in fact he had insisted she ring Astrid and apologise. There was a bunch of flowers and a huge box of chocolates waiting for her the next time she came and all was smoothed over. Now, it seemed that Astrid's artistic skills were not only being encouraged but rented.

By the time he had come downstairs, Astrid had left.

'I know what you're going to say,' pre-empted Charlotte as she covered prawns in crumbs, 'but I wanted it to be special tonight.'

Lew didn't argue. He was looking forward to having their friends over, with the notable exception of Regina. 'Can I do anything to help?'

'Nope, it's all done.' Right on cue the breadmaker gave a series of beeps. 'Oh, you can take that out, if you will.'

'What's the occasion that we need Astrid's zoo-towels?' Lew lifted the lid on the breadmaker releasing a delicious scent that made his stomach growl in anticipation. He hadn't eaten much all day because – marvellously – he'd been too busy. 'Is it anyone's birthday?'

'No occasion.'

'What time do the string quartet arrive?'

'Oh very funny, Lewis, not.'

Lew tipped the bread out onto the wire rack. He could have hacked off a slice, slathered it in butter and stuffed the whole thing in his mouth.

'It has been a long time since we've had one of these soirées, isn't it?' Lew tried to work out when it had been.

'Last time we were all together was at the Koh-i-Noor,' replied Charlotte, stirring something on the hob.

Lew shuddered. 'Ah yes, Indian Plattergate.'

'. . . Though I've been for coffee with Regina a few times in between.'

That surprised Lew. 'Really?'

'I like her, Lew. She's great fun.'

A picture of a great white shark flashed into Lew's head.

It often did at the mention of Regina's name. 'What about Gemma? Haven't you seen her at all?'

Charlotte shrugged dismissively. 'Maybe we're just growing apart.'

That saddened Lew to hear because Gemma was the nicest person in their group. The six of them usually met once a month and had done so regularly for the last four years, until Patrick and Regina's famous hoo-ha. Gemma and Charlotte had been best friends since school. Gemma was a sweetheart, Lew had always thought so, and had been Charlotte's bridesmaid and vice versa, and if either couple had had children, they would have been each other's first choice for godmother. But Gemma didn't want children; she had ploughed all her energies into her nail bar business, Sparkles. She had been married to Jason for ten years. He had been a jobbing car salesman until he took a gamble, leased a garage and started selling second-hand prestige cars and business was booming for him. Lew had always liked Jason, though if he were honest, he liked him more when he had less money. It had, as his mum would have said, 'all gone to his head a bit'. Jason, for the first time, felt able to engage in serious one-upmanship with Patrick, the world's most inveterate bragger. Lew was never interested in who had the best car, biggest house, fanciest holidays and he hadn't thought Jason was, until recent months proved him wrong. Patrick, an accountant, had been a business associate of both him and Jason. He was loud, brash, and extremely likeable but if you'd been to Sevenoaks, he'd been to Eightoaks; if you had double-vision, he had treble-vision. Regina was loud, brash and extremely unlikeable but Patrick's company was worth having, even if they had to include her. Still, as convivial a host as Lew was, he had to try really hard not to dread evenings in her company.

'It'll be good for us all to get together again,' said Lew, as Charlotte stripped off her apron. 'I can't believe you haven't seen Gemma in all that time. You haven't fallen out, have you?'

'No, not fallen out as such, but . . . Gemma . . .' Charlotte trailed off and made a nervous straightening-down her dress gesture.

'Gemma what?' He saw the gulp rise and fall in his wife's throat before she spoke again.

'Gemma's thinking about having a baby.'

'Gemma? Get away!' He was gobsmacked by that. Gemma had always said she never wanted children. And now? When her business was doing so well and Jason was giving his company everything he had.

'Yes, Gemma. She said it was like a switch going on inside her.' Charlotte wobbled her head a little as she quoted her friend with a brittle tone to her voice.

'Surely if Gem does get pregnant, that isn't going to affect your friendship, is it? It's been years since—'

'I know how long it is since my miscarriage, Lewis,' Charlotte snapped. 'And I'm fully aware I should be over it by now . . .'

'I didn't mean that.'

Charlotte clapped her hands. 'Let's change the subject; how was your new assistant?'

'She seems very good. Very knowledgeable and pleasant.'

'More than the other one? The thief?'

'Sooty was more knowledgeable than Vanda about antiques. I think fate was on my side this time.' Which was an understatement, seeing as his new assistant might just have saved his business and Charlotte need never know how close he had come to failing.

'Don't you miss being in charge of hundreds of people and not just one?' Charlotte asked with a loaded sigh.

'Not one bit,' said Lew. 'Especially if it means I might get to live longer.'

Charlotte nodded and said quickly, 'Of course,' as if she couldn't forget that the hugely prestigious job he'd once had had nearly killed him off. 'I'll go and freshen my make-up, they'll be here soon. You could open the Malbec if you like and let it breathe. Are you really wearing jeans and that top, Lewis?'

Lew gave her a crooked questioning smile. 'Yes I am, Charlotte,' he said. 'I'm relaxing after a day's work. With friends, not the royal family. If you want to wear Louboutins, go right ahead though.'

She turned on her swanky heel in the direction of the staircase and Lew wondered what was going through her head that she wanted him to put on a Ralph Lauren top to eat prawns in coconut breadcrumbs and a home-cooked steak and mushrooms in the company of friends. She was turning into Hyacinth Bouquet more and more each day.

# Chapter 13

Bonnie took a slightly different way home to the one she usually travelled, via Dodley. She wanted to drive past Starstruck's daughter's house. It hadn't been out of her mind since Starstruck had mentioned it though the flare of initial interest had been dragged down to earth by the weight of practicality. Wishing about leaving Stephen was easy, but actually doing it would take energy she wasn't sure she had, never mind the money. She really shouldn't open up the possibility of renting it because she was only setting herself up for disappointment. Leaving Stephen *was not the way of things*. He'd drilled that message into her head over the years and she'd blindly obeyed it. At least until she came to leave Ken Grimshaw she had.

When she first realised she'd made a huge mistake in marrying, it wasn't the right time because her dad was going downhill fast and her head had enough to deal with, but she'd made herself a promise to leave Stephen when her dad was at peace. By then, of course, she had no money to start again. Sometimes the resolve to walk out of Greenwood Crescent and never return would surge up in her like a tidal wave, only for it to immediately ebb from fear of the unknown and force her to shrink back into the dreadful familiar. Only once had she reached the point of actually telling him she was leaving him – and meant it and had her bag packed and her car keys in her hand ready to drive away for good. She hadn't known where she was going to, or how she would live . . . and yet she was still there.

She was trapped in her dull, dreary marriage. And even if she did find the guts to propel herself out of the door of Greenwood Crescent, she wasn't in a position to pay out seventy pounds a week for Starstruck's daughter's house, plus there would be utilities and rates and all the other bills added on. And she had no furniture either. She had a moment of wishing she'd kept hold of all the furniture in her dad's old house, but she'd had no use for it at the time and nowhere to store it, so it was sold along with the house which went to pay off the bills in the nursing home. If she left Stephen today, she'd have nothing to her name, apart from a couple of hundred pounds in her coin jar, and about seven hundred and fifty in her secret bank account and her clothes, books, photos, the ashes of her old dog Bear in a wooden box and a couple of pieces of jewellery, which she would never sell.

As it stood, she could just about afford to rent the house on Rainbow Lane for a couple of months, but what if Lew Harley turned out to be the sort of boss that made Ken Grimshaw look like the angel Gabriel? She'd only known him for two days. Or what if Lew conceded defeat and shut up shop, or sacked her because he decided that he couldn't afford an assistant after all?

But, despite the voice in her head telling her to drive past and not look, she overruled it. The house was easy enough to find, it was painted bright white and snuggled into the side of the old chapel as if claiming comfort from the old stone. It had a grey slate roof, a bright red door and an even brighter green gate. It was small and unspectacular from the outside, but Bonnie let herself imagine that on the inside, there would a furry, giddy red-coated dog waiting to greet her, a real fire glowing in the grate and an armchair waiting for her to drop into — and not a bloody beige cushion in sight.

Bonnie put her foot down and sped away before her little fantasy took root and became too hard to dislodge because its image was already sprouting sticky tendrils that threatened to burrow into her brain. She wished Starstruck hadn't said anything about the house; it had been on her mind all day, bouncing around on a string in her head, never taking centre stage, but always there in her peripheral vision, demanding attention.

Bonnie headed for 39 Greenwood Crescent and tried to force the idea of the little house in Rainbow Lane into a mental trash box. It was meant for someone else, not her.

# Chapter 14

Stephen was at home when she got in, watching the news. He turned around briefly and gave her the slightest nod to acknowledge her presence. She didn't expect an apology for what had happened that morning because she knew that in Stephen's mind, it was her fault it had happened. He was never wrong. His mother, the formidable Alma Brookland, had made him that way. She'd brought him up with the right to claim papal infallibility.

'The Shadow Foreign Secretary has resigned,' he said, adding with a sniff, 'not before time.'

Bonnie had nothing to say to that. Politics, as a subject of interest for her, was right up there with tin-mining and calculus. She slipped off her coat and got on with making the tea. There was some fish that needed using up which Stephen had taken out of the freezer. Bonnie wasn't really in the mood for it but she'd eat it for the sake of ease. She didn't seem to have much of an appetite these days, as if slowly bit by bit she was fading to nothing.

Bonnie drizzled the lemon sauce over the fish, careful not to let it touch the fine green beans on Stephen's plate. He was very particular about the components of his meal not encroaching on the space of any of the others. It was one of many of his little ways that she'd found odd but slightly endearing in the early days of their relationship; now she just found them odd. His father was the same, Alma once told her. He couldn't read a newspaper which had been opened by anyone else first, had an abhorrence for cleaning sponges and had to throw away his toothbrush on the last day of the month.

Bonnie remembered standing at the oven, cooking this same fish dish, feeling Alma's eyes boring holes of hatred into her back and knowing that she was about to be ripped to shreds. The sauce was too lemony, the fish too dry, the vegetables hadn't been cooked enough or too much. 'She's a perfectionist,' so Stephen explained his mother's rudeness away. Bonnie took it on the chin because her dad had always told her to answer rudeness with a smile, be the bigger person. He was full of sayings was her dad, his favourite being: *our family was born on the back side of the rainbow.* Luck had never been theirs, he said. The Shermans came from the side without the colours, only grey and shadows. Over the years, she'd come to think he might have been right.

'I take it you haven't phoned Mr Grimshaw?' Stephen asked, when they were seated at the table. He nudged a potato disapprovingly away from the lemon sauce.

'No I have not,' replied Bonnie.

Stephen took a large breath in through his nose and let it go the same way. 'Well don't say I didn't warn you when you find out that this . . . Lewis Harley person doesn't know what he's doing and you're out of a job with nowhere to go. What then, eh?'

Throw me out on the streets, Bonnie was tempted to say.

Maybe if he pushed where she didn't have the nerve to jump, she would have to learn how to survive.

'He seems reliable enough, otherwise I wouldn't have taken the job,' she said instead.

'"Seems" and "is" are very different things,' said Stephen, wagging his finger at her as if she were a child. 'Mr Grimshaw described him as a flash in the pan.'

And Ken Grimshaw is the fount of all knowledge, thought Bonnie. She wondered what else he and her husband had discussed, no doubt finding common ground in how ungrateful she was. She pressed down on the inner growl that his patronising tone was inspiring within her, though her clipped tone indicated with bells on that she hadn't forgotten what had happened between them that morning.

'Well, we'll just have to hope for the best then, won't we?'

He either didn't notice it or did and ignored it, because he then started to tell her an 'amusing story' about the previous day, which she knew would be anything but. He'd had to give a verbal warning to someone who'd told him to 'go away' in slightly more colourful terms after he'd told them to stay behind at lunch to finish off an account that refused to be balanced. Bonnie had often thought he might be the sort of boss that encouraged quite a few 'go away's under the workforce's breath.

As Stephen chewed each mouthful of his meal a customary minimum of twenty times, Bonnie tried to suppress thoughts of living in the little white house in Dodley. She always bought a Saturday lottery ticket but couldn't remember the last time she had won anything. Lottery wins were things that happened to other people, along with children and happy marriages and love.

It would have been Alma's eighty-seventh birthday on Monday, she suddenly remembered. She'd died five years short of it. Making the lemon sauce had stirred up thoughts about her mother-in-law, bringing them to the top again.

'Are you taking some flowers up to your mother's grave next week?' Bonnie asked Stephen as he placed his empty plate in the sink for his wife to wash.

'I don't think that's necessary, do you?' he replied. 'We've observed the anniversary of her birthday for long enough. Any more would be unnecessary and mawkish.'

He was letting his mother go then. Did that mean he might release her also?

# Chapter 15

Lew did a double-take when Patrick walked into the house. It might have only been two months since he last saw him but for all the changes in him, it could have been a lot longer. He'd put on weight, quite a lot of it too and Patrick never put on weight, because he was far too vain about his appearance. But that wasn't the biggest difference. Gingery-blonde hair rampaged wildly over his usually close-shaved face. With his Versace shirt on, he looked like a sort of posh Chewbacca. Charlotte commented on it because it would have been strange not to.

'My goodness, Patrick,' she said. 'Have you joined ZZ Top?'

'I'm reserve bass guitarist,' Patrick said with a meek smile and a voice full of gravel.

'Bloody hell, Pat,' said Jason. 'What's up with your throat? And more importantly is it catching?'

'That sounds sore,' said Gemma, with a tut of sympathy as she enfolded him in a hug of hello.

'Red or white, Reg?' asked Lew.

'White. Don't waste your sympathy on him,' said Regina,

air-kissing Charlotte. 'It was the AGM celebratory dinner last night and guess who decided to do the full repertoire of Louis Armstrong hits on the karaoke. No wonder he sounds as if his vocal cords have been grated.'

'Ouch,' said Lew, delivering the wine to Regina before holding up a bottle of Peroni and a bottle of Malbec for Patrick to indicate his preference. He pointed to the very cold lager without hesitation.

'And let's not even get onto his speech,' sniffed Regina. 'You might have thought as he owned the firm he'd have delivered inspirational words about the success of the company under his leadership but oh no, not Patrick Sheffield, who thought that it might be a great idea to make anagrams of his management team's names as an "amusing opener".'

They gathered by the way Regina said this and from how she flicked her long dark hair over her shoulder that this had not been a good idea and was about as amusing as a killer jellyfish invasion on Blackpool beach.

'What was it you came up with for Dean Walker, Patrick?' She turned to the others to deliver some background information. 'This is the guy my husband has been courting as a potential partner who came over especially for the evening from Jersey in his private jet.' She tapped her lip thoughtfully as Patrick gulped down half the bottle of lager in one. 'Ah yes, *Lead Wanker*.'

Everyone's 'no way' was drowned out by the next person's. Lew saw that Jason and Gemma were desperate to laugh but reined it in because Regina's eyes were flashing 'don't you dare' signals.

'I have never seen so much tumbleweed blow across a room in my life.' Regina pressed the cold glass of white wine against her forehead.

'It broke the ice,' Patrick shrugged.

'Oh yes, it did that all right.' Regina nudged up her artificial breasts with the insides of her arms like an upper-class Les Dawson. She dropped her bag onto the sideboard and Lew noticed how Charlotte's eyes rounded at the sight of it. It was as ugly as hell but he recognised it instantly as a vintage Henri Chaput. The designer was supposedly a protégé of Hermès.

'Is that a Chaput?' asked Charlotte, with breathless admiration.

'Sure is,' purred Regina. 'Farmed albino crocodile,' and she stroked it as if the animal were still alive and capable of receiving affection.

'Ugh,' Gemma shuddered. 'How can you enjoy carrying it around knowing that poor thing had such a shit life?'

Regina gave a bark of laughter. 'It's a bloody reptile not a kitten. It was fed and watered and lived in luxury all its life and had a good end. I probably saved it from starvation and poachers.'

'It would have been a damned sight cheaper for me if the skin had still been on its back,' sighed Patrick. Lew reckoned this was another present he'd had to stump up for to persuade Regina to forgive him.

'It's gorgeous,' said Charlotte.

'Get her an appointment with Specsavers,' Jason said quietly to Lew before turning to Patrick. 'How much did that set you back?'

Patrick blew out two slow cheekfuls of air. 'Don't ask. I could have bought a house for less.'

'Really?' Jason said and went for a second look. Lew suspected that it had now become a much more attractive *objet* to him. It amused him how money changed people, but he hoped it hadn't changed him that much.

'Everyone please sit down at the table,' commanded Charlotte after she had managed to rip her eyes away from the bag. 'We should eat straightaway before everything is overcooked so I hope you're all hungry.'

'Sorry, our fault for being late.' Patrick held his hand up. 'We had another row,' he added out of the corner of his mouth to Lew alone.

'Good because I'm bloody famished,' said Jason, shifting his gaze from Regina's handbag to her oddly hirsute husband as he sat down.

Lew had the same problem. Patrick didn't look like Patrick at all. Lew had only ever seen him with the faintest of designer stubble, if any, and cropped hair. And the whites of his eyes were creamy-yellow with dark shadows under them which told of more than a hangover from last night. Patrick looked drained.

Gemma dived into the bread and speared a butter curl with her knife. She loved her food and usually ran a lot so she could burn it off.

'I could eat this all night,' she said, closing her eyes and savouring the taste.

'Why are you drinking water, Gem?' asked Charlotte suspiciously.

'I'm driving home tonight. I'm up early in the morning because I have someone's nails to do for a wedding at six.'

'Really?' asked Charlotte. She gave a secret point to her stomach.

'Yes really,' said Gemma.

'You boring fart,' said Regina.

'It's all money in the bank, Regina,' returned Gemma. 'Weddings are big business for me.'

'Big business, nails,' chuckled Jason. Lew picked up an

unexpected scathing note in his tone but his observation was distracted by Regina's over-egging of the food-approval pudding.

'Mmm, fabulous prawns, Charlotte,' she purred, spraying panko crumbs over the tablecloth as she delivered her verdict. Considering she deemed herself tantamount to landed gentry, she had some very big holes in her manners. Talking with her mouth full was standard, as was ignoring any need to mind her Ps and Qs.

'So how's the world of antiques?' Jason asked Lew, pronouncing it *anti-queues*.

'Growing. Slowly,' said Lew.

'Lewis set another member of staff on,' bragged Charlotte.

'Oh really?' Regina sounded impressed. 'How many do you have now then?'

'Well, I still only have one,' explained Lew. 'I had to sack one for stealing and so I took someone on in her place.' He felt Charlotte kick him under the table.

'Anyone we know?' asked Patrick.

'I doubt it. She's called Bonnie,' said Charlotte.

Patrick shook his head. 'Don't know any of those.'

'Wasn't there a Blue Peter dog called Bonnie?' asked Jason.

'And is she?' asked Regina. 'Bonny, I mean, not a dog.'

'It would be very unfortunate if she was a minger with a name like Bonnie,' said Jason, dipping a prawn in the tiny bowl of dressing sitting on his plate.

'I had a temporary PA working for me once, an Asian girl called Priti,' said Regina. 'She was absolutely stunning, luckily for her.'

'Not good for Priti if she married someone with the surname Hideous though,' piped up Patrick, looking around the table for approval for the line. 'Or Awful.'

'Because there are loads of people called Mr Hideous and Mr Awful walking around, aren't there, so shut up, Patrick. Remind me, what was your slag called again ... Marlene Hunter, wasn't it? M Hunter – Munter for short.' And she laughed hard and Gemma and Charlotte, Lew and Jason all swapped glances and thought it would be best to change the subject matter as soon as humanly possible.

'So how's things with you, Jase?' asked Lew, noticing that Regina's glass was already empty. He stood up and tipped the bottle over her glass, filling it to just over half way.

'Good, good,' said Jason.

'To the top, Lew, I'm thirsty,' Regina instructed with a red-lipped smile that didn't reach her eyes. She was still angry with Patrick, Lew guessed. Still angry despite the big diamond, the holiday, the expensive bag. None of it could wash away the indelible stain that his affair had stamped on his marriage. He bet that Regina said her renewed vows in the Maldives beach service through clenched teeth.

'Oh guess what,' said Jason, after chewing vigorously to clear his mouth of coconut breadcrumbs. 'Pick up my brand new Porsche next week.'

'Nice.' Lew nodded approvingly, then waited for Patrick to wade in with a counter-brag. *Pick up a new Porsche, I'll raise you a Lambo.* Regina had never been so happy, since Lew had packed in his job in the City and they were now the number one high-earners in the group with Jason and Gemma in second place. But there was not a peep from Patrick. He really must be out of sorts. Lew snatched a glance at him, wiping his mouth with his serviette. His eyes looked as if they were drooping at the outer corners, like a sad Basset Hound's.

Charlotte stood up to clear the plates and Lew rose also to help her.

'He's bouncing around like Tigger,' chuckled Gemma, addressing the table. 'I don't get how a car can have such an effect on you boys. Jason's like a dog with two willies at the moment.'

'Gemma, darling, it's a Porsche,' grinned Lew.

'Totally unpractical if you're going to have a sprog, of course,' said Regina.

Gemma's eyes saucered and her voice came out whispery when she asked the question, 'How did you know about that?' Her glare slid to Charlotte whose cheeks flared pink with halogen speed.

'Sorry, I might have said something.'

Gemma shrugged. 'S'fine. It wasn't a secret.' But Lew noticed the clipped tone. Gemma wasn't stupid and knew they'd been talking behind her back.

'Are you pregnant? Is that the reason why you're on water?' asked Patrick, his face lit up like a Christmas tree.

'No . . . we're trying though,' said Gemma.

'You're not seriously thinking about having a brat, are you?' said Regina, as if Gemma had said she was considering getting a vaginal piercing without anaesthetic.

'Yes, Regina, we are,' replied Gemma, with a tone in her voice that said, 'so fuck off and mind your own business'. Lew knew that Gemma didn't like Regina for the same reasons he didn't like her; she was a spoilt, pretentious, nasty cow and, also like Lew, she put up with her because they all liked Patrick so much.

'Well, brat or no brat, you can't deprive a boy of his car toys, Gemma. His balls maybe, but not his car.' She snorted with laughter; Regina had a laugh ripe from the gutter.

Lew stood to fill glasses and hopefully steer Regina away from man-baiting waters. Charlotte took his lead and started loading up the dishwasher. It didn't have the desired effect.

'Never wanted brats,' said Regina. 'They're millstones round your neck for the whole of your life.'

'You were a child once, darling,' said Patrick.

'Oh shut up, Patrick.' Regina swept up her glass and almost drained it in one.

'I think you'd make a lovely mother, Gem,' said Patrick and raised his Peroni in her direction.

'Are you actively trying for a baby then?' asked Regina.

'Yes, we're at it like rabbits,' Gemma replied with a crudity that wasn't typical of her, and Lew could sense her annoyance.

Behind them Charlotte dropped a plate and swore.

'Gemma!' Jason's admonition was a hard growl. Lew leapt in with the first thing he could think of, diverting the conversation to Jason's plans to extend the garage whilst Charlotte brought the steaks to the table. Everyone had medium except for Patrick who preferred his well done and Regina who liked hers so blue it was still mooing.

'Help yourself to special sauce,' said Charlotte, indicating the jug on the table. Patrick was first to pour it over his steak.

'You'll have to try my special sauce next time you have dinner at ours,' said Patrick.

'You and Marlene both,' sniggered Regina.

Patrick ignored her. 'Whisky, cream and my secret ingredient, a dribble of honey.'

Regina wrinkled up her whole face. 'Don't bother, it's fucking awful.' She reached for the bottle of white in the middle of the table as no one was filling up her empty glass.

Patrick swivelled his head around to his wife who looked as if she were enjoying poking the tiger and under his breath Lew heard him say, 'Regina, stop it.'

'Stop what?' she answered at full volume. 'Stop telling people that you're no Gerald Randall. Well . . . maybe you are if the *Mail* is to be believed.'

Celebrity Chef Gerald Randall was headline news that week after it had been revealed his perfect Brady Bunch six-offspring marriage was a sham because he'd been having wild Fifty-Shades-of-Grey-type sex with a TV producer for twelve years.

'Oh for God's sake,' said Patrick, dropping his cutlery onto his plate, a gesture of tired defeat.

'And another thing—' Regina started up again, but the feeling of Lew's arm around her shoulder cut off her words.

He spoke softly into her ear. 'Reg, please. You're a guest in my house and so is Patrick. Don't spoil this evening.'

As if Regina had been jolted out of a groove and Lew's gentle admonishment had given her some perspective of how she was coming across, she conceded and gave him a slurry reply. 'Apologies, Lewis. I'll be a good girl.'

The bubble of tension that hung like an airship over the table seeped away. To everyone's relief, the rest of the meal was consumed with the usual camaraderie they'd enjoyed pre-Patrick's infidelity. After dessert, the women remained at the table with coffees and impressive chocolates and the three men went out onto the patio because Patrick was desperate for a smoke and Jason needed a vape.

'Thanks, Lew,' said Patrick, drawing on the newly lit Lambert and Butler as if it was an inhaler stilling the onslaught of an asthma attack.

'What for?' asked Lew.

'Having my back in there.' Patrick wiped his left eye with his knuckle and Jason flashed a look of 'oh heck' at Lew.

'It's fine, mate,' said Lew.

'She won't let it drop,' sniffed Patrick. 'It's wearing me down like you wouldn't believe.'

'As it would,' replied Lew, for the want of something better to say.

'It cost me an arm and a leg in "letting it drop" expenses but nothing's changed. It would have been cheaper and less painful if I'd let her cut my bollocks off.' He coughed and Lew saw two big splashes of Patrick's tears drop onto a flagstone.

A few seconds' silence ensued as Patrick smoked and Jason vaped.

'Marlene texted me last week,' said Patrick in a low voice. 'She said that she can't stop thinking about me.'

'Oh Patrick, be very careful,' warned Lew.

'I can't stop thinking about her either,' said Patrick.

'Just got to nip to your loo, Lew,' said Jason, quickly rising to his feet. That he didn't want to be party to this secret was quite obvious.

'I don't know what to do,' said Patrick, more tears dropping.

'Patrick, do you really want to start all that up again?' said Lew, his voice concerned but with a strong cautionary note. Regina wasn't his favourite person but that didn't mean that he condoned what Patrick had done to her. 'You hurt Reg very badly and it's going to take a lot of time to get her trust back.'

Patrick gave a sarcastic laugh. 'She doesn't want me to have her trust, Lew. She only wanted me to stay so she could punish me for the rest of my life. There are so many things you don't—' He cut off the sentence to draw the last of the nicotine from his cigarette. 'It wasn't a cheap fling you know. I fell in love with her. With Marlene. I miss her.'

'You'll get over it, Patrick.'

'You talking from a textbook or first-hand experience, Lew?' said Patrick, lifting his eyes to his friend.

'Are you seriously asking me that?' replied Lew. It shocked him that Patrick could think he'd been in the same position.

'All those years working down in London during the week. You must have had your opportunities.'

'Well I didn't,' said Lew convincingly, though it wasn't strictly true. There had been an extremely bright and beautiful graduate who had an obvious crush on him and he'd found himself more than once wondering what it would be like to hold her. But he was married and he hadn't even opened the door a sliver on that one. He'd made sure he was never alone with her, didn't flirt with her and never gave her the slightest inkling that unfaithful thoughts had flitted across his brain. He was only human after all and he couldn't do anything about involuntary reactions to her pheromones, but he could do something about not acting on what his perfidious brain was encouraging him to do.

'I understand. Charlotte's a good girl so why would you even look,' said Patrick. 'But Regina's poison, Lew. Treacherous. I'm so stressed I shouldn't really be drinking. It's a depressive, alcohol, did you know? Not that I think I could be more depressed if I tried. I've got an appointment at the doc's on Tuesday. I think I need Prozac or something before I end up throwing myself off a multi-storey car park.'

Lew's features assembled into a look of horror. 'Jesus, Patrick, are things that bad?'

Patrick lit up another cigarette. 'No, ignore me, not that bad. But I want to nip things in the bud before they get any worse.'

The sound of Regina's witch-like cackling resonated from inside the house and Patrick winced at the sound of it. It spoke volumes about how much that twenty thousand poundsworth-plus of reconciliation fees, not to mention a crocodile handbag, had been wasted.

In Tuesday's *Daily Trumpet* we printed an article about Freda's Café in the market and its child-friendly facilities. Freda Bagshaw, owner and proprietor, would like us to point out that she has not had the washroom designed to make the hanging of babies very easy for stressed parents, but changing of babies. We apologise to Freda and her excellent café.

# Chapter 16

Bonnie was awoken at four-thirty the next morning by Stephen pottering around downstairs. He was going fishing and so was filling up a flask and making some sandwiches to take with him. It would be cheese – mild cheddar – with a sprinkling of black pepper on wholemeal bread spread to the very edges with Flora because that's what he always had. She heard the van draw up outside which belonged to his friend Gerald, although 'friend' was pushing it a bit. Gerald was a pensioner whom Stephen had met on a river bank two or three years ago and they didn't socialise outside these Sunday morning outings. Stephen didn't have the sort of friends who invited them out as a couple for dinner or a drink at the pub. Bonnie used to have coupley-friends who wanted her and Stephen to join them but after too many refusals and excuses made, the invitations dried up and left her as socially isolated as he preferred to be. If it wasn't for the occasional coffee dates with Valerie, Bonnie thought she would have gone stark, staring mad.

As the van pulled away, Bonnie tried to shoulder her way back into the dream she'd been having before she'd been so rudely pulled from it. She was in a beautiful castle with fairytale turrets and every wall inside was painted with a different colour. There was a deep moat around it and the drawbridge was pulled up. Stephen was standing on the far bank screaming at her, but she knew with all certainty that she was safe from him, forever.

There was no point in wishing herself into a house like that, even if it was the first step to actually getting it, if her mother was to be believed. 'The Queen of Wishful Thinking', her dad said he used to call her. Her mum had been proof that wishing was a good thing, but only if you had the guts to back it up and go for what you wanted. She was born so premature, she shouldn't have lived and the doctors said she'd probably never walk – but she had. They said she would most likely not lead an independent life – but she had. They said she would never be able to bear a child – and she'd defied them in that too. She'd tackled every hurdle life had put in her way by imagining herself flying over it and then doing exactly that. Except for that last one which had been too high, too slyly positioned.

Instead of the huge castle, Bonnie's thoughts turned to something attainable: the little white house on Rainbow Lane. She imagined opening the green gate, walking down the path and in through the red door. She saw a table where she could sit and eat her dinner alone without having to look at Stephen chewing every mouthful of food, her things displayed everywhere in homely chaos without being forced into pattern and symmetry. She thought of waking up in a citrus-lemon bedroom with tangerine curtains and lime green bedding, of cooking in a kitchen painted every possible shade of blue and violet, of sitting in a huge scarlet chair, safe and content with the weight of a sleeping dog pressing on her feet. This wasn't a wish too far, this was doable if she backed it up with some action.

She should never have started thinking about the house because she knew now there was no way she would get back to sleep. She pulled on her dressing gown and went downstairs to make herself a coffee. As the kettle was boiling, she took out a pad and a pen from the drawer and started to jot down some non-committal figures. She wrote down her approximate secret savings and her expected basic wage. Usually she handed most of it over to Stephen for her share of the bills and savings. Now, with a new job, would be an ideal time to hand over less and keep more for her secret stash. He wouldn't be happy, but what could he do about it? Well, knowing him, he could ring up Lew and ask how much he was paying her but she didn't think Lew would tell him. Then she started to think about how she might earn some extra money on the side.

She had always said that she would leave her marriage without asking anything from Stephen but a quick divorce, even though she knew that he had inherited a considerable sum from Alma, and the insurance company had paid out over thirty thousand pounds, because she'd seen that on a letter he had once carelessly left lying about. Was there anything she could sell, she wondered. The only thing she had of any value was her parents' jewellery and that was unthinkable. Plan B: was there anything she could make and trade on the internet?

She unplugged her phone from charge and looked at the listings on eBay for some ideas. She'd always had very deft fingers, loved to cut up things and draw and stick when she was a child. She used to make all her own greetings cards for people, though she barely had anyone to send them to these days. She still had her large box of craft supplies which she hadn't touched for years. On the 'about to end soon' listings, some black cat confetti caught her eye. Seventy-five little cats for two pounds plus one pound fifty postage and packing. A silly idea came to her, but still one worth considering. What if she sold confetti in bags? A hundred pieces of it for two pounds fifty, including postage and packing? Her brain started spinning as she went back upstairs and pulled the craft box out of her wardrobe. She couldn't remember the last time she opened its lid. She took out the bag of German punches underneath all the paper. One of the dealers had given them to her dad to pass on to her. There was a cat design, a dog design, a reindeer head, various flowers, an owl, Happy Birthday, balloons ... lots of them, all needing a good squirt of WD40 and then a clean. It wouldn't make her a millionaire but it would be easy and every penny would come in handy. She still had a stock of unused coloured paper and the pound shop was good for craft materials. She could supply an upgrade on the usual confetti, press the cats out of glitter paper, draw red blobs on the reindeer noses – she had plenty of spare time to do that when Stephen had gone to bed. Bonnie felt an eel of excitement ripple through her. She could ask the traders at the antiques centre to keep their eyes open for unusual punches.

So, before work that day, Bonnie set up Paypal and eBay accounts calling herself The Rainbow Lady. It seemed appropriate.

# Chapter 17

Lew warmed up some croissants for Charlotte before he left for the Pot of Gold. Gemma and Jason had gone home at eleven the previous evening because they both had early starts in the morning. Charlotte and Regina had got totally blasted on Brandy Alexanders and Lew had broken out the Glenfiddich in the conservatory. He didn't drink much these days but he had a small one to keep Patrick and his triple measure company. Whilst his friend was talking about something banal, Lew had switched his hearing to the conversation happening nearby in the sitting room where Charlotte and Regina were bitching about Gemma getting all animal-rights about Regina's bag. He wouldn't ever dictate who his wife socialised with but, for the life of him, he hoped that Charlotte wouldn't replace Regina as her best friend. Though he felt disloyal thinking it, Charlotte was a chameleon and she absorbed the colour of the people she mixed with. When she hung around with Gemma, she was lovely and sweet, but since she had transferred her attention to Regina, she was taking on her snooty, rude ways. Well, much as he loved his wife, she wouldn't be getting a bag made out of a white crocodile from him – ever.

He delivered Charlotte's breakfast on a tray along with a pat of butter, a small jar of honey, a cup of milky, sweetened tea and two ibuprofen because he suspected she might have a hangover – and he was right.

'You should have made me drink some water before I went to bed,' said Charlotte, holding her head in an attempt to relieve the pain hammering at the front of her skull.

'I did. Most of a pint,' said Lew. 'So imagine what you'd be like if I hadn't.'

'Did you? I can't remember. I seem to have a blank after Regina suggested tequila shots. Did I have any?'

'No,' replied Lew. 'I told her that would be a very bad idea. Plus their taxi had just arrived.'

Charlotte glugged down the tea as if she'd been on a desert island for days without a drink and had just discovered an ice-cold lake.

'I wish I didn't have to go to work, even if it is only half a day,' said Lew, wanting to strip off and slip back into bed with Charlotte. 'When Bonnie has found her feet, I'll suggest that we do alternate Sundays.'

'Well to have a successful business, you'll need to put the hours in. Just like you did in London.' Charlotte pressed her teeth into her croissant like Regina's handbag must have once bitten into its meals.

'At least I'm home every night and all day Monday.'

'Yes and that's great,' said Charlotte.

She said it with less conviction than he would have liked to hear, and it wasn't the first time he had picked up on it either. 'Cheers,' he said, with a click of his tongue.

'What?' Croissant confetti dropped from Charlotte's lips.

'Sometimes I wonder if you like me being around more than I used to be.'

Charlotte put her croissant down on the plate, got out of bed, reached up and put her arms around her husband. She gave him a squeeze and then adjusted position so he was at arm's length. 'Lewis, a lot has happened to us in the past couple of years. We are adjusting.' She gave the word special weight. 'I know you want to build up your business and I respect that. I never moaned about you being away down in London, did I? Did I ever?'

'No,' he said, truthfully because she never had. He'd been working in the City when they first met and he'd been careful to set out his stall from the off that his life plan was to work bloody hard, rise to the top, retire in his early fifties and live a simpler, quieter life off the fruits of his labour. But still, he had often felt guilty about the time he spent away from Charlotte and that's why he compensated her with flash cars, a big house and a fat bank account for her to dip into at her leisure. He hadn't considered a spanner might be thrown into the works and set him on a different path. They had plenty of money in the bank, but not enough to indefinitely sustain the lifestyle they led when he was a big fish in the pool of high finance. He'd spoilt Charlotte too much, that was the problem. She wouldn't be content with simpler and quieter now, she wanted year-on-year bigger and better.

'So if it means that you have to put a lot of hours in so you don't slip into miser mode, I can deal with that,' added Charlotte.

Lew raised his eyebrows. 'Miser mode? What, because I told you to stop throwing money out of the window?'

'And what's next? We can't go on holidays and I have to

shop in Lidl?' Charlotte gave a dry skip of laughter and sat down heavily on the bed.

Lew looked at her incredulously. 'Where on earth is all this nonsense coming from?'

'We are now the poorest people in our social group.' Charlotte looked as if she was about to sob.

'No we aren't. My present salary might be decidedly lower than it was a couple of years ago, but we hardly need to start looking for the nearest soup kitchen.' He threw up his hands. 'Anyway, what does it matter who earns what? Why this current obsession with us not being group leaders in earnings? We didn't look down on Jason and Gemma when they were juggling bank loans, did we?'

She didn't answer the question directly, which said everything, but asked instead, 'Are you earning a lot of money in the shop, Lewis?'

It was a question she hadn't asked yet and he was dreading it coming up because he had never lied to his wife. Well, maybe a white lie when he was trying to stop her buying things because he'd already bought them as presents for her, but not *real* lies that carried a punch when uncovered.

He chose his words carefully. 'I've got a steady turnover, if that's what you mean.'

'Big profits?'

'No . . . not . . . really.'

'Any profits?' Her voice was fiercer now.

'Well, not yet.'

'Oh God.' Her hands flew to her head.

'It's early days, Charlotte. I'm starting from scratch and building up a clientele. It takes time to—'

Charlotte spoke over him. 'Regina asked me if we would like to go on a cruise with them to Alaska.'

'When?'

'Last night.'

'No, I mean when did she want to go?'

'September. But we won't be able to, will we, because it would cost too much money.' There was a fearful shake in her voice.

'The money isn't anything to do with why we won't be joining them,' Lew replied, half under his breath.

'We'll be holidaying in Butlins, won't we? Or a caravan. Well, I'd rather not bother.' She slipped back under the covers as if they gave her comfort from those particular horrors.

Lew bit back on saying that he'd had some great holidays in Butlins and caravans when he was a kid. In fact he was sure he remembered that she'd had caravan holidays with her parents. He took a deep breath before giving her the sort of reply she wanted. One she needed to hear.

'Charlotte, we have savings, we have a house with no mortgage on it, we have investments, financially we are more than all-right-Jack so don't panic. *But*' – he gave the word special emphasis – 'if you think I'm going to let you draw God knows how many thousand pounds out of the bank just to keep up with the Joneses – or Sheffields in this case – just to buy a handbag made—'

'Who said anything about a handbag?' Charlotte snapped.

'You did, last night. Or can't you remember? When Patrick and Regina had gone, you could barely stand up but you begged me to buy you a Chaput bag.'

'I only got drunk because Gemma started banging on about babies. You would have thought she'd have had more consideration.'

She bowed her head and Lew sat down on the bed and

put his arm around her, giving her a chivvying squeeze. Then he noticed the clock and realised he'd be late if he didn't set off now for the Pot of Gold.

'I'll have to go, but we can carry on this conversation when I get back.'

Charlotte sniffed. 'I'm sorry. I'm being silly, aren't I?'

He kissed the top of her nose. 'Yes you are. Stop panicking. *You* might have blown a fortune on fripperies in the past ... *I,* however, have been sensible.'

'Good job,' grinned Charlotte.

'Come here.' Lew attempted to kiss her full on the lips but she twisted her head and it landed on her cheek.

'I have revolting morning breath,' she giggled. 'Stay clear.'

Lew laughed and lifted up the breakfast tray from the bed, putting it on the table by her side. 'Go back to sleep for a couple of hours and get rid of that hangover,' he ordered. 'I'll close up early if we don't have any customers.'

'Have a nice day in your little shop,' said Charlotte, her head flopping heavily onto the pillow. Lew couldn't tell if that one word carried conscious or unconscious disdain, but it was derisive all the same. He leaned over, gave her a kiss on her head and set off for his *little shop.*

\*

Bonnie was waiting for him when he arrived, sitting on the bench in the middle of the square, below an enormous dome of an umbrella, each panel a different shade of the rainbow. She was dressed in a red raincoat, a dark pink shift dress with a white blouse underneath and blue boots on her feet. She smiled a welcome at him and it made him wonder when was the last time Charlotte had greeted him with a smile, or a kiss – as she used to when he came home from London. He recalled that her smile used to be very wide whenever he told her he'd received a banker's bonus.

'I'm not late, am I?' he said, quickening his pace whilst stealing a glance at his watch.

'Not at all,' replied Bonnie. 'I got up early because I couldn't sleep. I went to the little teashop in the corner and had a coffee and a toasted teacake. The sun was shining beautifully until five minutes ago, so I came to sit out here but it's just started to spit.'

'Good job you remembered your brolly, then.'

'Isn't it just.'

The rain increased its flow and fell with a soft shushing noise.

'Come on, let's get in,' said Lew, hurrying forwards. By the time they reached the Pot of Gold, the rain was falling in a sheet and there was a grumble of thunder in the distance. He quickly unlocked the door and Bonnie followed him in, after shaking the drops off her umbrella.

'April showers have turned up three weeks early,' she said, as he pressed in the code to disable the alarm. 'But it's Sunday, so don't worry about customers not turning up. This should be your busiest day.'

'Well it's not,' replied Lew, switching on the lights. 'That's why I'm only opening for four hours. I was going to suggest to you that when you've settled in, maybe you'd consider we do alternate Sundays. I'd like to spend some extra time with my wife.'

'I'm happy to work every Sunday,' said Bonnie quickly. 'Any overtime you have, I'll take it. Although if you get a lot more dealers in, you might find you need both of us on Sunday and someone else besides. In the good old days of

Grimshaw's, we didn't close until seven sometimes and needed all hands on deck.'

'Oh how I wish that for us,' said Lew. 'And yes, if you're up for an extra bit of cash in hand, I'll take you up on that offer.' That would appease Charlotte. They could go out into the country for a drive and Sunday lunch. And though there was the possibility that his new employee might be wanting the boss out of the way so she could steal all his stock, he was pretty sure she was no Vanda Clegg. Especially after two conversations he had that day with the traders.

The first was when he went over to help Vintage Valerie move into her new unit later that morning. He was assembling a clothes rail for her when Bonnie's name came up.

'I'm so glad that Bonnie is working here,' said Valerie, whose accent was so refined, she made Regina look like Hilda Odgen by comparison. 'You'll do no better for an assistant than her. Her father was one of the nicest men ever. A true gentleman and there aren't many of those left in the world, let me tell you.' She peered at him over half-moon glasses as if expecting him to disagree with that. Valerie had the air of a very strict headmistress of an extremely select girls' school. He wondered what her profession had been before she dealt in antique clothing, but he didn't ask.

'I hope you'll let me steal her away for a bite to eat next door,' she went on.

'Steal away. She's due a break.'

'Good.'

Then, when Bonnie was in the teashop next door with Valerie, Stickalampinit turned up with some more of his creations and conversation again steered itself to Bonnie. He had just dragged in a huge metal statue of an armless Greek goddess but instead of a face there was an oval clock. It was probably the most hideous thing Lew had ever seen, but he was careful with his words.

'That's an interesting piece, Stickalampinit,' he said.

'I don't think you'll be seeing this one for very long,' said Stickalampinit fondly. 'It's not a real clock but a colour-changing lamp. Totally weatherproof, so you can keep it outside.'

Lew didn't say that if he owned it, it would have to go outside because he wouldn't want it in the house.

Stickalampinit was obviously very proud of his creation. He was viewing it as if he were Pygmalion and it was Galatea and about to take a breath.

'No Bonnie today?' he asked.

'She's on a break. I think she's next door with Valerie.'

'Ah. Lovely girl is Bonnie,' he said. 'You've done well to get her working for you. She knows a lot.' He wagged a long finger as if to give his words emphasis. 'She should have had her own shop, not be working for someone else.'

'Should she?' asked Lew.

'Her dad used to part-own Grimshaw's,' said Stickalampinit. 'Oh, it was a proper shop was that once upon a time. It's full of shit now, but back in the day ... eeeh,' and he let out a very nostalgic sigh. 'She's had a poor deal, bless her.'

Just as Lew was about to ask what he meant, a customer interrupted them wanting to see an old teddy bear in Uncle Funky's cabinet.

'I'll get the key and be over in a minute,' said Lew.

'Nice teddy that, if it's the hump-backed one,' said Stickalampinit. 'I saw it myself and was going to buy it for our Sharon, but it's overpriced and the stingy old bugger won't come down more than ten per cent.'

'I need to learn more about toys,' Lew stated. 'It's not my strongest area.'

'Well don't let Uncle Funky teach you owt,' said Stickalampinit. 'We're talking about the guy who bought a job lot of *Jim'll Fix It* badges hush hush from someone in the TV company. He thought it would be his retirement fund.' He laughed heartily.

Lew went over to get the teddy bear, crossing paths with a woman who was walking towards Stickalampinit's ridiculous garden statue lamp and telling her husband that she simply must have it, simply must.

# Chapter 18

Next door in the teashop, Valerie and Bonnie were enjoying a bowl of home-made tomato soup, a warm plait of bread and a huge pot of tea after Bonnie had filled Valerie in on the details of her sacking. Valerie listened patiently, without interrupting, taking every word in. Only when Bonnie had finished did she comment.

'I think fate has intervened rather nicely for you, dear Bonnie,' she said, lifting the china cup to her lips and sipping delicately. Then she replaced the cup on the saucer before continuing, 'I am inclined to believe the rumours that Wendy Grimshaw got pregnant by another man, but Harry forgave her and brought the baby up as his own. Ken doesn't even look like Harry and he certainly doesn't act like him.'

Bonnie was shocked. 'You're joking. I've never heard that story.'

Valerie gave a small laugh. 'There's a lot you don't know, Bonnie.'

And she was right. For all the years Bonnie had known Valerie – and that was all of her life – she didn't *know* her at all. She knew that Valerie lived alone, had never married,

had no children, had once been an Oracy teacher in a private
school, though she didn't really know what that entailed.
She knew that Valerie had a sister who lived in Italy and she
went to a secret location in France once a year to stock up
on vintage clothes from a huge market there. And she knew
that Valerie and Jack Pitt, or Jackpot as he was known in the
trade, were very close friends. That was the extent of all she
knew about Valerie. But it was enough. Bonnie didn't need
to know anything more than Valerie enjoyed her company
and liked her as a person.

'I think Lew Harley could have a very successful business
in this square,' said Valerie. 'It's a wonderful location, plenty
of parking and, I must say, he is quite the charmer. Is he
married?'

'Yes, and happily so.' Lew had already told Bonnie that
he wanted to spend more time with his wife.

'Shame he's married,' said Valerie with a smile tugging at
the left corner of her mouth.

'So am I.' Bonnie lifted her hand with her wedding ring
on it and waggled it.

Valerie's lips assumed a serious line. 'Happily?'

'What?'

Valerie sat back against the scrolled ironwork of the chair
and studied Bonnie thoroughly for a few moments before
speaking again. 'We have an untypical friendship, don't we,
Bonnie, you and I? What is it – four or five years since we
shared our first pot of tea over a café table and yet I've
known you all your life and seen all the changes that have
happened in it. But we talk about the weather, the news and
we never pry into each other's business, do we?'

'I like that we do that,' replied Bonnie. 'I like that our
friendship takes me away from ... th ...' she struggled,

finding the right way to put what she meant '... from ... what I ... everything else.'

'And so do I, dear Bonnie. So do I. But that does not mean that I don't notice how pale you are, how little light there is in your eyes, and it concerns me greatly.'

It was the first time Valerie had lifted the veneer of their relationship to probe underneath it and Bonnie felt a stab of panic. If she opened up, even a little, everything would come pouring out and she couldn't let it.

'I'm fine, Valerie. Really. Working for Ken wore me down, that's all, and I've got new-job nerves.'

Valerie's slim hand closed over hers and gave it a squeeze. 'Dear Bonnie,' she said again and Bonnie knew that her wise old friend hadn't been at all convinced by what she had said but would leave it at that. For now.

# Chapter 19

Lew got home later than expected because there was a steady stream of customers in until three o'clock. He found Charlotte in a very chirpy and affable mood. She'd been shopping in Meadowhall with Regina who, despite her alcohol overload, had awoken fresh and fit for spending. Charlotte said that she hadn't bought a thing. Lew knew she was lying but he didn't press it. He didn't want to fuel any fire that he was a skinflint and he'd had too good a day to argue. He'd rented a couple more units out and sold some pipes to a delighted Pied Piper who had been lured to visit by tales of those Petersons. Stickalampinit not only sold the revolting statue but the woman who bought it wanted another as a garden pair. One man's rubbish really was another's treasure, thought Lew with a smile, and he thanked God that was the case.

Lew volunteered to cook and rustled up a simple pasta dish for them both – arrabiata sauce, olives, mushrooms, ham and loads of parmesan – and pushed a part-baked baguette into the oven. Cooking relaxed him, whereas it was just something on the chore list for his wife.

He spread the warm bread with chilli butter and put it on the table, then poured two glasses of crisp, cold Chablis.

'I had an amazing day sales-wise,' said Lew when Charlotte had taken her place at the table.

'Did you?' she replied, sprinkling the tiniest amount of extra parmesan over her pasta.

'My best day yet, I reckon,' he smiled.

'I bet your share price is just racing up,' sighed Charlotte.

'Ouch,' replied Lew, making light of the wounding comment.

'I'm sorry,' Charlotte said immediately. 'That came out as more sarcastic than the jokey way I intended.'

Lew suspected she meant it exactly as she had said it and felt a cloud drift across the sunshine of his mood. 'I thought you'd be happy that I'd put some money in my till.'

'I am, of course I am,' she tried to enthuse, but he wasn't fooled. What he had taken probably didn't even cover what she would have spent in Meadowhall. He'd bet his life on the fact that if he went on a search in her wardrobe, he would find a very classy designer carrier bag with a handbag or shoes in it. Possibly both.

It worried him that his marriage worked better when they saw less of each other. He'd read about other marriages suffering the same fate: women married to soldiers coping fine with their long-distance relationship, until the soldier left the forces and the extra contact broke them up. He hadn't made an issue of it, because the last couple of years had been full of pressure what with the house move and then nearly making Charlotte a widow. But things should have been levelling out by now. The shop was up and running, Lew's health checks were coming back with great big positives and their lives were as stress-free as they could be. But now they were together more, Lew had started to notice traits in Charlotte that he'd not been aware of before, especially how bitchy she could be; and though she'd always had the makings of a snob, she could earn a doctorate in pretentiousness judging by what he'd heard her come out with recently. In a couple of years she'd morph into a blonde version of Regina if she wasn't careful. He'd been sober the previous evening, unlike most of his guests, and he'd eavesdropped on some of the cruel comments his wife and Regina had been saying about Gemma and it didn't sit well with him. He liked Gemma immensely, especially for how she'd hardly changed at all over the years. She'd been behind Jason one hundred per cent when he left the car salesroom which he deputy-managed and struck out on his own, selling prestige cars. They remortgaged their house to buy stock, Gemma had doubled her hours in Sparkles to bring in extra revenue and had been the unheralded wind beneath his wings. And when the big money started to come to Jason, Gemma didn't give up work and spend her day gardening, playing tennis and blowing cash on crocodile handbags, but put even more effort into Sparkles. She was a grafter, a down-to-earth Yorkshire girl and she deserved a better set of friends, he was sad to admit.

Charlotte looked faraway as she was chewing.

'Penny for them,' Lew asked her, wondering what was making her smile so wistfully. He hoped it was him, but thought it more likely it was a purchase.

Her jaw froze and she looked at him as if he were slightly mad.

'What?'

'Your thoughts? You looked miles away.'

'I wasn't thinking anything.' The smile had dropped and been replaced with a scowl.

Lew was slightly taken aback at the sudden change in her. 'You okay? Something on your mind, love?'

'Like what?'

He shrugged, unsure why her tone had suddenly acquired a sharp, defensive edge. 'I don't know. Just . . . something?'

She stared at him with her large blue eyes and then, as if a thought had landed with a bump in her mind, she nodded. 'Oh I see, you mean because we haven't had sex for a while.'

Lew's eyebrows shot up his forehead at the same time as his jaw dropped open.

'I didn't mean that at all. It hadn't even entered my head.'

'Yeah right.' Charlotte's fork left her hand and clattered to her plate. 'I haven't been in the mood is the answer to that. I don't know why. Maybe I'm going through the change. Mum went through it at forty-two.'

'Charlotte, where's all this coming from?' He half-laughed at the ludicrous leap from her reflective smile to the symptoms of an early menopause. But Charlotte was so caught up in a loop, she didn't hear him.

'Maybe I'm still adjusting to our new circumstances even though I know I should have accepted them by now and I hear what you're saying about us being okay, but I can't help worrying when I know you can't claim your pension for years. Maybe I haven't got over the fact that you nearly died. Maybe I'm just a bit pissed off that my best friend wants the fucking baby that I'll never have and I don't think I'll be able to be around her if she gets pregnant.' Then Charlotte dropped her head into her hands and made a strangled noise of distress. Lew sprang from his chair and threw his arms around her. He kissed her hair and held her as her shoulders jumped as she sniffed. His poor wife. No wonder she was all over the place. They needed a holiday. Venice maybe – a city of beauty and good food where they could have some 'us' time and he'd buy her all the handbags she could carry if they stemmed the empty hungry hole in her heart.

\*

When Bonnie got home, Stephen was sitting at the kitchen table drumming his fingers impatiently on the surface. She wondered how long he'd been doing that. He could do it for a very long time when he was annoyed about something.

'Where on earth have you been?' he said, before she'd even got both feet through the back door.

'It was surprisingly busy at the shop,' she said.

'It closed at two.' His lips were a grim line of annoyance.

She forced herself to stay calm. 'It stayed open until three because there were customers.'

She saw him look at the clock, almost heard his brain whirring as it calculated that if the shop shut at three, getting home at twenty-past was reasonable.

'You should have rung,' Stephen said.

'I didn't see the problem,' replied Bonnie. 'We don't eat until seven on Sundays anyway. The timer's kicked in on the oven to cook the roast so what's the panic?'

'It's just not the way of things,' he snapped, before snatching up the newspaper and storming off into the lounge, muttering to himself the entire *Roget's Thesaurus* word listing for disorder.

*It was not the way of things* was his stock phrase. Anything that differed from the norm in Stephen's life threw him into a panic. She could blow his whole world apart by not having carrots with their Sunday lunch because that definitely was not the way of things. It was then that Bonnie was reminded how blown apart the 'way of things' would be when he came home and found out that she had left him.

# Chapter 20

As usual, Bonnie woke up early on Monday to breakfast with Stephen, wash up his cereal plate and cup and wave him off like a dutiful wife. Things were once again calm because order had been restored the previous night when she had served up a delicious dinner at exactly seven, with carrots, and then soothed any remaining ruffled waters by asking about his fishing expedition as they ate. He showed off the trout he had caught, gutted and frozen for next Saturday's tea and Bonnie had wondered if she would be still here then to have it.

When Stephen drove off to work, Bonnie sat at the kitchen table and began to plan out her future properly in an A4 pad. She wrote down all the things she would take with her and the bare essentials she would need to buy and found that she could get away with very little. She could make do with a flip out chair-bed that unfolded into a makeshift mattress. Even a sleeping bag would do for a couple of nights. She found a plastic box on a high shelf in the garage and put a couple of towels and some soap and toilet rolls in it, a few teabags, a pan to to cook from and to boil water in until she got a kettle, a spare toothbrush and toothpaste and one each of the following: a mug, a plate, a dish, a spoon, a knife and fork. She'd keep it under the bed for now, ready and waiting.

Then she pressed some confetti at the table and took photos of it, downloading them to eBay. The Rainbow Lady was open for business. She tipped her two-pound-coin jar onto the table and counted it to find that she had actually £304 in it. She nipped to the bank in Maltstone to update her passbook and found that with interest she had a few pounds more than she'd thought; not enough to go wild and buy the latest sort of smart TV, but every little counted. Her dad's voice came to her as the counter assistant was printing out her new balance, *Poor men throw away their pounds, Bon, and rich men look after their pennies.* She deposited the two-pound coins in her account so they were safe and started to feel a stir of excitement that she could really do this. She had taken the next step towards leaving Stephen, after merely wishing she could. There was a giant leap to the third, though; she was under no illusions.

She packed a few of her clothes in a suitcase and gathered up her treasures into a box: family photos, her parents' wedding rings, her mother's modest pieces of jewellery, her dad's notebook, his giant watch and the locket he had bought for her twenty-first birthday, plus Bear's ashes, and put it in the bottom of her wardrobe. Stephen thought it was oversentimental how she kept the ashes and gave her permission to put them in the garden if she must, but she didn't want to. She and Joel had bought Bear together as a pup. He'd been a tiny ball of red fluff that had grown into a huge teddy of a dog, as gentle a soul as Joel but with no crippling demons. She had cried into his fur when she found out that Joel had

left her and he had stood there, letting her use him as something to hold on to as if he knew that she might slip off the
edge of the world if she let go. Her father had loved Bear
and Bear had loved him too. Even when her dad sometimes
failed to recognise her, he always knew Bear. The place at
her side had grown very cold when she'd had to let Bear go,
and like Joel and her father – he had gone far too soon.

She had an eBay notification at two o'clock that she had
her first order: three packets of rainbow hearts for table
scattering. The money was already sitting in her PayPal
account. She pressed out the pieces at the dining table,
although she knew she wouldn't be able to fulfil any future
orders in front of Stephen, as he'd get annoyed by the constant clicking sound and he'd wonder what she was up to.
She packaged the order and took it straight to the post office,
rather than put it in the post box, so she could get a proof
of sending. A clear profit of about six pounds was hardly
putting her in the Alan Sugar bracket, but her little business
was up and running. As she hoped she would be soon.

There was a florist on the same row of shops. Bonnie
picked two bunches of freesias. Alma loved them. When she
was at the end of her life, she had a bunch on either side of
her bed so she could smell the scent. She'd been so very
poorly with that horrible imprisoning disease. *You get what
you deserve in life, I always say.* That's what Alma had said to
her once, deliberately provocative, when she heard that
Bonnie's father had pneumonia, on top of everything else.
She'd said it in front of her friend Katherine, her audience,
her witness. To this day, Bonnie didn't know how she'd
stopped herself from tearing across the room and slapping
her round, flabby face, sending her jowls juddering. *See that
look in her eyes, Katherine? She'd kill me if she could,* Alma had

smirked at her friend. And Bonnie had played right into her hands by answering, *Yes, Alma, right now I think I could kill you if I had the chance.* If only she hadn't.

Alma had hated her from the off. Even at her wedding, she had dressed from head to toe in black, refusing the pink carnation corsage which Bonnie had bought for her to wear. She'd done her best to ruin the day with her far from whispered remarks to Katherine, who'd been invited because Alma said she wouldn't attend otherwise. Alma had taken her son aside before they went into the registry office, but not too far away that Bonnie couldn't hear what she was saying to him. 'It will end in tears, Stephen. Do not marry this woman. You are worth more. She's after your money and she does not love you. It is not too late to back out. You've only known her two minutes and she's saddled with an invalid father. Look at him. And don't you be thinking now you're wed to her, you're going to stuff me in an old people's home like she did that poor thing sat dribbling who hasn't a clue where he is or why.'

It was her wedding day and she had said her vows with tears pricking at the back of her eyes. And afterwards, Harry Grimshaw, who had sat with her dad, holding his hand through the ceremony, had told her that he would drive her away right now if she wanted and help her undo the binds of the promises she had just made.

She should have taken him up on the offer and gone.

Bonnie gave her head a small shake to dislodge the picture of Alma from her inner vision because the tears it brought with it were clouding her eyes as she drove to the cemetery just outside the town centre. Despite all the money Stephen had inherited, he hadn't splashed out on a fancy stone for his 'beloved mother' as he'd called her in his eulogy at the funeral service. She rested in the next plot to her husband who had had a much taller, grander headstone, paid for by his widow.

Bonnie placed the freesias in the pot and tore up the long grass that was covering the dates and the words: *Alma Elizabeth Brookland. Into your Care, my God.*

'Happy Birthday, Alma,' said Bonnie. 'I came to tell you that I'm going to leave your son. As you knew I would.'

# Chapter 21

Jackpot was there bright and early at the Pot of Gold the next morning to set up his unit. He was a stocky, craggy-faced man with huge muscly arms and twinkling blue-green eyes. His voice was fag-ravaged, smoky and gravelly, his accent the broadest Yorkshire imaginable. Lew wasted no time in asking him about the Chinese items from Mrs Twist's hoard. He picked up the saucer with fingers thick as cigars.

'Very nice,' he said, pulling a loupe out of his pocket so he could view the character marks on the bottom. 'Where the 'ell did you get it?'

Lew smiled. 'An old lady brought it in with this.'

Jackpot put the saucer down and his hand reached out greedily for the cup.

'Bugger me,' he said, viewing that also through the loupe. 'It's as genuine as my arse.'

Behind him Vintage Valerie tutted her disapproval at his crudity. Jackpot threw her a look over his shoulder.

'Get back to hanging up your frocks, you,' he growled at her.

'No wonder they never called you to present the *Antiques Roadshow*, Jack dear,' she said with a haughty sniff.

Jackpot ignored that and switched his attention back to the Chinese duo.

'This is very special, lad. This is no fake. Get in touch with Christie's, look on the internet, there's a valuation process you have to go through. They've got an oriental specialist. Send them as full a description as you can, close-up photos of these two pieces from all angles, measurements, weight and if they're interested they'll come back to you. But I guarantee they will. They'll want you to send it down but I'd take it personally if I were you.'

Valerie came to peer over his shoulder and Bonnie noticed how she momentarily rested her long chin on it. Over the years she had witnessed rare little intimacies like this between them and it crossed her mind more than once to wonder if they had any shared history, only for it to be dismissed as nonsense. It would be like finding out that the Queen had a thing for Hulk Hogan.

'I've taken all the photos,' said Lew, feeling a quiver of excitement brush along his nerve endings. 'I was just waiting for your expert opinion. Bonnie said you really knew your onions.'

'I do that,' replied Jackpot, curling up his hand in front of his mouth as a thick cough came on. It sounded nasty. Behind him Valerie said, 'Ugh' loudly before returning to her unit where she was erecting a new shoe rack.

'You should have that looked at, Jack,' said Bonnie.

Jackpot waved the suggestion away. 'It'll clear up. I've been smoking since I were five, so I'm just grateful I'm still here.'

'Five?' Bonnie half-laughed, half-gasped.

'I wouldn't go to school unless me mam let me have a fag,' he chuckled.

Now Lew's jaw dropped.

'Oh go on, tell him about the lion and the cigarette,' Valerie called with a bored drawl in her voice as if it was a story she had heard many times before. 'I bet you're dying to. Someone who hasn't heard it before. Those people are so thin on the ground now.'

Not needing any more encouragement, Jackpot grinned and dotted his finger towards Lew. 'You'll like this one. Me dad had a lion. Used to guard our scrapyard. Leo, we called it. It used to take a fag out of me dad's mouth and spit it on the floor.' He laughed and the ensuing coughing fit made him bend over double.

Lew swivelled his head around to Bonnie who was nodding.

'It's true. Jack's dad Keith did have a lion.'

'Where did he live?' asked Lew, expecting the answer to be somewhere more exotic than Burton Street.

'We had a big cage for him in the back yard where he used to sleep. Broke my dad's heart when he died,' said Jack, recovering. 'Bloody vet gave him too much anaesthetic when he was taking out a hairball.' Jack's eyes glazed slightly as he slipped into a poignant memory. 'I can see me dad now, sitting in the cage and crying like a baby. He nearly wrung the bloody vet's neck. He never had the same zest for life after Leo died. It took four of us to dig the hole for his lion in the scrapyard. Me dad wanted him buried under where his cage were with the tyre he used to play wi'. We had to dig up a foot of concrete but we wanted it done proper. Me and my brother used to freeze sheep's heads for Leo, ye know. He used to eat them like a frozen lolly. He'd even go out with my dad in the truck, sit on the back seat with his head over my dad's shoulder looking out of the front window. He loved me dad did that lion.' He smiled fondly at the memory for a long moment, then pulled himself out of the past and into the here and now. 'So, there you are. No idea how we got from me coughing to our Leo but ... anyway, get them pictures fired over to Christie's. Whoever you got them bits off will be kicking the'selves. Let me know how you get on, lad. I'd be interested to find out.' And he clapped Lew on the arm with his meaty paw and went back to rearranging his pieces in his cabinet.

'I'm all right by myself if you want to do it now,' smiled Bonnie.

Lew glanced at his watch. 'It'll be your lunch in five minutes.'

'I can hang on,' said Bonnie. 'I'm not that hungry yet anyway and I'd rather be in here chatting to Valerie and Jack.'

'Okay, then, I will,' said Lew, grinning like a little boy who had just won a conker championship. He had no worries about leaving Bonnie to mind the shop, in the way he would have had misgivings letting Vanda Clegg. She fitted in the Pot of Gold, as if there had been a space waiting for her like a jigsaw with a missing piece, which she completed with her presence. He hoped she felt the same.

Bonnie did. She watched Lew walk into his office and felt as if she had known him for so much longer than she had. After only three days, the Pot of Gold felt as familiar to her as Grimshaw's. Yet at the same time there was change in the air, she could feel it and it thrilled her. She couldn't wait to see Starstruck. He'd be in later and she'd tell him that she was going to rent the little house on Rainbow Lane from his daughter.

Lew emerged from the office twenty minutes later with two mugs of coffee. Valerie and Jack had left – together, as they'd always left Grimshaw's – and the only customers were a man and a woman with a guide dog. Lew put the mugs down on the counter and watched Bonnie interacting with them. She was telling them about the musical box in which they seemed interested and he thought, again, what a lovely manner she had. She held so much information in her head about antiques yet never came across as patronising; she wasn't pushy but gently persuasive. And she was so likeable with her big curve of smile and bright eyes that people wanted to talk to her, ask her opinion and valued her guidance. He had no reason to believe that what he had seen in the few days since she had been here was not her standard way of operating.

'I hope it was okay to say he could bring the dog in,' said Bonnie, approaching the counter so that she could speak quietly to Lew. 'I recognise them. They used to come into Grimshaw's. The dog was never any trouble.'

'Of course,' said Lew. The dog was a cream Labrador, standing patiently as the woman described something to the man. 'Beautiful dog.'

'Lovely, isn't he?' Bonnie agreed. 'Do you have a dog?'

'No. I wish.' He'd suggested to Charlotte that they get a dog when a suitable time after her miscarriage had elapsed but she hadn't been keen. He thought it might have helped heal her, given her something to pour affection into but he hadn't pressed her in case she thought he was insinuating that a dog was the same as a baby. 'You?'

'No. Stephen – my husband – isn't an animal person.' She had never suggested they get a pet. She had picked up on his aversion to them listening to things he said about the neighbours' animals. Cats were merely things that urinated in his garden, dogs carried fleas and filth into houses. Both brought expense. She would have loved another dog. A red, fluffy one, a gentle giant like Bear that sat on her feet in the evenings and enjoyed being by her side, as Bear always had. That place had never warmed up since he vacated it, even after all those years.

'We had a couple of Alsatians when I was growing up,' said Lew. 'I think every kid should have a dog.'

'We had a greyhound,' said Bonnie. 'My dad bought him from a bloke in a pub because he thought the poor thing was starved. Turns out, however much we fed Flash, he always looked as if he hadn't had a meal in days. Dad was scared to take him out for walks in case people thought he was abused. I never thought I'd love a dog as much as Flash, until I got Bear.'

'Bear? What sort was he?' asked Lew, amused by the name. It conjured up an instant picture in his head of something large and furry.

'We have no idea,' replied Bonnie, 'though we reckon he was part-Chow because he had a blue tongue and a big smiley face like a Husky. He was just lovely, whatever he was.' She coughed away an onslaught of emotion hitting her throat. She had never quite got over losing him. 'I'll have another dog one day, I hope.'

'Oh, me too,' said Lew. 'Oh, Bonnie, before I forget, do you think you'd be all right to work next Sunday by yourself? Double pay. Say no if—'

'That would be great,' replied Bonnie quickly. 'Honestly, I'll do all the overtime you can throw at me.'

'Saving up for something?' Lew asked.

'Yep,' Bonnie said to him. A life, she said to herself.

She was serving a customer when Starstruck walked in. A woman was prevaricating over two tea services: a Royal

Albert Country Roses or a Midwinter Country Garden one. As patient as Bonnie usually was, this customer was driving her up the wall. Bonnie had been halfway through wrapping the Royal Albert one up when she'd changed her mind. She'd changed it again, just as Bonnie had put it all back on the shelf.

'Oh I don't know,' said the customer, tapping her lip. 'What do you think?'

'Well it has to be your choice,' replied Bonnie. 'I do always recommend you go with your first instinct, if that helps.'

'That would be the Country Roses then.' She nodded as if it was a full stop on the decision. 'Yes, the Country Roses. No . . . wait . . . Let me think about it. You must think I'm daft.'

'Not at all,' said Bonnie, convincingly.

'I'd better leave it,' said the customer. 'Yes, yes, until I know for definite.' She tapped her lip again thoughtfully, made to leave then turned back. 'You don't think they'll be sold before tomorrow, do you?'

'I would never like to say in this game,' said Bonnie. 'We do have quite a high turnover of sales and both tea services are very desirable because they're complete and in mint condition.'

'I'll probably come back tomorrow,' said the customer. She lingered for effect by the door then walked out of it. Bonnie knew she'd go home and decide she didn't need either. She could read this sort of customer like a book.

She tried not to race over to Starstruck, who was unpacking a double-signed pic of both Roger Moore and his second wife Dorothy Squires. He held it up in front of him, shook his head and said 'Poor Dorothy' on a long-drawn-out sigh.

'Hello Starstruck,' said Bonnie. Her whole arms were tingling with anticipation.

'Hello, Bonnie love. How are you settling in?'

'Smashing. Starstruck, about your—'

'I sold the Judy Garland photo, did he tell you?' He said 'he' in a not at all dismissive way about Lew, but a friendly, familiar one.

'He didn't, but I'll ask him about it.'

'They didn't even ask for the trade discount.'

'Great. Listen, Starstruck, about your daughter's house on Rainbow Lane. I have a friend who would be interest—'

'Got snapped up straightaway,' said Starstruck. 'But then I thought it would at that price.'

Bonnie's heart froze mid-beat and it felt as if something popped inside her: a little balloon of hope, maybe. *There are other houses,* said a kind voice in her head, but all her resolve had been tagged on to the one on Rainbow Lane.

'Oh ... that's good,' said Bonnie, pushing out a smile when she felt tears prickle behind her eyes.

'Tell your friend I'm sorry and to get up earlier next time,' asked Starstruck.

'I will.'

Starstruck's eyes drifted back to the photo. He kissed Dorothy Squires's lips and gave another sad sigh. 'She never got over losing him. Went into a proper spiral after he left her.'

At least Roger Moore had the courage to go, thought Bonnie as she turned from him and walked back to the counter as if her shoulders had suddenly turned to lead. The window of opportunity had closed, the rainbow had melted into the dark clouds as the sun had dropped from sight.

In the Arts and Entertainment section of last week's *Daily Trumpet* we mistakenly reported that Beyonce-Jade Smith (12) was playing the role of a courgette in the Kevin Glover Theatre School production of *Les Miserables*. We should have said that she was playing the role of Cosette. We wish Beyonce-Jane a very successful run.

# Chapter 22

'I don't know if I mentioned it,' Bonnie began with a nervous swallow, as they ate dinner that evening, 'but I won't be able to give you as much money for bills as I usually do.' She tried to make it sound as matter-of-fact as she could.

'What do you mean?' asked Stephen, after he had finished his obligatory twenty chews on his mouthful of food.

'My hourly rate will initially be less than it was at Grimshaw's.' She hoped she sounded convincing because she was a terrible liar. *You only have to remember one truth when you don't lie*, was another of her dad's sayings.

'I see,' he said, with a tone based very much in disapproval. 'Then it was very remiss to move, wasn't it?' He lifted the square of kitchen roll acting as a serviette from his lap and dabbed at the corners of his mouth with it. 'You've been deceitful, haven't you, Bonita? It's becoming a habit of yours.'

Bonnie reached for a slice of bread and butter aware that her cheeks were heating up. She was probably acquiring quite a visible blush, though one born of repressed anger and not embarrassment. She hated how he talked to her as if she were a rebellious teenager who needed sending to her room to think about her misdemeanours. He wasn't a stupid man, even if he was hardly the great intellectual he claimed himself to be but he had a hair-trigger for change and would fight against anything that threatened his establishment. She tried to smooth the edges of her revelation.

'There's no deception, Stephen, as I said *initially*. It's just for a trial period, a couple of months. I thought I had mentioned it, if I'm honest' – she hoped her nose wasn't growing – 'but the good thing is that there might be the chance of some overtime soon which would make up any shortfall.'

Stephen turned his attention back to his garden peas. 'Well, I hope for both our sakes that is the case.'

Bonnie felt a sharp stab of annoyance at his weary tone and couldn't help answering back. 'We're hardly on the breadline, are we?'

'That isn't the point, Bonit—'

'I mean, how much exactly do we have in the bank, Stephen?'

'I beg your pardon,' he said, as if she'd asked the most impudent question in the world.

'Well, I give you my money every month to put in our supposed *joint* savings account and yet I have no idea how much is in there.'

'That money is for living expenses, not frivolities. It is our safety net. Are you insinuating—'

'I'm not insinuating anything, Stephen. I just think it's odd that as a married couple I am not allowed to see what's in my own account.'

'*Our* account,' he corrected her. 'Why would you need to know? Do you not see the evidence of what it is being spent on? Food, bills, our yearly holiday. Your contribution alone would not cover a fraction of all the costs in running this house.'

'What about the money my dad left me?'

'What?' His face contorted.

'The money that was left after all his bills were paid. That's in there too.'

'The pittance, you mean.'

His neck was mottled with rising rage; Bonnie thought she had better back off. She wanted him to be aware of a slight financial change in their circumstances, but not lead him to start looking for others. But she was angry. Angry that the chance to leave had dangled in front of her face like a carrot and been snatched away just as her fingers had been about to close around it. More than that, she was angry at herself for not having the guts to change a life she was so unhappy with and make that leap from wishful thinking to actually going for it. Her mother would have done it, so why couldn't she?

'Of course, you're right,' she said, biting her inner tongue. 'You handle the money much better than I would. I'll put some extra in when I've completed my trial period and make up any difference, if you'd like to make a note of how much that will be.'

She hoped that would satisfy him, but she noticed that he was breathing hard. Her outburst had rattled him. She didn't for one minute think he was saving their money and blowing it on prostitutes and horses, but she did know that he was obsessed with feeling safe, secure, in control and would do anything to keep the status quo.

So many times she had laid in bed at night and wondered why she had agreed to marry him and what she had seen in him thirteen and a half years ago that made her say yes when he asked her to be his wife. And she had never come up with an answer. Then her head had been a mess. She was still grieving for Joel when her dad became markedly ill. He

THE QUEEN OF WISHFUL THINKING          139

started forgetting things, ringing her in a blind panic because he didn't know where he was, talking to 'the people in the wallpaper'. Bear was poorly too; the vet had found an inoperable tumour in his young, strong body and she felt as if she were sinking into quicksand. There was nothing in her world but aching uncertainty, doctors, vets, tears, bad news piled upon bad news and then suddenly a man appeared who offered to help her pick all her shopping up when the bottom of the carrier bag burst, sending everything rolling in the rain.

She couldn't even remember giving him her telephone number but when he rang to see if she was all right, she agreed to go out for a coffee with him. He was quiet and steady, attentive, sympathetic, everything her battered, bruised heart craved at the time. He said he could offer her companionship and security and help looking after her dad. He was a buoy to cling to in waters that wanted to drown her when it was time to call the vet to end Bear's suffering and her heart felt as if a pickaxe had pierced the middle of it. Four months after meeting Stephen Brookland she was standing in the registry office in a blue suit holding a posy of pink flowers ready to vow that she would love him and stay with him for ever. But she hadn't really known him at all when she married him. The *him* she thought she would spend the rest of her life with was a charming, caring veneer with a soft voice and a gentle manner and it had seduced her with its offer of a peaceful respite from the mad crazy world of pain she was inhabiting. The real *him* bound her in ropes of banal, boring, beige aspiring middle-class respectability and knotted them so tightly she couldn't remember the last time she could freely breathe.

*

Over dinner that night, Lew raised the subject of a dog.

Charlotte's fork stopped on its journey to her mouth.

'What do you mean, "do you fancy having a dog"? As a pet, you mean?'

'Well, yes. I didn't mean for dinner,' replied Lew with an involuntary snort of amusement.

'Absolutely no.' Charlotte delivered the suspended roast potato to her mouth and chewed.

'I thought it might be company for you.'

'No, really,' said Charlotte again after swallowing. 'I don't need company. I have friends for company.'

'We always said we'd have a dog one day.'

'*You* always said we'd have a dog one day. But you'll be working and it would be me who had to take it out and wash it and things.'

'Wash it? It's not a car, Charlotte.'

'They smell and wee everywhere.' Charlotte wrinkled up her nose.

'Puppies might have a couple of accidents. What about we go and adopt an older rescue dog then? One that's housetrained.'

'No,' Charlotte insisted. 'No, no, no. Why on earth would you think I might want a dog?'

'I just thought that . . .' *Careful,* warned a voice in Lew's head. 'I just thought . . . that it would be company for you during the day . . .'

'You said that already,' said Charlotte, her nostrils flaring slightly.

'. . . And that it might give you something to . . . to love. And to love you back.'

Charlotte's arms came to fold over her surgically enhanced bosom.

'Do you mean like a child?' she said.

Lew coughed. This was not quite going as planned. 'Of course not,' he said. 'But I thought as we can't . . . as we can't have . . .'

Charlotte held a beautifully manicured hand up to stop his flow.

'Lewis, if you think I'm jealous of Gemma, you couldn't be more wrong. I have had to come to terms with the fact that we will have a different life to the one we planned around being parents. My issue with her is that I very much suspect she will become one of those people who has no life outside motherhood and it will bore me rigid. She will want to talk about nappies and babies' first steps and I won't.' She ran out of breath, so dragged another one into her lungs. 'So, to clarify, I am happy to have a nice house without chewed wires and big doggy footprints all over my carpets and I am happy to have clothes without baby sick down the back of them. And there are other compensations, i.e. I have the same waist measurement I had twenty years ago, unlike Gemma is going to have. Now, would you like some more asparagus with your chicken because I made more than I should have?'

'No thank you,' said Lew.

'Okay,' said Charlotte, viciously piercing a baby corn. And that was the end of that conversation. At least verbally, because Lew didn't quite believe her, especially as only two days ago she sounded anything but over it. Even after eight years, she hadn't found how to cope with the loss of their child. He could have cried for her.

# Chapter 23

Two months passed and Bonnie still went home to Greenwood Crescent but she was not able to slip back into life there as if she were a snail sliding back into the familiarity of its shell, because it was as if the shell had changed into a smaller shape that caused her discomfort and threatened to burst open from the pressure. She wished it would, but in the meantime she secretly banked every penny she could and scoured the local newspapers for a place she could afford, but with no luck. A lot of the landlords required a substantial up-front bond or a long-term agreement. One of them was very cheap but in a horrible area at the other end of town. Then one came up which was situated perfectly but it was four-bedroomed and far too expensive. The Rainbow Lady had made over a hundred pounds profit through eBay selling and Clock Robin had sold her a box of interesting and unique craft punches from Eastern Europe for the princely sum of a cup of coffee and a couple of chocolate digestives.

Life in Greenwood Crescent ticked along with no great dramas. To keep Stephen happy, she tipped up an extra thirty pounds one week and twenty-five the next and told him she'd had bonuses because the shop had been doing so well. It stopped him nagging about her 'lack of contribution' as he so stuffily put it. She played the textbook dutiful wife, even though beneath her calm exterior there was a mutiny raging. Every day was closer to the one when she would shut the door of number 39 behind her and never return, and she was both thrilled and afraid about it, but she *would* do it and risk being bumped around on the sea of uncertainty. She was bored and lonely and restless and frustrated, but the main reason why Bonnie knew she had to leave Stephen was that she had fallen in love with her boss.

She hadn't planned it, she hadn't wanted it; it was a complication she didn't need because where could such feelings go? Cupid really was an evil little sod. She would have to press those feelings down, keep them secretly packed away in her heart and just be happy to be near him, moving in his orbit, working with him. When she was with him, she felt alive again, energised and smiley inside. He made her believe there might be another Lew out there for her who would cherish her and love her, as Lew obviously cherished and loved his wife. She had gathered through snippets of coffee-time conversation that Lew had been married for over fourteen years to Charlotte. They didn't have any children, which probably made them stronger as a couple, though it hadn't in her and Stephen's case. He was fair in business, the traders liked and respected him and he treated Bonnie as if he valued her help, her input, her knowledge, the way old Mr Grimshaw had. She liked Lew because he wasn't the sort of man to play around behind his wife's back. She might have imagined what it would be like to kiss him, but if he had done so in real life, she would have run a mile. The minute he crossed the line, he would have become someone she couldn't respect. But in her fantasies, he was single – and so was she – and her feelings were reciprocated.

Lew was kind to her, talked to her with warmth in his voice and wasn't above making frequent cups of coffee. He never flirted but she could guess by the way he treated her that he liked her too and it was enough for her. Bonnie was starved of affection; a little respectful attention was bound to enter her heart and flood it.

And because butterflies flapped in Bonnie's stomach whenever she saw her boss and her days were filled with brightness, her life at home felt all the more drab and stifling. Working with Lew had awakened something in her that mocked her situation, that she'd settled for so little, so quickly. The fear of being by herself was not a reason to stay with Stephen; she knew she could not be more lonely than she was in her marriage.

The box with the teabags, soap and towels still remained under her bed, her clothes were still waiting in her suitcase and her savings account continued to grow steadily and secretly. This time, when she was ready to leave, she would go through with it, she would be her mother's daughter and take that third step. There would be no repeat of what had happened before. When her brain was flashing the signal that all systems were go, she would close the door to Stephen's house behind her and she would not be pulled back through it. Not for anything. She had wished and thought of herself happy in a little house somewhere too much now to retract.

Lew was very happy with the way things were going in the Pot of Gold. He had a full complement of dealers now; all the renowned names were renting cabinets and space from him and there was even a waiting list. What a mad bunch they were too: Stantiques, Medal Mickey, Goldfinger, Vintage Valerie and Jackpot were fully settled in and making money enough to pay for their units plus profit and the footfall over the threshold was growing heavier with every week that passed. Lew had opened on the last two Mondays by himself to test what custom was like and it wasn't bad, not enough to merit two of them working there, but he thought it might in the coming months.

Lew was all too aware that working with Bonnie Brookland lent sunshine to his days. She was a lovely woman, and he suspected an unhappy one, an unfulfilled one. She didn't talk about her home life but he surmised that her marriage was less than perfect. Her husband was older than her by fourteen years, she'd let slip one day, and like him and Charlotte, they had no children. He thought she might be unloved and deserved more and something in his heart responded to her sweet vulnerability. *Tread carefully, my friend,* that wise voice in his head had warned because he didn't want to be lured by another woman's warmth to compensate for the increasing chill he was feeling at home. Charlotte was turning more and more into a mini Regina. She'd lost weight on a faddy no-carb diet, had hair extensions to ape Regina's at a cost that caused an argument, and even the way she spoke had acquired the impatient arrogance that Regina employed. And despite her dresses being lower cut on top and higher cut on the bottom to show off her new figure to everyone that cared to look, their sex life hadn't improved. It was as if the rest of the world were granted the sight of the curve of her boobs in public, but not Lew in private.

Is this what happened to Patrick, he had wondered more than once now. Unlike Patrick, though, Lew was not a flirtatious man. He kept his barriers up and his boundaries defined and Bonnie gave him no encouragement but still, he thought it would be very easy to fall in love with the woman with the beautiful hazel eyes who punched holes in pieces of coloured paper in the office during her lunch hour and sold the resulting confetti on eBay for peanuts.

That woman was now walking towards him with a cup of coffee and proffering a plate of fruit shortcakes but he was so caught up in his thoughts that he didn't register her until she spoke.

'You all right?' she said.

'Pardon?'

'You were on another planet then, Lew.' And Bonnie smiled and he mirrored it, aware that body language experts might say that was a sign of attraction.

'Sorry, you're right, I was. I was just wondering what the experts at Christie's were thinking about the Chinese cup and saucer,' he fibbed.

'I'm glad you took the pieces down personally,' said Bonnie. 'I wouldn't have liked to have trusted them to a courier. Plus the extra insurance you'd have had to fork out wouldn't have been cheap. When did you say they were going up for sale?'

When Lew had delivered the cup and saucer to London, he'd taken Charlotte with him and they'd spent the night in the Hilton Waldorf. They'd had an early dinner in the hotel and he'd surprised her with tickets for a West End show. The full-on day had tired her out, so she hoped he wasn't expecting sex, she said unromantically as they walked back from the theatre. He hadn't been. He had however arranged for a bottle of champagne, a dozen red roses and a box of chocolates to be waiting for them on their return, but her words poured a cold bucket of water over the evening and he wished he hadn't bothered.

Charlotte had felt guilty when she opened the hotel room door and found his gifts. She tried to make things right by suggesting they share a bath and open the champagne. Lew played along but his mood was squashed. The fizz made Charlotte squiffy and, ironically, amorous but Lew would have had more chance at singlehandedly raising the *Titanic* than he would at making love to his wife. There was something wrong with his marriage and he didn't know how to fix it.

He pushed that night in London to the back of his mind, aware that Bonnie was waiting for an answer.

'There's a specialised auction of oriental ceramics and works of art at the end of this month. With any luck they'll include our pieces.'

'And what would you do with the money if they fetched, let's say, five million?' asked Bonnie, hazel eyes twinkling.

'I wish,' Lew laughed gently. 'After giving you a very nice bonus, obviously ...'

'Obviously,' echoed Bonnie.

'... I'd ...' He thought and couldn't come up with anything. All the things he wanted, he couldn't buy: his child, a marriage on firm ground again. He made something up. 'I'd go on a round the world trip to the best beaches and build a wine cellar under my house. What would you do with your bonus then, Bonnie?'

*I'd ring an estate agent, rent the first house on the list however much it cost, go to Greenwood Crescent and grab my suitcase,* thought Bonnie, but instead she made something up. 'I'd buy a new car. Nothing flash though, reliable but one that no one had driven before me. And maybe . . .'

But she never did finish the sentence because the bell above the door tinkled and old Billy Boombox bumbled in as if he were drunk.

Long John, who was Windolening his glass cabinet doors, asked, 'You all right, lad?' which was ridiculous seeing as Boombox was twenty-plus years older than him.

'Am I 'eck,' replied Boombox. 'I've just heard that Jackpot's died.'

'Eh?' said Long John. 'He can't have.'

'When?' asked Goldfinger, appearing behind him.

'This morning. Stantiques rang me. He had a massive stroke apparently. He was dead as soon as he fell.' Boombox's voice dissolved in a croak.

'Oh no, not Jackpot.' Bonnie's eyes misted with tears. She'd known the man since she was a girl and he was amongst her favourites. She wondered how Vintage Valerie would have taken the news because they did all the same markets together and were the best of friends; they even bickered like a married couple.

Long John scrubbed a tear away from his cheek with the heel of his hand. 'I can't believe it. I did York market with him yesterday and he was right as rain. It's like he's been snatched off the earth by a big hand.'

'I'll pop on and see if his wife wants anything,' said Goldfinger, reaching for his weighty leather jacket. 'My wife and his go to bingo together. Bloody hell.' He shook his head at the thought of it. 'You never know what's round the corner, do you?'

No, thought Bonnie. Unless you live with Stephen

Brookland, then you can guarantee exactly what is around the corner and it will be grey and dismal.

A cloud settled on the day. Mart Deco and Stantiques came in just after one o'clock. and were full of the news. Mart said that he was going straight home and booking a holiday for him and the wife on the internet and Stan said that he was throwing all his cigarettes away instead of talking about it. Stickalampinit walked in and burst into tears. It seemed to make everyone in Jack's orbit sit up and take notice of their mortality.

Just before closing time, Lew walked into the back room to discover Bonnie having a quiet sob. Sensing his presence she pulled herself quickly together, produced a tattered tissue out of the pocket of her pinafore shift and blew her nose. 'Sorry,' she said.

'You've got nothing to be sorry for,' said Lew gently, blocking the instinct to put his arm around her to comfort her in case she thought it was inappropriate. 'It's been a sad day.'

'It has,' said Bonnie. 'It feels like I've known Jack forever. They're all like my uncles and aunts in this trade.' The tissue had disintegrated and she scrabbled in her bag for another without success. Lew reached in his pocket and handed over a pressed white handkerchief.

'I am one of the few men left in this world who uses them, I think,' he said. 'It's clean.'

'Thank you,' said Bonnie, taking it from him. 'I'll wash it and let you have it back.'

'There's no need,' Lew replied. 'I have hundreds of them. Executive presents. Most of them were either whisky or handkerchiefs. I don't give my whisky away though.'

Bonnie gave a spurt of involuntary laughter and wiped her nose on the enormous handkerchief.

'It's not an indication of nose size, I hope,' said Lew. 'I don't know why it's as big as a single bedsheet.'

'Perfect size for me then,' said Bonnie, giving the end of her nose a pinch.

'Nothing at all wrong with your nose,' replied Lew, with a smile. It had a little bump on the bridge, it wasn't perfect but it was perfect for her lovely face. No one would ever notice the flaw because her eyes were so pretty anyway. Not that he said that, because it would have sounded very flirtatious, and that would be disrespectful to his wife. And to Bonnie's husband.

'Look, forget about coming in tomorrow,' insisted Lew.

Bonnie had agreed to man the shop for him, even though Monday was her day off. It had allowed her to make the point to Stephen and say, 'Told you there was overtime available'. More importantly it would get her out of the house. Stephen was using some of his holiday entitlement and taking the first four days of the week to do some work in the garden.

'No, not at all,' she said. 'I'll be fine.' Plus she had some orders for confetti that she wanted to press out in her lunch break.

'Well, if you change your mind and don't feel up to it, just ring and let me know,' said Lew.

'Thank you, but I can assure you I won't change my mind.' Bonnie looked into his warm blue eyes and thought, for the hundredth time at least, how lucky Mrs Harley was.

# Chapter 24

'What on earth's the matter, Lewis? You look like someone's died,' said Charlotte when Lew walked in from work that Sunday afternoon.

'Someone did,' replied Lew. 'One of the traders. Jackpot. Lovely man, dealt in ceramics.'

'Oh,' said Charlotte, as if a trader constituted a lesser being. She was careful to leave a respectful few seconds of silence before speaking again.

'So have you had any more thoughts about the Alaskan cruise with Patrick and Reg?'

Lew lifted his head to stare at her in disbelief.

Charlotte's perfectly arched eyebrows tried to raise, but the secretly purchased Botox in her forehead forbade it. 'What are you looking at me like that for? You told me this morning you were going to think about it and let me know today.'

'No, you said you were going to let me think about it when I told you absolutely no. And even if I'd had a severe knock to the head that changed my mind, today has not been the day for thinking about whale-watching with Regina.' His voice carried a rare snap in it.

'I don't know why you're so upset,' said Charlotte indignantly. 'It's not as if you knew this . . . Jackpot man that well, is it?'

'No, Charlotte, I didn't know him well,' replied Lew, 'but it did bring it home to me once again how fragile life is.'

It hadn't just reminded him with a gentle tap, but with the thump of a sledgehammer. He'd been brought back from the brink though; old Jack hadn't. Well, not even 'old' Jack. He'd only just tipped over into his sixties and despite the fact a fug of cigarette smoke hung around him, Jack was like an ox, strong, hearty, full of life. That stroke hadn't just killed him, it had felled him like a well-placed axe on a Californian Redwood. No, today had not been a day for thinking about being imprisoned on a ship with Regina and Patrick. A holiday was supposed to be relaxing and unwinding. Patrick might be great fun to spend time with, but having to endure Regina's company for fourteen nights would pull every nerve Lew had so tightly he could have cut cheese with them.

Charlotte huffed impatiently. 'I really want to go to Alaska.'

'I would rather yank out both of my lungs and use them as an accordion,' said Lew, slipping off his jacket.

'Lewis. How could you say such a thing about a holiday with our friends.'

'Quite easily,' said Lew. 'Having dinner with the Sheffields is one thing, spending a fortnight with them glued to our side is another.'

'I would have thought that if anything, today would have taught you to grab the bull by the horns and live a bit,' said Charlotte, rather pleased with herself for thinking of that.

'Precisely,' Lew nodded. 'To enjoy ourselves and de-stress, which is why I wouldn't go on holiday with Patrick and Regina if they paid for us to go and threw the spending money in as well. And, in case you've forgotten, I don't need someone else's death to remind me of seizing the day, seeing as I almost had one of my own.'

'Of course I hadn't forgotten,' said Charlotte quickly. 'What do you take me for? I'll tell them no. I'll make something up and say that you can't take the time off.'

'We will have a nice holiday, just the two of us. Let's book a few nights in Venice. How does the Cipriani sound?'

'Venice again?' said Charlotte with a curled lip. 'God, no.'

And Lew thought, She's turning more and more into Regina with every day that passes.

*

'You're very sullen,' Stephen remarked at dinner. 'I've asked you twice to pass the condiments and twice you've ignored me.'

'Sorry,' Bonnie replied and passed over the wire basket which sat next to her containing the salt, pepper, vinegar and oil.

'Thank you. What on earth is the matter, Bonita?' Stephen said impatiently as he reached over to take it from her.

'One of the traders died,' Bonnie answered him. 'I've known him for years.'

'Oh,' said Stephen as if he'd expected more serious news. 'Well, we all have to go at some point.'

Bonnie didn't reply to that banal observation but carried on eating a Sunday roast she had no appetite for.

'And why are you so upset about it?' Stephen pressed, after a minute or so.

'I liked him,' said Bonnie. 'I liked him very much. He was a good man, a decent man. And the most knowledge-able person ever about ceramics.'

'Is he survived by a family?' asked Stephen, dabbing his mouth with the kitchen roll square tucked in the top of his shirt.

'Yes. A daughter. She was only married last month,' said Bonnie, putting down her knife and fork because the food was just rolling around in her mouth protesting against being swallowed.

'I do wonder how all these traders of yours manage to earn their living. I mean, is there actually money in dealing with pots?' He gave the words 'traders' and 'pots' all the disdain he could heap onto them.

Bonnie tried to keep the annoyance out of her voice as she delivered the line that she hoped would wound his snobbery gland. 'Yes, I imagine there is, seeing as Jack drove around in a brand new Bentley.'

'Hmm,' mused Stephen, wrinkling up his nose as if there was a bad smell underneath it. 'Fools and their money are soon parted.'

They ate the rest of their meal in silence. Then Stephen picked up his newspaper and went out into the garden leaving Bonnie to clear the table. Though Stephen wanted his wife to work full-time, at home he expected her to act like a traditional wife. His manly duties covered the gardening, the bulb-changing and general maintenance, the woman did the washing, ironing, cleaning.

As Bonnie filled up the sink with warm soapy water, she thought about Jack. He'd only just gone sixty-two and was far too young to leave the earth. But at least he'd lived. He'd been married to the same woman for over thirty years and he idolised his daughter. He had a big house and a series of expensive cars, he'd travelled all over the world and had a consuming passion for ceramics. He'd wrung the juice out of his life and drank it greedily. *And if you died tomorrow, could you say the same?* asked a voice in Bonnie's head. The answer was a very resounding no.

She couldn't wait to leave and start a new life. The day when all the planets aligned for her and she found a house that she could afford couldn't be that far away now, surely. But she knew she would be taking a huge risk in leaving because it wasn't financial worries or fear of the unknown that had really held her back, there was something else. Something that had stopped her from going before, four years ago when she'd had her bags packed and was about to walk out of the door for good. That was the something she was most afraid of.

# Chapter 25

Bonnie was cheered the next morning to find she had a message waiting in her eBay mailbox from a craft shop enquiring if she could supply fifty bags of assorted confetti. They wanted it at a ridiculous price, but she was still making a pound a bag clear profit, more if she dared to drive up the price a little. She sent a reply asking for another thirty pence per hundred, a counter offer came in for twenty and she accepted it. She loaded her handbag up with the punches and it clanked as she lifted it over her shoulder.

'What have you got in your bag that's making all that noise?' asked Stephen.

'Some craft stuff,' replied Bonnie. 'I get a bit bored in my lunch hour so I've been making a few cards.'

His eyebrows dipped in puzzlement. 'And what on earth are you going to do with them?'

'Nothing,' replied Bonnie. 'I just like making them.'

'Seems a very strange thing to do,' said Stephen, shaking his head. He rolled up his left sleeve to precisely match the length of the right one.

'Why is that strange?' asked Bonnie, irked that someone

with all his pernickety, peculiar ways could call anyone else odd.

Stephen looked shocked that she'd questioned him. 'Pardon?' he asked.

'Why is it so strange that I'm making some cards?'

'Well,' he cleared his throat with a cough, 'you've shown no propensity to craftwork before.'

'How do you know?' Bonnie cut him off. 'How do you know what I do when you're watching your stupid documentaries and I'm sitting in the kitchen?'

Stephen's eyes widened to the circumference of side plates.

'I don't think there's any need for using that tone, Bonita. You're being ridiculous,' he said in such a way that Bonnie had a sudden vision of him holding a handbag in his fingers and lifting it up in front of his chest with extreme indignation.

'I'm not being ridiculous at all, Stephen. I used to do lots of this kind of stuff when I was a kid. Thousands, millions of people around the world cut things out of paper, but because I do it, it's strange. Is it because "it's not the way of things", Stephen?' For once, she did not hide the fact that she was mocking his sad little ways. She'd had enough. Inside Bonnie was screaming and kicking against the walls of her marriage. He looked down on everyone, especially people in her world because they didn't sit behind desks and file paperwork. All that projecting herself outside of this oppressive set-up was making her brave. Maybe too brave. She wanted to shout at him that she was punching shapes out of paper in secret to fund a life away from this sham of a marriage so that she never had to see him or hear his boring diatribes again, but she knew she had said too much already. She needed to stay calm, focused, not give him any clue what she was really up to behind his back.

'I'm sorry,' she said, 'I didn't sleep very well and I'm a bit tetchy this morning.'

'Yes, you are, Bonita,' he replied, after a thoughtful pause. 'Maybe you need to drink less caffeine. I notice we are going through a full half jar of coffee per week more than usual.'

'Yes, it can't help, can it?' She forced out a smile but could only manage a weak, watery one.

Stephen slipped on his stiff gardening apron as Bonnie buttoned up her coat.

'See you later,' she said. 'Have a nice day off repotting your dahlias.' She hadn't meant it sarcastically, but unfortunately that's how it came out.

'Well really,' said Stephen to himself, hearing Bonnie's car start after the second attempt. He knew something was amiss. He wasn't fooled by her pleasantries which sounded forced, as if she were covering up a deep resentment. He detected a change in her, the same one he'd sensed four years ago. Back then, he'd known for days before she'd actually said the words that she was planning to leave him and he felt it again now.

Stephen slipped off his gardening shoes and went upstairs into Bonnie's room to make one of his periodic checks on her things. It didn't do any harm to be forewarned of her intentions.

On Thursday the *Daily Trumpet* mistakenly reported that local independent councillor Alan Stanley is a hermaphrodite. This should have read that he was a haemophiliac. The *Daily Trumpet* has made a donation to a charity of Mr Stanley's choice.

# Chapter 26

Bonnie ran the shop by herself for the next two days. On the Monday Lew was on a stock-finding mission in York. It wasn't really worth opening up as only three customers visited and didn't buy anything, but still it was much better than being at home with Stephen. On the Tuesday, Lew was at a giant antiques fayre in Newark. As Bonnie, in sole charge, walked around the shop, she let herself imagine that it belonged to her. That the Rainbow Lady earned so much profit she had bought it from Lew outright, or better still gone into partnership with him because her days would be much greyer without him in them. She had him to blame for her increasing agitation with her home life, for which she both cursed and blessed him. She'd thought it was possible to live without love. When Joel died, she'd tried to convince herself that life would be so much easier without having her heart broken over and over again. Emphasis on companionship rather than passion seemed the perfect way forward, but she'd been wrong.

There was a steady stream of customers that morning, but nothing that Bonnie couldn't manage. No traders came in to refill their units though, which was unusual. Vintage Valerie hadn't missed a Tuesday so far, but she wasn't here today. She and Jack had fallen into the pattern of going to the teashop next door for breakfast and Bonnie wondered how she'd be feeling. Valerie probably saw more of Jack than his own wife did. Bonnie had tried to ring her home a few times, but Valerie hadn't picked up.

Bonnie was just about to close a deal on a grandfather clock when in came a twittering couple of women, both very well-dressed and in heels, one blonde and one brunette. The latter was carrying a Chaput crocodile handbag, which Bonnie recognised immediately. It turned her stomach to think of the doomed life of the farmed animal from which it came.

'I have to confess that I pretended I wasn't in. Isn't that awful? I saw her number and I let the machine take it,' the one with the long blonde hair, tiny waist and springy boobs was saying to the other woman as she approached the counter with some urgency, scanning the room for the person in charge. Then she spotted Bonnie and marched over, interrupting her sales spiel.

'You must be er . . . I'm Lewis's wife Charlotte.'

*So this was the famous what-was-her-name*, thought Charlotte. And to think a couple of times she'd actually had stabs of jealousy that this woman spent so much time with her husband. She needn't have worried though. She was very average: neither tall nor short, slim but with no spectacular curves. She'd had no surgical intervention, that was clear. Unremarkable face, nose neither small nor large, Charlotte noticed a bump on the bridge that she'd have had ironed out had it been hers. This woman's lips looked naturally full and plump, without the duck-like fake protrusion that Regina's had. But it was her eyes that attracted Charlotte's attention the most: large and browny-green, fringed with thick, dark lashes. Those eyes lent an ordinary-looking woman more beauty than she should have had.

At the same time that Charlotte was appraising Bonnie, Bonnie was thinking, *So this was Lew's wife*. She'd expected her to be pretty, with a lovely figure and she'd been right. What she hadn't expected was her to look as if she had just come out of a mould with her cloud of blonde, lacquered hair and none-too-friendly red pout. She'd imagined Charlotte to be softer, fresher, smilier, not exuding snooti-ness through her high-heeled stance and granite-faced expression.

'I've left my purse so I'm taking some money from the till, okay?' Charlotte informed her husband's assistant, turn-ing on her fancy heel and flouncing back to the counter.

Bonnie's warning flags shot up. She wouldn't have thought Lew's wife would be the sort of person to walk in and make that kind of demand. Quick as a flash, Bonnie skirted around her and placed herself in front of the till.

'I'm sorry but you can't do that.'

Charlotte looked over at Regina who pulled a half-shocked, half-amused face. Then she turned back to Bonnie. 'I'm sorry, what?'

'You could be anyone,' said Bonnie. *What a horrid position to be put in*, she thought. She had no reason to believe it wasn't Charlotte, but without proof she couldn't allow her access to the till.

Charlotte smiled politely but impatiently. 'But I'm not just anyone. I'm the owner of this shop,' she said as she made to push past Bonnie. Bonnie barred her passage with her arm.

'Look, just to be on the safe side do you mind whilst I ring Lew?'

Regina gave a hoot of laughter and Charlotte's cheeks began to heat.

'I'LL ring my husband, LEWIS,' Charlotte emphasised and scrabbled in her handbag, a very expensive Burberry, noted Bonnie. She pulled out her mobile and tapped a lot at the screen, getting flustered as she entered the wrong pass code, then the wrong contact name. She crossed her arms waiting for Lew to pick up, but it went to voicemail. She tried again and this time let it record her voice.

'Lewis, can you please ring me urgently. And I mean urgently.'

Then she tried again and growled as once more it went to voicemail. She marched out of earshot and recorded a very angry message. 'Lewis, why aren't you picking up? I've tried both your mobiles and I'm getting nothing but your stupid answering machine. Your woman in the shop is refusing to let me get some money out of the till. She's totally ridiculed me in front of everyone so you better ring me back. NOW.' She pressed end call so hard that the phone flew out of her hand and she had to bend down to pick it up. By the time she had straightened herself, her face was as scarlet as her shoe-soles.

Bonnie stood resolutely by the till, even though the man with the clock was trying to get her attention.

'That is your boss's wife,' said Regina with a nasty little smile. 'I'd just give her the money if I were you.'

'I'm afraid I can't,' replied Bonnie.

'Just show her some ID, Charlotte,' huffed Regina impatiently.

'I haven't got any.' Charlotte ground the words through

clenched teeth. 'It's all in my purse which I've forgotten, which is why I'm here.'

'I'm sorry.' Bonnie shook her head. 'Unless I have permission . . .'

'Why on earth would I come in here and say it if I wasn't his wife?' Charlotte tried to keep the volume on her voice down but it seeped through on alternate words.

'I'm really sorry but I still can't let you open that till.'

'Absolutely ridiculous. This is stupid beyond stupid. *You* are stupid beyond stupid. Do I look like a shoplifter?' She spread her arms out and showed off her expensive linen swing jacket, the sharp cut shirt and skirt, the gold necklace at her throat, the newly touched up hair roots, immaculate nails, immobile forehead.

'I won't take that chance with someone else's money, I'm afraid.'

'It's my bloody money as well, you stup—' Charlotte's anger spilled over the top of the pan before she managed to slam the lid back on it. She was not only feeling humiliated in front of Regina but also a couple of other customers were showing interest in what was going on and looked primed to jump in to prevent a burglary. She stabbed her nail at Bonnie. 'You are in big trouble when my husband rings me, lady,' she said.

Regina, who ate shop assistants for breakfast and was bored with this impasse now, attempted to push past Bonnie with a well-aimed bony elbow in her side. 'For fuck's sake, get out of my way,' she snarled, but she was ill-prepared for Bonnie's slick body twist and seconds later, Regina found herself being fast propelled out of the shop with her arm twisted behind her back, Charlotte teetering behind in pinheels screeching like an injured parrot.

'Look, I'm sorry if you are who you say you are,' said Bonnie breathlessly at the door to Charlotte as Regina stretched the agony out of her arm, all the while swearing and growling as if possessed. 'But if you really are Lew's wife, you have to see it from my side. You wouldn't like me emptying the till into the hands of someone I don't know,' she said.

'You are so sacked,' said Charlotte, further infuriated by the sound of applause coming from the customers inside the shop. And if Lewis didn't sack the bitch, Charlotte would leave him.

# Chapter 27

Bonnie walked back into the shop to jokey comments such as 'Remind us not to mess with you,' and the man who wanted to buy the clock asked her if she was all right. She answered that she was, but behind the smile, she wasn't really. When the clock had been bought and the shop had emptied of customers, Bonnie tried to ring Lew's mobile from the office phone but he didn't answer. She copied the number into her own mobile so that she could text him an explanation, but deleted it. If that really was his wife, and the chances were that she was, he'd want to hear her version of events first anyway and he would be more likely to believe it, especially as the dark-haired woman was sure to substantiate what she said. On the off-chance that he didn't sack Bonnie on the spot, she could tell him her side of things and hope he accepted that she'd acted in the only way she could. Both of the women had been very angry and Bonnie was only glad she hadn't had to manhandle Lew's wife out of the shop. Her rib hurt where the dark-haired woman had rammed her elbow into her side. It felt so sore she was worried it could be broken.

She hadn't heard from Lew by the time she shut up shop and her anxiety levels were sky-high. What if he did sack her? She'd be back to having no job again and no contact with all her trader friends. And more importantly, all the plans she was setting in place for a new, happy, Stephenless life would blow away like the flossy seeds of a dandelion clock in the wind.

A fat tear rolled down her cheek as she slumped to the chair in the office and held her head in her hands. That woman had put her in an impossible dilemma – damned if she did let her at the till, damned if she didn't. Charlotte, if it was her, might have ruined everything just for the fifty-pound float that had been in it. Just like last time, her escape had been thwarted at the final hurdle.

Bonnie had been married nine years when she eventually plucked up the courage to leave Stephen. Her marriage was dry dust, her days were colourless and there was barely any interaction between them. Surely he couldn't be happy either?

She made a nice dinner – his favourite – pork loin, broad beans, chantenay carrots, roast potatoes, hoping it would set an amiable scene. They were adults, they could talk through this reasonably. After all, there was no one more sensible than Stephen. She wouldn't ask for very much from the divorce, far less than the law would say she was entitled to. She just wanted enough to rent a small place until she was on her feet. He would agree to that, she was sure, as long as it was put in writing so he could feel secure that she wouldn't renege on any deal they agreed to. Bonnie had pored over the right way to open this discussion for days; it was a knotted ball of wool with no suitable beginning, so the only way was to take hold of it, break it and make a start to it.

'Stephen, I need to talk to you,' she said as he sipped a post-prandial cup of tea.

Maybe there was something in her tone that intimated what was coming because he visibly stiffened, put down his mug and made to stand.

'I need to dig out the hyacinth bulbs and wrap them in newspaper for next year. They won't do it themselves.'

'Please, Stephen, just sit for a moment.' He relented, back ramrod straight. She saw his Adam's apple rise and fall on a gulp before he spoke.

'What is it, Bonita?'

Now it was Bonnie's turn to swallow. She felt as if she had planned to dive off a platform but only now, when she looked down, could she see it was much higher than she had first thought and the water below had the suspicious shadows of rocks in it.

'Stephen, I think we should separate. I think that . . .'

She had imagined he would listen to her in stony silence, that her words would sink in and swirl around until they formed a digestible shape. Then he would nod when he realised that she was giving him the opportunity to let her go easily, cleanly without biting greedy holes into his financial safety net. She had thought that he would then instigate the disassembling of their marriage fairly and without drama. She could not have been more wrong.

'Separate, separate?' Stephen bellowed, springing to his feet, his face suffusing with blood. 'What madness are you spouting? We are married and we are not going to separate. Why would we separate?'

'Stephen, we have nothing in common, we don't even share a bedroom, there's no love . . .'

'Love?' He pushed his face into hers and screamed the word. 'Love, sex . . . that's what you had with *him*, isn't it, and where did that bloody get you? An idiot bastard depressive who led you a merry dance, didn't he? DIDN'T HE? Look, you've made me swear. I don't swear and you are making me do it.'

He made her wince with the volume of his words, the stream of obscenities that poured from his lips, and then he seized hold of her arm, tight, his fingers digging in her flesh. 'Shall I pour pills down my neck that turn me into a zombie? Shall I fuck around and break your heart? Shall I disappear and leave you to go out of your mind with worry? Is that the sort of *relationship* you want again, you silly, silly girl?'

Bonnie wrenched her arm away from his hold and saw the imprint of white fingermarks. She opened her mouth to remonstrate, but he was in full flow.

'I picked up the pieces of you when that . . . mental patient had brutalised your spirit and when you needed someone to help look after your father. You had nothing, you were a mess, you needed my help and I gave it to you and so you'll stay. You owe me.'

'I owe you?' Bonnie threw the words back at him, indignation rising like a surfer's wave inside her. 'I don't owe you anyth—'

'After what you did? You expect me to stay silent about it? Oh yes, that's shut you up, hasn't it? I have protected my wife. If you aren't my wife any more, then I have to tell and you will be punished. Everyone will know the truth about "sweet little Bonnie", won't they? You'll be a pariah.'

Bonnie paled before his eyes.

'You will not leave and that is an end to it. You owe me,' he said again. And Bonnie knew that she would stay because what she had done had bound her to him forever, if that's what he wanted to happen.

Bonnie lifted her coat down from the peg and put it on, ready to finish what might be her last shift ever. Lew had probably spoken to Charlotte by now. She had no doubt Charlotte would put her own twist on the truth and he would believe her, because she was his wife. She would be sacked and what then? Stephen would be ready with a barrelful of 'I told you so's, indignity heaped on indignity. How could she leave him without a job to fund her new life? Her hope was being crushed under the weight of the day. She was fooling herself anyway with these daft plans because Stephen would never let her go, not even if she had a million pounds in the bank.

She was just locking up the office when the phone inside it rang. Quickly as she could, she opened the door, ran inside and snatched up the receiver. Her hand was shaking as she held it against her ear. Lew's voice poured out of it.

'Bonnie? What on earth has been going on?'

Her heart didn't know whether to stop or race. His voice was distant, fuzzy, he was ringing from the car.

'Lew, I had no idea . . . I am so sorry . . . I . . .' The words tumbled out in a jumbled mess.

'Bonnie, Bonnie . . . just . . . just calm down.'

'Sorry . . . I . . . sorry.'

'Bonnie. Shh. Now start from the beginning.' His voice, calm and soothing but more importantly, not angry.

'Two ladies came into the shop around lunchtime. One said that she was your wife and wanted to take money out of the till. I couldn't . . . I didn't know if it really was her or not . . .'

'No, of course you didn't,' he interrupted her, irritation in his voice, but she knew it wasn't aimed at her.

'What if it hadn't been your wife and I let them walk off with all the money? What if I'd given her the benefit of the doubt and you were angry with me . . . I just didn't know what to do so I did what I thought was right . . .'

'Bonnie, stop panicking,' said Lew, hearing the distress in her voice and he wished he were there to put his hands firmly on her arms and look into her eyes so she would believe him when he said, 'You did absolutely the right thing. I am so sorry you were put in that position.'

Bonnie didn't realise how much tension she was holding in her shoulders until they dropped in relief.

'Really?'

'Yes of course, really. I have no idea what my wife was thinking of.'

The big question. 'You aren't going to sack me then?'

'No, not at all.' He laughed that she'd asked that. 'Why would I sack you? I rang to make sure you were okay.'

The relief was insurmountable. 'I'm fine,' she managed, her insistence belied by the wobbly croak in her voice. 'I love this job so much, I was so worried . . .'

'I know, I thought you might be but you have absolutely nothing to be worried about. I'll see you tomorrow. And again, I apologise.' He could visualise her pale and anxious face and it angered him to think what Charlotte and Regina must have put her through.

'Thank you, and yes, see you tomorrow.'

Bonnie put down the phone, sat heavily onto the chair and burst into a flurry of relieved tears. She stayed there for a few minutes until they passed, breathing deeply to steady herself. She couldn't even let herself think what her life would have been like had she been cut off from the lovely job and the special man she worked for who had just become even more wonderful in her eyes in the past few minutes. If that were possible.

Lew walked through the front door of his house more annoyed than he could remember feeling for a long time. Although he tried not to let things get to him, this one he wouldn't fight against. It would spill over and rightly so. He'd rung Charlotte as soon as his phone was charged, to find out why he'd had thirteen missed calls from her, expecting a dire emergency. He'd had to end the call and tell her he'd speak to her at home because his stress levels were spiked listening to her ridiculous narrative and he didn't want to have a second heart-attack whilst negotiating twisty country roads.

Charlotte was sitting at the kitchen table filing a nail when he entered the kitchen. She momentarily stopped, looked up at him, then resumed filing.

'If you don't sack her, then I'll leave you,' she said, calmly, menacingly.

'Will you really, Charlotte? Will you really pack up all your designer gear into your Louis Vuitton cases and head off to the nearest B and B?' Lew countered confidently.

She threw down the file onto the table. 'I've only just had these done and I broke two corners off picking my phone up from your floor,' she said, waggling her left hand.

He ignored that. 'Whatever possessed you to walk into the shop and try and take money out of the till?' he said, pushing back the dark waves of his hair with an exasperated comb of fingers. 'You knew I wouldn't be there.'

'If you'd bothered to answer either of your phones when I originally rang you, we wouldn't have had any of this.'

Lew held his hands up. 'I will apologise for that. I left my number one phone in the house and didn't realise my work phone was out of charge.'

Charlotte leapt on the opportunity for blame. 'What if there had been an emergency? What if I'd fallen down the stairs or something?'

'Luckily you didn't,' Lew replied.

'I could have though. You always answer the number one phone. Until today, when I really needed you to answer it.'

'Look, Charlotte, we are both alive and well, thank the Lord, but what you did today was out of order. And no, I will not sack the woman for not opening my till and giving out money to anyone who says they are my wife.'

'But I AM your fucking wife,' Charlotte screamed at him.

'How would Bonnie know that?'

'She would have done if you'd picked up your bloody phone and told her I was!'

Lew looked at her and for a moment saw Regina, not Charlotte. He decided the time had come to say something about that.

'Can I tell you something that might hurt you?' He didn't wait for her to answer. 'You're spending so much time with Regina lately that you're turning into her.'

'I suppose you'd rather I were like Gemma then,' snarled Charlotte. 'Nice little Gem-Gems who wouldn't say boo to a goose.'

'I'd rather you were like Charlotte Harley actually,' replied Lew. 'The lovely girl I married.'

Charlotte rose angrily from the chair, pushing it back with her legs. 'Oh, so I'm not nice now, is that it? Not as nice as Bonnie who calls you Lew.' She screwed up her face and put on a pathetic little girl voice. 'No, I'm not letting you have Lew's money. He wouldn't like it.'

Lew stared at her scrunched-up features and for a moment time seemed to freeze and he thought, *I don't know my wife any more.*

More than once recently he had wondered if the Charlotte of old had been replaced by an alien. Or was the Charlotte of old always going to evolve into this one? Was it his fault for indulging his wife so much through guilt at working away that his sweet and pretty Charlotte had turned into Regina mark II? Had she been bored and unhappy after packing in her job to take up the role of a housewife? Then again, as he remembered, she hadn't needed much persuading to become a lady of leisure. She'd dropped her job in the shop faster than you could say P45.

'You're being ridiculous,' said Lew, turning to leave, needing to get out of this space and take a shower to wash away a day that had slid from a wonderful time buying in Newark to surreal madness.

'You might not think it's ridiculous when the police come,' said Charlotte, crossing her arms smugly across her chest.

Lew halted by the door. 'Police? What do you mean, the police?'

'Assault,' said Charlotte, smirking. 'Your precious Bonnie assaulted Regina. Dragged her out of the shop. I bet she didn't tell you that, did she?'

Having seen Regina in full dangerous harpy mode, this revelation nailed Lew's attention. He hadn't realised there had been a physical battle as well. Bonnie was bound to have come off worst faced with Regina's talons, and he wouldn't put it past her bringing her teeth into action either.

'What happened?' asked Lew.

'Your assistant grabbed her and pushed her violently out of the shop.' Charlotte gave a dramatic nod, a gesture of 'so there.'

'What – she just grabbed her for no reason?'

'Yes.'

Lew dry-laughed. 'Yeah, of course she did.'

Charlotte gasped. 'You're actually defending her, against our friend? Against me?'

'Come on Charlotte, I've seen Regina in action. What did she do that made Bonnie throw her out of the shop, because whatever it was, it wouldn't have been "for no reason"? Did Regina wade in with her fists flying?'

'Not ... no ... she ...'

'She what?' Lew hurried an answer out of her. 'She attacked Bonnie first, did she?'

'Is that what she said? She is a lying cow because Regina hardly touched her ...'

Lew's jaw tightened. 'Bonnie never said a word. Lucky guess.'

'For God's sake, she only caught her with her elbow as she tried to squeeze past to get to the till ...' Charlotte's jaw clamped shut as she realised she wasn't helping her case.

'So, let me get this right,' mused Lew. 'Regina elbows Bonnie out of the way and makes a grab for the till and Bonnie stopped her?'

'That's not what I said,' said Charlotte, gnawing on her lip.

'That's exactly what you said. I shall be checking with Bonnie tomorrow that *she* doesn't want to press charges of assault. So you'd better tell Regina to back off. Was anyone else in the shop?'

'I didn't notice anyone,' grumbled Charlotte under her breath, though he saw the side of her mouth twitch as it did when she was lying.

'So, possible witnesses were in the shop who saw everything, were they?'

Charlotte shrugged like a recalcitrant teenager.

'Charlotte, I will not be sacking Bonnie and I do not want you ever going into my shop and putting my staff in that position again. In fact it would be the decent thing for you to go there tomorrow and apologise.'

Charlotte let loose a bark of disbelieving laughter. 'You are joking.'

'No I am not. The poor woman thought she was going to lose her job for actually doing her job. She was worried sick,' snapped Lew.

'Good.' Charlotte blew down her nose like a furious horse.

'Not a nice feeling is it, Charlotte? I seem to recall you coming home in tears one night before we were married, when a woman you sold some make-up to tore a strip off you because she'd had an allergic reaction. Remember that?'

'No,' said Charlotte.

'I do. In glorious technicolour. You thought you were going to get the sack because you'd told the woman you couldn't guarantee she wouldn't have an allergic reaction but she bought it and did and then came storming into the shop asking for your head on the block. And your manager stood up for you.'

Charlotte shrugged and that brief half-smile appeared again, the one that told him she was evading the truth. She wasn't even aware of it, but Lew was.

'Well I am not apologising to a paid assistant,' groused Charlotte, stamping down on that seepage of smile.

Lew had to stop his jaw from dropping open.

'So people who work in shops are lesser beings, are they, Charlotte? Is that what you were when you worked in Debenhams?' He pretended to think for a moment and placed a thoughtful finger up against his lip. 'Yes, actually you might be right. Maybe I should sack her, then.'

Charlotte gave an open-mouthed sigh of relief.

'Hallelujah. That's the first sensible thing you've ...'

But Lew hadn't finished.

'... and because I need an assistant, you can do the job. You're experienced, you know how to sell things and it's about time you worked for a living.'

A squeak came out of Charlotte's throat, as if a mouse had become trapped there and made a cry for help.

'How dare you. I clean this house so it's nice for you to live in and come home to,' she screamed.

'Astrid cleans our house so it's nice for me to live in,' Lew screamed back. He gave a growl of frustration and realised he needed to get away from Charlotte before he really gave her both barrels. 'I'm going to have a shower,' and once again he turned in the direction of the door. And once again he stopped short of it as something came to him. A niggle that he needed the answer to.

'Tell me, Charlotte. When you couldn't get through to me on either phone, did it occur to you that the reason might be that I'd had an accident or been taken ill?'

'Of course. That's why I was so stressed.'

But there had been too much of a pause between the end of his question and the beginning of her answer for him to believe it.

# THE STARS ARE TURNING OUT FOR JACK

The *Daily Trumpet* is very sad to announce the sudden death at the weekend of popular antique ceramics dealer Jack 'Crack' Potts. Jack's father, Keith 'Pott' Pitt the elder was a scrap dealer and local character best known for having a lion as a bodyguard. His brother Keith 'Pitt' Pott the younger is a former area heavyweight boxing champion who has a boxing gym built on the site of the family crapyard. The funeral will take place this Thursday at the Church of the Blessed Virgin and will be attended not only by his family and friends but also celebrities Cristiano Ronaldo, star striker of Real Madrid and Jason Orange of Take That fame.

# Chapter 28

The funeral of Jackpot took place four days after his death, on Thursday at the Church of the Blessed Virgin. Lew shut up shop at lunchtime because he insisted that he and Bonnie should both be there. Bonnie brought black clothes to work to change into. Jackpot's wife was a devout Catholic who had organised a sombre pomp and ceremony service with no modern fripperies such as dressing in bright colours; everyone attended in their darkest finery. Four black-plumed, black horses pulled the carriage bearing his huge black coffin covered in an explosion of white lilies. His widow and daughter were in black, his daughter, tall and wide like Jack, in floods of tears being supported by her new husband. In contrast, Jack's small, bony wife Dolores was dry-eyed and hard-faced. It was the first time Bonnie had ever seen Jack's wife and she was surprised at his type. She didn't look a match for Jack, though they'd been together for over thirty years. *That's twice in one week that I've failed to pair the right wife with the husband*, Bonnie thought. Mrs Pitt strode regally into the church and the huge procession of mourners followed.

Lew walked in behind Bonnie thinking how pale she looked in black. Even the rich brown of her hair looked as if it had lost its vibrancy today. He had never seen her wearing black before; the colour swallowed her up, sapped all the life and energy from her.

Bonnie's eyes were leaking tears which she soaked up with a store of tissues. He had the handkerchief which she had returned, washed and pressed, in his pocket, ready to hand to her if she needed it.

Valerie waved at them both to sit next to her. Her eyes were dry but she reached for Bonnie's hand to draw badly-needed comfort from it. Valerie's fingers were frozen to the bone.

The ceremony was hymn–heavy and Bonnie noted that Lew didn't mime them, as so many did, but had a rich, deep singing voice. At the other side of her Valerie's voice rang out like a tuneful bell and she sang the words as if she meant every one of them. Only on the last lines of the final hymn did Bonnie hear her falter.

*Be still, my soul; when change and tears are past,*
*All safe and blessed we shall meet at last.*

After heartbroken eulogies from his daughter Mandy and his craggy-faced weeping brother, Keith the younger, which filled the room with emotion, Jack's coffin was solemnly lowered into his grave. Then everyone trooped across the road to Jack's local, the George and Dragon, where corsets were loosened and the mood was much more relaxed and convivial. Whereas the service had been about mourning Jack's death, the wake was all about celebrating Jack's life. Trays of drinks awaited guests and a buffet that took up four long tables. Through one of the windows, Bonnie noticed that Valerie had taken herself off and was sitting alone on a wall, smoking. Bonnie gathered a plate of finger-food for her and walked outside to deliver it. As she neared Valerie, she was surprised to see how aged and tired she looked in the sunlight.

'Hello, love,' said Valerie, blowing out a plume of smoke and tapping the ash off the end of her cigarette with a long finger.

'I brought you some sandwiches,' said Bonnie.

'I'm not hungry, darling. But thank you. You eat them,' said Valerie, smiling politely though her usually bright blue eyes were dull today. 'Come and sit on the wall and keep me company. I don't want to go in there.' She pointed her cigarette in the direction of the pub.

Bonnie put the plate down on a nearby table and shooed a fly away just before it landed on the square of quiche.

'Do you know why Jack's dad called his lion Leo?' asked Valerie eventually in her beautiful, vintage BBC announcer's voice.

'No idea,' said Bonnie, preparing to be enlightened.

'He called it Leo after my mother,' said Valerie, pulling smoke into her lungs. 'My mother had the most beautiful red hair and Keith Pitt used to say that she looked like a lion. Her name was Elsie but he called her Leo. He was in love with my mother.'

'Really?'

Valerie looked straight ahead, though she could feel Bonnie's eyes trained on her face.

'My father was a bastard, Bonnie. A real, hard, nasty bastard and my mother was going to leave him for Keith Pitt. But she caught TB and it killed her before she could. Keith was never the same man after that. When he got that lion, he called it after my mother because he was convinced she'd come back to him in it. That lion loved him so much. It was as tame as a kitten with him. And that's why he was heartbroken when it died. It felt like he'd lost her all over again.'

Bonnie noticed that a stray tear was dropping down Valerie's cheek. She let it weave down her face, unhindered.

'My family's fate is entwined with the Pitt family's,' smiled Valerie, crushing the light from the cigarette butt on the wall. 'I fell in love with Jack when we were at school.'

'Did you?' asked Bonnie, never realising she and Jack went back so far.

'And Jack fell in love with me. We were going to be married.'

The tear was joined by another.

'I didn't know you went out with each other,' said Bonnie.

'Not many did. But we fell out and I did a stupid thing and kissed someone else, knowing it would drive him mad with jealousy. Jack was so angry . . .' Valerie reached into the pocket of her long black jacket for another menthol cigarette. 'So he slept with someone to get back at me. Once. And she got pregnant.' She gave a mirthless chuckle. 'Oh the daft games people play that have such dire consequences.'

'God . . .' gasped Bonnie for the want of anything better to say, though she felt that Valerie just needed to hear something, anything to know she was being listened to.

'She's in there now, feeding her fucking rosary through her ever-so-Catholic fingers and pretending she's above us all,' Valerie lit the cigarette so elegantly she made it look like an artform, '. . . but she couldn't drop her knickers fast enough for him back then. And he had to marry her because it was so Jack to *do the right thing*,' she snarled. 'But he never stopped loving me, did you know that, Bon? He married that dried-up twig but it was me he wanted and he never stopped wanting me.' More tears joined the ones that were now dropping off Valerie's chin onto her black silk skirt where they spread into sad blossoms.

'Oh Val. I'm so sorry.'

'He wouldn't have left her whilst Mandy was growing up. He adored his daughter. Then Mandy had all sorts of problems that some girls have, throwing up and dieting and he said he couldn't leave whilst she was ill . . .'

Bonnie's eyebrows creased in confusion. 'You mean that you still . . . were together all the time he was married?'

'Oh yes,' nodded Valerie. 'We never stopped being lovers. He didn't get anything from *her*. He only stayed for Mandy. She gave him a reason for being, but I gave him a reason to *live*. I loved him with my whole heart.' Bonnie handed her a tissue and Valerie thanked her and blew her nose on it. 'Anyway, Jack said that as soon as he'd seen Mandy down the aisle, that was it. He was leaving Dolores and coming to me. He was going to tell her on Sunday. The day he died. He'd ordered white roses to be delivered to me the next day, the first morning we would wake up together as a proper couple again. This is one of them.' She reached into her bag and pulled out a white rose, now limp and crushed. 'I wanted to throw this into his grave but I didn't dare. He always bought me white roses. I have his roses, Bonnie. They arrived on Monday morning with his card that said "Val, my love, my life for always." But I don't have him.'

She pulled smoke out of the cigarette as if it were oxygen and she needed it to breathe.

'Oh Valerie,' Bonnie spoke softly. 'Did Dolores know he was leaving her?'

'Not a chance,' huffed Valerie. 'She wouldn't have let me within ten miles of that church if she'd known there was anything going on between us. No one knew. No one. And I'll have to keep it secret forever now, because what's the point in saying anything? I'd hurt Mandy for no reason and Jack won't be waiting for me up there if I do that because he'd be furious.' Her shoulders slumped and she sobbed, then immediately recovered.

Bonnie tried to put her arm around Valerie but she pushed her away.

'Don't, Bonnie, darling. Because I'll disintegrate. This cigarette is the only thing holding me together. I'm sorry. And I'm sorry for burdening you with this. We both have been carrying a lot of secret baggage, I suspect, but I wanted ... had to tell someone that it was *my* Jack that got buried today. Mine. He was mine, all mine.' Her voice dissolved, her lips were quivering with grief.

'I understand, Valerie.' Bonnie flicked a tear from her own eye. She noticed that little flies were all over the plate of buffet food now.

'We thought we had time,' said Valerie, her throat thick with emotion. She took a long draw of her cigarette, dabbed her cheeks with the back of her hand, then she looked Bonnie straight in the eye. 'Promise me that you'll take your chances when you can, Bon. Grab them with both hands and run with them and don't wait. I know you aren't happy in your life and you should be. Don't end up like me. Promise me,' she insisted.

'I promise you, Valerie,' said Bonnie. And she meant it.

'Now, go on and leave me for a bit. I want to think and remember. There's a good girl.'

Bonnie nodded and gave Valerie's arm the briefest touch, yet it carried all the weight of her affection before she walked back towards the pub. Starstruck was getting some air by the door. It was weird seeing him in a suit, his usual wild hair greased back, the top pushed forward into a quiff as if he were a Teddy Boy. She smiled at him.

'All right, Starstruck?'

'Yes love, are you?'

He caught her arm just as she passed him.

'Bonnie, love, it's not the time nor the place I know, but our Alison's house is up for rent again if your friend's still interested. Bloody tenants did a moonlight—'

'Yes, she is, it's me.' Bonnie heard the words come out of her mouth before she'd even planned to say them. 'I'll take the house, Starstruck. I'll rent it.'

# Chapter 29

Bonnie made small talk with her antique dealer friends for the next half-hour but her brain was anywhere but in the snug of the George and Dragon. Starstruck said he would come over to the Pot of Gold first thing the following morning to give Bonnie the key for the house on Rainbow Lane. This time tomorrow, she would have left her grey, cold life in Greenwood Crescent. She couldn't think straight. It was like being blind and opening her eyes for the first time to be assaulted by the full spectrum of colours in their brightest intensity. She was actually going to do it. Leave. Whatever happened afterwards she would have to deal with.

She got into Lew's Audi with her head spinning as much as if she'd had three glasses of wine. She was glad she hadn't had any because she needed her brain to be clear and focused.

'You all right?' asked Lew, turning to her as they joined the main road. 'You look very pale, Bonnie.'

'Is there any chance I could come in late to work tomorrow?' asked Bonnie. 'A hour; two, tops.'

'Of course.' He didn't pry but he wanted to.

Then Bonnie burst into tears. She hadn't meant to, they came from a strange, agitated place within her, a lake of adrenalin filled with pockets of fear, excitement, fascination, energy; a whole gamut of emotions, all vying for supremacy.

'Let me find somewhere to pull in,' said Lew, concerned.

This had to be connected with what had happened in the shop between her and Charlotte, he figured. He'd hoped Bonnie had been totally convinced that she had done the right thing and had absolutely nothing to worry about, but evidently not.

Regina had not called the police; she would have made a fool of herself if she had. Lew had told Charlotte in no uncertain terms that if Regina did that, he would sever all social ties with the Sheffields and tell them why. He overheard Charlotte ringing her later, telling her to put it behind them because 'that Pit Bull woman just wasn't worth getting aereated about.' Then between them they'd arranged a dinner for this weekend at Regina's house for the six of them. Lew really didn't want to be anywhere near the woman for now but on the other hand it would be nice to see Gemma and Jason again.

'I'm so sorry.' Bonnie was horrified at herself. She couldn't stop crying, although at one point she started laughing at the ridiculousness of such an emotional explosion. I'm going mad, she thought. Maybe she had been so trapped in Stephen's mindset of 'being in order' that her system couldn't digest the many changes that would be happening to her over the next hours and her brain was trying to vomit them back out in case they poisoned her.

'You have nothing to be sorry about. There's a pub near

here.' Lew took a left down a country lane and pulled into the car park. Ironically – given the conversation she'd just had with Vintage Valerie – it was the Red Lion. 'A small and friendly traditional pub' according to the wording on an A board standing next to a cluster of alfresco wooden benches and tables.

'Come on, let me buy you a drink,' said Lew, getting out of the car. 'I think, after this week, I owe you a big one anyway.'

'You don't . . .' Bonnie started to protest but Lew wasn't having it.

'What would you like?'

Bonnie made her way to one of the outside tables. No one else was there so she had the pick of them all. Lew returned a few minutes later with half a lager for himself and a glass of Diet Coke for Bonnie.

'I asked for a bottle because the stuff that comes out of those taps is revolting,' said Lew, putting it down in front of her.

'It's more expensive though,' said Bonnie.

'I'll take the difference out of your wages,' said Lew, eyes twinkling.

'Thank you,' said Bonnie, hoping her eyes weren't as red as she imagined they'd be, and that her mascara hadn't run.

Lew sat down opposite to her and thought again how ashen Bonnie looked in black, as if the colour had sucked out her soul.

'So . . .' he began. 'Look, if you're still worried about what happened on Tues—'

Bonnie cut in. 'That's not why I . . .' She took a bolstering breath. 'I'm leaving my husband,' she blurted out. 'And I have to go quickly and cleanly because he . . . I . . .'

Lew leapt to the obvious conclusion. 'Is he violent?'

'No, no,' Bonnie shook her head, though that slap he gave her still sat at the forefront of her mind. 'He's needy, sticky . . . he gets upset by change and what I'm about to do is likely to blow all his fuses.'

Lew's brow furrowed in concern. 'He could be unstable then, is what you're saying?'

'I don't know.' She wanted to tell him that he was stable in his unstability. He would hit the roof but at the same time he would know exactly what to do. 'He will probably resort to emotional blackmail and tell me that I owe him and I probably do . . .'

'You sound as if you're paying off a debt,' said Lew, tilting his head at her.

Bonnie swallowed hard before answering. 'I think that's what I have been doing.' She took a sip of her Diet Coke and gulped it down along with the rising tears. She didn't say it was a debt that she could never clear. Or that she might be running from a life from which there was no real escape.

'Have you been unhappy a long time?' said Lew, his voice gentle and Bonnie knew that if she wasn't careful she would offload the last thirteen years into his lap. He held up his hands, palms forward. 'I don't mean to snoop. You have full permission to tell me to butt out.'

'I should never have married Stephen,' said Bonnie, looking down at the ground. An ant was scurrying along the flagstone with a crumb of something on his back.

'So why did you?'

'I loved him,' said Bonnie. 'Or at least I thought I did. He was everything I needed: kind, steady, attentive. He was in the beginning, anyway.'

She coughed away the sudden dryness in her throat and

took another drink. 'I lived with someone before Stephen. He was lovely, was Joel. We'd known each other since we were kids. He was full of life, crazy, a tour de force. But he got lows as deep as the highs were high and over the years they got worse. He was never . . . *even*. We were either living life at a hundred miles per hour or in slow motion. I loved him so much but it was like being on the worst sort of fairground ride. Medicines either didn't work or drugged him senseless, until he did a trial on a new one and it balanced him more than he'd ever been. We had six beautiful months of believing that we could be a couple like anyone else. He got a job in a warehouse, nothing flash but it was a massive leap forward for us. We went walking in the park with our dog and we started planning for the future. Then the drug was suddenly pulled because it was causing an adverse reaction in some patients and he was weaned onto another one which was useless . . .' Her voice faltered. She took a deep breath before continuing. 'I came home from work to find him gone. There was a note on the table saying sorry, just that one word. We looked everywhere for him and I mean everywhere. A dog-walker found him hanging under a bridge near Ketherwood three weeks later. The police said he'd probably killed himself the day he left me.'

Lew didn't know what to say. 'I'm so sorry,' was what fell from his lips.

'My whole life was so focused on Joel that I hadn't realised my dad was slipping away from me too. What we'd both put down to just daft "getting older and forgetful" stuff was far more serious and he'd kept it from me, not wanting to add to what I was going through. I walked in one day to find him putting the electric kettle on the open fire to boil telling her to leave all the arrangements to him and he'd make sure he looked after her.

'You're probably wondering why I've stayed with him so long,' said Bonnie, but she guessed he'd just think she was stupid.

'It's not hard to guess,' said Lew, which surprised her. 'It's a huge task leaving a marriage when you have nowhere to go to and no energy to carry you.'

'Dad's nursing home took almost every penny from the sale of the house and the little savings he had, and Stephen took the rest and put it in our joint savings account that I don't have access to,' said Bonnie. 'I nearly left Stephen once but—' She stopped. She couldn't tell him the truth of why she stayed. She couldn't tell anyone. 'I wasn't quite brave enough to go through with it.'

'It doesn't sound like a happy marriage, Bonnie,' Lew said, just stopping himself from placing his hand over hers, to comfort her.

'It isn't a marriage in any sense of the word,' said Bonnie. 'I didn't even feel giddy or excited at my wedding. My dad was there and I wanted him to see me settled before he died, but he didn't even know who I was . . .' She'd had dreams about her wedding over the years, distorted images of everyone in black, Harry Grimshaw pulling on her hand to leave but her feet being glued to the floor, her dad drooling, Alma laughing at him and Bonnie slapping her face hard over and over again until her hands stung, but still she wouldn't stop cackling like an old witch.

She'd presumed what she felt for Stephen was just a different sort of love from the one she'd had for Joel. When he'd been well, they'd talked about getting married and she'd been filled with joy and excitement about it all. He

it. Dad went from nought to sixty with dementia a[...]
he stayed at sixty for years. He was a huge man [...]
couldn't handle him when he started lashing out. I h[...]
put him in a specialist care home.' She flicked away the [...]
that were pumping out of her eyes. She could still hear A[...]
speaking to Stephen at three hundred decibels, *Don't thi[...]
you're going to stuff me in an old people's home like she did tha[...]
poor thing sat dribbling who hasn't a clue where he is or why.* 'It
was something I said I would never do to Dad, whatever
happened, but I had to. That ... that horrible disease kept
him alive and fit and strong everywhere but in his head.
Then my lovely dog got a tumour and I lost him too.'

'And in the middle of all that along comes your husband?'
guessed Lew.

'Yep.' Bonnie gave a dry chuckle. 'He couldn't have timed
it better if he'd tried. I dropped all my shopping in the rain
and this man appeared at the side of me like a knight in
shining armour. He gave me tea and sympathy and attention
and he drove me up to see Dad and helped me sort out all
those little things that were weighing me down, forms to
fill in, Dad's house bills to sort out, car repairs. He said we
should get married then he could look after me properly. I
was so drained, so grateful and he was so kind ...' She
cringed at her own stupidity. 'Looking back, I wasn't in the
right place to make big decisions like that. We were married
so quickly I hardly had time to draw breath ...' She rapped
on her head with her knuckles. 'Idiot, eh?'

'Not at all,' said Lew, his voice soft, understanding.
'Sounds a little as if you were manipulated.'

Was I? thought Bonnie. She hadn't thought of it that wa[...]
she'd always blamed herself for being needy. She coul[...]
even recall Stephen proposing. She just remembered [...]

must have said a million times how much he loved her, yet she couldn't remember Stephen saying it once. It was a *different sort of love*, all right.

'And why now?' asked Lew. 'What's finally made you decide to go through with it?' He reached into his pocket and passed his handkerchief over. 'Getting to be a habit, this,' he laughed softly.

'Thank you,' smiled Bonnie, pressing her face into the soft material. She didn't say that she was in love with her boss, that meeting him had wakened and warmed up her heart more than she thought possible. And that just being around him had given her the energy to risk leaving Stephen in the hope that she just might outrun the darkness that would surely follow her. Instead she answered, 'Timing. Starstruck's daughter has a small house for rent nearby. It's affordable, if I'm careful with my money. He's bringing the keys around tomorrow and I'm going to move in whilst Stephen is at work. If I tell him I'm leaving, he'll make it awkward. I can take what I need in the car, one trip. I can have everything packed and be out of the house in an hour, max.'

'Do you need any help?' asked Lew.

'No, thank you. I'm better off doing everything alone,' replied Bonnie. She didn't want Lew near the house. She was scared what Stephen might tell him.

'Where's the house you're moving into?' asked Lew.

'Dodley Bottom. It's on Rainbow Lane, next to the old Duck Street Chapel. It's only a tiny place but it'll be perfect for me, I'm sure. I'm hoping I won't be that late to work. I'll make up any time . . .'

'Oh don't be silly, Bonnie,' Lew remonstrated. 'Why don't you take the day off?'

'No, I'll need something to keep my mind occupied.' She was adamant on that.

'Then I'll follow you after work and help you lift things in.'

'No, really, you're okay. I'd like to do it myself anyway. On my own.'

Something in her tone convinced him that she wasn't just saying that, she really did mean it, so he relented with a nod.

'Tell me if you change your mind, and I'll leave it at that.'

'Thank you.'

'Can I ask you something, Bonnie? I don't want you to get worried, I'm just curious. I heard that you manhandled Regina out of the shop like Bruce Lee. Is it true?'

Bonnie's eyes snapped up to his face to find that he was wearing a lop-sided smile. She'd noticed that his 'business-smile' was a regular one, his lop-sided one was the genuine article. It gave his face extra handsome points.

'Dad's friend had a nightclub and when he was a young man he used to do a bit of doorwork for him. He was handy, my dad, and he taught me a few moves just in case I ever needed them.'

'Ah, I see,' said Lew, noticing that Bonnie's cheeks had a pink flush to them. 'You said he was a big man, didn't you?'

'In every way you can think of,' said Bonnie. 'Six foot six tall with massive shoulders. He was lovely.' She pictured him holding her hand, walking her to school and remembered feeling proud that he was her dad. Sometimes she had to work hard to force the pictures of him in the grip of dementia from being the dominant ones in her memory album: of him going berserk in the house, smashing things in frustration, of him being an empty shell in the home, drool down his shirt. 'If I ever get like that, shoot me, Bon,' he'd once said when they were watching a documentary about dementia on the TV. 'I hope to Christ I never end up like one of those poor buggers.' And he had. Cruel, cruel disease.

'Well, your dad did you a favour there. Though I hope you don't come into contact with any more undesirables who need ejecting from the shop, but it's good to know that the Pot of Gold is in very safe hands,' grinned Lew. He was glad to see that he'd made her smile with that. She has such a beautiful smile, he thought.

Lew took Bonnie back to the Pot of Gold where her car was parked. She went home knowing that the next time she drove it, it would be away from Greenwood Crescent forever. It all felt too easy, too smooth, especially for a Sherman, who was born on the back side of the rainbow, as her dad always said.

# Chapter 30

Stephen was standing by the sink washing up a plate when Bonnie walked in. He looked over his shoulder at her and smiled and she thought how odd that was, because she couldn't remember the last time he'd greeted her with a pleasant expression.

'Did it go well?' he asked. Again odd, because he never asked about her day, only told her about his.

'As much as could be expected,' replied Bonnie. 'It was very well attended.'

'Burial or cremation?'

'Burial. Then a wake.'

'I have no idea why people expect to be fed and watered after a funeral,' said Stephen with a sniff.

You wouldn't, thought Bonnie, casting her mind back to Alma's funeral. There had only been a few mourners because Alma had alienated most people. Not even Katherine, her so-called best friend, had attended it. The few pensioners who turned up uninvited to the church were shocked to find that no sandwiches had been laid on for after the service. Bonnie had argued it was the decent thing to do, but Stephen had called it an unnecessary expense.

'A lot of people travelled a long way to pay their respects to Jack,' said Bonnie.

'Then they should have fortified themselves with a hearty breakfast.'

Bonnie made a face behind his back. To think that this time tomorrow she would be in another life sent a thrill fizzing through her down to her bones. She didn't know how she'd managed to stay with Stephen for so long; she'd only been in the house five minutes now and already wanted to scream.

'I've defrosted some pork loin medallions for tea,' said Stephen, pumping some hand-cream out of the dispenser at the side of the sink and rubbing it into his palms.

'Yes, fine,' said Bonnie, though something was rattling around in her brain. *They rarely had pork and it was always pasta on Thursday, never anything else.* He'd broken with the pattern and that small thing concerned her because Stephen never did that. It meant something, but she didn't know what.

'I'll go up and change before I start dinner,' said Bonnie.

'There's no rush.' Stephen poked the pork chops through the cling film. 'They need another half-hour before they're fully thawed, I'd say.'

Bonnie went into her bedroom and stripped off her black dress. She opened the wardrobe to hang it up and her scalp prickled as if something wasn't right, in fact the feeling was as thick as sauce in the air. She flicked through her clothes, looked on the empty top shelf and down below on the floor where her case sat but nothing looked amiss. She was unduly anxious, she concluded. Her nerves would be in shreds by the morning if she didn't pull herself together. She had one more night to endure, one more meal sitting opposite

Stephen and his relentless chewing, one more morning waving him off to work. She had to act normal and claw through the next sixteen hours. It sounded hardly anything and at the same time, an eternity.

\*

When Lew got home he walked into a wonderful aroma of beef cooking in red wine and a smiling Charlotte standing by the hob. It was a welcome sight given the wrong foot they'd been on for the past weeks. Lew walked over to her and gave her a kiss, intending it for her mouth but she gave a little twist at the last minute and it landed on her cheek.

'How did it go?' Charlotte asked.

'As good as these things can, I suppose,' said Lew, placing his jacket over a dining chair back and loosening his tie. 'There were loads of people there and the wake was cheery enough. The service was a bit heavy though and very black.'

'I want everyone to dress in light blue at my funeral,' said Charlotte, stirring the cooking pot.

'What did you have lined up for me then, when I had my heart attack?' asked Lew, realising that he'd never actually asked her this question before.

'I . . . I didn't even think about that,' said Charlotte. 'I always knew you'd be fine.'

He had a sudden vision of Charlotte going shopping in Meadowhall for a very expensive black ensemble, including hat and new handbag. She'd have had her nails done black as well, he bet. Then the thought of a younger Bonnie in black knocked the image of Charlotte out of his head. He imagined her at Joel's funeral, a picture of quiet dignity, her emphasis set on letting her lover go on to wherever he was destined rather than being the belle of the black ball.

'I'll go up and change,' said Lew. 'I might have a shower if I've got time.'

'Loads,' said Charlotte. 'This will be half an hour at least. Oh and did I say that we're going to Patrick and Regina's for dinner on Saturday?'

'Okay,' said Lew, but he hadn't heard her. His thoughts were still taken up with Bonnie. It sounded as if she hadn't had a great deal of luck in life. Luck, he'd found, was not a commodity that was fairly distributed. He'd had more than his fair share: money, breaks, success, even the heart attack that didn't kill him but gave him the wake-up call he needed to begin a career he was loving that brought him into contact with the mad, motley bunch of wonderful dealers. Charlotte would think that people like Starstruck were common and not worthy of her attention, until she found out he had a holiday home in Barbardos, of course. Even then he couldn't see Charlotte enjoying his stories and throwing back her head and laughing at them, like Bonnie did. He couldn't imagine Charlotte wanting to mingle with Long John and Uncle Funky or being interested in anything they sold.

She was missing out. He'd had more fun in the past three months than he had in the past three years. He loved the camaraderie of the traders, their banter, their expertise, their familial-type warmth towards each other. And most of all, he looked forward to the company of Bonnie with her brightly coloured clothes and her huge rainbow umbrella and her beautiful autumn eyes.

Lew stripped off his suit and had a shower. He turned the cold tap to full to chase away the pictures in his head of Bonnie and her lovely but sad face.

# Chapter 31

The evening passed ordinarily enough for Bonnie. After they had eaten, Stephen went into the lounge to watch a documentary about fish wars in the world's oceans and she watched the clock's hands crawl round to the time when Stephen would announce he was going to bed. Bonnie left it half an hour after that before retiring herself. Then, with the water running into the bath in her ensuite to mask any noise, Bonnie pulled the suitcase out of the bottom of her wardrobe to put the rest of her clothes in it.

When she opened it, she found it was empty.

Her mind tumbled. She had half-filled it, she knew she had. She plundered her memory bank for evidence and she found it: hi-def footage of her putting in underwear and her jeans, her flowery dress. She flicked through her wardrobe again and found the clothes that should have been packed away hanging there and she knew that was the reason why she'd done a double-take when she changed out of her black dress. She looked around for the box holding Bear's ashes and her family treasures and couldn't find it and she knew then that Stephen had been in her room, in her wardrobe.

He had found the half-full case and realised that she was planning to leave him. It must have happened whilst she was at the funeral, because she would have noticed the flowery dress there, next to the empty hanger for her funeral outfit. Her lips pulled back from her teeth in boiling rage. She wanted to fly into his bedroom like a bullet and scream into his face: how dare he touch her things, how dare he take her precious belongings, but she forced herself to be calm and think. She sat on the side of the bed and willed her heart to stop its wild, angry beating. He knew that she wouldn't leave without her treasure box; it was his way of trying to anchor her here. She cursed herself for talking back to him recently. It had set his warning flags running up the pole.

*Think, Bonnie, think.* She closed her eyes and concentrated. She needed to formulate a codicil to her plan of action. Stephen would be back at work in the morning. As soon as he was out of the door, she would hunt for her missing possessions and she would find them, then she would go. The morning could not come fast enough for her now. She might be crushed if she left, but she would definitely be destroyed if she stayed.

Silently and quickly, she packed all the clothes and possessions that her suitcase, the plastic box and a large holdall could carry then she got into bed and invited sleep to come, but her hatred for Stephen drove it back for hours.

# Chapter 32

By lunchtime the next day, Bonnie had still not arrived at work and Lew was worried about her, especially after their conversation the previous day. He had no doubts that she told him she would be coming into work with her car packed full of her belongings by mid-morning at the latest. Starstruck had already been and gone and left the key for the house on Rainbow Lane. Something didn't feel right. Lew found her home and mobile numbers from a file in the office and rang both, but there was no answer. He left a voicemail asking her to ring the shop. By one o'clock he had still heard nothing and he had no idea what to do. It would be rather odd for a boss to go over to a member of staff's house enquiring where they were, he thought, and could even be seen as harassment. Maybe she and her husband were having an eleventh-hour reconciliation and ringing in to work was the last thing on her mind. But somehow he didn't think so because he was sure that Bonnie would have let him know, had her plans changed. Lew didn't work on hunches usually, but he could not shake off the suspicion that Bonnie might be in trouble. She'd said her husband was 'sticky', hadn't she? He was certainly manipulative, if her story was to be believed. He decided that it would be better to risk coming over as interfering and over-zealous than have her come to harm because of propriety.

Lew waited for a loitering customer to leave the shop, then he closed the door quickly behind her and scooped up his car keys.

*

Bonnie had woken a full hour before her alarm went off. She washed and dressed for work as normal and tried to suppress the current of adrenalin surging through her system. She needed to be out of this house as soon as humanly possible. Yesterday she had wondered if guilt would have followed her out of the door, leaving Stephen silently and without notice, even though she knew that was the only way she could avoid his barbs sticking into her, trying to drag her back. But when she had discovered that he had emptied her case and confiscated her things, she knew she would sail out of the front door devoid of any sympathy for him at all.

She could hear him moving around in the kitchen. She took a deep breath before taking the stairs and another before she walked into his airspace to say her customary and polite, 'good morning'. She tried not to react when she saw that he was dressed for another stint in the garden.

'I thought you were back at work today?' she said, a thumping heartbeat in her throat.

'Yes, I was supposed to be, but I have a headache. The fresh air will chase it away, no doubt.'

'Oh.' She wanted to scream at him *Where are my things?* She pushed down on the words with all her might and said instead, 'I'll make some tea. Would you like one?'

'No thank you,' he replied.

Bonnie crossed to where the tea and cups were kept and clicked the kettle on. It could have been her imagination, but she felt his eyes on her back, watching for signs of rebellion. It took every bit of self-control she had not to turn around and launch the tea caddy at him.

'I did notice that the front borders were looking less than sharp,' Bonnie said, pouring boiled water over a teabag in a cup. 'Is that what you're going to be tackling today?'

'That's one of the jobs, yes. In fact, that reminds me, where's my lawn edging tool?' He mused, chewing his lip in thought. 'I haven't used it in a while.'

Bonnie thought she might have left it in the garage when she used it to nudge the plastic box off the top shelf. She leapt on the moment to buy herself some time, not much, but it might just be enough.

'My guess would be the shed,' she said, keeping her voice light. 'Knowing you, it will be with all the other gardening equipment.' She sat down casually at the kitchen table. 'Chicken casserole or cacciatore do you think for tonight because we haven't had either in ages?'

'Cacciatore,' said Stephen, pronouncing the last 'e' both as acute and as if correcting her. He lifted the shed key from the hook on the wall and walked out of the back door, heading down the garden. Bonnie bolted from the chair and up the stairs as if she were spring-loaded.

She threw open the door to Stephen's bedroom and began looking around. She never came into this room, not even when she was cleaning because he insisted on doing it himself and he was so finicky that she didn't argue. The room was showhouse perfect: the carpet, which was laid over twenty-five years ago, looked brand new, though the pattern was hideously old-fashioned. The mirrors on the wardrobe didn't have a single finger-print, the clothes brush, comb and various toiletries on his dressing table were artfully positioned, even the bed had been made precisely and every crease smoothed out to an icing finish. Bonnie dropped to the floor to look under the bed, but there was nothing. She opened all his drawers and tried not to disturb the carefully placed con-tents to see if her box was there, but it wasn't. The wardrobe was locked, which was interesting. She first looked on his dressing table and struck lucky because she found the key in a glass lidded dish, with a couple of other keys for the windows and assorted enamel lapel badges. She quickly unlocked the wardrobe and checked the base where there was an ordered stack of boxes containing his shoes except for the second one from the top which had all her missing treasures in it. *The bastard,* she thought. *The arrogant bastard,* she amended that to, because he'd presumed she wouldn't dare enter his secret lair, other-wise he would have hidden them elsewhere. She grabbed the whole shoebox, locked the wardrobe door and wiped her dull fingerprints from it with her sleeve and then put the key back in the pot. She crossed to her own room, put her most precious possessions in her case and zipped it shut. She was ready to go now. She couldn't stay another minute in this house.

She heard the kitchen door opening with a cheerful two-tone 'Avon calling' alert. Stephen shouted her name, a note of panic in his voice. Bonnie loaded herself up with her case and holdall. She'd need to come back for the plastic box, but if she had to leave it, she would do. She took a deep breath, ready for the inevitable confrontation. She heard his hurried footsteps taking the stairs. She opened her door to find him standing there, tall and wiry, drained of colour and wearing an expression she had never seen before; one of disbelief and confusion, the whites of his eyes laced with red as if blood vessels had exploded in them. She had lived with him for thirteen years and yet at that moment he looked like a stranger.

'What are you doing?' he said, his voice a breathy whisper.

By comparison Bonnie's voice was iron. 'I'm leaving, Stephen. You will not keep me here by hiding my things. How dare you even try. Now don't make this harder than it is, because I am going and you cannot stop me this time.'

He looked as if a puff of wind would have blown him over, but when she stepped into the narrow gap between his body and the door, he was unyielding. She looked up at him and he appeared taller than she pictured him being, as if he'd grown inches in minutes.

'Get out of my way, Stephen.'

Without a word, Stephen's palms came out and pushed her backwards with such force that she landed on the bed. He grabbed the handle and slammed the door shut. Bonnie righted herself and lunged for the handle on her side but he was holding it firmly on the other. She wrenched on it with everything she had and it gave slightly and through the gap she saw that he was doing something with a rope. It slammed shut and when she tried it again, it was as if it had been sealed. He had tied the handle to the one belonging to the airing cupboard next to it.

'Let me out,' she screamed.

'You can't leave, it's not how it's supposed to be,' Stephen screamed back. *It's not the way of things.*

In yesterday's article entitled 'The Stars are Turning Out for Jack' we mistakenly reported that attending the funeral of popular antique ceramics dealer Jack 'Pott' Pitt were celebrities Cristiano Ronaldo, star striker of Real Madrid and Jason Orange of Take That fame. We should have said Chris Ronald, striker for Rotherham FC and John Lemon, silver expert and friend of the deceased.

# Chapter 33

Bonnie had been trapped in her room for hours when Lew pulled into the estate where she lived. The back, where Bonnie's bedroom was, looked out onto long fields of yellow rapeseed. There was no house opposite and no chance of being seen waving madly out of the window, unless the small boy who lived five houses down happened to be flying a drone or the local farmer decided to cut his crop early. Her phone was downstairs in her handbag. The key to the window which was always on the sill was missing, Stephen had taken it as a precaution, presumably. She had tried reasoning with him through the door, calmly, offering to talk things through, even lying that she wouldn't leave, but he hadn't answered. He was past responding to anything she might say, she'd decided after a couple of hours so then she'd tried to smash the double-glazed window with a cup then a perfume bottle but it hadn't worked. She looked around but there was nothing she could have picked up and launched at the glass to smash it; her only hope was to wrest the sink from the wall of her ensuite and try that. She sat on the bed and thought it was ludicrous that she could be trapped in a bedroom with no means of escape. How would she get out if there was a fire? She had to treat this as if it were the same because she was sure as hell she would get out if her life were in immediate danger. She had just started looking for something to help prise out the sink when she heard the front doorbell ring, followed by a tattoo of heavy knocking. She raced to the bedroom door and pressed her ear to it, hearing the muted notes of an exchange of voices. Only postmen, Jehovah's Witnesses and old Gerald at stupid o'clock on Sunday mornings ever called. Any of them would surely find a woman screaming was cause for further investigation. So she filled up her lungs with as much air as they could take and screamed.

*

Lew had already seen Bonnie's Vauxhall parked on the drive as he approached the detached house in an estate filled with samey-samey others. The style of the house didn't fit her at all, he thought. He imagined her in a cottage setting with non-conformist windows and a riot of coloured flowers bursting from crowds of pots and window boxes. He strode up the path and rang the doorbell, following it with a series of staccato knocks that no one on the inside could miss. It was almost immediately opened to the length of the attached security chain by a tall, wiry man with short, thick greying hair and a long, gaunt face. Stephen, her husband, presumably. Something else that didn't match her.

'Is this where Bonnie Brookland lives?' asked Lew.

'Who wants to know?' asked the man cautiously.

'I'm her boss. She didn't turn in for work today and I . . . I wondered if she was all right.'

Lew's ear picked up a high-pitched sound, as though he'd inadvertently switched on his phone in his pocket and someone were screaming down the earpiece. A woman's voice.

'She's fine. She's ill,' said Stephen paradoxically, closing the door so his face was just a slice of skin and one grey eye.

*Help. Help me. Get the police.* Was Lew imagining this or could he really hear it?

'Is there any chance I could have a quick word with her? She's got a key of mine that I really need,' he said, thinking on his feet.

*More screams.* He felt vibrations on the edge of his radar now, as if someone were stamping their feet.

'I'll ask her to ring you.' The door was closing.

*Help me. I'm locked in.*

Lew's hand shot out to stop it.

'There's someone shouting for help in your house.'

'Go away,' said Stephen, putting his full weight against the door, but Lew was younger and, thanks to his post-trauma healthy exercise regime, stronger than he had ever been in his life before. He countered Stephen's effort with his shoulder, giving it everything he had. Stephen fell back, the door swung fully open as the chain broke. The shouting was louder now and unmistakeably Bonnie's voice.

Lew strode over Stephen's prostrate form. 'Bonnie?' he shouted, trying to trace the source of her distress call.

'I'm upstairs.'

Lew took the stairs two at a time and there at the top of them were the door handles bound with figures of eight rope.

'Bonnie, it's Lew. Are you all right?' he asked, deftly

unlooping it. He checked behind him for her lunatic husband but there was no sign of him. He threw the rope onto
the carpet and opened the door and there stood Bonnie,
ashen-faced, her hazel eyes large and shiny with anxiety, her
hand holding up a metal nail file as a weapon.

'Oh Lew.' She ran to him in relief and his long, strong
arms closed around her. She could have stayed there forever,
breathing him in, the scent of his unnamed cologne mixed
with his warmth.

'I have to get out of here,' she said, gulping as if she had
been starved of oxygen. She moved out of his hold to pick
up her things.

'What do you need?'

'The case, the box and the holdall. That's all I'm taking.'

'Let me go first,' he said. 'You get the bag, I'll manage
the rest.'

Lew tucked the box under his arm and walked tentatively
down the stairs, not unconvinced he'd be met at the bottom
by Bonnie's soon to be ex-husband wielding a bread knife.
Any man that locked his wife in a house was going to be
unpredictable. But Stephen Brookland was slumped at the
kitchen table, a cloth pressed to his rapidly swelling cheek-
bone. He didn't lift his eyes when Lew walked past him.

'I need my handbag,' said Bonnie, darting past Stephen
towards a row of hooks on the wall where a line of coats
were hung. As Bonnie checked through the contents of her
bag, Lew looked at him hunched and pathetic and his lip
curled instinctively. He couldn't imagine anyone more
unlikely for her to be married to.

Bonnie took her two coats down from the pegs and lifted
her umbrella from the stand. She could have taken more
now, but she just wanted to get away.

'Can I have a minute?' she said to Lew. 'Please.'

'Really?' Lew said with disbelief. He didn't want to leave her alone with this brute if he could help it.

'I won't be long.'

'I'll be just outside the door,' said Lew, dragging his eyes away from the contemptible creep.

When he had shut the door, Bonnie stood squarely in front of Stephen but his eyes remained downcast, his hand still pressing the cloth against his cheek. He looked old and disgusting and she shuddered at the thought that she was joined to him in marriage. She pulled her wedding ring off her finger and set it on the table in front of him.

'It didn't have to be like this, Stephen,' she said. 'I don't want anything from you, just a divorce.'

'Don't worry, you won't be getting anything from me,' said Stephen, flicking his eyes up towards her for a second. 'Not a single penny.'

'Let's do this quick and painlessly, for both our sakes.'

Then his head rose slowly and she saw a smirk spread across his dry, thin mouth.

'Quick and painlessly, eh?'

She picked up her things feeling panic wash over her like a cold shower.

'You'll be back. There will be no life for you if you don't, as well you know,' he went on.

She rounded on him. 'Stay away from me, Stephen. I mean it or I'll get the police onto you. You wouldn't want them calling around here, would you? Setting all the neighbours off talking?' His respectability was important to him, he would find that excruciating.

But the warning bounced straight off him and that smirk remained, twisting up the side of his mouth. A nasty, rotten, smug smirk that burned itself on her eyeballs so fiercely that she would see it for a long, long time.

'Call the police, would you? Pass me the phone and I'll ring them for you.'

She turned quickly, half-running towards the door, slamming it hard behind her, striding down the path away from his voice that was intent on following her.

*You know what you did, you bitch, and I'll make sure everyone knows as well.*

# Chapter 34

Lew had put the case and the box in his car. The boot was still open for the holdall.

'Put it in here and let me drive you,' he commanded. 'We can pick up your car later.'

'No,' said Bonnie. 'I want to take it now so I don't ever have to come back here.'

'Are you all right to drive?' She didn't look it.

'I'll be okay. I'll take it steady.'

'You go first,' he said. 'I'll follow close behind and make sure he doesn't come after you.' Lew thumbed behind him at the house. 'What sort of car does he have?'

'A blue Mondeo,' Bonnie informed him and reeled off the reg number.

Bonnie turned the engine and immediately stalled it. Her leg didn't seem to have a bone in it when she pressed down the clutch. She forced herself to concentrate and not look any more of a fool in front of her boss than she did already. She adjusted the rear-view mirror and caught sight of her face. Death warmed up didn't even touch on it. What on earth must he think of her? Shame rushed into the spaces which the adrenalin had vacated. She looked every inch the wreck outside that she felt inside.

She pulled up in Spring Hill Square car park with Lew at her rust-bucket heels in his polished Audi. She felt shaky and weak as she placed her feet on terra firma but she willed some strength into herself. She couldn't bear that he might see her as a victim.

'Let's take your things into the shop where they'll be safe. You okay?' asked Lew, opening up his boot. The warm concern in his voice made her feel even more embarrassed that he'd seen her so low and needy.

'I will be,' she said, trying to smile and fearing she looked demonic instead.

'Come on.' He handed her the holdall and they walked towards the shop where, once inside, he locked the door behind them and didn't turn the closed sign around to open. 'I'll put the kettle on,' he said.

'Oh don't keep the shop closed because of me, I . . .' she protested, but Lew was having none of it.

Bonnie sat down on the chair behind the counter and let the tension relax in her body. She was out of that house yet half an hour ago she had been trapped in a room about to try and pull a sink off the wall. It felt as if she had just slid out of a bad dream too fast and was disorientated. She shouldn't have tried to threaten Stephen with the police. He would see that as a battle line being drawn. She should never have mentioned the police. *He wouldn't,* her mind argued. *He wouldn't do what he could do. He would be damaged in the process.* But didn't bees sting even though they knew they would kill themselves too?

Lew returned with two mugs of milky coffee.

'I think you might need this,' he said with a gentle chuckle.

Bonnie smiled, wishing he wasn't looking at her so intently. She wouldn't want to view herself through his eyes.

'Thank you,' she said. 'I don't know what I'd have done if you hadn't come. There's no one else who would have realised I was missing. Not for days anyway.'

'You haven't told any of your friends what you were planning?' asked Lew, pulling a packet of Florentines out of his pocket and peeling the opening strip.

Friends? One by one she'd lost them all over the years. There was just Valerie and she wouldn't have wanted to burden her with all this.

'No, I didn't tell anyone,' said Bonnie.

'Have you put any furniture in storage anywhere?'

'All I have, I brought with me.' Bonnie looked at the holdall at her feet. The handle, resting on top, looked like the curve of an upside down smile, as if it knew it held a pathetic dearth of possessions for the life of a forty-two-year-old woman.

'What are you going to sit on? Or sleep on?'

'I'll go shopping,' said Bonnie.

'Do you want me to come with you?'

'God no,' Bonnie protested. She didn't want Lew seeing her buying crap, cheap sticks of furniture. 'But thank you anyway,' she added quickly.

Lew was about to press his offer to help but stopped himself. Bonnie was a woman with much-valued pride in tatters and he knew she must be feeling uncomfortable and ashamed, though she had no reason to be: he genuinely wanted to help her. He'd have driven her up to Houseworld in Penistone and bought a bed, a sofa, a table for her, but he knew she would never have agreed to it. He wondered what the outcome of the scenario with her husband would have been had he not driven up there, and was so glad he'd followed his instinct.

'There's someone looking in the window,' said Bonnie, pointing to a couple outside. 'You'd better open up.'

'I will, but I want you to go home,' said Lew. 'To your new home.'

'No,' said Bonnie. 'I had a plan. To get out, come to work and then go to my new house when I finish. Please. That's what I really want to do. To get back on today's track. As I wanted it to be.'

Lew waved at the couple and unlocked the door, greeting them warmly as they entered. 'Yes, we're open, we were just finishing off a stock-check,' he said as an excuse.

Bonnie recognised the couple. They'd been in the previous week asking about the Queen Anne-style walnut writing desk. They smiled at her when they saw her.

'I'm so glad you're here,' said the woman. 'We'd like to buy the desk. I could have kicked myself when we came away without it. I haven't been able to stop thinking about it. We didn't know if you were on commission so we wanted to make sure we bought it from you, just in case.'

'Bless you,' said Bonnie, warmed by their thoughtfulness. 'Well, it's here and still available, but it's certainly been a piece of interest.' She had slipped into work-mode, which was a blessing for her because it was normal and normal was tantamount to a home.

# Chapter 35

Lew insisted that Bonnie leave at four.

'Lew, I can't afford to lose any more pay,' Bonnie said.

'Do you actually think I'm going to dock your wages?' he asked. 'Please!'

'Ken Grimshaw would have.'

'I'm not Ken Grimshaw,' said Lew sternly.

*No, you're most definitely not*, said Bonnie to herself. Ken Grimshaw didn't have deep blue eyes, the colour of a twilight sky, or thick black-brown waves of hair that her hands wanted to plunge into. Ken Grimshaw didn't smell like a fresh forest and have a smile that make the heat rush to her cheeks. Ken Grimshaw didn't make her heart feel as if there were something on this planet worth beating for.

'Make sure your phone is charged up and do not hesitate to call the police if your husband turns up. Does he know where you'll be living?'

'No,' said Bonnie. 'Not yet. But it won't be long before he finds out.'

Lew picked up one of the business cards from the counter and scribbled on the back of it. 'Here's my personal mobile number. Only a few people have it and I'll always pick up if it rings.' *Apart from one notable occasion*, added his brain for his ears only.

'Thank you,' said Bonnie, reaching out for it and then pulling her hand back quickly before he caught sight of the state of her nails, which had been bitten down to the quick when she had been locked in the room. They had pulsed with pain all day.

'I'll get your luggage out of the back room.'

'Lew, you've done enough, I'll—'

'I'll get your luggage out of the back room.' He was insistent. They walked across the square to her car and Lew lifted the bags into the boot for her.

'I'd better not forget to give you these,' he said, pulling out two sets of keys tied together with ribbon. 'The blue ones are for the back door, the red for the front.'

Bonnie took them from him and felt a fizzy thrill zip around inside her. She'd done it. She'd actually done what she had wished she could do. These were not only keys for the doors of a little house, they were keys to a new life, a life without Stephen. Her freedom. She wouldn't be going back to him, whatever he said, whatever he did. A Queen of Wishful Thinking would only ever move forwards.

'You take care,' Lew said and bumped her shoulder because he'd wanted to touch her in some way to convey his concern and it wouldn't have been right to close his arms around her again as he had that morning. He would swear he could still feel the imprint of her against his chest.

With every yard she covered towards the house on Rainbow Lane, Bonnie felt a further notch of exhilaration, like a child on her way to see Santa. She knew that when she walked in, the house wouldn't be the same as the one in her head, an explosion of cheerful colour, but it didn't matter. She parked up in front of the green gate and took the keys out of her pocket, having another moment of disbelief that she was actually here and about to open the bright red door. *Her* bright red door. Inside, instead of the huge cosy inglenook fireplace of her imagination, there was a small low tiled one in the lounge and the carpet was dark brown, the walls magnolia, but it was still lovely. She brought in her luggage and shut the door behind her. She was home, and her lungs expanded and she breathed in the slightly damp air and it felt wonderful. The kitchen was tiny, but it did have a two-ring hob set in the work surface and a small fridge underneath it. She switched it on and it whirred merrily into life. Upstairs there was one large bedroom with built-in wardrobes either side of a chimney breast. The window afforded a view of a considerably overgrown square of garden, two posts standing upright and a droopy washing line strung between them. There was a bathroom with a cheap but new-ish white bathroom suite. It felt wonderfully unfamiliar.

Now came the part she had been waiting for, the exciting part. She needed things and, thanks to The Rainbow Lady sales, she had extra in her budget to buy them with. She set off down to the small retail park just outside town where the big Argos was. She already had the product codes saved on her phone for a kettle, a single quilt, cover, pillow and the flip-out bed that doubled up as a chair. The bed, in the brown colour only, had twenty pounds off. The colour didn't matter to her at all. The young male assistant kindly carried it to the back of her car for her. Then, across the road in Asda, Bonnie bought some milk and coffee, bread and butter and basics, including a can opener that she realised wasn't on her list. She found a toaster for ten pounds and when she saw a microwave with a large scratch on the side for the discounted price of thirty-five pounds on a gondola end, she couldn't resist. She unloaded her new purchases at home as if she were unwrapping surprise birthday presents. Her evening meal consisted of a cheese toastie and a mug of tomato soup and it was a feast because she didn't have to eat it opposite a man chewing his jaw off and pontificating about subjects he pretended to know more about than he did.

She was tired out by ten o'clock and settled down on her new bed in the front room, which wasn't the most comfortable thing on the planet, but she didn't care. She snuggled under the cheap quilt, rested her head on the pillow which was soft and bouncy with its newness and savoured a different sort of quiet from the one in Greenwood Crescent. She hadn't realised the sounds her ears registered there, until she could no longer hear them: Stephen's muted padding across his carpet, the faint play of voices or music coming from the radio in his bedroom, the neighbour's garage door opening and closing when he arrived home from work. Here there was only a sporadic rumble of cars on the nearby High Street, but she didn't mind that at all.

She would wake up in the morning not having to see Stephen over the breakfast table. It really would be the first day of the rest of her life, as the old saying went. Further thoughts of him flittered to her brain, like moths drawn to a light. She thought about what Lew had said about him manipulating her and she explored that from her new safe vantage point in the little house. She rolled back to thirteen and a half years ago and again tried to fathom what had made her so thirsty for the attentions of a man like Stephen Brookland. She'd been a wreck, on the precipice of a nervous breakdown. Physically she was so drained that Harry Grimshaw had sent her home on full pay for a fortnight to have a good rest. Mentally she was so wired she was barely sleeping, yet she was exhausted. She was battered too from the beatings she had given herself for not being able to help Joel or see through the 'I'm perfectly fine' act her father had put on. He'd been her rock, her daddy who had brought her up with all the love he had to give and made sure she had the best of what he could afford. All that to cope with and Bear's illness thrown on top. She had loved her dog so much and had to watch him growing weaker as the silent, sly cancer took hold. And though she'd known her final kindness to him had been to let the vet send him to his forever sleep, it had still been a hard duty. If she closed her eyes, even now all these years later, she could still recall him falling backwards into her arms and see the light draining from his eyes. She could still imagine her face pressed into his darling fur made damp with her tears and the voice of the vet above her saying 'Sorry for your loss.'

Stephen was fourteen years her senior, but she hadn't felt the age difference until they were married. She'd been adrift, floating around helplessly, about to drown and he'd appeared like a lifeboat and led her into a harbour. No wonder she'd fallen in love with him. He had designed himself to make her do that.

Funnily enough when she had a ring on her finger, he hadn't been as keen to help her with her duties to her father. And his chivalrous ways were sadly lacking when his mother attacked her for not being good enough for her son, for being a gold-digger (that amused rather than hurt), for being a leech. There had been a slow slide from treating her like a lady to a housekeeper then further down the scale to a mere sounding-board for his inflated theories and pompous opinions on everything.

Even with less than a day's distance from Stephen, she could see clearly how she might very well have been manipulated, as Lew had said. The real Stephen had been the one post-marriage, the fake one had led her to the registry office with a crumb trail of kind words and gallantry. He didn't even want to sleep with her before they were married and she'd presumed he was an old-fashioned gent. She'd been so easily hoodwinked. And why? Just so that he didn't have to be alone? She'd been nothing more than a pet to him. And not even one that he'd treated with any respect, or love.

And so what would he do now that they were apart? She pictured him today in an empty house with no familiar smells of Friday chicken coming from the kitchen at teatime. He would have made himself a sandwich and eaten it at the table with no one opposite to speak at – not to or with: she was there to speak *at*. He would have watched the Discovery or History channel, as per normal but his plate would not be washed up when he went into the kitchen to lock the door at half-past ten. He would have retired to his bedroom then to listen to the radio with the precisely placed socks in his drawer and his boxes of shoes in the wardrobe, and his mind would be spinning on the events of the day, just as hers was now.

Mental exhaustion soon made her eyelids shutter down and sleep drifted towards her in thickening mists. Just as she was surrendering to it, she heard Stephen's voice cut through them, as sharp and loud as if he were beside her, his lips close to her ear.

*You'll be back. You'll have to be back. There is no life for you if you don't, as well you know.*

And she shuddered because it was not the *way of things* that she went and she had absolutely no doubt that he would be planning how to restore order.

# Chapter 36

'Please don't forget that we are going to dinner at Regina's tonight,' said Charlotte as Lew opened the door to leave for work the next morning.

'Promise I won't,' he replied.

'Can't you come home early and just leave thingy in charge if she's so wonderful,' said Charlotte.

'Bonnie. And no, not at the moment, it would be unfair ...' Lew instantly regretted saying it because Charlotte leapt on it.

'What do you mean "unfair"?'

He batted away the subject with a wave of his hand if it were of no importance. 'Just personal problems, I don't know all the details.'

'Huh. This from the man who said that personal problems should never interfere with work,' humphed Charlotte.

Lew looked at her in puzzlement. 'When did I ever say that?' He knew he hadn't because it wasn't something he believed was true. 'Personal problems do impinge on work life sometimes, it's inevitable.'

Charlotte shrugged. 'Oh well, if it wasn't you it was

someone else, but it's true though, isn't it? You get paid to do a job, not mope around. Besides, work should take your mind off things. What's up with her anyway?'

'I don't know.'

'Yes you do, Lewis. Why so secretive?' There was a suspicious note in her voice.

'Her marriage has ended,' said Lew, feeling slightly disloyal that he was discussing Bonnie's business. Even to his wife.

'No wonder. Bet her husband is out partying now,' smirked Charlotte.

'What a horrible thing to say,' Lew barked, which made Charlotte's mouth drop open with shock.

'Lewis!'

'You have no idea what the woman has gone through, have you? Not everybody has your privileged easy life, Charlotte.'

'Lewis!' she said again, but he hadn't finished.

'You've got a bee in your bonnet because of the other day—'

'I have not . . .' Charlotte gave a shrill protest.

'You might live in a grand house and have a gold visa card, Charlotte, but that does not give you the right to treat people like shit. You came from a semi on the edge of Ketherwood, or have you conveniently forgotten that?'

'Will you stop shouting at me,' Charlotte screamed at him. 'I'm having a really rotten time at the moment with Gemma and that whole baby thing and I could really do with you and me being on the same side.' Her hands shot to her face and her shoulders started shaking.

Her distress threw a bucket of cold water over him and he felt instantly annoyed at himself for being so insensitive.

'I'm sorry,' he said and rushed over to give her a hug. She turned into his shoulder and he buried his lips in her hair.

'I thought you said you weren't upset by Gemma trying for a baby, love.'

'I lied,' said Charlotte, sniffing hard. 'I didn't want you to think that I was petty and jealous. But obviously I am. I'm a horrible person.'

'Oh don't,' said Lew. 'You're not.'

She pulled herself away but kept her head down. 'Go on, get off to work. I'll see you tonight.'

'I won't be late and we'll have a lovely time this evening.' He placed his finger under her chin and lifted it up, then he kissed the tip of her nose.

It was only when he got to the car he realised that for all her sobbing, Charlotte's eyes had been totally dry.

*

As Bonnie started to wake up on that first morning in Rainbow Lane she felt as if something were holding her against her will and her arms pushed against the force and, as she came to full consciousness, she realised that it was only her quilt that was pinioning her arms. But the sensation had freaked her, because it signified something she already knew: that her new-found freedom was an illusion. She had run from Greenwood Crescent and she would divorce Stephen, but he had an ace card and she knew he would use it. He would do everything he could to try and bring her to heel or grind her beneath it if she resisted.

She lifted her left hand and looked at her ringless finger. She could still see the faint groove in her skin where the gold band had sat and she rubbed it and hoped it would smooth away so there was no trace of it. She wondered if Stephen was still wearing his, but she reasoned that he would be because he had complete confidence that he would keep his marriage away from the divorce court. She sat up and looked around her. She might have to leave this little house for a prison cell, but she would not leave it to go back to Greenwood Crescent.

Her limbs felt jittery with nervous tension as she drove to work because she expected to see Stephen's car parked on Spring Hill waiting for her. But it wasn't there and that surprised her. She started second-guessing what he might have planned instead but reprimanded herself. There was no point in leaving him if she were to bind herself to him mentally.

She had forgotten that she would need an iron. Her shirt was creased and she was embarrassed about it. She had put on a long dark cardigan to cover it up but the sun was bursting out of the sky and she looked ridiculous. Lew was already in the shop, sorting out the till float. He raised his head when he heard her open the door and smiled.

'Good morning. And how are you today?' he asked.

'I'm fine,' she said, returning the smile.

'How was your first night in your new living quarters?'

'Wonderful,' said Bonnie, 'although there's a lot of paperwork to sort out now that I've moved. Council rates and water and driving licence, and I've got to find a solicitor. I'm filing for divorce as soon as I can.'

'I can give you the name of the firm I use,' said Lew. 'The divorce solicitor there is a woman and she's very good. And thorough. She'll get you what you're owed.'

'I'm not bothered about taking any money, I just want it

all to end quickly and smoothly,' said Bonnie, trying not to notice that Lew was shaking his head at that.

'Let her deal with it all for you. She will do the negoti-ating on your behalf, but you should start your new life with what you're due. Here . . .' He pulled his mobile out of his pocket and looked up the number, then he scribbled it on a piece of paper and handed it to her. 'Adriana de Lacey is her name.'

'She sounds expensive,' said Bonnie, raising her eyebrows.

'She'll be worth every penny you pay her. She often works Saturdays too so you've got a good chance of speaking to her today if you wanted to set the ball rolling.'

Bonnie hadn't considered how much a divorce would cost her. As if Lew could read her mind he then said, 'I think you're looking at around a couple of thousand pounds, in case you're wondering. It won't be much cheaper with anyone else either so take my advice and use her.'

Bonnie's eyes rounded. She hadn't expected it being any-thing like as much. Would she have to pay it all or would Stephen be liable for half? She guessed the former.

'Look,' Lew began, scratching his newly shaved chin, 'Bonnie . . . please don't be offended but if you need me to advance you some wages or even to borrow money—'

Bonnie held up a protesting hand. 'No, I don't want to go down that road—'

He interrupted back. 'All I'm saying is that the offer is there should you need it. Okay?' She nodded, grudgingly, but both of them knew she wouldn't ask. Some people weren't used to taking because they had so little experience of it.

'I'll put the kettle on,' he went on. 'You nip next door to

Leni's for a couple of toasted teacakes so we can toast – if you'll excuse the pun – your first day of freedom. What do you think about that?'

'That sounds smashing,' said Bonnie, but she couldn't quite believe it was freedom. Not yet. More of a fool's paradise, knowing Stephen.

# Chapter 37

There had been a steady stream of customers in the shop all morning, but at one o'clock it was empty, except for Valerie who was in her unit unpacking some clothes and steaming them on their hangers with her iron. Lew had gone out to the supermarket in Penistone for some wine for the evening. It was the first chance that Bonnie had had to talk to Valerie. She looked terribly pale and aged, thought Bonnie. Grief was weighting her features, pulling her lips downwards into a sad arc.

'You all right, Valerie?' asked Bonnie.

'Thank you, as well as can be expected,' she replied, pressing the steam button to remould a felt hat.

'I didn't think you'd be in for a while.'

'I have to carry on and earn a living,' said Valerie, with a loaded sigh. 'My world is a little grey at the moment, Bonnie dear, but slowly some colour will come back into it, I'm sure. I'm going to stay with my sister in Italy for a couple of months. Hence why I'm here, replenishing my stock so there's plenty for you to sell in my absence.'

Bonnie wanted to throw her arms around Valerie and hug her, but she wouldn't. Valerie wanted to keep her composure intact, even if her heartbreak was obvious.

'Valerie, would you mind if I borrowed your iron for two minutes please?' asked Bonnie. 'Whilst the shop is empty? My shirt needs a press.' She checked to make sure no one was about to come in.

'Go behind my changing curtain,' commanded Valerie. 'I'll do it for you. Go on and take it off.'

Bonnie did as she was told.

'I've never seen you with a creased shirt before,' said Valerie as Bonnie handed it to her. 'In all the years I've known you, you've never been less than immaculately presented. Now why is that, I wonder?'

'I left my husband,' said Bonnie from behind the curtain. 'I only took the bare essentials with me.'

Valerie didn't miss a beat. 'And when did you do this?'

'Yesterday,' said Bonnie, peeping around the curtain. 'After what you said at the funeral about taking your chance, I took mine yesterday.'

Valerie pressed the short sleeve of the blouse. 'Jack always said you weren't happily married. Harry Grimshaw once told him that he didn't like your husband.'

'Really?' said Bonnie. Harry had never interfered, apart from what he'd said at her wedding, and she'd certainly had no idea that he'd spoken about her to anyone else.

Valerie went on, 'Of course Harry was too much of a gentleman to gossip but he did once tell Jack that he thought you had rushed into things.'

'I did,' sighed Bonnie. 'I made a mistake.'

Valerie handed the shirt back to her.

'Not so easy to leave a marriage. I know this, of course,'

said Valerie with a sad smile. 'Especially when you are held there by ties of loyalty.'

Bonnie nodded slowly. Valerie was talking about Jack; she didn't know how true that was of Bonnie's situation too.

'Where are you living now, Bonnie?'

'I'm renting Starstruck's daughter's house on Rainbow Lane in Dodley Bottom.'

'I'll leave the iron for you. I won't need it if I'm going away. And take the ironing board too. Are you short of anything else, other than that? I have a few bits of extra furniture at home.'

Bonnie smiled. 'That's very kind of you, Valerie, but I'll not put you to any trouble. I'll buy pieces here and there when I can afford them.'

Valerie's hands flew to her hips in a gesture of impatience. 'Do you have a bed? Sofa? Table? Chairs?'

'I have one of those chair things that flops out into a bed.'

'That will be no good at all for your back,' Valerie tutted. 'Leave it with me.'

'Honestly, Va—'

'Can I tell you something, Bonnie?' Valerie cut her off with a snap in her voice.

'Go on,' said Bonnie. Valerie was a formidable creature and when she demanded people's attention, she usually got it.

'Your father was a gentleman. When I first started off in this game, I fell behind paying my rent in his shop because someone bounced a large cheque on me. He gave me three months free on my unit so I could get on my feet and I think he'd have given me more if I'd needed it. I survived because of his kindness and I never looked back, and I don't forget things like that. I've made a good living at this game and

I've loved it, and I have your dad to thank for extending his hand of friendship towards me when I needed it most. And it isn't just me that feels like that. Your dad helped Stickalampinit out with a lot of things, and Jack and Boombox and Stan. They all thought a lot of your father and they wouldn't see his daughter in need.'

Bonnie recalled how many of them went to visit him in the home, just to pass some time with him. Even though he mostly didn't recognise them, they still went and sat and talked to him.

'You have customers,' said Valerie, shooing Bonnie away just as she was about to open her mouth and protest. Bonnie saw how shiny and full of tears her friend's blue eyes were before she turned back to steaming the hat. 'Bonnie, go and attend.'

# Chapter 38

Patrick and Regina's behemoth of a house stood behind presidential-style electric gates. Jason and Lew privately referred to it as 'the White House' because Regina had had the facade of it painted a blinding shade of white a couple of years ago so that it would stand out from the other five clone houses on the prestigious cul-de-sac. She also had an eight-foot fountain installed in the front complete with stone cherub posed in arrow-shooting mode on top.

'You look nice tonight,' said Lew as Charlotte took his arm when they got out of the taxi, because the pebbles on the drive weren't compatible with her heels.

'Thank you.'

'Haven't seen that bag before, is it new?'

Charlotte stopped in her tracks. 'What's that supposed to mean?'

'It means have you bought yourself a new bag, because I haven't seen that one before. It's called conversation.' Mentally Lew threw up his hands in exasperation.

'Do you mean "we're on an economy drive so you

shouldn't be buying anything"?' she replied tightly, resuming walking, but her grip loosened on his arm.

'Okay, I'm sorry I asked,' replied Lew, refusing to be pulled into an argument and setting a sour note for the evening. 'If it is or isn't new, it's nice . . .'

'It's not new,' said Charlotte, but he knew she was lying because that nervous smile was playing at the corner of her mouth.

'I wouldn't begrudge you a handbag, Charlotte. Just not one made out of a white crocodile.'

'It's. Not. New,' she insisted through clenched teeth.

Lew rang the doorbell and Patrick greeted them looking even heavier and hairier than the last time they'd seen him. He'd gone past Chewbecca and advanced to Bigfoot. 'Come in and what can I get you both?' he asked, rubbing his hands together.

'I'll have a glass of red,' said Charlotte.

'Same for me, please,' added Lew, noting that Charlotte hadn't said please. Another one of Regina's less desirable influences, thought Lew. People of class and distinction didn't have to say please, would have been her ridiculous justification.

They were the last to arrive. Regina, who was directing things in the kitchen, came out to greet them warmly. She made no mention of what had happened during the week in the shop and Lew had put it to the back of his mind so that it wouldn't encroach on his enjoyment of the soirée. Then they joined Jason and Gemma who were in the garden under the pergola, glasses in their hands: wine for him, Shloer for her. Patrick was the best host and, as Regina liked to show off, she usually pulled all the stops out when it was their turn to hold a dinner party. Lew hoped – for once – they'd have an evening that passed without incident. They were all well overdue that privilege.

Gemma and Jason jumped up to greet them too. Gemma, especially, looked delighted.

'We aren't meeting up enough,' she said, settling back onto the big rattan outdoor sofa. 'We must be due a shopping trip soon, Charlotte.'

'Absolutely,' said Charlotte. 'But I'll have to check my diary, it's mad busy at the moment.'

Mad busy? thought Lew. With what? he wondered. Gemma hadn't bought the lie either if the small shrug of her shoulders and the withered 'Okay' were anything to go by. It was funny that as soon as Regina rang, there wasn't anything that his wife wouldn't drop to accommodate her. It saddened him. He hoped that Gem and Jason did have a baby and that she met more deserving friends with children.

Lew and Jason had a quick catch-up. Jason was expanding the business to include American vehicles, Lew learned. He started reeling off figures of what he was paying out and his expected profits but Lew couldn't quite concentrate because he was watching how Jason's forehead didn't seem to move when he spoke. Jason, it appears, was worshipping at the altar of the Botox god these days. And he'd had his eyebrows shaped.

Regina appeared and plonked herself down next to Charlotte and Lew noticed how wide and genuine his wife's smile grew, as if she was at school and the head girl had just picked her out to be her friend. Patrick followed and sat on the chair arm next to Lew.

'Shouldn't you be putting the chip pan on, Reg?' laughed Jason.

'Fernanda has everything in hand in the kitchen. I'm better off out of the way,' she replied.

'Fernanda's leaving us soon,' put in Patrick. 'She's getting married and is going back to live in Brazil.' He looked sad about that.

'Lovely for her, but sad for you, I imagine,' said Gemma. Fernanda had been their live-in housekeeper for three years.

'We will miss her a lot,' agreed Patrick, scooping up a handful of vegetable crisps from a bowl on the table.

'You'll miss looking at her arse,' chortled Regina, swigging back the last of the wine in her glass. Patrick didn't respond, as if he was so used to these sorts of comments now, they didn't even flash up on his radar.

'Jason's just been telling me he's expanding the business, Gem,' said Lew, moving the conversation away from women's arses and back to the much safer subject of cars.

'Tell me about it. I never see him these days,' Gemma replied, rolling her eyes but smiling at the same time.

'As you gentlemen know, you have to put in the time to build up the business,' said Jason, winking at his fellow entrepreneurs.

'Excuse me, and women as well,' said Gemma, jabbing herself in her chest.

'I'm talking big business not trimming someone's fingernails, Gem,' laughed Jason, but there was too much derision in there for Lew's liking. He was reminded that the last time they'd met, Jason had also said something in front of them all that put his wife down.

'Cheers,' said Gemma with a good-humoured tut. She hadn't taken offence by the sounds of it. Maybe I'm being over-sensitive, thought Lew.

'Yep, it's all going really well,' said Jason. 'So if you want to get rid of that old banger of an Aston Martin, Patrick, I'll give you a couple of thou' for it.'

'In your dreams,' said Patrick. 'She's the love of my life.'

'Apart from Regina, obviously,' put in Charlotte.

'Of course,' nodded Patrick, but not very convincingly.

'I might come and see you. I need something more satis-factory than I have at the moment, Jason,' said Charlotte. 'A little less conservative and more racy.'

'Anytime. Just come in my office when you're ready,' he replied, quirking a waxed eyebrow. 'Always go for speed above comfort, that's what I say. I can sort you out, no problem with that.' A click of the tongue, a cheeky wink. Lew wondered what the hell had gotten into him. Had a little money gone to his head so much? A bottle of dye had also gone to his head, he noticed. The grey hairs that had been sprouting at his temples were now as dark as the rest. He was turning into Boycie from *Only Fools and Horses*.

'So how's Sparkles doing, Gem?' Lew enquired. As soon as he asked, Jason started another conversation about cars, leaving Lew and Gemma to it.

'Very well, thank you,' she replied. 'I'm building it up as much as I can and training up a manager to take care of things for a while when I catch on.' She crossed her fingers and raised them.

'Any luck yet?' Lew asked, casting Charlotte a quick, concerned glance, but she was too busy listening to what the others were talking about.

'Alas no,' she said. 'Jason's always knackered when he gets in. His working hours aren't conducive to my tem-perature chart.' She chuckled. 'I can't believe I've been bitten by the broody bug at forty though. I mean, what's that all about?'

Jason and Charlotte groaned loudly at something Regina had said, which led Lew to think she'd made another joke at Patrick's expense.

'I'm a big believer in there being a right time for some things, Gem, and not always when you'd expect it,' said Lew. 'Now, when the baby comes, you'll have some money at your back and security and age and experience that you didn't have before.'

'You'd have made a nice dad, Lew,' said Gemma, giving his hand a sudden squeeze and his gut a hell of a sucker punch.

*

Bonnie was spending the night quietly tucked up in bed with her book after a Chinese takeaway from the restaurant around the corner, and a large glass of red wine, or rather a mugful, because she hadn't brought any glasses from Greenwood Crescent. It didn't matter what she drank from, but she felt that she wanted to toast her new life properly and she had. Wishful thinking and having the guts to back it up with some action had got her this far, she had to believe they would help her keep it.

When she went to pick up her chow mein from the take-away counter, she could see through to the restaurant which was full of couples and groups all smiling and eating together and she wished she were part of the scene. Maybe in time she might meet a kind, sociable man with good friends and a great line in banter. It was something else to wish for. She pictured Lew at a table with his buddies that night, laughing, drinking wine, though not from mugs. She imagined him turning to her, grinning at her. She imagined feeling lucky that he was hers and the person she'd be going home with that night.

*

Fernanda sounded the dinner gong and everyone filed back into the house, seating themselves around the amazing glass and metal dining table which Regina had custom-made by a Japanese designer. The chairs were stunning polished chrome, although Lew always thought they became very uncomfortable to sit on after an hour, however impressive they were to the eye.

Whilst Patrick refilled everyone's glass, Fernanda served up the starters: exquisite parmesan crisp baskets filled with a warm bacon and avocado salad with tiny quail eggs sitting on top.

'Fernanda, Fernanda, they are not going to let you go,' said Jason. 'You are too good.'

'They should lock you in the house so you can't get out,' added Gemma, which sent a shiver tripping down Lew's spine.

Fernanda chuckled. 'I have to go, Mr Whiteley. My fiancé needs me to cook for him.'

'He's a very lucky man,' said Patrick, tucking straight in as if he hadn't eaten for days.

'No wonder you're on course for doubling your weight by next month,' Regina remarked.

'I've starved myself all day for Fernanda's cooking,' came Patrick's retort.

'You — starve yourself?' said Regina, with a loud 'ha'. 'Yeah, looks like it. You're turning yourself into a hog roast.'

'Children, children,' said Gemma, raising her glass.

'Come on, let's toast something. I know, what about friendship.' She raised her glass and everyone lifted theirs to join with it in the air. She chinked it against Lew's and the thought came to him that out of everyone around that table, at that moment in time, he liked her the most. In all the years he'd known her, she'd always been sweet and uncomplicated, hard-working and smiley. She'd been a rock for Jason and never bragged about anything she'd accomplished. Lew hoped that Jason appreciated what a gem he had in Gemma.

Regina had made Patrick change seats so she was sitting next to Charlotte, interrupting the boy-girl, boy-girl, boy-girl pattern. She'd made such a fuss about it that Lew hoped Gemma didn't feel put out that they were cosying up to each other so obviously.

'That's a lovely bag you have, Charlotte,' said Gemma, noticing it parked on the urban-chic sideboard behind her.

'Lulu,' Regina answered for her. 'Love a bit of Lulu.'

'Guinness?' asked Gemma.

'Well obviously,' laughed Charlotte. 'You didn't think she meant the singer Lulu, did you?'

Lew stopped himself barking at Charlotte for being rude.

'I bartered the price down for you, didn't I, darling?' said Regina with smiling pride and wagged her finger whilst imparting some words of wisdom: 'You always have to be prepared to walk away.'

Lew couldn't help himself asking, 'Oh yes? When was this then?'

'Thursday,' said Regina.

Charlotte cast him a laser-like stare.

*So it was new then.* Charlotte had lied. As Lew already knew.

'I have no idea about designers,' said Gemma, shaking her head.

'You don't say.' Gemma didn't hear Regina mutter that to Charlotte, but Lew did.

'My wife does,' said Patrick. 'I don't recognise her without a dozen carrier bags in her hand.'

'And I don't recognise you without fucking love-bites on your neck,' Regina spat, throwing an icy bucket of water over the conviviality.

'Take it easy, Reg.' Even her new best friend Charlotte winced at that.

'I was only joking, so chill everyone,' said Regina, flapping her hand and reaching for her wine glass. 'Fernanda, we're all finished, I think.'

Fernanda arrived to gather up the dishes.

'Fernanda is going to have plenty of babies with her husband,' said Regina, grabbing hold of the young woman and jiggling her stomach. Fernanda laughed it off, but she looked horrified.

'I wish you lots of luck, Fernanda,' said Gemma, who looked as disturbed as Lew did by Regina's manhandling of her.

'Any development with you two on that front?' asked Patrick, addressing Jason and Gemma.

'I don't know why you're bothering,' said Regina. 'Have a drink and forget about having a sprog. You're too bloody old for a start.'

'No she isn't.' Lew stepped in. 'Women are having babies later and later these days.'

Regina guffawed, reaching for the decanter of wine on the table. 'You'll be the oldest mother in the schoolyard, Gem. Everyone will think you're the granny.'

Gemma's smile of amusement looked strained.

'I can't think of anyone who will look less like a granny at the school gates,' Patrick said with warmth and feeling.

'Totally agree,' added Lew, watching Regina drink her fully replenished glass down in one.

'Steady on,' Patrick warned his wife. She gave him a very nasty look and snatched up the decanter again.

Fernanda delivered two plates in front of Regina and Charlotte. Mains was halibut in lobster sauce with a colourful fan of vegetables on the side of the plate.

'It's nice to hear that someone is getting attached. Everyone we know seems to be splitting up,' said Gemma. 'Our neighbours, two of my clients plus the cleaner at Sparkles and she's in her late fifties. Mind you, she looks great on it. She's got a toy-boy, dropped two stone and started wearing clothes from Top Shop.'

'Good for her,' said Patrick.

'You should go down to Sparkles, Patrick,' sneered Regina. 'You'll be trying to shag her next seeing as you have a penchant for older women. GILFs I think they're called.'

Lew felt the hairs on the back of his neck start to rise.

'I read a very interesting thing in the *Mail* yesterday,' Gemma said quickly, doing her best to guide conversation to a safe harbour. 'It said that if most people were offered the chance to be truly happy, but they had to forfeit all their possessions, they wouldn't do it.'

'How can you be happy without any possessions?' replied Charlotte, wrinkling up her nose.

'Surely the point is that you are, because that would be the deal,' said Patrick, coming to Gemma's defence.

'No one would agree to that deal though, would they?'

put in Jason, with much the same expression on his face as Charlotte had. 'It's just stupid.'

'I think I would,' said Patrick with some force.

'You? You're the most materialistic person I know,' mocked Jason.

'Am I now?' Patrick threw back, locking eyes with Jason. 'Maybe I was once upon a time but I think you might have wrested that crown from my head, Jase.'

'What's that supposed to mean?' Jason laughed, but there was little amusement in it.

Lew turned to look at poor Gemma who had meant to extinguish any flames, not throw petrol on them. He mouthed a silent, 'you okay' message at her. Her husband, however, wasn't so caring.

'See what you've started, Gemma?' he hissed at her, sounding so much like Regina that Lew began to wonder if she was a virus.

Gemma's head dropped and Lew felt a sudden jab of anger. Friend or no friend, he was being a knob.

'Oy,' he warned.

The usually jovial Jason twisted his head sharply towards Lew. 'What do you mean, oy?'

Patrick pulled the heat back to himself. 'Gemma sweetheart, alas for some, happiness *is* a Chaput farmed crocodile bag, though obviously not for the poor doomed crocodile.' He swivelled around on the chair so he could address his wife directly. 'Isn't that right, darling? So the argument for them is a paradox.' He poured Regina a glass of water and she looked at it in disgust.

'What the fuck is that?'

'Water. Don't worry, I'm pouring everyone a glass and not just singling you out.'

Regina picked up the glass and threw the contents over her shoulder, where it splattered all over their Osborne and Little wallpaper.

Patrick sighed despairingly. 'For God's sake, Regina.'

'Fuck you,' came the reply.

Lew speared a lance of buttery asparagus, hearing a clock in his head start to count down to a full repeat of the Koh-i-Noor night, although instead of a mixed platter, Regina would start missiling baby courgettes and Jersey royal potatoes. Her eyes had started to roll; she was pissed and dangerous.

'This is lovely,' he said.

'So it should be, the amount I pay Fernanda. Hey Fernanda, don't I pay you well?' Regina barked in the direction of the kitchen, sounding more fish-wife than society hostess.

'Not enough for her to put up with you treating her like a slave,' said Patrick out of the side of his mouth.

'Er ... what was that?' Regina rounded on him. 'What was that, you fucking prick?'

A surge of tension charged the air as if the room had just been plugged into an electric socket.

Patrick wiped his brow with weary fingers 'Regina, please just—'

'Don't you Regina me. You and your unfaithful tiny organ.' She grinned nastily and looked around the room for allies to join in laughter with her. She found one in Jason who snorted then tried to cover it up as a cough, payback for Patrick's recent dig at him, Lew surmised.

'My organ only looks tiny when it's playing in your bloody massive St Peter's Basilica of a vagina,' Patrick threw back at her. 'Although "playing" implies pleasure and trust me, there is nothing pleasurable about fucking you.'

His words hung in the air, echoes clinging to them. Even Regina was stunned into silence, at least for a few seconds, though it felt much longer.

'What did you say?' she said, in a Regan MacNeil *Exorcist* growl.

'You heard,' said Patrick, snatching his napkin from his lap and throwing it down onto the plate of fish. He stood up, gave a short burst of mirthless laughter, then shook his head. 'I give in,' he said. 'I finally give in. I don't want to be here any more.'

His eyes swept across the table at all the people sitting around him and, before he spoke next, they came to rest on Lew, as if he knew he would be assured acceptance there.

'I should have left. I should have had the balls to pack my cases and go to Marlene. I loved her. Correction, still love her. She's beautiful, she's kind, considerate – and do you know how we met? Fucking swinging, that's how. And it was her bloody idea.' He extended an accusing finger in his wife's direction.

A collective gasp sounded in the short silence that followed that disclosure before Patrick carried on, not allowing Regina a millimetre of butting-in space.

'Yes, folks, Snow Bloody White here, Mrs Butter-wouldn't-melt-in-her-enormous-gob, or so you all think, decided that our sex life wasn't interesting enough so she signed us up to a swinging club in Leeds. I hold my hands up' – and he did physically too – 'I agreed to it, though not as enthusiastically as you might think because I said to her that this could all blow up in our faces and, oh boy, did it. So she ended up screwing this bloke's brains out in one room and I ended up with his wife who had been dragged along like I was and didn't really want to do anything. So we talked. And we talked the next time we met as well. Then the next time we kissed because she's gorgeous but I respected her too much to try anything else. That's how it started. She left her husband for me but I didn't leave my wife for her because I'm one of those dicks that didn't think I'd be really happy without possessions.' He locked eyes with a startled Gemma and went on in a voice that was raw with feeling, 'But I was so wrong. Things don't make you happy, people do. Which is why I am walking out of this door now and leaving.'

He turned to Regina who, for the first time in her life, was mute and addressed her directly. 'I do not love you. I've no doubt you'll rip up my suits and smash my watches but I do not fucking care.' Then he walked out of the door and in his wake the room was sucked into a vacuum of silence for a long, long moment as if they had all witnessed a nuclear bomb land in their midst and were waiting for the ensuing shockwave to hit them. Then the moment of fallout occurred and all hell broke loose. Regina turned into a monster from *Doctor Who*, lashing out her arms, spitting, vomiting a string of f and c words as Charlotte tried to comfort her. Jason started darting around the room as if he should be doing something but didn't know quite what. Fernanda busied herself with a cloth, dabbing the wall and picking up everything that Regina started to throw around. Only Gemma was inanimate and sat glued to her chair, eyes wide as a petrified deer's.

'Was that all my fault, Lew?' she asked.

'Absolutely not, Gem, don't even think that.' It should have been her husband comforting her, but he was buzzing to and fro like Roadrunner. 'I'm going to find Patrick.'

Lew hurried down the long hallway and caught up with him at the front door, just as he was putting on a jacket and loading his pocket with keys and his wallet from the hall-stand drawer.

'Patrick, are you all right, mate?'

Patrick turned around and it was the oddest thing, but he looked ten years younger than he had five minutes ago.

'I don't think I've been this good in years, Lew,' he replied. 'Thanks.' And he smiled gratefully, his eyes glistening with emotion.

'Thanks?' Lew asked, confused. 'What for?'

'For this. For just following me to the door to see if I'm all right. It means a lot.'

Lew felt the heavy weight of Patrick's hand coming to rest on his shoulder and he thought, as if he had received some psychic message from the contact, *this is a man so starved of kindness that he doesn't know what to do with it when he receives any.* Then Patrick pulled him into a hug and slapped his back hard, trying to masculinise the tender gesture. When he pulled away his cheeks were wet.

'Look after yourself, Pat,' said Lew.

'I will. And you. Life's too short to struggle on when you know you're in the wrong place. See you around. Keep in touch with me. Please.'

And before Lew could say that of course he would, Patrick, like a hirsute Elvis, had left the building.

# Chapter 39

After Patrick had left, Lew returned to the dining room to find Fernanda racing around with a sweeping brush and Jason flapping because he had tried to pick up some broken glass and half-slashed his wrist in the attempt. Charlotte had transferred her attentions to him to try and stop the blood and Gemma had taken over trying to stop Regina hyper-ventilating; but she pushed Gemma rudely away because she didn't want to calm down, she wanted to scream then cry then tell everyone again how small her husband's penis was, how much of an arsehole he was and how much she hated him, all on a continuous loop. Lew tried to stop her drinking more wine and received a string of abuse for it. After half an hour he was tired and bored by Regina's floorshow and so was mightily relieved when the wind dropped behind her vitriolic sails because she had exhausted herself. Charlotte decided to stay with Regina in the hope of preventing her destroying their house and doing things she might regret like cut holes in everything of Patrick's that had a crotch; although knowing Regina, she wouldn't regret that at all. Charlotte insisted that Lew go home, especially as he was so obviously in the Patrick camp, so Lew rang a taxi home and shared it with Jason and Gemma. It would be a bit of a round-the-houses trip because they lived at opposite ends of town, but taxis were thin on the ground at that time on a Saturday night. Gemma looked beat. It hadn't been a pleasant evening for any of them, but Lew thought she'd had a particularly rough deal.

When the taxi arrived, Lew presumed that Jason would have got into the back to be with his wife, but instead he hopped into the front seat and started talking to the driver about something car-related. Cars and money and the spending of it was all he seemed to have in his conversational repertoire at the moment.

'Bet you wished you'd stayed in and watched a film,' Lew said, nudging Gemma's arm.

'Oh God, I need a piss,' said Jason loudly, to the driver. 'Can you stop for a minute?'

The driver pulled around the corner so that Jason could race out and empty his bladder behind a row of hedges.

Gemma leaned close to Lew to impart her next words. 'Do you want me to let you into a secret, Lew? I've never really liked Regina. I'm almost glad this evening happened because it's given me the excuse not to see her again.'

Lew smiled. 'Want to know a secret – me too.'

'She looks down on me,' confided Gemma. 'I couldn't give a toss about handbags and I don't know a Vivienne Westwood from a Clint Eastwood. I was only ever of any interest because I'm Jason's plus one. Another man for her to flirt with.'

'Well I hope you don't think that's how we see you,' he said.

'Of course not,' tutted Gemma. 'I liked Patrick though. Even if he did have a habit of talking to my chest.' She chuckled. 'I hope he does find some happiness with Marlene.'

'So do I,' said Lew. And he did.

There was a moment's silence, then Gemma giggled. 'Swinging eh? Who'd have thought?' She gave him a poke in the rib. 'Fancy it, Lew? Let's do swapsies.'

Lew chuckled. 'Anytime, Gem.'

Gemma blew out her cheeks. 'I wouldn't wish Jason on my worst enemy at the moment, never mind my best friend.'

In all the years Lew had known Gemma, he had never heard her say anything derogatory about her husband so something was obviously on her mind. And as she hadn't drunk any alcohol, it couldn't be blamed for easing the passage of her concerns into the open air.

'What's up, lovely?'

Gemma's head was bowed. 'He's changed, Lew. He snaps at me all the time, I don't feel good enough for him any more.'

'Don't talk rot,' Lew stepped in.

'And he's gone all metrosexual. He doesn't buy his underpants from Asda any more. Forty-five quid for two pairs of Calvin Kleins. And his toiletry shelf is bigger than mine.'

'He's taking some pride in himself, Gem, that's all,' said Lew. 'Nothing wrong with that.'

But Gemma wasn't listening. 'And . . . it's like he wants to outdo everyone all of a sudden. He was never like that when we had no money but now he's obsessed with being the best wage-earner, having the flashiest car. He's even looking around for another house. We could never afford one as big as Patrick's but he wants one bigger than yours and those were his actual words.'

'Oh,' said Lew. That didn't sound like the Jason he knew. 'Maybe he's nest-building, Gem. Maybe he wants to give the baby the best he can when he comes. Or she.'

Gemma humphed. 'Well look out for the shepherds and wise men because I think you have to have sex to have babies, unless I've got that wrong.'

The taxi driver in the front started fiddling with the radio buttons and whistling, embarrassed.

'I lied when I said we were at it like rabbits, in case you haven't guessed. Twice in three months. It's even crossed my mind that he's—'

She cut off her words as Jason threw open the car door, loudly declared, 'That's better,' and the taxi set off again.

'Sorry, I shouldn't have said all that,' Gemma said after a while.

'Oh don't be silly, Gem. I'll have forgotten by the morning anyway,' said Lew, though he wouldn't have.

'Who does the maintenance for your taxis?' Jason asked the driver and they began a discussion about MOTs.

'The other reason I don't like Regina is that she's taken my friend away from me,' Gemma said for Lew's ears only. 'I barely see Charlotte now. I can't remember the last time we went for a coffee.'

Lew winced inside. Should he tell Gemma why his wife was avoiding her?

'I rang Charlotte a couple of weeks ago, you know, Lew,' Gemma went on. 'I needed to buy an outfit so I thought we could go shopping in Leeds and have lunch and a catch-up but she said she had to stay in all day and wait for something to be delivered for you. So I nipped to Meadowhall by myself because it was nearer and she was there, with Regina, having lunch in House of Fraser. I never told her I saw her, but it really hurt me, Lew.'

She looked hurt too; her brown eyes were shiny with gathering tears. 'It would be nice to have my friend back. I miss her. God, listen to me, I sound like a thirteen-year-old kid.'

'No, you don't.' He should tell Gemma. 'I totally understand.'

'When it's Charlotte's birthday next month, I'd like to invite you around for a meal. Just the four of us. Unless you're taking her to Firenze or somewhere else.'

'That sounds lovely,' said Lew, and it did. It hadn't been just the four of them for ages and their foursomes had always been so much more preferable to the sixsomes.

'I'll really push the boat out and I'll make a fabulous cake. And I'll put decorations up and everything. Like the thirteen-year-old kid I am.' She smiled, but it looked sad rather than happy. 'I don't know if I've done anything to upset Charlotte, but if I have, I'll make sure that her birthday puts us on a new footing.'

Lew really did have to tell her.

'Gemma, love, look . . .' *God, where to start.* 'Charlotte should have told you this . . . she's finding it difficult at the moment . . . with you and Jason talking about having a baby. She doesn't want to say anything and spoil it for you, but that's probably why she's keeping her distance from you. It's just stirred things up for her a bit. She'll come round, and please don't tell her I told you because she'd be horrified to think she'd upset you.'

Gemma didn't react except to give the slightest nod of her head. It flagged up as odd that she didn't say anything, but the whole evening had been bonkers. Then the car swung into her and Jason's estate and the moment was forgotten.

Lew felt wired when he got into his own house. He poured a small neat bourbon and drank it in the silence of his vast, empty kitchen letting his mind drain itself of the awful night. He shouldn't have left Charlotte there, he thought. He texted to see if she was okay and she replied that he was not to worry and she was perfectly fine and parked on one of the two giant sofas in the lounge reading this month's *Cosmo*. Regina was on the other snoring her head off.

As his eyes shuttered down to sleep, the last image in Lew's mind was Patrick's face, skin smoothed, eyes bright; even his beard looked glossier for his having been amputated from his gangrenous marriage. Even if Marlene didn't welcome him back with open arms, Lew knew that he and Regina were finished for good.

# Chapter 40

A sharp rapping on the door woke up Bonnie the next morning at seven-thirty. Panic gripped her throat with a cold hand, she daren't move. Who could be knocking at that time on a Sunday morning but Stephen? He'd found her.

The letter box flap opened inwards. 'Bonnie, love,' a familiar voice called through it. 'It's me, Stan.'

Bonnie kicked off the quilt and checked through the window to see that it was him and his large white Stantiques van was idling behind him.

'Hang on,' she called and grabbed her tracksuit bottoms and a baggy top, wondering what on earth he wanted her for.

She opened the door to find him talking to someone in the back of his van.

'Sorry to call so early, Bonnie love, but I'm off to Cleethorpes with the missus in an hour and if I didn't drop this stuff off now, you wouldn't get it until later on in the week.'

'I have no idea what you mean, Stan,' said Bonnie, her face pulled into all sorts of confused shapes.

'This furniture.'

'What furniture?'

There was a bang from inside the van. 'Floyd, for God's sake, watch it,' shouted Stan before turning back to Bonnie. 'Valerie rang round us all saying you needed some stuff. We've got a load of furniture for you. She said you had nowt.'

Bonnie's mouth dropped open and she could feel herself colouring. A single mattress still wrapped in plastic appeared out of the back of the van, presumably being pushed by Stan's son Floyd.

'That's brand new, that is. Goldfinger bought a single for his lad but he wanted a double so it's been sat in his garage. He said you could have it no problem. Oh, and Starstruck said you could either have a signed photo of Tommy Cooper or a month's paid rent on the place. I made the decision for you: in other words, I ain't bringing you a chuffing picture of a bloke wearing a fez. Now,' he manoeuvred Bonnie out of the doorway, 'I'm presuming you want it upstairs. It's one of them divans with a drawer in it. The lads will set it up for you.'

Bonnie watched as the gargantuan Floyd carried the mattress into the house over his shoulder and then Stan's second son, Evander, appeared from the van carrying two Arne Jacobsen retro-style chairs.

'Uncle Funky's sent you those. There's a table as well. Stickalampinit's sent you one of his best.' He rolled his eyes and reached into the back of the van, pulling out a two-foot-tall glass bottle with a cluster of coloured bulbs sprouting from the top.

'He must think you've moved into a disco,' Evander called over his shoulder.

'He's a crank,' tutted Stan, carrying the lamp and the coffee table he'd brought for Bonnie into the house.

There was also a pretty two-seater vintage cottage sofa from Valerie, a pair of bedside cabinets from Long John and a bedside light. There was an old stripped pine chest of drawers from Mart Deco and finally a portable TV and video recorder combo from Boombox.

'He says it's working, even if it is as old as God's dog,' laughed Stan. 'Make sure you get a licence though, you don't want to be spending all this on a fine.' And he pulled an envelope out of his back pocket. 'The ones that didn't send owt put some money in this for you. Here, lass.'

When Bonnie's hand didn't come out, Stan lifted her arm, opened up her fingers and placed the envelope flat on her palm. 'Don't insult anyone by refusing. Your dad was a cracking fella and we know it would have brok' his heart to see you without. So you take this, Bonnie.' And Stan leaned towards her and placed a gentle kiss on her cheek.

'Now if I don't get off, I'll be going to Cleethorpes with no knackers,' he said. 'Get yourself in, Bon, and make yourself a cup of tea and sit on your new sofa.' And with that he slammed the back door of the van shut with his two hefty sons inside, waved and drove off, leaving her staring at the envelope in her hand with tears in her eyes.

# Chapter 41

Lew slept in fits and starts until a text from Charlotte woke him up at half-past seven asking him if he'd pick her up. She looked drained and puffy-eyed when he collected her from Regina's house. In her severely creased L. K. Bennett dress and carrying her Lulu Guinness bag, she looked like some sort of designer zombie. Half-way through the journey, he had to stop the car on a quiet country lane so that Charlotte could throw up behind a tree. She returned to the car very white-faced, holding her head and sighing a lot.

'I'm taking it you had a few more drinks after I left last night,' said Lew.

'I had a Jack Daniel's, just one, with Regina,' came Charlotte's fierce retort. 'I thought it might help me sleep. It didn't sit well with the red wine, obviously.'

'One? Really?' said Lew, turning the car onto his drive.

'Honest,' said Charlotte, the corner of her mouth twitching.

'Pint of water, two ibuprofen and bed for you, my darling,' said Lew, when they walked in through the front door.

'I think we need a bit of distance from Regina and Patrick, if he comes back or not,' said Charlotte, kicking off her shoes in the hallway. And Lew thought, *Hallelujah for that*.

The *Daily Trumpet* would deeply like to apologise to the Mayor for the error which appeared in the 'Spotlight on Derek Trubshaw' article. 'Mayor Trubshaw extols the virtues of a firm mistress at night for daytime work efficiency. "I've had a couple of bouncy ones in my time and not got much sleep so I've invested in a big fat one that will last me for years."' We did of course mean mattress, not mistress.

# Chapter 42

Lew couldn't wait to spend a normal Sunday in the Pot of Gold after the madness of the previous night.

'Ah, you timed that perfectly, the kettle has just boiled,' said Bonnie, greeting him with a warm morning smile, and she retreated into the office to make him a coffee. When she handed it to him, she tilted her head to study him tentatively before saying, 'Everything all right?' He took from that that he looked less than fresh. He opened his mouth to answer and found that he didn't know what to say. He laughed instead, an 'I-have-no-words' sort of laugh.

'Sorry, I didn't mean to pry,' Bonnie said, sensing his awkwardness.

'You weren't prying,' Lew replied quickly. 'I just wouldn't know where to start. The worst evening I have ever spent in my life just about sums it up.'

'That bad?' Bonnie grimaced.

'Oh, way beyond bad.' He remembered that she and Regina had crossed paths, so she probably wouldn't be surprised that drama courted her. 'The woman you ejected from my shop so masterfully last Tuesday hosted a dinner

party and had a total meltdown. Her husband left her right
after the main course was served, which was a real shame as
it was a fantastic bit of halibut. There was more, much more,
but I doubt you'd believe it.'

He heard a snort from Bonnie who had covered up her
mouth. 'I'm so sorry,' she excused herself.

Lew chuckled. 'When Regina blows, as you might
imagine, she blows. I'm surprised her house is still standing
this morning.'

'And you say her husband left her? For good or . . . just for
the evening?' Bonnie offered him a dark chocolate digestive
from a newly opened packet and he took two.

'For good, I hope. I don't think he's been happy for years.
He had—' He just stopped himself in time from saying that
Patrick had an affair, because it hadn't been as straightfor-
ward as they had all been led to believe. He'd taken the
blame for it, but it hadn't been all his fault. Patrick had been
more of a gentleman than they'd credited him for.

'He had . . .?' Bonnie prompted.

'They both had . . . relationships outside the marriage.'
He glossed over the details. 'It's complicated. They tried to
patch things up in the beginning but there wasn't enough
marriage left to stitch back together, if you know what I'm
saying.'

'Oh yes,' said Bonnie, with emphasis.

'Oh Bonnie, I'm sorry. I didn't mean . . .'

Bonnie flapped her hand. 'Don't be silly. There's no point
in staying together when there's no love. And sometimes not
even love is enough.' A picture of Joel drifted across her
mind. 'There has to be love and trust and . . . all sorts of
other little ingredients.' Love was just the bricks of the wall.
The other stuff was the cement.

'You're very wise, Mrs Br—' Lew bit off the 'Brookland'. 'Are you going to keep your married name?' he asked, but he could guess the answer to that one.

'Not a chance. I'm having all my documents changed back to Ms Sherman. "As in the tank", as my dad used to say.' She smiled and Lew again thought how attractive she was. There was a blush of colour in her cheeks today and light dancing in her hazel eyes.

'It's nice to see you in such a cheery mood, Bonnie,' he said.

'I am,' Bonnie replied. Today had reminded her just how much good there was in the world, to counterbalance the bad. There had been a lot of rain in her life and now the sunshine was coming out at last, and making a bright arc of rainbow in her sky. For however long it lasted, at the moment it was hers to enjoy.

The Pot of Gold had to stay open until five because there were so many customers. Bonnie sold two of Stickalampinit's lamps and Butterfly Barry came in just before closing time and bought over four hundred poundsworth of various bits which Bonnie had put aside so he could have first choice of them. He took the lot, then he gave her something of his own: an envelope with money inside and he overrode the protest she made.

'I want you to have this,' he said, 'with my love. Your dad would want us all to help you.' It had fifty pounds inside. The envelope which Stan had given her that morning had contained four hundred and twenty pounds. Bonnie didn't know what to say, so she threw her arms around him. He smelled how she would imagine Hercule Poirot to smell, a curious mix of scented tea, floral cologne and face powder.

'Thank you, Barry.' She pulled away before she stained his pristine white collar with make-up.

'You're worth every penny, darling,' he said and gave her cheek a soft pat with the palm of his small, smooth hand.

Lew watched Bonnie closing the window blinds with a smile on her face and it brought a smile to his own. He imagined Patrick's Marlene being like Bonnie, a woman with kind eyes and a gentle heart and no affectations at all.

'So, what are you up to on your day off tomorrow?' he asked her.

'I'm seeing your friend Adriana,' Bonnie replied. 'I'm filing for divorce.'

Lew nodded. Thank goodness she hadn't had second thoughts, he said to himself.

'Has Stephen been in touch?'

'Nope. Which is slightly worrying.'

'Not what you expected?'

Bonnie's smile was fading now. 'No. It's not like him to . . . to let go so easily.'

'You have my number if you need it,' said Lew as they walked out to their respective cars. 'It's always best to expect the unexpected.'

Last night had told him that much.

# Chapter 43

The next morning Bonnie woke up in a proper bed in the bedroom upstairs. She'd had a wonderful night's sleep and a dream about Lew. In it, he'd admitted that he really liked her and she'd felt giddy and pretty and the feeling had followed her into the day and started it off very nicely.

The little house was full of furniture now. She had drawers to put her things into, a table to have her breakfast on and use for pressing her confetti and she'd attached the old TV to the aerial socket and found that it worked, though she'd have to get a licence sorted or she'd be in trouble. Her appointment with the solicitor was at nine-thirty so she had a bowl of cereal and set off for the office in Maltstone, from where the firm of Redfern, Darlow and De Lacey operated.

Adriana de Lacey was nothing like Bonnie expected. She'd imagined someone young, Amazonian and glamorous with cascades of copper hair. In reality, she was a tiny wizened woman of nearly pensionable age, with Alexis Carrington shoulder pads, steel-grey hair, bright bird-like black eyes and a deep and powerful voice. She exuded

Chanel No. 5 and a 'don't-ever-fuck-with-me' presence. Her office was a chaos of paper and files, apart from the desk surface which was bare except for an iMac, a telephone, a Mont Blanc Meisterstuck pen and an A4 pad open at the first blank page. Seconds after Bonnie sat down, Adriana's secretary brought in two cups of milky coffee and a sugar bowl.

'Would you prefer tea?' asked the secretary. 'It's no trouble if you do.'

'Coffee's fine,' said Bonnie. 'Thank you.'

'Mrs Brookland,' began Adriana, dropping three sugar cubes into her cup and stirring them slowly to aid their dissolving. 'Or would you prefer I called you Ms Sherman?' She fixed Bonnie with her beady little eyes below their heavily mascara-ed lashes. Those are eyes that can see into people's souls, Bonnie thought.

'Yes please. Bonnie Sherman,' she replied. 'I don't want to be ever called Brookland again if I can help it.'

'Women tend to keep their married name if they share that surname with their children,' said Adriana, lifting the cup to her lips and slurping noisily.

'I have no children,' said Bonnie. Her hand was shaking when she lifted up her cup and she had to bring her other hand to it in order to steady it.

'You're understandably nervous,' said Adriana. 'That's completely normal. We are starting off a process that will change your life as you know it, hopefully for the better. There's a lot to get through but every piece of information you give me will be one step nearer to your divorce and I'm figuring that's what you want and why you're here.' She quirked a pencilled eyebrow and Bonnie nodded, instantly put at ease.

'So, let us begin.' Adriana poised her pen over the page. 'Is your house in both names?'

'No. It was Stephen's before we married so I know I'm not entitled to—'

'Well you're wrong there because you are. Is there a mortgage on the house?'

'No but I . . .'

Adriana was determined to override any nonsense Bonnie had about not claiming any financial entitlement. She wanted details of bank accounts, investments, pensions, incomes. Bonnie felt embarrassed that she had so little knowledge of Stephen's side of things. Adriana said that it didn't matter that she didn't know now, they'd find it all out. Stephen wouldn't be able to hide anything away. Not from Adriana de Lacey he wouldn't anyway. It wouldn't do him any favours to try either because the courts hated that.

Bonnie would be divorcing Stephen for unreasonable behaviour. Adriana was understanding when Bonnie was loath to cite too many examples of it for fear of appearing vindictive.

'It's common to feel disloyal, even in cases like yours,' said Adriana, 'but the fact that you're here tells me that you've had enough. The courts need to know what exactly it is that you've had enough of. And trust me, the further into the divorce process you venture, the less you'll worry about protecting his sensitivities.'

It was with joyous relief that Bonnie received the information that she need have no further contact with Stephen if she didn't want to. It would make her divorce easier and cheaper if both parties were compliant, Adriana said, but more often than not, that ideal wasn't possible.

'What if he won't divorce me?' asked Bonnie. Her biggest fear was being tied to him forever now.

'He can contest it, of course, or stick his head in the sand, but he will be dragged eventually to the end of the process,' said Adriana. Words which Bonnie was more than glad to hear.

Read back to her, Bonnie's statement felt cold and out of perspective, even though it was completely factual and in perfect perspective.

'... I have had no sexual relations with my husband since the first month of our marriage ... I am not allowed to know how much money there is in our joint bank account ... I am not supported emotionally by him ... I do not love him ... When I tried to leave, he locked me in the bedroom until I was rescued by my boss ...' Bonnie worried how Stephen would react when he received her statement in the post and what it would move him to do. She felt sick when she left Adriana's office.

Lew listened to Charlotte's side of the phone conversation with interest.

'... I can't, Regina. Lewis is off today and we're going out ... No, I can't later either because we don't know when we'll be back ... I can't this week, I'm really busy sorting out decorators ... I'll ring you. Next week ... we'll do lunch. Bye ... bye.'

She put down the phone and let out a long breath.

Lew raised his eyebrows. 'Decorators?' he questioned.

'I couldn't think what else to say.'

'You are pulling back from her, aren't you?' Lew was impressed.

'She can be hard to say no to though.'

'But you managed. Anyway, you didn't tell me what happened when everyone left on Saturday.' Lew slathered blackberry jam on his toast. 'Did you talk some sense into her? Did she tell you any more about the swinging scene?'

'Nothing happened or I would have said,' Charlotte replied. 'I calmed her down, we had a chat and a couple more ... we had a nightcap and then we fell asleep on the two sofas.'

'What did you talk about?'

'God, Lewis, I don't know, I can't remember. I'd had a drink and I was knackered by then,' Charlotte snapped. 'What is this, Twenty Questions?'

Lew held his hands up in a sign of peace. 'Whoa, I'm only making conversation. I was curious to know if she'd realised that Patrick had left for good.'

'I imagine so. Banging noises woke me up. When I went upstairs to see what she was up to, she'd already cut holes in everything hanging in his wardrobe and was smashing his watches.'

'Oh God.' Lew gave a despairing sigh, but he'd expected nothing less from Regina. He wondered if she knew yet that Patrick was going to engage Adriana as his divorce solicitor. He'd texted Lew that morning to ask if he could recommend a good firm of solicitors. He had taken up temporary residence in the local Holiday Inn but he and Marlene were reunited. He didn't tell that to Charlotte though, just in case she let it slip to Regina before she was supposed to know.

'I need a break from her,' said Charlotte. 'She's too intense, too needy.'

Amen, thought Lew.

# Chapter 44

The happy little bubble in which Bonnie existed burst on the Thursday of that week when the postman arrived at the Pot of Gold. Lew picked up the mail, sifted through it and handed a letter to Bonnie which had been addressed to her there. Bonnie immediately recognised the writing on the envelope and prickles of tension ran up her arms. She paled before Lew's eyes and he guessed it must be correspondence from Stephen.

'You all right?' he asked.

Bonnie nodded, but it was an obvious lie.

'Go and have five minutes to yourself,' said Lew, thumbing towards the back room. 'You can bring two cups of coffee back with you.'

Bonnie felt light-headed as she carefully tore the top of the envelope as if its contents might leap out and attack her.

Bonita,

I have received correspondence from your solicitor, which I have read with great amusement. You do not seriously expect me to comply, do you?

I have not contacted you because I hoped your

nonsense and temporary insanity would work its way
out of your system. I know that women of your age
can experience hormonal problems and would advise that
you visit a doctor and discuss.

So far as this ridiculous situation is concerned, I
will grant you until the end of the month to return to
your senses and to this house. If you do not, I will be
forced to tell the authorities what happened on March
15th at approximately 7 p.m. five years ago and I do not
think you would want me to do that.

I have been your guardian and support for almost
fourteen years. Your disloyalty in the face of my
devotion is inexcusable but I am sure given time I will
learn to forgive you.

Yours
Your HUSBAND Stephen.

Bonnie could hear the pompous words in his supercilious
voice, menace couched in his magnanimity, that shouted
status of 'husband' as if to remind her that she was his property and she felt the contents of her breakfast stir in her
stomach. It had begun. Seeing the threat in cold, hard print
crushed her temporary illusion of being free of him. She
didn't want tears to make an appearance but they came rushing to her eyes, pulled there by panic and frustration and fear.

Lew's head popped round the door and he caught her
madly trying to wipe the tears from her eyes faster than they
fell. And when she saw him, though her first reaction was
to turn away, her body betrayed her with a huge hiccup of
a sob. She dropped her head into her hands and hadn't a clue
what to do when she felt his arms close around her.

He hadn't meant to touch her. He'd expected to walk in

and see her putting the kettle on, letter thrown down on the desk with the contempt it deserved, but he'd found her crying, looking lost and so very vulnerable and it had been instinct, not conscious thought, that had made him clear the distance between them in long strides to comfort her. She felt so breakable and she smelt of summer flowers and he knew that he shouldn't be holding her like this, no matter how much he wanted to. Warning bells were sounding, pictures of Charlotte flashing in his head; he had pushed against a boundary and must step back.

'What did he say?' Lew asked, releasing her, moving things to a less intimate plane.

'He received the letter from Adriana. He thinks I'm bluffing and he wants me to go back to him,' said Bonnie, wiping her eyes and stuffing the letter into her bag. She couldn't let him see it. 'If I do, he'll try to forgive me.'

Lew gave a dry chuckle.

'I bet he would.'

Bonnie continued to look worried.

'You wouldn't go back, would you?' asked Lew, tentatively.

'God no.' She looked sickened at the thought. 'But I know that ignoring him will inflame him and yet if I respond he might think he's reeling me in.' She closed her eyes and shook her head. 'I don't know what to do for the best.'

Lew folded his arms over his broad chest. 'He's done exactly what he wanted to do with that letter: worm into your head.'

'I know.'

'It's his way of clinging on. Let Adriana deal with it for you. And give her the letter, because it might be useful.'

'Yes, I will,' said Bonnie, knowing she wouldn't. She couldn't let anyone else see it because they would ask questions.

'Adriana will tell you, Bonnie, that the law isn't very tolerant of people trying to dodge it and thinking they can outsmart it.'

Which wasn't as good news for Bonnie as Lew might expect.

After work, as Lew approached his house, he noticed that Regina's white Mercedes was parked outside and it infuriated him. He couldn't imagine that Charlotte, in her present mood, had invited her there, especially after telling her on the phone that she'd be far too busy all week to see her, which meant Regina had forced her unwanted company on his wife. He geed himself up for getting Regina out so he could relax with Charlotte but as he opened the door he could hear Regina's screech from down the hallway.

'. . . he can fuck off, I tell you. Dad's solicitor is a bastard. He'll be singing soprano by the time he comes out of the divorce . . .'

'Oh hi,' Charlotte greeted Lew with obvious relief when he strolled into the lounge.

'Hello love, hello Reg,' he went over to kiss Charlotte on the cheek. 'I thought the decorators were coming this afternoon to talk you through things.'

'I rang to cancel them,' said Charlotte, grateful for his collusion. 'Regina needed me so I'm hoping to see them tomorrow instead.'

'And how are you, Regina?' Lew said, bending stiffly to kiss his guest politely on the cheek and being immediately overpowered by the poisonous combo of spicy perfume and hairspray which clung to his lungs as he breathed her in.

'Seen anything of my errant husband?' Regina asked. She'd had a spray tan and was two shades nearer to mahogany than she was the last time he'd seen her and her spirally, black hair was at least a foot longer. She was dressed as if she was going out clubbing: short skirt, leather jacket, thigh-length black boots. She looked like someone who couldn't decide whether to go to a fancy dress party as Cher or Dorian from *Birds of a Feather* so opted for a hybrid of both.

'Nope,' said Lew, noticing the four empty coffee cups on the table; so she'd been there for a while then. 'Have you?'

She humphed by way of an answer. 'I've been trying to drag your wife out for some badly needed retail therapy but I get the feeling she's avoiding me,' she went on with a smile on her lips and flint in her eyes.

'I doubt she's avoiding you, Reg,' said Lew, unable to mask the irritated tone in his voice. 'We're about to start decorating the whole house so she hasn't got time at the moment as she's supposed to be picking out colours. I thought she'd already told you that.'

'Oh, do you have books, Charlotte? Let me see,' said Regina, clapping her hands excitedly. 'I have the best eye for colour.'

Lew felt his skull prickling with annoyance. He made a deliberate show of checking his watch.

'Look, Reg, I hate to be a party pooper and Charlotte won't say because she wouldn't want to come across as rude but we're going out to dinner tonight with a business client and you – ' he addressed Charlotte ' – don't have long to get ready.'

Regina planted her cup on the table and stood. 'Charlotte, you should have said.'

'I didn't want you to think I was shoving you out of the door. I know you're upset,' Charlotte sighed, though Regina looked the least upset person Lew could imagine. 'I'm sure that the ... your clients can wait if we're late.' She widened her eyes at Lew, imploring him to play ball and he wondered what the hell she was playing at. 'We've time for another coff—'

Lew cut her off sharply. 'Darling, bless you for being sweet and Reg knows we wouldn't say this if we didn't mean it, but I've been waiting to screw these people down to a date for a long time and turning up late will give them an initial impression I would rather they didn't have of me.' He zapped his own message via his eyes to his wife: *work with me on this, not against me.*

'Going anywhere nice?' asked Regina, picking up that horrible white crocodile bag.

'Client's house, near Castleton.'

'That's a long way,' said Regina, giving Charlotte an air kiss at either side of her cheek.

'Worth it, I hope,' said Lew, letting her repeat the double *mwah* against his face as he held his breath. They both escorted Regina down the hallway, although she looked more as if she were heading for a dancing pole than the door.

'Take care, Reg,' he said.

'I'll see you both very soon.'

*Not if I can help it,* said Lew to the back of the door when it closed on her.

Charlotte almost slid down the wall in relief.

'I didn't think she'd ever go. She's been here two hours.'

'So why the bloody hell were you asking her to stay longer?' Lew raised his eyebrows in puzzlement. 'I was giving you a lifeline and you were preferring to drown.'

'I don't want to upset her,' said Charlotte.

'She's got the hide of a galvanised rhino. You can't possibly upset her. She doesn't want Patrick, she just can't stand the idea that someone else has him.' He shuddered at the thought of having Regina as his wife. It would be like being married to a giant lamprey.

'She's found out that he and Marlene are together and he's employed a divorce solicitor so she's had a giant bonfire and burnt everything Patrick left in the house.' Charlotte winced.

'Ouch. I hope he sues her for criminal damage. You know, I'm looking forward to going out with just you and Gemma and Jason in the near future. And one day soon maybe Patrick and Marlene too can join us.'

Charlotte gave him a horrified look. 'What if Regina found out?'

'What if she does?' said Lew, kicking off his shoes.

'Well . . . nothing. Just wouldn't want to get on the wrong side of her. She can be . . .'

'Evil,' Lew supplied the word for her. 'I imagine she would be deadly when wounded. Oh I hope his solicitor goes for her bloody jugular.'

Charlotte nodded heartily in agreement. 'She will say anything to damage Patrick, don't you think? She'd lie and manipulate to get what she wanted. I wouldn't trust a single word she says. I think she enjoys causing troub—'

Lew cut her off. 'No more talk of her, please. Now, shall we really go out and have dinner somewhere nice and nod to the fact that we actually enjoy being married to each other?'

He felt a sudden and overwhelming need to celebrate that he didn't have all the problems that Patrick and Bonnie had and that he was damned lucky he wasn't going to be another client of Adriana de Lacey. He needed to give his wife some attention and chase away the thoughts he was having about Bonnie that really shouldn't be anywhere near his head.

# Chapter 45

Bonnie sat at her table filling up the last of twenty bags of sunflower table confetti for a wedding. She had pressed the shapes out and then dotted the middles with a brown pen. It had taken ages, but they looked lovely and it was nice to offer a more detailed service than others did. She'd spent her whole day off pressing out shapes and building up some stock. She'd treated herself to a fish and chip lunch and when she went into the Co-op on the High Street, she found they were giving out free samples of new salted caramel latte sachets. The woman had given her a handful. 'It's your lucky day,' she had said to Bonnie.

She was on her third – they really were too nice – as she began stapling her Rainbow Lady label to the tops of the confetti bags. She had a Will Ferrell film playing on the TV in the background to keep her company and she'd giggled to herself at some of the lines and hearing herself, had marvelled that it was possible to be so content with so little. If only it could last, because she knew that no amount of wishful thinking would stop the brightness draining out of the rainbow that had coloured the last two and a half weeks for her. It would soon be back to 'Sherman grey' with no gift of a pot of gold at either end.

She hadn't heard from Stephen since the letter had arrived, eleven days ago. Adriana had told her exactly what Lew had: that Stephen was trying to make her dance as if she were his marionette and that the only way to thwart him was to ignore him. And Bonnie had wished that it were all that easy. None of them had any idea what he could do to her.

She'd received a postcard from Valerie that morning which had cheered her. The words were written in her beautiful scrolling hand:

*My dear friend, I hope this finds you well and happy and living safely in a house full of fine furniture. I am in a good place where I can bear now to savour my memories and appreciate how loved I was. Despite everything, I consider myself one of the lucky ones. Life offers no promises and chances should be taken when they fly close enough to catch. I have not booked a flight yet, but you will be the first person I shall call on when I'm home. I am thinking of you. You have more friends than you know, Bonnie. Do not be afraid to ask for help if you need it. Now back to the sunshine. Wishing you the best of everything and thinking of you.*
*Valerie x*

It made Bonnie realise how fond she was of the older woman and that by the time she had returned from Italy, their friendship would have changed. It would either be closer and deeper or not exist at all.

There were four days until the end of the month. Bonnie wondered how many of those friends would be shaking their heads at the thought that a man like Brian Sherman could have produced such a daughter.

# Chapter 46

The next day, Lew was in the back room, searching on the computer for gift ideas for Charlotte's birthday at the weekend, when he realised the date: it was today that the Chinese cup and saucer would be auctioned off. How the hell had that slipped his mind? Then again, there were plenty of things in his head serving to divert his attention. Charlotte wasn't herself. She was jittery, nervous, upset about something, though she insisted she wasn't. Regina was making a bit of a pest of herself and Charlotte, for some reason, was reluctant to tell her to get stuffed. So much so that when Lew said he was quite happy to do it for her, Charlotte reacted very strangely, jumping to Regina's defence. She argued that Regina was more upset about Patrick than she was letting on and it would be cruel beyond measure. Lew didn't get it at all; one minute Charlotte wanted to extricate herself from Regina, the next she was letting herself be pushed into spending the day at the Trafford Centre with her. He threw in the towel and told Charlotte that if she wanted to go out and social-ise, he wasn't going to stop her, but if she made any arrangements which included him, he would not be going.

And Bonnie was on his mind too, much more than he wanted her to be. She turned up for work every morning dressed in bright colours – not a designer name amongst them – and he couldn't help that his spirits lifted every time his eyes came to rest on her. And it worried him that his heart liked her so much and that his thoughts drifted to her so often, as if they were magnetised.

Stephen was resisting the divorce and the strain was telling on her. She was as smiley and friendly with the customers as always, but sometimes he caught her off-guard, staring into space and wondered at the activity going on in her head. She looked lost, stunned and so dreadfully tired when her mask slipped.

He could hear her now talking to Stickalampinit and his girlfriend who, despite being a rather big girl, exploited her passing facial resemblance to Sharon Stone with great aplomb. She was known (secretly) amongst the other traders as 'Sharon Seventeen Stone'. Today she was Catherine Tramelled up to the nines with a very short, sleeveless, high-necked dress on and her hair greased back from her – it had to be said – very pretty face. Stickalampinit didn't have a very scintillating line of chat but Bonnie always listened to what he had to say as if he were as interesting as Jeremy Paxman. She had a way of making people feel special and he was glad that the traders had made her feel special too with their recent kindness of a load of furniture and enve-lopes of money.

It was no hardship for Bonnie to listen to Stickalampinit enthuse about his latest creation or moan about his back. He was part of the antiques world which had embraced her and which she loved so much in return, and whilst she was in the Pot of Gold there was always plenty to occupy her and keep her mood buoyant. But there were now only three days until the end of the month.

When Stickalampinit and 'Seventeen' eventually left, Lew went next door to the teashop and bought a selection of toasted sandwiches for himself and Bonnie, hoping she'd feel obliged to share them with him.

'This is a nice treat,' she said. Leni's sandwiches were always lovely. 'What's the occasion?'

'It's the auction today,' returned Lew. 'My nerves are in shreds so this is displacement therapy.' He wasn't lying.

Bonnie had forgotten too. Her brain had been too full of junk to spare a corner for the fate of the Chinese cup and saucer. 'You need something to do to take your mind off it. Go and buy some more bubble wrap, that'll waste a good hour,' she suggested.

The traders all bought their bubble wrap from a bloke in Hillsborough called 'Bubble Wrap Rashid'. He operated from the garage at the back of his house, cash only, obviously.

'Great idea,' said Lew. 'Will you be all right by yourself?'

'It's quiet, go and get yourself away,' Bonnie smiled.

Lew left her with the sandwiches. They were delicious, but he was too wired to eat them.

Bonnie didn't eat them either. They were lovely, but she had no appetite at all.

# Chapter 47

Bonnie had just pushed the sandwiches to the bottom of the bin in the back room when she heard the bell tinkle above the shop door. She emerged with her shop-smile intact, which dropped instantly when she saw who was standing there. Stephen looked as if he had aged since she last saw him. His usually neat hair was untidy and needed a trim and he was wearing the zip-up beige jerkin that she always thought made him look like an old man. But the biggest difference was his face: he'd lost weight and his cheeks were dark and hollowed out; his eyes looked more hooded than she could remember and the hair in his eyebrows sprouted off in all directions like wayward wire. Bonnie crossed her arms in front of her, an unconscious defensive movement and he registered that and enjoyed the fact that she felt threatened by him.

'Bonita,' he said. 'You didn't reply to my letter.'

She forced herself to drop her arms to her sides, hoping to convey by that that she might have been momentarily cowed by his presence, but she was over it.

'I have nothing to say to you, Stephen,' she said slowly

and carefully. 'My solicitor will convey everything to you and your solicitor when you engage one, as you should.'

He shook his head slowly in disappointment. 'Have you forgotten all I've done for you, dear?' Despite the endearment, there was no affection in his voice. His tone was patronising and arrogant.

'Have you forgotten all I did for you?' she replied, fighting the waver in her voice. 'Years of cleaning your clothes, cooking your meals, being a presence in your house to stop you from being lonely? A housekeeper would have done the same job, Stephen, but obviously you'd have had to pay her for that.'

'You silly little girl ...' He took a step towards her. Bonnie retreated two.

'I *will* divorce you, you know,' she said, despising him. How could she have ever thought she loved him? He'd conned her. He'd reeled her in like one of the fish he caught, lifting her from a chilled lake to a smaller, colder bowl.

Stephen took a deep steadying breath. 'I will not let you divorce me, Bonita. You do not have the money to complete the process if I do not agree to it and you certainly won't be getting any of mine.'

He was trying to intimidate her with lies, she knew. Adriana had assured her that whatever tactics he might try, he was only delaying the inevitable and she would be divorced from him. He could not prevent it.

'I don't want your money, Stephen. I don't want anything from you. I just want a divorce. And I will have one, with your agreement or without it. It was never a proper marriage and so it won't take much dissolving.' She felt bitterness seep into her tone like acid. 'Now please get out of here. We have nothing else to say to each other.'

Stephen's eyes narrowed and then he unleashed a gush of invectives that she had never thought him capable of. He sounded possessed, mad. He was slavering, '... *Bitch* ... *whore* ...'

Then the bell above the door sounded and the couple with the Labrador guide dog walked in and Stephen sliced off his vitriolic stream. The woman picked up that something was wrong and looked from Stephen to Bonnie and asked if she was all right.

'As I said, till the end of the month,' said Stephen, feeling the heat of the couple's attention on him, but still he strolled slowly out of the shop with his shoulders back and his head held high.

'He looked a bit shifty,' said the woman.

'Awkward customer. Nothing I can't handle,' said Bonnie, sticking on a smile, but how she doubted her own words.

# Chapter 48

Lew burst into the shop an hour and a half later with an enormous roll of bubble wrap.

'Have you looked on the auction site?' he asked.

'No. I was waiting for you,' said Bonnie.

'Did we have any customers?'

'The couple with the guide dog and a group of six ladies. They bought your writing slope and a vinaigrette from Long John's cabinet.' She didn't mention the other visitor.

Lew dumped the roll and pushed Bonnie into the back office. The auction would have ended now and the sale price would probably be listed on Christie's webpages.

'What do you think, Bonnie?'

'Jack thought it might fetch ten thousand.'

'That would be fantastic, wouldn't it? But let's not get our hopes up. Or should we? I'm not sure I dare look.'

'I'm not sure you'll be able to stop yourself though,' Bonnie chuckled.

Lew threw himself into the captain's chair at his desk and pulled the spare over to his side for Bonnie. 'Okay, here we go.' He logged into the Christie's site, found the latest auction results, marvelled briefly at some of items listed before his impatience speeded him up, and then he came to a picture of the cup and his lungs froze.

'I don't believe it,' said Bonnie, more breath than sound.

Lew looked at the figure on the right of the screen, under 'price realised'.

'I know this, but I'm asking anyway: that means the sold price, doesn't it?'

'Yes,' said Bonnie weakly.

'Thirty-five thousand pounds for that cup and saucer, that's right, isn't it?'

'No. That's just the cup. The saucer must be listed separately.'

He turned quickly to her. 'That can't be right.'

'Lew, it is.' She extended her finger to the wording. 'That is one item. They weren't sold as a pair.'

'Oh boy.' He shook the shock of pins and needles out of his hands. 'So, I'll ... go onto the next page ...'

'It's there,' yelled Bonnie, immediately apologising for nearly deafening him.

'Holy f ...' He didn't have enough voice for the rest of the expletive because there, on the page, was the little Chinese saucer with the staples and a price realised of forty-eight thousand pounds. The figure didn't sink in. Lew's brain seemed to be trying to push it back in case it entered and blew all his neurons.

Beside him, Bonnie was as still and quiet and disbelieving.

'That's wrong. That has to be wrong. Is it sterling or some other currency where there's three million to the pound?'

'Lew, it's sterling. It says. Thirty-five and forty-eight, I can't add them up.'

'Eighty-three thousand pounds.'

Bonnie gulped. 'I'll bet the same person bought both.'

'I'm in shock,' said Lew.

'Obviously there will be fees to take off that figure.'

'I get that.'

Bonnie's outstretched hand crept into his peripheral vision.

'Congratulations, Mr Harley.' Her slim fingers closed around his and she shook it. But he didn't want to shake her hand, he wanted to leap up into the air and pick her up and dance around the room with her and he didn't know how he stopped himself from doing it.

'I'm in shock,' he said again and Bonnie laughed. She was thrilled for him, and he knew that because her eyes were smiling as much as the curve of her soft, plump lips.

'You sent that old lady to me,' he said. 'You are in for such a bonus, Mrs . . . Miss Sherman.'

'If anyone should get a bonus, I think it should be Mrs Twist, rather than me.'

'Don't you worry about her. Mrs Twist was always going to get something extra if the pieces were valuable. I kept her details just in case. And there's the white jade pieces in the August auction to look forward to too.'

'I think you'll have spontaneously combusted before then, Lew.'

'And I think my wife is in for the handbag of her dreams for her birthday,' he smiled. Although it wouldn't be white or made of crocodile. That would never happen.

'She's a lucky lady,' said Bonnie. She bet Charlotte Harley didn't appreciate just how lucky she was.

Lew arrived home with a bottle of champagne and a huge bouquet of flowers. News of the amazing sale surprisingly shifted all traces of Charlotte's depression and they made love that night for the first time in months.

Bonnie sat in the little house in Rainbow Lane and filled in some more forms which had arrived from Adriana, then she punched out five packets of Happy Birthday pink confetti which Lew had ordered from her for the weekend.

# Chapter 49

A lady was waiting for Lew to open up on the Saturday of that week. She had a hoard of ink pens and said that she'd been told he'd give her the fairest price for them, which pleased him immensely because he had finally established a reputation in the business. Lew knew a lot about pens so he was on safe ground here. Amongst the collection was a vintage Waterman Art Deco fountain pen and a fake Mont Blanc. The body of the pen was a fair copy, but the nib gave the game away. The woman thought that the Mont Blanc was the real prize and Lew knew that he could have sent her away to try her luck elsewhere with it and bought the rest off her for fifty quid, but he just wasn't built like that. He took time to explain to her why the pen was worthless and though she probably believed him deep down, she kept it and sold him all the others. He gave her much more than she had expected for them and Lew knew that he could sell them on straightaway for a substantial, easy profit. He was starting to have some excellent sales – the Pot of Gold was very well named.

As the woman walked out, Bonnie hurried in, splashed

with rain from the summer morning shower. She was wearing her yellow mac again and the words 'Bonita Banana' pinged into his brain, and he smiled.

'Morning,' he greeted her.

'Good morning. She was an early customer.' Bonnie thumbed behind her.

'She wanted to sell me some pens. What do you think?'

'Wow.' She spotted the Waterman immediately. 'What a beauty. You have to show this to—'

'Criss-cross. Oh yes. I'd be mad not to,' Lew finished off her sentence.

Crispin Crossmoor-Innesworth was as posh as he sounded. He was a man obsessed by quality pens and mechanical pencils which he bought to add to his already vast private collection. And, even better, he bought everything with cold hard cash.

'Wonderful. If only every transaction could be like that. I'll give him a ring if you like. I'll pop the kettle on, shall I?' said Bonnie.

'Yes please,' said Lew, thinking that despite the sunshiney smile, her eyes were puffy as if she hadn't slept very well. He called after her as she disappeared into the back office, 'There's an envelope on the desk for you from me.'

'P45?' she quipped.

'Got it in one,' he replied. His ear traced the sounds of the kettle building to a boil, the fridge opening, a ting of metal spoon stirring inside the cups, an envelope being torn open and then silence. Then Bonnie appeared with two mugs, walking slowly because her hands were shaking. She put them down on the counter just in time before she dropped them.

'You're joking, right?' she said.

'Nope. It's your cut.'

'My wage is my cut,' said Bonnie. 'You're the boss.'

'So I say what happens,' said Lew. 'And I want you to put that cheque in the bank.'

Bonnie shook her head. 'You haven't even got the money from Christie's yourself yet. What if for some reason the buyer retracts . . .?'

'He won't and you know he won't,' said Lew. 'The market is strong, and even if he does, as you and I both know, another Chinese bidder will snap those items up. Probably for even more. I wanted you to have the money now. I won't argue.'

'I don't know what to say,' said Bonnie, blinking hard. She couldn't look him in the eye and she knew that he knew she was close to tears. Seven thousand pounds was a fortune to her.

'You don't have to say anything. Just don't leave. My luck changed when you walked in through the door.' He hadn't meant it to sound as loaded with tenderness as it came out, but it didn't matter that it did, because that was what he felt.

'I won't, I promise,' said Bonnie. She wouldn't dream of leaving this place, if she didn't have to. But she might have to. Today was the first of the month and she hadn't gone back to Stephen. He wouldn't have made a threat if he didn't mean to carry it out. She had dressed in her brightest colours today hoping to ward off his darkness but it wasn't working. Not really.

When Lew left work later, he drove straight to Meadowhall to collect Charlotte's birthday present: the bright red version of her favourite black Lulu Guinness handbag, along with the matching purse. He also bought a huge bottle of her favourite perfume, a pair of Manolo

Blahnik strappy shoes and some Tiffany earrings. He had spent far too much, but what the hell. He felt as if his home life was turning a corner, just as the shop had. He and Charlotte hadn't had a cross word all week and they were going to spend a lovely birthday evening tomorrow with Gemma and Jason, without the viper that was Regina. He hoped Charlotte was going to be thrilled by the surprise party.

At home, Bonnie pinned the cheque to the noticeboard in her tiny kitchen. The money would finance her divorce first and foremost, which was far more important than anything else she could spend it on. She'd bank the rest. She might need it for more legal fees.

She wouldn't see Lew until Tuesday now. He was having the day off tomorrow as it was his wife's birthday. She imagined he would spoil her with all sorts of romantic, feminine gifts: gorgeous shoes, a designer handbag, perfume, flowers, champagne. He would take ages in choosing a card for her with lovely words that meant something. He wouldn't buy her presents like old-fashioned slippers, practical dressing gowns, dull hardback books that she *should* read like Stephen had for her.

Stephen. She shuddered as she thought about him and the loaded gun that he was holding to her head. She could feel the cold steel press against her temple, hear his finger play on the trigger, drawing out the moment of cocking the mechanism for full effect. She closed her eyes and imagined what it would be like when he finally let the bullet fly and blew everything in her world away. She wondered if she would feel release more than pain.

She was ready. Let it come. Let it all be over.

# Chapter 50

Stephen Brookland savoured the ten-minute journey from his house into town because – or so he'd convinced himself – at the end of it he would be doing the right thing, even if it was long overdue. He had taken care over choosing the right clothes for his forthcoming task as if it were a sacred ritual: polished shoes, charcoal trousers, light blue polo shirt and a casual grey jacket. The combination said, 'this is an upright, law-abiding citizen whose word is to be believed.' He would never have admitted, not even to himself, that the prime reasons for his actions were vindictive, devious, and vengeful. A crime had been committed and he was obliged to do his civic duty and report it, whatever had forced his hand.

He parked the car and walked down the road towards the police station, feeling a shot of adrenalin course rapidly through his veins, as if someone had fully released the tap on the gland where it came from. It was the first of the month and a Saturday night; he hoped the station would be busy. Under his arm he had tucked the A4 folder full of information which the police might find useful: a handwritten account of what had happened five years ago signed and dated, people to contact to verify his allegations, even a photo of the house where Mrs Brookland was now living. He had followed her home one night, at an unseen distance. There was also information about where she worked, a copy of her passport and her National Insurance number.

The front office area was crowded but he didn't mind waiting, because it all added to the drama and was very interesting, like a real-life *Jeremy Kyle Show*. Someone respectable, like himself, came in to report a stolen car, everyone else in the queue was loud and foul-mouthed and obviously lower working class, though he used the word 'working' loosely because he doubted any of them had ever had a job. Then it was Stephen's grandstand moment.

'Yes sir, can I help you?' The counter clerk was civil but dour, suffering the impatience of someone who was at the end of a very long, hard shift.

'I want to see a senior police officer, please,' said Stephen, pushing down on the pressure he felt inside him, which was not unlike that of a shaken bottle of champagne.

'Can you give me some details?'

'Certainly,' he replied, his brain preparing to register the impact of his words. 'I'd like to report a murder.'

# Chapter 51

Lew walked into the bedroom with a tray scattered with some of the pink Happy Birthday confetti which he had commissioned from Bonnie. The rest was sprinkled elsewhere in the house and he'd have some serious vacuuming to do later. Also on the tray was a full English breakfast, coffee, juice and a cut rose in a glass on the side. He trilled the 'Happy Birthday' chorus before he rested it at her side on the bed.

'How lovely,' she grinned, reaching for the orange juice. 'But I can't eat it. I'll be as fat as a pig if I do.'

He leaned over and gave her a kiss full on the mouth. 'Yes you can. There are no calories on your birthday. Happy Birthday, darling.' Then he disappeared into the dressing room and came back out with an armful of presents. 'A good fortifying breakfast will set you up for the day but you'll be hungry again by dinner. We're going out.'

'Where?' Charlotte demanded with a sharp intake of excited breath.

'Surprise,' said Lew.

'Firenze?' She clapped her hands together expectantly and

Lew knew then that – sadly – she would probably be disappointed by what he had planned for her. At least initially.
He hoped she would be charmed by the fuss that everyone
made of her and declare it afterwards to be the best birthday
she'd ever had.

'Just wait and see.'

Charlotte was grinning because she was absolutely certain
he had booked Firenze. It was her favourite place and Lew
knew that, so he would have made a reservation there, of
course he would.

'Open your presents,' he said and she tore into them,
declaring undying love for the Tiffany earrings which
matched the necklace he had bought her for Christmas, the
gorgeous shoes, the perfume and some other fripperies,
although he was keeping the bag and the purse for later. But,
apart from a few nibbles on the toast, she didn't eat any of
her breakfast.

*

Stickalampinit was telling Bonnie all about the holiday he
and Sharon Seventeen Stone were going on in four days'
time. They were off to a little place on the Costa Brava for
a fortnight, staying in the Hotel Sunshine, their favourite,
apparently and it was well situated, being across the road
from the beach and next to the police station, so there were
no pickpockets about. They were only having bed and
breakfast, he explained, because they knew lots of dirt-
cheap cafés in the back streets. The hotel had a huge
swimming pool with a waterfall and a sunken bar and spa
facilities. He sounded like a talking travel brochure. Bonnie
envied him so much, flying far away from here on easyJet

to a guaranteed good time with someone he loved. His brain would empty of everything but the feeling of sun on his skin, the smell of Hawaiian Tropic and the taste of San Miguel. Bonnie wished she could rip out her brain and throw it as far away as possible, because it felt full of worms that were squirming into chambers she had kept locked for years. She'd always suspected that Stephen had gone against his mother's wishes to be cremated in case the day ever came when they might have to exhume her. She knew that Stephen would have been into the police station by now. The worms were telling her that he would have relished every second of his visit.

'We go to a place called Antonio's. You can get a full fry-up for next to nowt. We love it.' Stickalampinit dragged her back to the here and now. 'You should go and get some colour in your cheeks because you look white as a bleeding sheet, Bonnie, lass. You ailing?' He gave her cheek a light pinch and she gave him her fake smile and told him that she was fine.

'Right, I'm off. I'm going to pack. It'll tek me ten minutes, it takes Sharon three days.'

'You have a lovely time,' smiled Bonnie. 'I'll see you when you get back.'

'One pair of Sharon's knickers will take a full case up,' said Long John from behind her, when Stickalampinit had gone. 'He's right about something though, you're the shade of boiled shite. That dickhead husband of yours causing you hassle?'

Bonnie wasn't surprised he knew that she wasn't divorcing on the best of terms. The compost heap of gossip amongst the traders was rich and fertile. How Valerie and Jack's affair remained undiscovered was nothing short of a miracle.

'I'm okay, John,' replied Bonnie. 'I'll just be glad when it's all done and dusted.'

'Where's Lew today?'

'He's having his Sunday off. It's his wife's birthday.'

'Nothing better than having a good partner,' said John, polishing a silver lighter with a soft yellow cloth, 'and nowt worse than having a bad 'un. I've had both. I felt like I'd been let out of prison when I got divorced from Satanic Sandra.'

Bonnie smiled, but her mind was troubled. Prison, police . . . the words were haunting her, or maybe preparing her. The worms teemed excitedly in her head. She wished the police would just come and be done with it. She had to let the weight of what happened that night drop soon, because she had carried it with her like Jacob Marley's chain for too long and it was breaking her.

\*

Lew left Charlotte soaking in the Jacuzzi whilst he slipped out to Tesco to buy some bottles of pink champagne, which he thought might be a nice addition to Charlotte's surprise party. He didn't tell Charlotte where he was going or why, which all added to the intrigue. Then he was worried that her expectations might be building up to a ridiculous level. She was probably expecting a private jet to take them to Paris for the night.

Who should he bump into down the booze aisle but Gemma, who was studying the label on a bottle of non-alcoholic wine, as he discovered when he perched his chin on her shoulder and scared her half to death.

'You silly dog,' she grinned, recovering from the shock.

'Non–alcoholic wine?'

'I was just wondering if it tastes as crap as it sounds,' she replied.

'What are you doing here anyway?' Lew asked, thinking how lovely she looked: fresh and healthy and smiley. 'I thought you'd be slaving over a hot stove. You've only got' – he made an elaborate show of checking his watch – 'seven hours until we're at yours.'

'You have nothing to worry about. Room is decorated, the table is half-set, the cake is made but I dropped the tub of cream getting it out of the fridge, hence I am here to replenish stocks.'

'On your own?' asked Lew, twisting around, looking for Jason.

'Of course. He's working. As per usual. He was out of the door before I woke up this morning.' Then she added, as a private thought spoken aloud, '. . . which was a shame, really. Oh well.' She gave herself a little shake. 'Anyway, how's the birthday girl? I did text her this morning but I haven't had a reply.'

'I don't even think she's looked at her phone. She went straight for a bath and that girl can soak for England when she's in there reading magazines,' said Lew, rolling his eyes and hoping he sounded convincing. It was rude of Charlotte not to answer, and might make it awkward for tonight. 'In fact, I'm sure she turned her phone off in case Regina rang,' he added for good measure. 'Charlotte has come to her senses at long last and has had quite enough of her. Especially after "Swingergate".'

'Don't blame her,' said Gemma, with a hoot of laughter. 'I hope Regina doesn't scrape the bottom of the friend barrel and try and latch on to me if Charlotte's given her the brush off.'

'Tell her to sod right off if she does,' said Lew, leaning down to give her a see-you-later kiss on the cheek.

'Don't you worry, I will. With bells on,' said Gemma.

Gemma almost laughed when she turned the corner into her road and saw, too late to do a crafty backwards manoeuvre, a white Mercedes sports parked outside her house and an all too familiar figure about to get back in it. When Regina spotted her, she bared her porcelain veneers in a dolphin-unfriendly smile and Gemma cursed the unfortunate timing. Only sixty seconds later and she would have missed her.

'Hello Regina, to what do I owe the pleasure?' said Gemma, her tone flat but polite.

'I was in the area and, as I haven't seen you for ages, I thought I'd call by and say hello.'

Gemma didn't buy it at all. Regina had never once popped by to visit her humble abode.

'Oh, really,' she said, opening up her boot and scooping up the shopping which had spilled out of the carrier bag: a packet of chocolate cake sprinkles, three lemons and some Happy Birthday candles.

'Someone's birthday, is it?' trilled Regina as Gemma slammed the boot shut.

Typical self-obsessed-and-bugger-everyone-else Regina, thought Gemma with an inner huff. She never remembered anyone's birthday until at least a fortnight after the event. Even when they'd all arranged to go out expressly to celebrate Gemma's birthday last October, Regina had forgotten to buy a card and a gift.

Presented with an opportunity to cause mischief, ordinarily Gemma would have passed, but she was irked by

Regina's cheek of just turning up unannounced and expecting the red carpet. So, on this occasion, Gemma acted against type and said, 'Yes. It's Charlotte's birthday. Today. She and Lew are coming up for dinner.' And she let that information sink in.

'I see,' said Regina, trying not to let it show that there was more than a possibility of life going on without her. 'And would there be a spare place for me? Or has everyone dropped me like a hot shit now that I'm not half of a couple?' She was smiling but it was a horrible one; more like a grimace from a long-dead cadaver.

Tonight was more special than Regina could ever know. The idea that Gemma would even consider allowing her across the threshold was laughable so the answer to that one was easy.

'No you can't come tonight, Regina,' said Gemma. 'And let me tell you why. You have single-handedly ruined most evenings that I have spent in your company. You have always talked to me as if I am something you are trying to flush away and yet here you are *just calling by* for the first and only time because everyone else is avoiding you and you presume I am thick enough to believe you actually want my company.'

Regina's jaw dropped.

'We have never been friends, Regina. Don't kid yourself that I even showed up as a blip on your radar.'

And with that Gemma turned her back on Regina and walked up her path.

# Chapter 52

Lew was now feeling that his plans for the evening might not have been the wisest. Charlotte was dressed in her new towering birthday shoes, an obviously new and very expensive black dress and wearing more rhinestones than a roomful of guests at a joint Elton John and Liberace convention.

'You're not wearing that, are you?' asked Charlotte, looking at Lew's open-necked shirt, even if it was a Hugo Boss one.

'Yes I am,' said Lew. 'I'm perfectly dressed for where we are going.'

'So we aren't going to Firenze then?' Charlotte's bottom lip started its customary curl.

'No, we aren't. Just let the surprise unfold, please,' Lew said. 'You'll enjoy it. I promise.' *Oh God*, he sent a silent message upwards. *Please make her enjoy it.*

He shooed her out of the bedroom and down the stairs so that he could leave the Lulu Guinness bag and the purse on the pillow for her to find when they got back home later that evening, along with more sprinkles of Bonnie's confetti.

He made her close her eyes for the length of the taxi journey and only open them when they pulled up outside Gemma and Jason's house. He watched her face drop when she saw where she was.

'Please, trust me,' he said, observing her mouth move over a jumble of silent swearwords. 'We want you to have the best evening. Gemma's gone to a lot of trouble.'

Charlotte got out of the car, slapping away his offer of a helping hand. Her jaw was twitching as her teeth clenched, but when Gemma gushed out to greet her, Charlotte forced a smile and let herself be pulled over the threshold into Gemma's warm and welcoming kitchen. Lew followed with carrier bags full of clanking bottles which he handed over to Jason, making a joke about them being relabelled Lambrusco.

'Happy Birthday, dear friend,' said Gemma, holding Charlotte at arm's length and studying her. 'We have been bezzies for thirty-one years in September, did you know that?'

'Really?' said Charlotte, smiling awkwardly at the OTT greeting.

'Yep. And I'm not giving you your present yet, you'll have to wait. What did Lew buy you then? Tell me all.'

'These shoes, some earrings, perfume, a scarf, a reed diffuser . . .' Charlotte reeled off.

'. . . Fondue set, cuddly toy. Bloody hell, it's like the conveyor belt on the *Generation Game*,' Jason guffawed like a man twice his age. 'Though, obviously I am far too young to remember that first-hand.'

He didn't look too young though. He was wearing a green-and-yellow Paisley shirt with a pink V-necked jumper over it and red slacks, as if he had dressed either to play golf

with a bunch of posh old farts or to present a relaunch of
*Rainbow.*

'You spoil her, Lew,' Gemma laughed. 'You're totally
ruined, Charlotte Harley.'

'Drink?' said Jason. 'Shall I crack the top off some champers or do you want a beer?'

'Oh please, champers for our guests,' Gemma said. 'I'm
on the non-alcoholic stuff so I can coordinate all this properly,' she swept her hand across the busy work surfaces and
hob, full of pans and plates. 'But I can have half a glass
because I want to toast my very good friend Charlotte's
birthday.'

Gemma is acting a bit odd, thought Lew, though no one
else seemed to notice.

Jason popped a cork and cheered, then poured out four
flutes of pink champagne.

'Let me do the toast,' begged Gemma. She lifted up her
glass. 'To friends and lovers,' she said, wearing a smile of
such gigantic proportions it almost split her face in half.
'How fortunate we all are to have each other.'

# Chapter 53

Detective Sergeant Bill Henderson had been the lucky man who had interviewed Stephen Brookland the previous night. Mr Brookland had insisted on taking his allegation right to the top but a DS was the highest rank he was going to get on a Saturday night. Even if Johnny Depp had walked in with a hand grenade, Henderson would have been the man drafted in to deal with him. He had listened to Brookland's story, delivered with relish, taken a formal statement and now he was on his way to interview Mrs Brookland. Even though it was a five-year-old historic case and he doubted somehow that Mrs Brookland was the devil incarnate her husband had inferred, DS Henderson decided to check it out sooner rather than later. With him was Detective Chloe Barrett, who had been uniform for two and a half years and had recently transferred to CID. Barrett could have done far worse – and not much better – than to have as a mentor the well-seasoned Henderson, who thought she'd make a good detective in time. She did, however, in his opinion, tend to see things in black and white and could do with a few lessons in recognising the shades in between.

Henderson got out of the car with his battered blue A4 daybook under his arm which had all his notes from the meeting with Brookland in it. He had a feeling this case was going to fill most of the pages. He noticed the sparkling clean windows of the house on Rainbow Lane when Barrett knocked on the door. The thought came to him that his mother always judged a person's character by the condition of their front windows and he suspected a little of that must have rubbed off onto him, because he paired those respectable windows with the woman who answered the door. She looked absolutely terrified to find them standing there and he knew instinctively that this woman had never been in trouble with the police in her life before.

'Mrs Bonita Brookland?' said Henderson.

'You're the police, aren't you?' she said, hazel eyes wide and worried. She immediately stood aside. 'Come in. I've been expecting you.'

# Chapter 54

The snug dining room was decorated with huge bunches of Happy Birthday balloons, pink heart-shaped balloons and ones with Charlotte's name on them; there were Happy Birthday banners Blu-tacked to the walls, streamers draped over the arms of the big light – in short, Gemma had done her friend proud. The starter of buttery potted shrimps was divine, though loaded with calories and Lew knew that his figure-conscious wife would probably be living on fresh air for the next couple of days to compensate. The next course was a creamy fillet steak stroganoff, the best Lew had ever tasted. The food was fantastic, the company was great, the atmosphere stress-free. Lew was in seventh heaven. It was soul-refreshing to have a normal evening with normal friends with neither the prospect of any food-flinging nor the A–Z of name-calling on the horizon. Charlotte's initial faux smile had relaxed into a real one. Even Jason seemed more like his old self now with this smaller group dynamic.

'Dim the lights, Lew,' ordered Gemma, disappearing into the kitchen and pulling her husband in there behind her.

'Uh-oh, I feel a surprise cake coming on,' chuckled Lew,

twisting the knob on the wall. 'At least I hope I do.' He squeezed Charlotte's arm and whispered to her, 'You okay? I'll take you to Firenze this week, promise.'

'I'm good,' said Charlotte and Lew knew that she meant it.

'Happy Birthday to you . . .' sang Jason, walking in and carrying a large pink lit candle like a gaudy choirboy. He pointed behind him at Gemma. 'She says she's not sticking it in the cake because it's too big. Looks like a bloody dildo to me.'

Charlotte and Lew chuckled.

'Sing, Jason and Lew,' ordered Gemma, following Jason in and carrying a cake of gigantic proportions. '. . . Happy Birthday to you. Happy Birthday, dear Charlotte. Happy Birthday to you. Blow, Charlotte.'

Charlotte blew out the big pink candle which Jason was holding in front of her. Lew cheered. Jason twisted the light back up. Gemma put the cake in front of Charlotte so she could see it. Charlotte registered the word BITCH spelt out in cherries couched in inches of cream a mere second before it was pushed up into her face.

# Chapter 55

'Can I get you both a drink? The kettle's just boiled,' said Bonnie, a tremor heavy in her voice.

'Please,' Henderson answered for both of them. 'Coffee, white one sugar, times two.' He knew that talking to the lady with a hot drink in his hand humanised the situation. Some cases required the heavy approach, emotional ones like this needed more of the gentle touch.

'I'll be a couple of minutes. Please sit down,' said Bonnie, darting into the kitchen and getting cups out. The detectives heard something fall on the floor, a spoon probably. She was jittery.

Henderson looked around at the décor. She owned a proper mish-mash of furniture styles and colours; nothing matched but the effect was homely rather than junk-shop. There was a stack of small plastic bags and bits of paper on the coffee table and he reckoned they'd interrupted her doing something crafty, though not in the same 'crafty' sense he usually found people. He picked one up and found it was full of tiny umbrellas with a fold of cardboard at the top reading 'The Rainbow Lady'. Bags of confetti. It made a nice change from what he was used to finding in small plastic bags in houses he visited.

Bonnie came back into the room with two cups of coffee, put them down and scooped up all the small bags. 'Sorry for the mess,' she apologised.

'You don't know what mess is, love,' Henderson wanted to say to her, but instead he said, 'Thank you.'

Bonnie sat down on the brown 'flip-out bed' chair, knees together, hands clasped tightly as if in prayer, her whole body stiff with tension.

'You said you'd been expecting us,' said Henderson, with a friendly smile. 'Why's that then?'

'You're here to arrest me,' said Bonnie, smiling back. A strange smile. A smile almost borne of relief. It was the smile of a person who had done something wrong and the guilt weighed so heavy on them that when the police finally caught up with them, they rushed towards the chance to atone with open arms. He'd seen it before; not many times, but enough to recognise it.

So to business. 'There's been an allegation made against you . . .' Henderson began.

'My husband, Stephen. He said he would,' Bonnie interrupted him. Her eyes were shiny with tears now and she pressed them back with her fingers. 'Sorry. I'm a bit nervous.'

Stephen Brookland had insisted she should be charged with 'first degree murder'. He'd been watching too many American dramas. Henderson pitied the woman they had appointed as his FLO – the family liaison officer, whose duty it would be to keep him updated of the events. He'd be a daily pest, Henderson was sure of it. He could smell the neediness coming off the older man in waves.

'We're not here to arrest you, but we would like you to come into the station on a voluntary basis and make a statement,' Henderson said, adopting a calm, avuncular tone. He took a sip of the coffee. The cup had Mondrian coloured squares all over it. Barrett's featured Van Gogh's *Starry Night*.

'I'd rather come now,' said Bonnie. 'Please just arrest me.'

'I'm not going to do that, Mrs Brookland,' said Henderson, kindly but firmly. 'The police cells are not pretty places. You don't need to go there when you can sleep soundly in your bed here and see us in the next couple of days.'

'I haven't slept soundly in my bed for a long time. Just let me face this now, I'm ready. It's the right thing to do,' said Bonnie, flicking tears from her cheeks. Henderson knew she was forty-one but she looked fifteen. Her eyes were huge and full of pain.

'Trust me, you really don't—' began Barrett, before Bonnie interrupted her.

'Please. I don't think I could bear for you to leave me here by myself now that it's started. I don't know what I'd do . . .'

'Is there anyone you can call to come and stay with you, or you stay with them?' Henderson's concerned tone pulled more tears from her eyes, one after the other like a stream of magician's scarves.

'No,' said Bonnie. 'There's no one.' *There's no one.* It sounded so sad and pathetic but it was true, there was no one. Not really. 'Please,' she said again. 'This has cast a long shadow over my life.' She knew she needed to force their hand. 'I won't turn up of my own accord so you'll only have to come back and arrest me, so you might as well save yourself a job.' She tried to sound bolshie but failed. Her head fell into her hands. 'You have no idea how much I've dreaded this day.' She had already been imprisoned for five years in her mind; one more night would not make a difference.

Henderson felt Barrett look at him for guidance. Henderson really did not want to arrest this woman but neither did he want to risk what she might do to herself and she was presenting as unstable and vulnerable. She needed help, not arresting. These emotional cases were the ones that stayed in his brain when he was trying to get to sleep at night. He put his empty cup down on the coffee table, said thank you and stood up.

'If I arrest you, you might end up spending hours in a cell and they aren't nice, Mrs Brookland,' said DS Henderson, trying again to put her off. 'There's a toilet with no seat in the corner of the room, no sink and don't even get me started on what the food they'll give you is like. You'll be searched and questioned and if you end up having to stay until the morning, as well you might, you won't get a wink of sleep. There's no need for any of that, now, is there?'

'There is,' begged Bonnie. 'Please. Help me. There is.'

# Chapter 56

There was a stunned silence in which no one spoke and it seemed to last for minutes, rather than the seconds it actually was. Strangely enough, Charlotte was the last to react. First was Lew who grabbed serviettes and started scooping the cake from Charlotte's face and shoulders, his brain telling him that Gemma must have slipped. Second was Jason who leapt up from his seat with a 'What the fuck . . .?'

'Fuck? Fuck . . . oh yes, let's talk about fucks and fucking and fuckers.' Gemma gave a hard forced chuckle.

Charlotte had now stirred into life and was spitting out cream and wiping herself with her hands whilst making strange noises of distress. Lew's skull was prickling; Gemma never swore. He knew something had been amiss with her. He'd felt it as soon as he'd laid eyes on her tonight.

'What are you talking about?' growled Jason, but there was something in his tone that inferred he might know exactly what his wife was talking about.

'I had a visitor today,' said Gemma, calmly licking a lump of chocolate-sprinkled cream from her finger. 'Lovely cake. What a waste. Regina. Came to crawl up my arse because no one else was speaking to her. Wanted to wangle an invite for this evening but obviously I told her to stuff off. So guess what she told me, Jason?' Gemma stared hard at her husband, then swivelled her head around to Charlotte, who looked as if she were metamorphosing into a snowman. 'Sh . . . Harlot?'

Charlotte was silent under her cake mask. Jason was struck dumb, wide-eyed and his face was turning redder by the second. Lew was silent too but his brain was sparking, trying to work out what was going on.

'Regina told me that you two had been screwing. My husband and my best friend, fucking like minxes,' Gemma went on, calmly as if she was talking about the price of potatoes rather than the ultimate betrayal.

'Regina is fucking evil,' said Charlotte now, spraying whipped cream like a snow machine as she spoke. 'I can't believe that you'd actually take her seriously.'

But whilst Lew was listening to his wife's reasonable response, he was looking at Jason, who had gone past red and was heading for purple. Jason hadn't opened his mouth and Lew thought, *If that were me, I would be screaming a protest.*

'You know, Charlotte, that's exactly what I said to myself to begin with. But I have to admit, she was pretty convincing.' Gemma's composure began to slip now and her voice started to rise. 'She said that the night Patrick left her, the two of you got wrecked on Jack Daniel's and you fessed up to her, you bitch. As for you . . .' Gemma's attention swung to Jason. 'Guess what I did this morning? A pregnancy test. I'm pregnant. I'm pregnant to a wanker who is fucking my best friend.'

Jason folded like a concertina that had been kicked in the

bollocks. 'Oh no. God, I'm so sorry,' he said, face creasing like a five-year-old who had just been told Christmas was cancelled.

'What are you sorry for? Nothing happened,' screamed Charlotte at him. 'Tell them Jason, nothing bloody happened.' But Jason had his hands on his head as if performing a penance for a teacher and he was saying absolutely nothing as he rocked backwards and forwards.

Lew stood as if in the eye of the storm, the cool, clear part that saw the disaster surrounding him, and none of it was making sense. Or rather it was and his brain was repulsing it, refusing to let him accept what his eyes were seeing and his ears were hearing.

'Jason, tell them nothing happened!' Charlotte was shrieking like a harpy, but he was dissolving in front of them, sinking to a chair, sobbing.

'You pathetic shit,' Gemma bawled at him. 'You make me feel sick. What should have been the best day of my life, ruined. And as for you – ' she screwed up her face at Charlotte ' – it's a good job you never had kids, you selfish—'

'That's enough, Gemma. Do not go there,' Lew cut in sternly. Whatever mess they were all in, that was just cruel.

'Oh, oh,' Gemma laughed almost manically. 'Of course you don't know, do you?'

Charlotte sprang from the chair, pushed past Lew and lunged at Gemma. 'Don't, Gem.' Charlotte pressed her hand over Gemma's mouth. Gemma prised it off.

'You do know that while YOU thought you were trying for a baby, SHE was on the pill. She only came off it because you thought something was wrong and wanted to send her for medical tests.'

'What?' Lew's eyes tennis-matched between Gemma and Charlotte.

'You lying bitch. Lewis, don't listen to her, she's mental.'

'Am I now? You're painting me out to be the bad guy, are you?' Gemma guffawed like a panto villain. 'Bad news usually comes in threes, so guess what the third one is, Lew. SHE had an abortion, not a miscarriage.'

'She's lying, Lewis. You fucking bitch.' Charlotte grabbed a handful of Gemma's hair, Gemma reached for Charlotte's, Lew threw himself between them and it was Charlotte he pushed away and Gemma whom he closed his arms around and whom he held firmly whilst she slumped against him and sobbed as if her heart was breaking up inside her.

He couldn't remember how long he stood there holding her, giving her comfort, claiming comfort for himself from this terribly wounded woman. Later when he tried to recall the events of the evening, there were gaping black holes in his memory. He couldn't remember what happened between standing there with Gemma and getting into a taxi with Charlotte. He could remember paying the taxi driver and storming up the path whilst Charlotte trailed behind, carrying her shoes.

Then they were in the kitchen and he recalled pouring himself a whisky and throwing it down his neck and he remembered how the burn on the back of his throat felt good, real, after the numbness of the last half-hour/hour . . . however long it was, he had no idea, his brain was scrambled.

'Is it true?' he said eventually, coming 'back into the room' as if a hypnotist had clicked his fingers.

'No, of course not,' snapped Charlotte, bottom lip pushed out so far Tom Daly could have dived from it.

'She made it all up? Really? Did she?' he bellowed and she jumped back a step.

'Yes.' That stupid giveaway nerve was jerking on the edge of her lip.

Lew picked up the glass and threw it across the room where it smashed against the wall clock. He walked straight up to bed with the thought in his head that he'd never liked the bastard thing anyway.

The *Daily Trumpet* would, once again, like to apologise to the Mayor Derek Trubshaw for the report in our weekend edition supplement. When asked what he considered was the greatest gift in life, his worshipfulness was sadly misquoted as saying 'A penis'. This should have read 'Happiness.' We wholeheartedly accept responsibility for the error.

# Chapter 57

Everything seemed distorted and dreamlike when Bonnie entered the police station with the detectives: the custody sergeant behind the wide elevated desk appeared huge, built of different proportions to a normal man. The shouting from the smartarse drunk in front of them in the queue hurt her ears, the rancid body-odour of the man with the tattooed face whom she had to sit next to in the waiting room made her feel sick. None of it appeared real, yet at the same time she knew it was very real and she was here and it was every bit as grim as the detective sergeant had told her it would be. The rhetoric he and the arresting officers used brought it home to her that she was in terrible trouble: *Due to the seriousness of the offence . . . refused to comply with voluntary attendance . . . arrested on suspicion of encouraging and aiding the suicide of her mother-in-law.* A woman police officer snapped on some blue gloves, took her into another room and searched her before returning her to the custody sergeant. She had her fingerprints scanned to be compared to those recovered from crime scenes. Her necklace, watch, dress-belt and handbag were put into a bag. The policewoman suggested she put her cardigan in there as well just to be sure, the inference being that she could hang herself with it. She was given a rip-proof grey sweatshirt to wear instead for warmth. She was told she had the right to free and independent legal advice and could look at a book which detailed how she should be treated by the police. She was asked if there was anyone whom they could inform of her arrest. She said that there was no one.

The detention officer led her to a cell. He was putting her in the one at the far end, which would be the quietest, he said. She had to leave her shoes outside the door. The cell was small and square with glossy yellow wipe-clean walls; a Crimestoppers telephone number was stencilled on the ceiling and a steel toilet stood in the corner. There was a wooden bench with a plastic-coated mattress little more than an inch thick. It smelt so strongly of cheap disinfectant and sweaty trainers that she could almost taste it in the back of her throat. When the door shut with a loud, heavy clang, Bonnie truly realised what had been set in motion now. She made it to the toilet just in time to vomit. There was nowhere to wash her face afterwards or swill her mouth or sponge the splashes off her dress.

Minutes later, the flap on the door was pulled down and eyes appeared in the gap. Then the flap slid down further and a flimsy green blanket was pushed through. 'Just in case you feel cold. And I've got some food and a hot drink for you. Do you take sugar?'

'No thank you.'

'Here you go then.'

Bonnie got up to receive the polystyrene bowl with soggy chips, a square of grey fish and congealed beans and a cup of weak coffee through the hatch.

'Try and get your head down. The duty solicitor says you'll need a specialist because she can't handle what you've been brought in for but he won't be here until the morning. Little tip, we'll check on you every hour so if you want a bit of privacy to use the toilet, go and use it straight after we've been.' The custody officer didn't extend the courtesy of his advice to everyone, but he felt this lady should have it.

'Thank you,' replied Bonnie.

She couldn't eat the meal but the coffee was welcome. She was shivering. The cell wasn't cold but the chill was bone-deep, borne of panic and desolation. She felt numb at the core of her, but at the same time her senses were hyper-aware. Her ears sifted through the layers of sound outside the cell: shouting, doors clanging, banging, people talking, swearing, echoes falling from them all. So much for this being the quietest cell.

She curled into a foetal position on the wafer-thin mattress and knew the policeman was right and that she wouldn't sleep. She wanted to be at home in the bed that Goldfinger had given her, snuggled under her cheap Argos quilt with a salted caramel latte swilling in her stomach and she tried to wish herself back there now, looking forward to waking tomorrow morning on her Monday off. She had planned to fill some of the plastic pots which she had found in the tumbledown shed with the flowers she had bought that day from the florist in Spring Hill Square. She'd left them outside the back door and they'd be dried out and dying by lunchtime. She should have watered them before she left. Then she thought how ridiculous it was that her anxiety levels were spiking over a fiversworth of marigolds when she could be charged with murder.

Because that's what assisted suicide was really, wasn't it? And she was guilty but she would have done it all over again if time had been rewound. So it was right that she should be here in this cell with despair and fear solid in her gut like a dense boulder. She should have walked into a police station as soon as Alma died. She had wanted to . . .

She closed her eyes and thought back again to that night, but it was like a well-worn recording and she wasn't sure if she was remembering it properly any more. Guilt and emotion had warped it.

She had waited by Alma's side until Stephen returned from wherever he had been. She'd heard once that the newly deceased were often disorientated by their new state and so she talked to her, hoping she could hear her and be comforted by her. Then, when Stephen arrived, Bonnie left them alone. He was dry-eyed at his mother's passing, which was ironic, though she hadn't thought about it until now: her devoted son emotionless, her despised daughter-in-law, heartbroken.

'She went the way she wanted to go, Bonita. She had a good death,' Stephen had said.

'I think I should go to the police,' said Bonnie.

Stephen had rounded on her fiercely. 'You will not tell ANYONE that you helped my mother end her own life. You will not damage her memory in that way. There will be no fuss, is that understood?'

There had been a warning in the way he said it. 'Go and sort yourself out before the doctor arrives.'

She had not known then that her involvement in Alma's death would be his insurance policy against her leaving him. He wanted it known that his mother died naturally until he needed to expose the truth to benefit himself.

As grim as the police cell was, it was nothing compared to the prison that had been her marriage to Stephen Brookland.

# Chapter 58

Lew lay fully dressed on top of the bed in the spare room, but there was no way he would be able to sleep. He didn't know what to do with himself. The events of the evening were tumbling around in his head like a washing machine on a high spin setting. He traced the sound of Charlotte trudging up the stairs, sniffling hard, sobbing dramatically but it did not move him one bit. It was as if his brain had built up a wall around him to keep out all emotion to stop it engulfing him like a tsunami. But it was already crumbling, realisations were pushing through the weakest cracks in the brickwork: *she screwed your friend, she didn't have a miscarriage, she lied, lied, lied . . .*

There was an almost indiscernible knock on the door and a, 'Can I come in?' Charlotte's voice was tear-heavy. He didn't answer. She came in anyway. He sat up, swung his legs off the bed and watched her shuffle towards him, as if she were ancient. Her face was blotchy, eyes puffy, hair loose, wet and greasy from the cream.

'Lewis,' she hiccuped. 'Can we talk, please?' She sat down on the bed at a distance from him, looking sideways at him for his reaction. Other than a tightening of his jaw, there was nothing. Her hand came out towards his arm and he flinched back from it.

'Don't,' he said, 'just don't.'

'I'm sorry,' she bawled.

'For what?' His head pivoted round to her. 'For trying to touch me, for continually lying to me, for screwing my friend or getting rid of our child? Which part of all that are you sorry for?'

'Lewis, stop,' said Charlotte, her voice a weary croak.

Lew jumped up from the bed. He didn't want to be near her. He couldn't even feel the betrayal of her sleeping with someone else yet because there was no room for it in his head. He had to get out of the house. He went to his wardrobe, dragged his cavernous sports bag out of the bottom and began to stuff it with jumpers, jeans, socks.

'Lewis, please,' she sobbed, throwing herself at his back, her arms forming a weak band around him. 'Please, don't leave me.' He pushed her away and she crumpled onto the bed, her body limp but her lungs in fine fettle as she howled loudly. He packed the bag until it was full, then at the rasp of the zip, she sat up bolt upright.

'I'm begging you, Lewis, I'm sorry, I won't know what to do if you go. Please, we can get through this. Don't leave me on my birthday.' He was at the door; she screamed at him, 'Pleeease.'

'Why did you marry me, Charlotte?' Lew turned.

'What?'

'Why did you marry me?' He tilted his head at her, waiting for the answer.

'Because ... because ...' Charlotte sniffed, swallowed; this was her chance to turn the tide where her full emotional display had failed. '...you were clever, handsome, smart, ambitious, kind. You treated me like a princess. I knew we'd be good together, I knew we'd make a great team. And we did, Lew, we are so good tog—'

'I married you because I loved you,' he said. Even when he had asked Bonnie why she had married Stephen, she had said that she loved him.

'I love *you*,' said Charlotte, emphatically. But it was too late. He knew that she probably did love him but it was a by-product of the money and the luxury and the comfort, something that had grown like an incidental weed in the garden of their marriage.

He walked out of the room leaving her wailing like a bargain basement Regina.

# Chapter 59

Sleep did not come easily to Bonnie, but despite the adrenalin zapping around her system and the constant noise,
nervous exhaustion closed the shutters on her brain and she
was awoken by the detention officer pulling down the hatch
on her door.

'Bit of breakfast for you. And your solicitor will be here
in about twenty minutes.'

Sausage, beans and scrambled egg fresh from the microwave and a coffee. Bonnie had never gone to bed without
brushing her teeth before and her mouth felt dry, her breath
rancid.

'Thank you,' she said. She'd been lying on her arm and
it was stiff and painfully prickly as the blood flow increased.
She couldn't eat but drank the lukewarm coffee in thirsty
gulps. She used her hands as a comb and tried to plait her
hair, then licked her fingers to wipe around her eyes and
mouth then sat on the bed and waited. She thought of Lew.
Would she ever see him again? She couldn't remember what
the police said would happen now. Did someone tell her that
she would be up in front of magistrates or was she mixing

that up with television programmes? Stephen would make sure she was in the newspaper: *Bonnie Brookland, aged 41, arrested for murdering her mother-in-law.* She would have to give up her lovely little house, the Pot of Gold and Lew. What would he think when she didn't come into work tomorrow? Would the police let him know she had been arrested? Her horizon was colourless, black, nothing beyond it but more black and her dad's grey rainbow.

The door opening dashed away all thoughts. 'Come on, love,' said the detention officer. *Love?* He would never know how much that one little warm word jerked Bonnie back from the lip of a very deep well.

'In you go.' He opened the door to a dingy, windowless room, bare except for a table and four chairs which were screwed to the floor. A man rose from one of the chairs, hand extended. He was tall, slim with thick salt and pepper hair, aviator glasses and a smile. He introduced himself.

'David Charles. I've been asked by my colleague to help you in this case because you have a specialised need. Duty solicitor would have been neither use nor ornament to you. Please sit down.' He gestured towards the chair opposite to his own. Bonnie stumbled over the leg and it set all her nerves jangling. What must he think of her? She looked a mess and she knew she smelt of sick.

'Try not to worry,' he said, clicking the top of a pen. 'Easier said than done, of course. Why exactly were you brought in? You should have been advised that you could attend on a voluntary basis.'

'I was,' said Bonnie, nudging her hair back from her face because her plait had unravelled already. 'I wanted to meet it head on. I did what I'm accused of.'

'Ok-ay,' said David Charles. 'Mrs Brookland, the law is a

set of complex rules and it's not what you think you've done, it's whether you fit within the framework of the offence. And it's not for you to say whether you're guilty but a court to prove that you are. If it gets that far, of course.'

There was a knock on the door and the detention officer appeared with two coffees and sachets of sugar. When he had exited, David Charles took a sip and grimaced. 'Kenco eat your heart out. Right, Mrs Brookland, or can I call you Bonnie?'

'I'd prefer it if you did,' she said.

'Shall we start from the beginning?' said David Charles, pen poised.

'Please,' replied Bonnie, more than ready to offload what had been sitting inside her like a rotten, festering egg for five long, cold years.

# Chapter 60

Lew was awoken by the flashing light of a text coming through on his phone. Ironically it was Patrick.

> Hi Bud. New address alert. I'm at Marlene's flat.
> 5a Jasmine Court. Flockton. Must get together
> soon. Life is good. Pat.

So Patrick had vacated the local Holiday Inn, where Lew now found himself and he wondered if the place was being bankrolled by estranged partners.

When he examined his phone, he found that he had missed eleven calls from Charlotte, four voicemails and had six waiting texts from her – all of them asking him to meet up and talk. He was going to delete the voicemails without listening to them but changed his mind. She was crying on all of them, borderline hysterical on the second, angry on the third, contrite on the fourth. *Please come home, I love you.* He felt nothing but bitterness and anger and that was all he wanted to feel because it was all-consuming and kept hurt and grief at the door.

He sat up and pressed his temple where a stress headache was drilling into his skull. He needed ibuprofen, coffee, toast and his car. He had felt stone cold sober when he left the house but he was over the limit thanks to the celebratory champagne consumed at Gemma's so he'd sat in his car and ordered a taxi which had taken over half an hour to arrive. The drive had taken him through a sleeping Dodley and his thoughts drifted to Bonnie, tucked up in her little house in Rainbow Lane, before he switched them off because she had no place in the present black state of his mind.

He showered, wishing the water could wash off the filth he felt crawling under his skin. He turned the tap to cold and let the spray pulse against his temple, battering at the persistent throb. He dressed and went down for breakfast amongst couples and businessmen. He ate toast, drank coffee and then ordered a cab to take him back to Woodlea to pick up his car. He didn't even look at the house but drove away from it then he parked up around the corner from where he texted Gemma. He needed to talk to her.

*

Half an hour later, the detectives came into the room: Barrett and Henderson, with his trusty A4 daybook. Many recent notes had been added to it, information supplied by the family liaison officer. She had only just been appointed and already Brookland had phoned her a number of times to feed things through to the detectives which might be of interest to them.

Bonnie sat with her hands clamped between her knees. She looked as if she had shrunk overnight, thought Henderson.

'What was the relationship like between you and your mother-in-law Alma Brookland?' he began, after he'd told her he hoped that she'd had not too bad a night, and a brief exchange with David Charles.

'At the beginning it wasn't good, in fact it was awful,' replied Bonnie. 'She didn't like me at all and she'd belittle me at every opportunity. I could never do anything right for her: my cooking was always substandard, she'd drag her finger over everything trying to insinuate I didn't clean properly, telling me that I looked as if I'd put weight on, criticising what I wore, and she always called me Bonita even though she knew I hated it. It doesn't sound much I know, but she was continually pecking at me, breaking me down. She was very protective over Stephen, my husband, her son. She thought I was a gold-digger. And before you ask, no I wasn't. My dad was in a home because he had dementia. He'd put savings away all his life to make sure I'd be well set up. Dad died when I'd been married nearly four years. What he left me was mostly eaten up by costs for the home.'

'Did you ever say that you wanted to kill her?'

Bonnie nodded slowly.

'For the benefit of the recording, could you please answer that verbally,' said Barrett.

'I'm sorry, yes I did, I admit it. I'd just found out that Dad had pneumonia and Alma said that you got what you deserved in life. She was goading me into saying something in front of her friend. She was pointing at me, smirking, telling her friend that I looked as if I wanted to kill her and I said that I did. I'd given up trying to make her like me by then. She was hateful. She knew that my dad was my weak spot, you see, and that I felt guilty about having to put him in a home. He was six foot six and had arms like a windmill when he got upset and didn't know what he was doing.'

Tears were coursing down Bonnie's face, too fast to wipe away and snot was dribbling from her nose. Barrett leaned over the table between them and handed her a tissue.

'Thank you,' said Bonnie, giving her nose a well-needed blow. 'She came to the house every fortnight for tea and I used to dread it. I know she told everyone who'd listen that I was using her son and that I'd wormed my way into his life and that I wanted her put in a home out of the way just as I'd done with my dad.'

'And did you?' asked Henderson.

'God no,' Bonnie protested, raising her head, looking him in the eye. 'I can't tell you how much it hurt me when she used to say that, but Stephen never spoke up for me. He just said he couldn't stop his mother believing what she wanted to believe and I shouldn't let it bother me. But it did. Alma was very good at mind-games. I know she enjoyed ridiculing me, especially in front of an audience. Before she got ill, that was; then things changed.'

'How did they change?' asked Barrett.

'She became frightened, needy.'

'What exactly was wrong with her?' asked Barrett.

'She was diagnosed with progressive bulbar palsy. It's a neurological disease, very aggressive. When she could speak she told me that she'd thought what had happened to my dad was the worst thing that could happen to anyone: that their body remained fit and their mind died. What she had did the opposite, her body closed down whilst her mind stayed alert and aware. She said it was worse for her that way round.'

'How long did she live at ...' Henderson checked the address from his notes '... Greenwood Crescent with you?'

'Just over two months. She started getting ill about three months before that. I noticed that Alma had started using her left hand to lift a cup. I suspected she wasn't well but Stephen hadn't noticed anything and told me not to fuss because she wouldn't like it. Then she started to go really downhill very quickly and Stephen was forced to take her to seek medical help. She didn't want to go, she was terrified of hospitals and doctors. She had self-diagnosed on the internet and had a good idea what sort of disease she had.'

'Were your husband and his mother close?'

'She was very close to him,' Bonnie replied. 'He was . . . dutiful towards her.' She chose the word carefully and Henderson asked her what she meant.

'There was no warmth from him, no overt affection. She was scared and she wanted someone just to hold her and give her comfort but he didn't want to do things like that. Even when she died, I never saw him break down, he just got on with things. He was like that though with everyone, very dry emotionally. But she idolised him.'

'So Mrs Brookland did attend hospital?'

'Yes, she had tests and they more or less confirmed what she knew already. She didn't want anyone to know or see her degenerate. She even managed to keep it secret from her best friend Katherine. She didn't see Alma for the last three months of her life because she always went to Spain just before Christmas to stay with her daughter who lives out there. No doubt you'll be speaking to her though.' Bonnie shook her head slowly from side to side. 'She won't shed a very kind light on me. She had Alma bitching about me into her ears for eight years.'

'Did Mrs Brookland have any visitors when she was at your house?' asked Henderson.

'Other than a doctor and a couple of nurses at the beginning, no. Katherine was her only real friend. I think she scared everyone away. She had plenty of Get Well cards from people at the church and the bridge club she liked to go to but no one actually came to see her.'

'Whose idea was it to ask her to move in?'

'Alma asked. It was a massive thing for her to admit that she couldn't cope and so she asked Stephen if she could move in with us.' She gave a small huff of sarcastic laughter and Henderson questioned it.

'He said no. He told her it was me that didn't want her there. I know that because I found out the next day when she got a taxi over to the shop where I worked. She was in a terrible state and she begged me to let her stay with us, which was so out of character for her. I was fuming – at Stephen not Alma – but I didn't want her to think badly of her son so I pretended and said that I'd changed my mind. I made up the spare room for her and when Stephen came home from work, she was already *in situ* and he couldn't exactly throw her out. She was so grateful she cried. I'd never seen her cry before. To be honest, I didn't even think her capable of it.'

'What were his reasons for not wanting her to stay?' asked Barrett, exchanging knowing glances with Henderson. There were a lot of contradictions between Mr and Mrs Brookland's stories. Stephen Brookland had insisted that it was very much his idea to have his mother move in with them.

'He said it was impossible because we were both working. But I think he was a bit revolted by the idea of having to nurse her, wash her, feed her, that sort of stuff, because she refused point blank to have strangers come in and do that for her. So I did it all.'

Barrett was confused. 'You're saying that she didn't like you, but yet she let you look after her. Doesn't sound right to me.' She huffed sarcastically and Henderson gave her a sideways glance.

'I think it might be appropriate to have a short break,' announced David Charles in a clipped tone, also casting a warning look at Barrett.

'I don't want a break,' said Bonnie, turning to the solicitor. 'I want to carry on. Really.'

Henderson nodded. 'Okay, let's carry on then. You were saying that she let you look after her.'

'Yes she did,' said Bonnie. 'Better the devil you know.' Then she puffed out her cheeks, because that probably wasn't the best thing to say in the circumstances. 'My boss then, Harry Grimshaw, let me take unpaid leave to look after her. I sat with her and I read to her and we watched TV in her room together. She loved to do quizzes.'

'You became friends, did you?' asked Henderson.

Bonnie smiled. 'I don't know if she ever saw me as a friend, but she softened towards me. I suppose she just got to know me properly. She trusted me. She must have.'

'What do you mean?' asked Barrett.

'Because she told me about her suicide plan before she told Stephen.'

The detectives exchanged loaded glances. This was not the sort of interview they had been led to expect. Stephen Brookland had told them that his wife would deny everything. They were not to trust a single thing she said, either, because apparently she was an expert liar, as murderers usually are.

'When was this?'

'About a fortnight after she moved in. She could speak

well then but by the month after there were times when she was barely intelligible. She showed me a package that she kept in her bag. There was a sheet of instructions and a plastic bottle with liquid in it. She'd bought it from Mexico on the internet. I can't remember what it was called but I know it was some sort of veterinary drug, it was obvious even from the Spanish wording. She wanted me to tell Stephen for her. I think she thought he'd be upset.' Although she had wondered since if Alma hadn't told him first because she thought he might *not* be upset. It hurt her that she knew he didn't love her as much as she loved him.

'She wanted to end her life whilst she still had some control. She was terrified of Stephen seeing her as a burden.'

The two police officers and David Charles shifted nervously in their seats at this revelation. The word 'burden' was a word that might infer this was a self-serving crime rather than a compassionate one.

'Did you see her as a burden?' asked Henderson.

'No I did not,' Bonnie returned adamantly. 'I saw her as a frightened old woman in pain.'

'So, what was Mr Brookland's reaction when you told him about his mother's plan to end her own life?' Henderson unconsciously leaned forward, interested in the answer to this one. Stephen Brookland had said that he had no idea his mother had contemplated suicide until he found her dead and his wife confessed to being party to knowing.

'He didn't believe me at first, he said that I must have misunderstood, so I took the package out of Alma's bag when she was asleep to show him. She was hoping that she wouldn't have to use it and she would die in her sleep. She used to cry in the mornings when she woke up to another day.' Bonnie realised she was straying from the question and apologised. 'He was angry, I could tell, but he didn't say much, only that it was absolutely ridiculous and he told me to put it back in her bag.'

*If he was so incensed, why didn't he destroy it himself*, thought Henderson and scribbled that on his pad.

'You said there was a sheet of instructions.' Henderson herded her back to that point. 'Typed or handwritten?'

'Her writing, very clear capitals, a line to each point. It was written as if . . . for . . . written to someone' – this was going to sound very wrong – '. . . to someone who would do it for her, if she couldn't manage it herself.'

Barrett raised her eyebrows. Henderson didn't react. 'Can you remember what it said?'

'At the top there was an instruction in very large letters that under no circumstances should she be resuscitated. Then a line denoting a new section which was about using the drug: that it had to be administered orally, on an empty stomach and that all evidence should be destroyed so that no one would know she had ended her own life.'

'Why didn't she want anyone to know that?' asked Barrett.

'She thought suicide was a weakness and a sin against God. She fell out with someone quite spectacularly at the church she attended after spouting her theories on that after their son had hanged himself. It caused a lot of trouble.'

'Whose computer did she use to buy this drug on?'

'Presumably her own,' replied Bonnie. 'It was an ancient Hewlett Packard, a hulking great thing. Stephen smashed it up when she died and took it to the dump because he didn't want anyone accessing his mum's personal stuff.'

'And what happened on the day of her death?' asked Henderson, his voice low, gentle, coaxing.

'Can I go back to the previous day?' asked Bonnie and Henderson nodded. 'Just before she went to sleep, she found she couldn't swallow. She went into a total panic and started coughing and choking and I rang 999 but Stephen grabbed the phone from me before it connected. He said that his mother had told us that she did not want to be resuscitated and we had to respect her wishes so we had to stand there, watching her struggle for breath and I didn't know what to do so I held her and she came out of it. It was horrible, horrible.'

Bonnie folded forwards. The memory was intense and disturbing.

'I really think my client might need a break,' insisted David Charles.

'No, I'm fine. Please.' Bonnie blew her nose and took a deep breath. 'It scared Alma so much, it was the signal she was waiting for. When I tried to settle her for the night, she was agitated because she was trying to speak and it was very hard for her to be understood. I had got used to the sounds she made though, so I was pretty sure she was trying to say "tomorrow". I repeated it back to her to make sure and she nodded.'

'And what did you think was going to happen tomorrow?' asked Barrett. Her tone was flat, disbelieving.

'That it was the day when she was going to kill herself,' said Bonnie. 'It couldn't mean anything else. If you'd been there with her, seen how this disease was stripping her of her every dignity, you would have known that is what she was telling me. She was scared of dying, but after that episode, she was more scared of living.'

'So we come to March the fifteenth,' said Henderson. 'What happened on that day?'

'I woke up, had breakfast with my husband and then he went out to work . . .'

'A normal day then?' asked Barrett.

'Well . . .' Bonnie lifted and dropped her shoulders. 'As normal as it can be with the possibility of what might happen sometime during it.'

'Your husband went to work, you say. Did you tell him that his mother had made noises that she wanted to die on that day?' Barrett's tone was overtly derisive and David Charles's annoyance showed in the way he tapped his pen on the table, warning her.

'Yes of course I told him and asked him to take the day off. After Alma had nearly choked, I was scared to be alone with her because I wasn't sure that I could watch her go through that again without ringing an ambulance. I would have been cursed if I did and cursed if I didn't. I hadn't slept very well, I couldn't get the image of her panicking out of my head.'

'But he didn't take the day off?' Barrett pushed, wanting an answer to this particular question.

'No. He said that he couldn't. He had an important meeting to go to.'

Barrett raised her eyebrows. She didn't know it but she was thinking the same as the solicitor and Henderson: if what she was saying was true, Stephen Brookland was an insensitive arsehole at best.

'I imagine you were very tired by this stage,' Henderson said softly.

'I was, yes,' said Bonnie. And she had been. When she wasn't working at Grimshaw's, she was cleaning, feeding and keeping Alma company or cleaning the house and feeding Stephen. Even when she was asleep, her ear was permanently cocked for signs of distress from Alma's room. She was mentally and physically exhausted by then.

'And how was Mrs Brookland that day?'

'Weak,' said Bonnie. 'She wouldn't eat anything. She was scared of triggering off that swallowing thing again, I think. She let me put a sponge to her lips with iced water on it.'

'Talk us through the day,' said Henderson.

'I changed her, gave her a wash with a flannel, she liked to be clean. She . . .' Bonnie had been about to tell them what Alma had said to her, but they wouldn't believe her. Besides, it was a private moment and for no one else's ears but hers. 'She . . . I mean I brushed her hair, patted a bit of her powder on her face. We watched a couple of antique and home restoration programmes because she liked those, then she had a nap and I hung out the washing – she needed clean sheets on her bed at least once a day. I checked on her every twenty minutes and when she was awake, just after two-thirty, I brought her some soup but she couldn't eat it. So I read to her. *Persuasion*, by Jane Austen. The last quarter of the book. Then Stephen came home from work and had his tea.'

He hadn't been very pleased that it had been some of the broth that Bonnie had made for Alma and not the customary meat and two veg, but she didn't mention that trivial detail to the police.

'Then he went up to see his mother just after seven and when he came downstairs, he announced he was going out.'

'Did he say where he was going?'

'No, just out and that he would be back at ten. He never went out in the evening. I was sure he was deliberately . . . getting out of the way.'

Brookland had said that he had been out watching a

football match in a pub, though he couldn't remember which pub or which match. He'd been upset about how poorly his mother was and wanted some time away from the house to recharge his batteries, he'd explained. Henderson had thought at the time that it was his wife who was the one that needed her batteries recharging. If what Bonnie Brookland was telling them was true, Stephen Brookland had left her to deal with it. Nice.

'So after your husband had left the house, what happened then?'

'I went back upstairs to sit with Alma. She was upset when I went in. I think it was because she knew that she would never see her son again.' She gave a sudden gasping sob. 'He should have been there with her. He should have been there for his mum. My dad died when I wasn't there but Stephen had the choice to be with her right at the end.' Barrett passed Bonnie the rest of the pack of tissues that she had in her pocket and Bonnie apologised for her outburst. She dabbed her eyes, as she had dabbed Alma's when she found her crying. 'I tried to wet her lips with the sponge, but she wouldn't let me. She pointed to her bag and I knew what she wanted. I really didn't want to get it, but she was ready. I could see that she'd had enough.'

Bonnie lifted her head and saw the two police officers waiting for her to continue. She knew they dealt in facts and not suppositions. If only she could have shown them the pictures in her head of Alma's determined face, the strength shining in her usually dull eyes.

'I passed her the bag. It took her a long time to open it because she couldn't flick the clasp but she kept trying until eventually she did it. Then she dragged the packet out and the bottle and tried to screw off the top but she couldn't do it. So she pushed it across the quilt to me.'

All eyes were on Bonnie now because this was the kernel of the story.

'. . . and I opened it for her. I took off the lid and gave it back to her.'

Which is why they'd find Bonnie's fingerprints on the bottle that Stephen Brookland had produced. He said that something about his wife's account of what happened hadn't rung true and so he'd had a feeling that he should keep it safely stored away.

'There wasn't much liquid in the bottle but she couldn't lift it to her mouth and was struggling. It was awful to watch. Then she looked up and said, "Bonnie". It was the first time she'd ever called me Bonnie and the word came out clear as a bell. She was asking me for help, I have no doubts on that.'

'And did you help?' asked Henderson.

'Yes,' said Bonnie. 'I lifted it to the height of her mouth but I was very careful to leave a gap; it was she who leaned forward and put her lip against it and she nudged at it like this—' Bonnie demonstrated, butting her mouth against a hand curled around an imaginary bottle. 'She swallowed all the liquid, then she sank back against the pillow and I sat on the bed next to her with my arm around her. She drifted off to sleep and didn't wake up. I don't know exactly when she died. I was still there when Stephen came in but she had gone.'

'What happened then? As precisely as you can, please.'

'He walked into the bedroom and I told him that she had slipped away, very peacefully, and he said that she had a good death and went the way she wanted to go.' She thought he might have kissed his mum then, let down his emotional fence, but he hadn't. 'Then he asked me to tell him what had happened, so I told him from her pointing to her purse onwards. He said –' her voice faltered '– I must have tilted the bottle because she would never have been able to drink it otherwise.'

Henderson shifted in his chair. This was a game-changer. This tipped the case from assisted suicide to murder.

'You can't remember if you tilted the bottle?' he asked her.

'I was sure I didn't. When it was happening I was so careful to let her take the lead, but when Stephen said my account of things wasn't likely, doubts crept in . . .' She passed her hand wearily across her eyes.

'Jesus Christ,' said Barrett, louder than she'd intended, which caused David Charles to tap his pen against his notepad with overt annoyance.

'And what happened then?' prompted Henderson.

'I panicked that he was right and I was wrong. I wanted to ring the police and tell them that I'd helped her commit suicide but Stephen said that I wasn't to do that because no one must know. He said that it was unthinkable that I should even consider it when Alma had gone to so much trouble to do what she had done secretly and that the details didn't matter really because her aim had been achieved in the end. I told him that the details did matter but he wouldn't discuss it any further, he just ordered me to go and sort myself out whilst he rang for the doctor.'

'What do you mean "sort yourself out"?' asked Barrett, wrinkling up her nose.

'Well, I took it to mean wash my face, brush my hair. I looked a bit of a wreck. Just before I left the room, he asked me where the bottle was. It was on the bedside table.'

'What happened to it then?'

'He said he'd move it. And he obviously did because it wasn't there when I went back in there later.'

Henderson turned to a new page in his pad. 'I understand that you and Mr Brookland have recently become estranged.' *And lucky for you*, he thought to himself.

'I've started divorce proceedings, yes,' said Bonnie. 'I was going to leave him before but Stephen said that he would report me to the police if I did, so I stayed. I'm glad it's happened. It's been hanging over my head for far too many years.'

'Sorry, you said *before*. When was this?' asked Henderson, thinking that this was noteworthy.

'Four years ago. I told him I was leaving, I hadn't a clue where I'd have gone but I couldn't stand living with him any longer and I had to get out. He told me that I owed him for his silence.'

It was certainly starting to look to Henderson as if Brookland knew more about his mother's death than he was saying, but he'd bring that up with him at their next meeting.

'So, you left your husband recently, can you remember the date?'

'May the tenth.'

Barrett checked her notes. 'And so let's go to the conversation you had on that day with your husband about your mother-in-law. How exactly did that start?'

Bonnie looked at her blankly. 'What conversation?'

Barrett licked her lips. 'The conversation in which you admitted to Stephen Brookland that you had forced the liquid in the bottle down his mother's neck because you were fed up of looking after her. You've already said how much hard work she was.'

Barrett's words flapped in the air as if they were bunting. Bonnie was momentarily stunned into silence.

'I don't understand. Forced? I never . . . Why would I . . .?' she said eventually, her eyes travelling from the detectives to the solicitor and back again. 'I did help her do what she wanted to do and Stephen knew that all along. But Alma was never mentioned on the day I left. Honestly. I tried to get out of the house without him seeing me because I knew he'd try and stop me going. But he locked me in my bedroom. My boss came round when I didn't turn up for work and he heard me shouting for help.'

*Well, Brookland hadn't mentioned that,* thought Henderson. If it was true, of course.

'And your boss is?'

Bonnie closed her eyes against the thought that she might have just dragged Lew into this mess. She gave a heartfelt sigh and answered, 'Lewis Harley. The Pot of Gold antiques centre in Spring Hill Square. If you don't have to contact him, please don't. I don't want to lose my job.'

Henderson recognised the name. Brookland had called him 'her fancy man'. He made Bonnie no promises though. He wouldn't go and see Lewis Harley if it wasn't relevant to the enquiry, but he would if they uncovered something that might make a visit essential.

'You say you left your husband on Friday May the tenth. Are you definite about that?'

'Oh yes. I couldn't forget it.'

Henderson tapped his fingernail on the desk as he weighed something up in his head. So there were over three weeks between the date when Stephen Brookland said his wife revealed she had murdered his mother and the date when he walked into the police station to report it.

'And was that the last time you had contact with your husband?'

'No. That was last Tuesday – the twenty-eighth. He'd sent me a letter a couple of weeks before when he realised that I'd filed for divorce. He wanted me to change my mind by the end of the month or he said he was going to the police about me. I didn't respond so he came into the shop on Tuesday and started shouting at me but then customers came in so he went.'

Brookland was emotionally blackmailing his wife then, thought Henderson. It said something that she would rather be arrested for a possible murder than return to him.

'Do you still have the letter?' asked Barrett.

'Yes.'

'Can you let me have that, please?' asked David Charles eagerly.

'Yes of course,' replied Bonnie.

David Charles insisted then that Bonnie have a break. They were all ready for one.

Henderson couldn't wait to see Stephen Brookland again, in the light of this interview, and Katherine Ellison, the friend. Historic cases were always a nightmare though, too many false memories and missing details. He was looking forward to going home already, and it wasn't even anywhere near lunchtime yet.

Bonnie was escorted to the toilet and Barrett, Henderson and David Charles sat in the interview room, backs relaxed against the chairs.

'Could you perhaps have a quiet word in Mr Brookland's ear that it would be best if he ceased from contact with his wife,' said David Charles, raising a brace of hopeful eyebrows at Henderson, who nodded by way of response. He'd be more than happy to do that. Brookland fancied himself as Columbo and Quincy combined and that sort of prat could easily damage an investigation.

'She's very keen to spill all the beans, isn't she?' said Barrett. 'Too keen. I'd call that suspicious.'

'Would you now?' David Charles dismissed Barrett's deduction with acute disdain.

That annoyed Barrett so she sniped, 'Yep. It's looking more like a murder than an assisted suicide to me.'

'It's not your place to be judge and jury, is it?' said David Charles, clearly irritated.

'Pardon me for speaking,' tutted Barrett, looking for support from Henderson, but finding none.

'She doesn't have to prove she's innocent, *madam*,' said David Charles, loading the word with scorn. 'You have to prove she's guilty. That's how it works in this country and you should know that.' He stood up abruptly and left the room to have a word with Bonnie before she came back in. He wanted to check she hadn't felt coerced into saying things she shouldn't.

Barrett sat in a cowed silence, with warm pink cheeks.

'Word of warning, don't try and be a smartarse with David Charles,' said Henderson. 'He will chew you up whole and spit you out in bits. And keep your theories to yourself.'

'Lesson learned,' said Barrett, saluting him.

'Go get some teas in,' Henderson ordered. 'I've never been as ready for one in my life.'

After Bonnie had read and signed her statement, she sat in the interview room and drank the last of her lukewarm brew whilst being told what would happen next.

'You're being bailed to come back to the police station, pending further enquiries. It'll be about six weeks, you'll be given the actual date before you leave. You and I will be in touch, obviously. The police will probably appoint you a Family Liaison Officer to—'

'I don't want anyone,' replied Bonnie. 'I just want things to take their course now.'

'Okay.' David Charles didn't press her on that. She might decide that she did need one after all when the high intensity had settled down. 'Let's go and get your possessions signed for and then you can go home.'

Bonnie looked at him in confusion. 'Really?' She had expected to be there for hours more at least.

'You aren't going to run off anywhere, are you?' asked Henderson, with warmth and just the right amount of humour.

'No, not at all,' said Bonnie quickly.

'The police now have to gather evidence and present it to the Crown Prosecution Service, who will judge whether it is in the public interest to prosecute you. We can talk it through in more detail when you come and see me,' added David.

'The tea's rubbish here, isn't it? Get yourself home and have a proper cup,' said Henderson after Bonnie had been reunited with her belongings. She had been booked to return to the police station on 5 July. Henderson watched her leave the building cautiously, as if she expected alarms to start going off and policemen to start running at her. He had an old copper's hunch that this woman's version of events was much closer to what actually happened than what her husband had said. It sounded to him as if Stephen Brookland quite deliberately put doubt in her mind that she'd tilted the bottle and doubled his chances of controlling her. If he couldn't manage to incriminate her, then, as a person with a conscience, she was likely to incriminate herself. Then again, he'd been fooled a couple of times over the years. Some people were masters of spinning a convincing yarn. His job was to gather every piece of relevant evidence and let the CPS do the rest. Stephen Brookland was a despicable man, but that didn't mean he wasn't telling the truth.

He didn't say it aloud, but he wished the woman well because if what she'd told them had been true, the next few weeks at least were going to be hell for her. Decent people found it very hard to live a normal life with a possible trial hanging over their heads, especially one that could send them to prison for fourteen years.

# Chapter 61

Gemma looked absolutely terrible as she walked towards Lew. She had swollen eyes and appeared totally battered by life in stark contrast to twenty-four hours ago when he'd met her in Tesco and she'd looked radiant, beautified by her secret pregnancy and was looking forward to having a fun evening with some of the people she loved best in the world.

Lew stood up to greet her and kissed her on the cheek, but her arms wrapped around him and she held on to him tightly.

'Come on, sit down, Gem,' he said, pulling the chair out from under the table for her. He'd picked a quiet corner one on Higher Hoppleton Garden Centre's terrace. 'You all right?' he asked, though it was a daft question.

'Lew, I'm so sorry,' said Gemma. 'The one person I shouldn't have hurt was you. You didn't deserve it.'

'I got us a pot of tea,' said Lew, pouring it out. 'Hope that's okay.'

'Fine, thank you.'

They both drew comfort from the warmth of the cups as

they cradled them in their hands. Neither of them knew what to say.

'So, where to start?' said Lew eventually because otherwise they would have been sitting there in silence for ever.

'Have you spoken about it to . . .?' asked Gemma. She couldn't bring herself to say Charlotte's name.

'No. Have you and Jason talked?'

'We haven't done anything but talk,' said Gemma.

'Does he know you're here with me?'

'Yes. I think he'll try and get in touch with you . . .'

'Tell him not to bother,' said Lew, jaw tightening. 'We have nothing to say to each other.'

'I'm so angry,' said Gemma, ripping a serviette out of the holder on the table in preparation for the tears that were pressing against the back of her eyes. 'I punched him after you'd left.'

'You need to remember you're pregnant, Gem.'

'I don't want to be a single mum,' said Gemma, lowering her head and Lew saw tears splash on the surface of the table. 'I hate him, I hate him so much. What a mess.'

Lew reached over and squeezed her arm. 'You don't have to make excuses, Gem. It's not up to me if you leave him or not.'

'Will you leave Charlotte?'

'I don't know,' he lied, because he did know.

Gemma sighed deeply. 'It was supposed to be his day off yesterday. I was going to surprise him and do a pregnancy test as soon as we woke up so we could sit and watch the lines appear together but he got up early and went into work. So I did it alone because I couldn't wait to find out. I've kept thinking, if only I'd woken up earlier, I'd have persuaded him not to go in, we'd have had such a great morning, we'd have gone to tell our parents and I'd have missed Regina calling. I'd never have known . . .'

'Let me stop you right there,' said Lew. 'Regina would have told you at some point.'

'Do you think?'

'Of course she would. She must have been desperate for an opportunity and she'd have made one if she hadn't found one.'

Gemma said resignedly, 'Yeah, you're probably right.'

'So what exactly did she say to you? Please don't hold anything back, Gem. I need to know it all.' He knew that Gemma was the type to soften things at the edges so they didn't hurt so much. Usually. 'Please. Don't do me any favours.'

Gemma nodded. 'Then I'm so sorry for anything I'm going to tell you today. I will try to say it all exactly as it happened.'

'Thank you.'

Gemma took a fortifying breath. 'Regina was waiting for me when I came back from the supermarket. She said she was just calling by. I knew she must be desperate for company because she had never done it before. I told her that she and I were not friends because she'd always treated me like a lesser being and then she started spitting like an old cobra. That was when she told me that Charlotte wasn't my friend either because' – Gemma drew speech marks in the air – '"She's been screwing your husband for months." My heart stopped, Lew. I asked her what the hell she was talking about because my first thought was that she was lying, shit-stirring, being Regina, but too many things rang true. She told me that when Charlotte stayed over after Patrick walked out, they'd both got pissed together, played some daft truth and dare game. Charlotte decided to share her big secret that she could be every bit as wild and wanton as swinging Regina. She was probably so hammered she thought it might impress her. I don't know why she did that to me – and you – but I do know why Jason shagged your wife, at least I do if he's telling me the truth.'

Jealousy. He wanted some of what Lew had, it was obvious to him. A modern-day equivalent of a cannibal eating someone to absorb their qualities. Plus daring, laddishness and a soupçon of excitement with an attractive, well-preserved woman. Even though he had a beautiful woman of his own, who was a much nicer person than Charlotte.

'He told me everything,' said Gemma. 'It started about six months ago. Just after his business had really begun to take off. It was just sex, no-strings thrills, they didn't actually go out on dates or anything. I don't know if that makes it better or worse.'

That they risked hurting their partners for something they could both have had at home . . . that made it worse in Lew's book, but he didn't say it aloud. Something danced on the edge of his thoughts about the dinner party at Patrick's and Regina's: Jason and Charlotte talking about cars: *I need something more satisfactory than I have at the moment. A little less conservative and more racy.* They'd been flaunting it in plain sight, enjoying their sordid little secret. *Come in my office.*

'I don't want to ever see Charlotte again,' said Gemma. 'I know that it takes two to tango but I have to hate her for the both of them. I expect you feel the same about Jason.'

Lew gave his shoulders the merest shrug but if he was honest, the 'affair' paled into insignificance against the other truth he'd learned. He was wounded by Jason's duplicity and petty jealousy and he knew that if he suddenly appeared in front of him, Lew's testosterone levels would spike and his fists would bunch, but everything was drowned under the weight of what Charlotte had done to their child.

Lew's voice was a croak when he spoke next. 'Tell me the truth about my baby, Gemma.'

'Oh God, Lew, I am so sorry. I couldn't tell you, I swore to her that I'd keep her secret. She put me in a terrible position when she asked me to go with her to the clinic.'

'You went with her?' Lew's tone was disbelieving, laced with disappointment.

'Please don't look at me like that, Lew. I was her best friend and I was there for her but – I know this sounds really bad – until yesterday, until I saw those two lines on the test, I didn't really grasp the full impact of what she'd done.'

Lew put the cup on the table before it fell out of his hands. 'Why did she do it?'

'Oh God.' Gemma shook her head slowly from side to side. 'This should come from her.'

'How can I trust her to tell me the truth?' said Lew. 'Tell me, Gemma. No lies. I've had years and years of them.'

'She changed her mind.' Gemma blurted out the words as if they were too hot for her mouth.

Lew let the words sink in. 'Changed her mind? Like it was a handbag?'

Gemma licked her lips nervously as if lubricating the way for the words which would come out next. 'She said that she didn't want to be left alone with a baby whilst you were working away all week. She said she'd mistimed this pregnancy and she would be better off having a child later on.'

'But we talked about what would happen. She wouldn't have been alone. I would have got another job, come back up north . . .' Gemma raised her eyes to him and Lew thought how strange it was that you could read so much in two round circles of colour, almost a psychic message. Gemma didn't need to say anything; her stare said it all. 'I would have come back up north . . .' The penny dropped. '. . . for less money. That's why, isn't it?'

'I told her, Lew. I told her that it wasn't right. I'm so sorry. You are the loveliest man I know. You deserve better.' She slipped her hand into Lew's and felt how cold and limp his fingers were. Dead as the rest of him was. Dead as his marriage because there was no way back from this.

# Chapter 62

David Charles kindly dropped Bonnie off at home, right to the door. He had told her that best case scenario, the CPS would find there was no public interest in a prosecution even if there was enough evidence to bring this case to trial. But if it did and she was found guilty, she could face a maximum of fourteen years in prison. It was, however, unlikely she would get the full fourteen, she could get ten which would mean she was out in five and the last couple of years would probably be served in an open prison. If she was found guilty and sent down, they would appeal against the conviction. He didn't want to scare her but he had to give her all the facts. She only had to read the newspapers if she wanted to inform herself what might happen. Recently there had been a highly emotive case of a man who had assisted his elderly sister to end her life. The prosecution had gone for his jugular, insisting he had murdered her for personal gain and the jury had bought it. The subject of euthanasia polarised opinion and in the present climate, the courts were definitely swaying towards intolerance of it.

When Bonnie got out of the car, everything seemed too

bright in the sunlight and she scuttled inside, seeking the dark
and security of the dear four walls of her rented home. She
felt dazed and battered, as if she had been hauled over painful
coals of her past. She'd told the truth to the police and could
swear to all of it but the part where she lifted the bottle to
Alma's lips. Then again, she'd been so careful to let Alma call
the shots at every stage, she wouldn't have done what Stephen
said she must have and taken the lead. Now it appeared he
was accusing her of more: of declaring to him that she had
forced the bottle's contents into Alma's throat. It was beyond
lying, but a jury would believe him above her. He would be
so much calmer and less emotional in a court. And boiling all
the surplus meat of the story away, she *did* screw the lid off
the bottle for Alma and she *did* lift it up for her to drink and
she would have to admit to that because it was the truth. So
they'd be bound to believe her capable of murder.

She went straight upstairs, stripped off and had a shower
but no amount of soap would wash away the stain of shame;
it was underneath her skin, indelible, a constant reminder
that people could think she had killed a vulnerable old lady
because she was a burden.

Later she realised she needed milk but the thought of
going out to the shop terrified her. What if she was in the
*Daily Trumpet*?

'Oh God, oh God.' Her heartbeat started to race and her
shallow rapid breaths were making her light-headed. She sat
down on the sofa and tried to force her breathing back to a
regular rhythm. There was nothing for it, she had to go out
to the shop now or she might never be able to leave the
house again.

She picked up her bag and stepped out into the sunshine
feeling as if it were a huge spotlight above her head, picking

her out so everyone could see the criminal. Her eyes darted to everyone in the supermarket, checking to see if they were looking at her. She approached the newspaper cube with caution, wondering if she would see her photo on the front page, but the lead stories were all about yet another politician caught with his trousers down. She bought milk and a *Daily Trumpet* and paid for them using the self-service till. This is what agoraphobics must feel like, she thought, glimpsing a world of anxiety and super-awareness. The little house on Rainbow Lane had never felt like more of a sanctuary than it did when she got back to it. Her hands were shaking as she ripped through the pages of the *Trumpet*, but nothing was immediately obvious. She pored over the smaller articles, but couldn't find any mention. She would have to buy a *Trumpet* every day to check: forewarned was forearmed. In a panic, she took out her phone and rang the number of David Charles from the business card he had given her. He answered via the Bluetooth in his car.

'David, I'm so sorry to bother you, it's Bonnie Sherman. Look . . . will I be in the newspaper?'

'Possibly,' he answered. 'The newspapers don't always have the full info so it could either not be in at all because they don't know about it or need the space for other stories, or it might just be a couple of lines to say that a woman from Barnsley has been arrested for assisting a suicide and released on police bail. They could mention your name. It won't be in today though, it's too early.'

Bonnie felt sick. 'What about the national papers?'

'Hardly likely unless you're a celebrity or it's a very slow news day,' replied David. 'The police are now conducting an enquiry. Any reportage is likely to prejudice the outcome of a trial so if anything, you'll be given bare minimum coverage.' He didn't want to raise her hopes and tell her that the *Daily Trumpet* would probably leave it alone. The new editor was keen to stop ruffling feathers, though he'd need to sack every reporter he had in order to do that. 'Try to stay positive, Bonnie, and carry on with as normal a life as you can, because that will help you maintain some control. I'll be in touch when I have any information, and if there is anything else you need to ask, you know where I am.'

Bonnie's stomach dropped as much as if she'd been on the downward leg of a roller-coaster. All she could do was try to survive each day. Until this mess was over, one way or another.

# Chapter 63

Lew went back to the hotel to make some calls before he set off to the marital home, including one to an estate agent. He wouldn't be sorry to say goodbye to Woodlea, not in the way he had to The Beeches which had been full of his dreams and ambitions. The house he was about to sell was just four walls and a roof to him, full of stylish furniture and deep expensive carpets. It was both warm and cold, beautiful and ugly at the same time because it said to him that it was a house for a couple who would never have children running around it, recording their height against the doors. It was a house of failure – and now lies.

As Woodlea came into view, he wished he could fast forward one hour, when what he had to do was done. He wasn't looking forward to seeing Charlotte at all. She would launch a full emotional offensive; she would cry and beg and scream and absorb the blame, then vomit it back out in his direction. She would make Regina look like Anne of Green Gables because she was desperate to hang on to her comfortable no-maintenance life. He felt drained after a night of rubbish sleep and then having to hear what Gemma had to say; thoughts had been whirring around in his head and the task of dismantling life as he knew it felt enormous. It would be so much easier to talk it through, accept there had been mighty mistakes made, draw a line and continue as normal, purred his brain. Splitting up was a massive task, physically, financially, emotionally. At least he had the money to move out and create distance between him and his spouse whilst the arduous task of extrication took place. No wonder it took Bonnie so long to leave her unhappy marriage.

As he turned up the drive, he noticed Astrid the cleaner's battered Volvo parked there. He wondered if Charlotte had forgotten to cancel her, or was just carrying on as normal in the hope that the act would force all the jigsaw pieces back into the picture they were supposed to make. Well, I'll find out in a moment, said Lew to himself, pulling on the handbrake and slipping the ignition key into his pocket.

He walked in through the front door to find Astrid on her knees cleaning the skirting boards. It was a change to look down on her as she was six foot four and used to be a loosehead prop for Frankfurt rugby union club.

'Guten Morgen, Mr Harley,' she smiled up at him. 'Isn't it a luvverly day? I vish you had more cleaning to do on der outside of your haus. I'd get a reight sun-tan.'

'Yes, it's very sunny, Astrid,' he replied. He'd miss seeing Astrid, he realised. She was a lovely – if formidable – girl and incredibly hard-working. He'd never considered it before, but he wondered now what she really felt about the pampered wife who flittered around her house booking hair and beauty appointments whilst she dusted skirting boards and scrubbed toilets.

Charlotte appeared at the top of the stairs, coiffured and

made up, wearing heels and looking more as if she were going out to Firenze than sitting on her backside reading *Cosmopolitan*. 'Oh hello, Lewis,' she said. 'How was your conference last night?' She flashed a warning at him in her baby blue eyes to play along with the charade. She was pretending that he'd been away on business so that he wouldn't cause a scene in front of Astrid. *Is she actually serious*, said something sarcastic and scathing in his brain that had its arms crossed and was shaking its head in disbelief.

'I have no idea what you're talking about,' he replied, his tone measured and firm. 'As you well know, I spent the first of many nights in a hotel because I've left you.'

Astrid's eyes were screwed to the skirting board but her ears were as pricked and receptive as a twelve-foot satellite dish with radar attachment.

Charlotte was, as expected, horrified. Her eyes were firing missiles at her husband, though her mouth was set in a very stiff smile.

'Oh Lew, you are funny. He's only joking, Astrid.'

'No he isn't, Astrid,' he rode over her silent command not to wash their dirty linen in front of the cleaner.

Clinging on to her composure, Charlotte descended the stairs in her heels with rushed steps. 'Stop teasing and let's go into the kitchen and you can tell me why you didn't answer your phone over coffee. I was worried sick. I thought you'd had an accident.'

'Well, as you can see I'm perfectly fine,' said Lew, admiring the shine that Astrid had put on the parquet flooring. The new buyer would admire that floor because it cost a fortune. Say what you like about Charlotte but she had a flair for décor. 'And no, I don't want a coffee.'

They stood at either end of the hallway like two gunmen at the OK Corral.

'Well let's just get out of Astrid's way then.' Her teeth were starting to clench more now.

'Don't worry, I shall be getting right out of Astrid's way and yours,' said Lew. 'Astrid, I'd like to thank you for working for us because my wife was too lazy sitting on her toned arse, filing her nails and arranging assignations with her lover to have cleaned it herself.'

Astrid's eyes were now superglued onto the same part of the skirting that she'd been wiping for minutes now.

Charlotte squeaked. It was just audible but another semitone higher and it would have been firmly on the canine aural frequency spectrum.

'So are you going to tell me why you did screw Jason?' Lew addressed his wife, who was striding towards him now, trying to herd him into the kitchen but he wouldn't budge before he had apologised to Astrid. It was unfair of him to make her feel uncomfortable.

Astrid nodded a confirmation that she'd heard the apology and then, and only then, did Lew walk into the kitchen and close the door behind him and his wife. He lost no time in repeating the question.

'So?' He stood arms folded, waiting.

With no one to keep up appearances in front of, Charlotte's shoulders slumped as if she had been held up by strings which had suddenly lost their give. Lew prepared for her full Greek Tragedy onslaught.

'I didn't plan it,' she returned, with her volume switched down. 'I was lonely ... Please, Lew ...'

'We've never spent as much time together as we have done these past couple of years so that argument doesn't hold water does it, Charlotte? You wanted something *less conserv-ative and more racy* if I remember rightly from what you said at Patrick and Regina's party. I'm so sorry that life with me was so monotonous for you.'

'I ... you ...' Charlotte's face flooded red. She couldn't defend herself so she launched an attack. 'I was bored. Your job has always been more important to you than I am.'

'I've been working away all week in London since before we met,' he replied, calm and collected, at least on the out-side. Inside his emotions were raging currents, splashing against his ribcage, hammering on his chest wall to get out. 'I have never heard you once tell me that the arrangement bothered you.'

'I couldn't, could I?' spat Charlotte. 'You loved your job. You'd have hated me if you'd had to leave it for me, wouldn't you?'

'You didn't want me to leave it though, did you, Charlotte? You loved the big money I brought home. So much so that you got rid of our baby to keep on having it.'

She gasped and flapped her hand in front of her mouth as if it had the double purpose of fanning more oxygen her way and batting away the accusation. 'That is not what happened.'

'So tell me, what *did* happen?' Lew was as controlled as she was now agitated. 'Why did you abort our baby?'

'I was terrified of childbirth. You weren't around to talk to. You were always in London ... I wasn't sure I'd make a good mother ... You pushed me into it, Lewis.'

Lew listened to her and had a sudden vision of her picking excuses written on little notes from a tree. He would never get the truth from her because she was too ashamed to admit it, even to herself.

They'd been a couple for sixteen years and yet he was looking at her now as if she were someone he recognised but didn't know at all. The whole fabric of their relationship had been built on a foundation of lies. She had paid only lip service to their plans to have a family and had she ever loved him more than his money? He thought not. He had comforted her and worried about her so much since her supposed miscarriage. It had contributed to the stress that nearly killed him.

'I'll tell you what's going to happen now, Charlotte,' said Lew calmly. 'I have an appointment with a divorce solicitor this afternoon.' He half-wanted to laugh that he'd been so adamant he'd never be one of Adriana's clients. 'And I've already instructed an estate agent to deal with the sale of this house. I'll be showing him round in exactly twenty minutes. Feel free to stay or get out of the way for an hour.'

'Nooo ... Lewwwisss.' Charlotte dived on him, threw her arms around him, sobbed into his polo shirt. He carried on talking, arms by his sides, making himself heard, even above his wife's wailing. She appeared to have forgotten that Astrid could hear every word.

'It will happen, Charlotte, so make this as painless for yourself as possible. Sign the papers when they arrive and return them. I advise you to get your own solicitor, though you'll be paying for it yourself. I've stopped the credit cards so don't use them, oh and you won't be able to draw any money from the joint bank account – that will remain open to pay household direct debit bills only. You can stay here until the house is sold and I'll move out, or you can move out and I'll stay here, your choice. Obstruct me at all, do a *Regina* and I'll do my damnedest to make sure you'll get the bare minimum of what I have to give you. Play ball and I'll be more fair than you deserve because I want out of this marriage as soon as I can possibly extricate myself.'

Charlotte threw herself back from him angrily. 'You heartless bastard,' she said, and her hand came out to strike his face but he caught her wrist and held it firmly.

'I have never struck a woman in my life,' he said, rage stinging in his eyes, 'but I am closer to it now than I ever thought it possible to be. Now I'm going upstairs to pack some more of my things.' And he pushed her a little to the side yet she careered dramatically into the wall, yelping and holding her arm.

'It wasn't a baby yet. It was just a little blob. I'm not a monster,' she screamed. He didn't even grace that with a reply as he threw open the kitchen door and strode out to where Astrid was wringing her cloth in her bucket.

'Just in case you're wondering, Astrid, I didn't lay a finger on her.' He could guess that Charlotte might resort to an accusation of assault, especially if it might lead to more money and sympathy for her. The gloves were well and truly off now and their inner ferals would out. Sadly.

'I nivver zort that you did, Mr Harley. I am very zorry to hear zat—'

'Just get on with your bloody work and keep your fucking nose out,' Charlotte shouted at her cleaner, tottering out of the kitchen and clutching her arm as if it had been broken in fourteen different places.

'How dare—' Lew began, but his gallantry wasn't needed. Astrid had two inches and three stone on him. She straightened up, dropped her cloth in her bucket and put her hands on her hips.

'Nobody speaks to me like zat,' she said. 'I am eine cleaner not eine slave.'

Lew reached into his pocket and pulled out his wallet. He took out five of the twenty pound notes that were in there and pressed them into Astrid's hand.

'Astrid, you go home early. I won't be needing your services any more in this house because it's going up for sale. Please take this as a little thank you for all the folded toilet rolls and the towel animals, you've been a real lady.'

'Oh Mr Harley, zank you. You ev been a gentleman.' Astrid's eyes filled up with tears and she threw her considerable arms around Lew and hugged him. 'I shell miss you.' Then she released him, picked up her bucket and strode past Charlotte with an obvious 'humph' to collect the rest of her cleaning kit from the kitchen.

'I hate you, Lewis Harley,' yelled Charlotte, picking up her handbag and scrabbling around in it for her car keys.

'Anything else you want to say to me, do it through my solicitor,' he said coldly, heading for the staircase.

'I'll tell you why I slept with Jason,' she bawled at his back. 'Because I could.'

Lew didn't miss a beat. He'd heard so many lies from her that might be true or not. Either way, he was relieved and strangely fascinated to find that he really didn't care.

# Chapter 64

The editor of the *Daily Trumpet* put down the phone on yet another complaint, from the head of the council this time, missiling expletives at him down the line and as hopping mad as a rabbit with rabies. And it had been his fault this time, because he'd personally proof-read the article about the mayor spending the day interacting with local school children, only somehow it had landed on the newsstands as Derek Trubshaw spending the day *interfering* with children. The trouble was, more people bought the damned paper for the mistakes than they did for the news which was great for sales but not for his personal reputation. He had come to the *Trumpet* to turn it around into a respectable newspaper. He might as well have been Canute trying to hold the bloody sea back.

He found himself now on the horns of a dilemma about tomorrow morning's issue: should he publish the details he had of the woman who was accused of helping her terminally ill mother-in-law to shuffle off this mortal coil or give the woman a break and just nod to it? Could he really do with all the calls telling him he was a heartless shit as well as an incompetent one?

The phone rang again. The mayor was thinking of suing.

*Daily Trumpet* 4 June

A Barnsley woman was arrested at the
weekend on suspicion of assisting her mother-
in-law to commit suicide. She was released on
police bail pending further enquiries.

# Chapter 65

Bonnie picked up a copy of the *Daily Trumpet* from the newsagents after dropping off the letter Stephen had sent her into David Charles's office. She flicked through its pages before driving on to work. She found the mention on page nine, tucked into the left near the bottom just above an advert about a furniture sale. Bonnie could have wept with relief. Her name wasn't mentioned, there was no detail, no age, no address. She felt as if a tight belt around her chest had slipped a notch. She might still feel its presence, but she could breathe. Stephen would have seen it, she knew, and that worried her because he might feel duty-bound to highlight who the Barnsley woman was, but then again, he wouldn't want to prejudice the case that the police were presently building against her. Stephen would be pouring all of his poison into files containing his 'evidence' against her, she was sure of it, because that was the sort of thing he would do, but he would have to stay silent *sub judice*. The same legal system preparing to prosecute her, ironically, would be keeping her safe for now.

*

Lew walked into the Pot of Gold and breathed in the dear familiar scent of old things, polish, wood, must. It was the smell of normality, sanctuary, home. His late parents had barely a modern stick of furniture, everything was carved and heavy, and had previous lives in other people's houses and he loved the solidity of all the pieces he grew up amongst. It would be good to get back to work. Yesterday had been spent setting in motion the deconstruction of his married life: showing an estate agent around his house, a full hour with Adriana de Lacey, preparing a financial statement for the settlement, then a meal for one in the hotel bar and watching TV in his room. He'd stay there for now; he hadn't got the energy to look for somewhere to rent.

The huge longcase grandfather clock announced an accurate nine o'clock and on the third chime in walked Bonnie. Lovely Bonnie, part of this world that he knew would keep him tethered to sanity. She smiled a welcome at him but it sat tenuously on her lips.

'Good morning, Bonnie,' he called. 'Good weekend?'

How could she answer that honestly, she thought. 'Not bad. And yourself?'

Oh how to answer that, he thought. He went for the keep-it-simple approach, marvelling at his own composure. He felt as if he were wearing a mask, a hard tight one with a manufactured pre-painted smile. 'Yep.'

She took off her yellow summer mac and he noticed that she had on a navy dress with polka dots underneath. It wasn't like her to wear something so dark which made her look washed out and awfully fragile. There was something about her that made him not want to lie to her. He didn't think he had it in him to pretend that his life was just the same as it had been when he last saw her three days ago.

'Actually, it was a crap weekend, Bonnie. I left my wife. I might as well tell you just in case I get more phone calls on the office number than usual.' He shrugged his shoulders. 'C'est la vie.'

Bonnie didn't react immediately. There were a few moments' silence when the only sounds were the clocks, tocking their comforting rhythms, before she spoke.

'I'm so sorry to hear that, Lew. I'll make us a coffee, shall I?'

'A coffee would be good.' He gave her a smile of appreciation. She walked a step in the direction of the office, then turned back.

'I'm sorry. I didn't know what else to say.'

'I get that, Bonnie.' He gave a soft chuckle.

She didn't say that her natural reaction would have been to put her arms around him, press her warmth into his skin in the hope that it would find its way to his heart.

'We reach for the kettle as people, don't we?' she laughed gently. 'When we know we can't feed a soul, we look for the next best thing to comfort.'

'We do.'

When she went into the back room, she immediately noticed a copy of the *Daily Trumpet* on the desk. She wondered if his eyes had taken in the snippet about the anonymous woman who had helped her mother-in-law kill herself, not knowing it was she. Should she tell him before the police came calling, or Stephen painted *murderer* over the building in red paint? She hadn't ruled out that he might. But there were security cameras outside the building: he wouldn't risk being seen, surely? She was torturing herself thinking of all the ways Stephen Brookland could ruin her life. She no longer thought of him being connected to her, but as a vindictive stranger. She knew he wanted to punish her for leaving him, for upsetting his *way of things*. It was only a matter of time before Lew knew what was going on in her personal life. She should tell him first, before he heard it elsewhere with all its distortions. She gave herself the length it took the kettle to boil to decide what to do. When it clicked off, she knew she couldn't tell him. Not yet. She had confessed everything to the police, but she needed some respite for herself, a safe island of normal to stand on in the middle of the torrent. Being here in the shop was the happiest she had felt for many years. She just wanted to hang on to it a little longer.

As Bonnie handed Lew the coffee, she noticed immediately that he wasn't wearing his wedding ring. It had been his wife's birthday on Sunday. Bonnie got the impression he had spent a fortune on her in presents. And yet sometime over the weekend his marriage had crumbled. Hers had been falling brick by brick for years; Lew's seemed to have been instantly dynamited. She wouldn't have asked him how it had happened, but she wondered.

'Thank you,' he replied, taking a long sip, wondering how a mere instant coffee could taste so good. She always made them just right.

'Is there anything . . . I can do, silly question I know . . .' Bonnie asked, immediately chiding herself. 'Stupid of me, of course there isn't. Ignore that.'

'Bonnie.' Lew put down his coffee and turned to face her. He put his hands on her arms and looked into her huge hazel eyes. 'I just want everything to be as it usually is in here. With Stickalampinit bringing in his ridiculous creations, Long John spending an hour polishing one item of silver, Starstruck reciting anecdotes about film stars and you being you, holding it all together, making this place work. That's what you can do for me.'

Bonnie nodded. 'I understand,' and as much as she wanted his hands to remain on her, to savour the thrill of his contact, she stepped away from him on the pretence of needing to check something on the shop floor, because she couldn't bear the thought that if he relied on her to be stable and unchanging, she was going to let him down very badly.

# Chapter 66

Both Stephen Brookland and Katherine Ellison had the option of being interviewed in the comfort of their own homes and though the latter had accepted the privilege, Brookland had insisted on attending the police station so that he would put the police to as little trouble as possible. Henderson expected he would. Brookland was a grandiose man who was enjoying the theatre of it all, despite whatever tripe he said about being helpful. The family liaison officer had told Henderson that he was already driving her mad asking for updates every day.

'Thank you for coming in again, Mr Brookland,' Henderson smiled politely.

'Pleasure,' returned Stephen.

*I'll bet*, thought Henderson. 'Just a few points I'd like to clarify with you.'

'Certainly, Detective Sergeant. I'd like to be as much help as I can.'

Henderson couldn't understand how Bonnie Brookland had managed to live with him for thirteen years. Then again, he'd had one hell of a hold over her for the past five at least. He had control freak stamped all over him.

Barrett brought in three coffees. Henderson wanted Stephen Brookland to think they were all pals. Those eager to impress often 'forgot their script'. Niceties ensued. Was Brookland coping? Had the FLO been of assistance? Then, with the atmosphere greased, Henderson slid into the grist.

'So, Mr Brookland.' He leaned on the desk and templed his hands together. 'You say that you didn't know anything about your mother's plan to take her own life.'

'Absolutely not,' confirmed Stephen. 'I would never have let her. As I said to you, I only have my wife's word that she did. She is very plausible, I'm sure you've found that. All nicey-nicey, butter-wouldn't-melt. You should ask her last employer why she got the sack: dishonesty—'

Henderson cut off his vitriol with a respectful but controlled interjection. 'If we could keep to answering the question that would really help for now. The clearer the details, the stronger the case.'

That herded him back in line, as Henderson knew it would. 'Of course, Detective Sergeant. Well, no I didn't know. And of course when I walked in and saw my poor dear mother deceased, I was understandably shocked, which is why I didn't properly take it all in then. Naturally I believed my wife's version of events wholeheartedly at the time, but soon after I began to wonder.'

'Which is why you kept the drug bottle.'

'Indeed. My wife nursed my mother very adequately but I began to suspect that it had all been an act. For eight years she hated my mother and suddenly she couldn't do enough for her; it's odd, don't you think?'

'And yet you let your mother be cared for by her?'

'Well, yes.' Stephen shifted position in his seat. 'I was

working full-time, Mother didn't want any strangers around her. Bonita was the lesser of two evils.'

*I bet he's delighted to have used that line*, thought Henderson. 'Why did you save the bottle, Mr Brookland? Why not destroy it?'

'I was going to,' said Stephen. 'I was distraught enough to find my mother dead and then my wife drops the bombshell on me that she died by her own hand. I couldn't think properly. My wife left me alone with Mother to say my goodbyes. As I was doing so, the thought came to me that something was very wrong here. Firstly, my mother would not have committed suicide, she thought it was a disgrace. You can check with the church she attended, she upset quite a few people with her views on it. Secondly, my mother and I were very close. She would not have done something like that without my knowledge. Nor would she have chosen to confide in Bonita. And it was very suspicious that my mother supposedly committed suicide when I was out for the evening. She would have wanted me by her side, don't you think, rather than a woman whom she had always despised and who had always despised her. My mother was an inconvenience to my wife. All this flashed through my mind as if my mother herself had put the thoughts there for me, so before I sent for the doctor, I decided to get a plastic bag and keep the bottle just in case.'

'Just in case what?' asked Henderson. *Just in case you wanted to bring your wife to heel*?

'Just in case there was a post mortem, of course,' Stephen said imperiously.

'But your wife had admitted to you that she had handled the bottle, hadn't she?'

'Yes, as I said, she had. She was too candid in my opinion. I found that very questionable.'

Barrett made an unconscious noise of agreement, which pleased Stephen. Henderson didn't react but he made a mental note to mention later to Barrett to try not to let her personal opinions bleed into interviews.

'So, when there was no post mortem and your mother was buried, why didn't you destroy it then?'

Stephen crossed his legs and folded his arms slowly, a gesture that gave him a few seconds to think of an answer, Henderson deduced.

'Forensic scientists are coming up with more and more advances each day. I kept the bottle because I thought that maybe in the future it might produce evidence to say that my mother had been murdered.'

'Like a voice recording?' Henderson kept his face serious.

'Like some sort of chemical that humans give out when being forced into doing something against their will, I mean,' said Stephen, not recognising that Henderson was being facetious.

'I see,' said Henderson, nodding in agreement.

'What I will say is that my mother would have been horrified that anyone thought she had committed suicide. She might have been a very old lady and incredibly ill but she was very sharp up here.' He tapped his forehead. 'She should have been a politician, she could run rings around anyone verbally, was meticulous in detail, a master bridge player, she made sure she covered every eventuality when she organised anything.'

'She sounds a wonderful woman,' said Barrett, with sympathy.

'She was. I loved her very much,' said Stephen. He bowed his head and apologised for having to take a second to compose himself before continuing. 'My mother walked towards death with her head held high, which is why it is ludicrous to think that she bought a veterinary drug from Mexico to end her own life.'

'You presumably are the sole beneficiary of your mother's will?'

'Yes, although she left a small legacy to her bridge club for them to buy new chairs.'

'She had a life insurance policy?'

'Yes, I think I told you that before.'

'You did. Would the insurance have been voided by suicide?'

There was a pause before Stephen answered. A swallow.

'I don't know. I didn't check.'

'It would have been fraudulent to claim, surely, if you knew that your mother had committed suicide?' said Barrett.

'I wasn't sure that she had though.'

'So you suspected your wife of murder but you didn't go to the police?' Henderson raised a mental high five to himself.

Brookland rubbed his head as if it were Aladdin's lamp and a genie would come and take him away from this question trap.

'I had no evidence to prove either suicide or murder. In the end I decided that I should support and protect my wife. My mother would not have wanted to be stained with the stigma of suicide so that seemed the only course of action at the time. I had to honour my mother's memory and as for my wife . . . I vowed for better for worse in front of a registrar.' His voice was rising, he was rattled.

'But now, of course, she's left you.'

Yes.' His jaw muscles were spasming. 'And if you are insinuating this is some sort of vengeance, then you are very wrong. I would not have betrayed her if she had not told me when she walked out of the door, as a vicious parting shot, that she had killed my mother: "forced the contents of the bottle down her neck because I was fed up of nursing the old bat but you'll never be able to prove it" were more or less her exact words. My goodness, Sergeant. I was so glad that I'd kept the bottle then. I wanted to smash it into her laughing, disgusting fa—' He recovered quickly. 'I apologise. I'm very upset. And I have to admit, I feel as if I'm on trial myself.'

'No apology needed, Mr Brookland. But if this does come to trial, a barrister will be asking these sorts of questions. It's a complicated and emotional case and the devil is in the detail.'

'Oh yes, the devil,' humphed Stephen Brookland, as if he knew it so well because he'd been married to it.

'Yet you didn't come straight to the police after she said this to you?' Henderson delivered the line smoothly.

'Pardon?'

'You left it over three weeks.' Henderson noticed Brookland's neck was blotchy at the collar.

'There was a reason for that. I . . .'

'You wanted your wife to go back to you,' said Henderson, nodding as if he understood and agreed. 'Presumably we wouldn't have met if she had.' He turned pointedly to Barrett and asked, 'Do we have the copy of Mrs Brookland's letter yet?'

'Erm . . . not sure if it's arrived yet but her solicitor was going to email it over, I believe,' came the reply.

Brookland sat up straight in his chair, tension coming off

him in waves though he did his best to hide it. 'What you have to remember is that I was in shock when she told me. I thought they were just words meant to wound, we did have quite a heated row after all. I am not the sort of person to act rashly, I needed to process it all. It was very painful going over the events of my mother's death, but essential and I'm afraid to say that I became convinced my wife had blurted out the real truth at last. I thought by sending her that letter I might force her to confess to the authorities before I reported her, therefore making your job easier. As you know, she did not turn herself in to you, so what does that tell you about her, hmm? My hand was forced at that point. But at least after five years, the truth is known.'

Very well improvised, thought Henderson. 'Thank you for clearing that up. I think that's all for now,' he smiled, checking with Barrett who nodded in agreement. 'Thank you for coming in. It's much appreciated.'

'You need to speak to Mrs Katherine Ellison if you haven't already,' said Stephen. 'I'm sure she will convince you that there is skulduggery afoot.'

Who the hell talks like that, thought Henderson as he assured Mr Brookland that they would indeed be speaking to his mother's best – and, it seemed, only – friend.

# Chapter 67

On the Friday of that week, Mart Deco staggered into the shop like a drunken bumble bee with a large square electrical appliance, which he almost dropped by the counter. He was purple-faced when he straightened up again. Mart might have been a massive bloke but he had 'a glass back'. He was waiting for an operation on a disc.

'Martin, what on earth . . .' Bonnie rushed towards him. 'You'll be doing yourself a mischief. Here, sit down.' She pulled a fiddleback chair from under a nearby table and pushed Mart down on it whilst he took his asthma inhaler out of his pocket and drew the spray into his lungs.

'It's a washing machine,' said Martin, in between puffs.

'Shut up talking for a minute,' Bonnie commanded.

Martin nodded and then when he got his breath back he continued. 'As I was saying, it's a washing machine. It sits on your work surface. It's a couple of years old but it works smashing. It's the wife's sister's. She's just won a proper one in a competition. Dead lucky she is. She won a week in the Isle of Wight in April. Anyway, she said that it was a waste to dump it because it's a cracking little thing and I said I know just the home for it. She's cleaned it up and the instruction book is inside.'

'Oh Mart, that's so lovely of you. How much do you want . . .?'

'I don't want owt for it,' Martin tutted. 'It'll save me a trip to the dump. And it would have been a shame, because as I said, it works.'

Lew appeared from the back room where he'd been taking a private call from the estate agent telling him that Woodlea would be up on their website within the hour.

'Mart's brought me a washing machine,' said Bonnie, attempting to pick it up and move it out of the way. It was a dead weight though and it didn't budge.

'Whoa, you'll do yourself an injury,' yelled Mart and Lew together.

'Stand back please and leave it to the experts,' said Lew, lifting it far more easily than either of the others. 'I'll put it in the back room for now.'

'Or I can put it straight in my car?' suggested Bonnie.

'You won't be able to lift it out at the other end though, Bonnie. I'll drop it off for you after work,' said Lew.

'I don't want to put you to any troub—'

Lew cut off her protest. 'I insist.'

'Eh, did you hear that Grimshaw is packing up?' said Mart, suddenly excited. 'He's bought a bar abroad. He's sold the shop to a bloke who does kitchens.'

'That's an end of an era,' said Bonnie with more than a hint of sadness. Her world was changing beyond recognition. Even Grimshaw's shop, as dingy as it had become, was familiar and it was those constants that gave her reference points of stability. They were buoys in cold, uncertain waters whose current was dragging her every day towards the edge of something that made Niagara Falls look like a trickle.

As soon as Bonnie got home, she scurried around the house straightening things, hanging up the cardigan she had left draped over the arm of her sofa, gathering up all the pieces of craft items she had left out on the coffee table, giving the work surface in the kitchen a wipe down, spraying some Febreze into the air to mask the faint damp smell. The little house was clean and tidy but it was a few country miles away from what Lew was used to and Bonnie felt slightly shamed that he'd see her in the midst of all her hotch-potch. He arrived at the door five minutes after she had with the washing machine in his arms and she guided him through to the kitchen. It took up half the available work surface but there was nowhere else for it to go. And it would be a big improvement on washing things in the sink and drip drying them on the short line outside.

'Thank you,' said Bonnie, rubbing her hands together nervously. 'Can I get you a coffee or something?'

'A coffee would be lovely,' said Lew. Anything to delay going back to the Holiday Inn for a very long evening alone.

Whilst Bonnie went to fill the kettle, Lew sat on the sofa and looked around. What a mix of furniture, he thought with a smile. And yet strangely, all the pieces sat harmoniously with each other. The table and chairs were the perfect size for the recess at the side of the kitchen door, the sofa was snug under the window, the coffee table just right for the space available. Bonnie had hung some curtains at the window, Lew recognised them from a house clearance haul he'd acquired. They were dark blue velvet, and she had secured them to their tie-back hooks with red rope twists.

The small hearth had a burst of fake flowers where logs would crackle in winter. The mantelpiece above had photos on it in frames: an old colour photo of a couple at their wedding; a big stocky man in a suit, a little girl, about seven he reckoned, in a new school uniform holding his hand. There was an adult Bonnie cuddling a large red bear of a dog. Next, a mother in bed holding a newborn baby, a father cradling the same baby. That last image seared on his retina and even when he looked away, he could still see it.

He shifted his attention to Bonnie's profile in the tiny kitchen, spooning coffee into two mugs as the kettle boiled beside her and just looking at her warmed his heart. She was so . . . understated. What you saw was what you got with her. She displayed more of a reaction over the old second-hand mini washing machine than Charlotte did over the Tiffany earrings. She brought the drinks through and set them on the coffee table.

'Would you like a biscuit?' she asked. 'I think I've got some KitKats in the cupboard.'

'No, I'm fine thank you,' said Lew. 'I don't want to spoil my appetite. At the prices they charge for dinner, it's best if I'm very hungry to enjoy it.'

'They?' asked Bonnie, sitting on the brown bed-chair.

'Sorry . . .' He realised he hadn't told her any details about his new living arrangements. 'I'm staying at the Holiday Inn.'

'I see,' smiled Bonnie. 'Very nice for a couple of nights but I imagine it's not so relaxing if you don't have your own things around you.'

'I'll swap you,' said Lew. The coffee was good. He suspected it was flavoured with the lovely surroundings in which he was drinking it. 'Your house is very cosy.'

'I like it,' said Bonnie, looking fondly around at all the things so kindly donated. 'I love coming home to it in the evenings. It feels . . .'

'. . . Welcoming,' supplied Lew. 'Woodlea is a new build and there's no imprint of lives lived in it, if you know what I mean.'

Bonnie nodded. Stephen's house had been a new build when he bought it and it had only absorbed his energy. It had refused to soak up any traces of her.

'The house I had before that was a hundred and seventy years old. It creaked at night and one of the rooms was always extra-warm when you walked into it, and I mean when there was no central heating on. And it was north-facing. Odd, wonderfully odd.' Lew smiled, as he always did, when he thought of The Beeches.

'The house I grew up in was like that,' said Bonnie with a sigh. 'Victorian, with a monster staircase. If I stood half-way up on the turn, something used to ruffle my hair, like a summer breeze. I know it was haunted, but by something benign. We didn't mind sharing with it.' She smiled. She used to stand there sometimes, close her eyes and pretend it was her mother touching her.

'I suppose really I ought to go and find somewhere to rent. I'm fed up already living in a hotel.'

'There's no—' Bonnie cut off what she'd been about to say and apologised.

'Go on,' urged Lew.

'I was going to say . . . there's no chance of a . . . reconciliation then?'

'None,' said Lew. 'Absolutely none.'

'I'm sorry about that. I had no idea your marriage was in trouble.' She sipped her coffee.

'Neither did I, Bonnie,' said Lew. 'But I found out on the same day that not only had my wife been sleeping with her best friend's husband, but that she'd been lying to me for years about miscarrying our baby when she'd aborted it because it would have been too inconvenient to have it.' His tone was bitter, arctic cold.

Bonnie opened up her mouth to say something, realised she had no words and shut it again. Lew gave a long apologetic sigh.

'I didn't mean to say that, forgive me.' He should go before he made her feel even more uncomfortable.

'It must have been ready to come out,' said Bonnie kindly. 'Don't worry, it won't go any further.'

'I don't doubt that,' said Lew. His eyes drifted again to the photo of the dad and the little girl in the school uniform. If his baby had been a girl, she would have been about the same age now. He coughed away a throatful of emotion. He shouldn't burden this woman with his worries and really ought to leave because sitting here with her felt too comfortable.

'I can't imagine what a shock that must have been for you, Lew,' said Bonnie, gently, carefully.

'I'm not even sure I've taken it all in yet,' he replied. 'My brain is still spinning from all the lies she told me over the years.' He pushed the waves of his hair back with his fingers. 'I've chewed it over and over in my head, Bonnie. Did I want a child so much that I ignored what she wanted? She said I pushed her into it and though I *know* I didn't, I'm starting to doubt myself. I couldn't have, I wouldn't have . . .'

He stood up quickly because he could feel tears pushing at the back of his eyes. 'Sorry, I don't know what's the matter with me.'

'I do, you're grieving, Lew,' Bonnie said. She pulled at his hand for him to sit down again and he did. 'Let me top up your coffee.'

And because Lew felt as if this little house was wrapping its arms around him, he said, 'Thank you. That would be nice.'

*

Stephen Brookland was in ecstasy. He thought he'd got it wrong about his wife and her boss. He'd been doing spot-checks on them both since she walked out but he hadn't seen any out-of-work meetings between them until now and he really had begun to think they weren't carrying on after all. But now he knew his instincts had been correct. Bonita wouldn't have left him off her own back. He supposed they'd stayed away from each other so they could do what other cheating bastards did, pretend that they'd only got together respectably when their previous relationships had ended. But he knew that Lewis Harley was now living in a hotel. It was obvious that he had left his wife for his tramp of a mistress. It would have been too much of a coincidence for his marriage to have broken down for any other reason. He was doing what the family liaison officer advised him to, i.e. not harassing his wife, but he could still do his own undercover investigations. The more damning evidence he could find on her, the more mud would stick because he knew the case against her wasn't definitive.

He checked in his book the time that Harley had arrived and carried in that white block, whatever it was. He'd been in there over an hour. Even allowing for a cup of tea he

should have been on his way by now. He would have left
had it all been innocent and above board. Yet he was still
there.

*

In Bonnie's cosy little lounge, Lew spilled the whole of the
sorry story of Charlotte and Regina, Patrick, Gemma and
Jason. And she listened patiently.

At the end he apologised yet again. 'I'm not used to baring
my soul, Bonnie,' he said. 'Never mind two full loads of
dirty washing. I'm more your bottling-up sort of guy.'

'Maybe that's why you had a heart attack,' she replied.
Then her stomach grumbled really loudly and they both
burst into some well-needed laughter.

'I'm keeping you from eating,' said Lew, draining the last
from his third cup of coffee.

'No, you're not. I always have a Chinese on Fridays. They
don't open for another ten minutes anyway.'

'It's been ages since I had a Chinese,' said Lew, thinking
how good that sounded. He stood up to take his mug into
the kitchen and by the time he had returned an idea had
come to him.

'Can I share a Chinese with you, if I buy it? It feels only
right I should use some of the money from the Chinese cup
and saucer sale.'

'Er, yeah,' Bonnie said, unable to think of an excuse why
not. She pulled the takeaway menu out of the retro magazine rack at the side of the TV and whilst Lew was choosing
from it, she remembered something with mortifying
embarrassment.

'I've only got one plate and one fork,' she said. He

THE QUEEN OF WISHFUL THINKING          395

chuckled and said he'd be sure to pick up some chopsticks and they could eat their meals out of the cartons.

As Lew was waiting in the Great Wall of China on the High Street, it came to him that he'd chewed her ear off and not asked her about her own situation, something which he decided to rectify when he arrived back at her house and they were opening up the banquet that Lew had bought.

'We'll never eat all this,' gasped Bonnie.

'We can have a good go at it,' grinned Lew, popping a whole prawn won ton in his mouth and crunching down on it. Then, when he could speak again he asked her, 'Have you seen anything of your husband?' Which was ironic as, unbeknown to him, Lew had just passed him hiding in his car around the corner. Stephen had sold his Mondeo and replaced it with a black Aygo so he could spy on her unnoticed.

'No, thank goodness,' said Bonnie. 'He isn't playing ball in the divorce, which is no less than I expected. He hasn't signed the papers but Adriana says I haven't to worry about it. He can't stop it happening.'

'She's very thorough, you're in good hands,' said Lew, expertly picking up a mound of egg fried rice with his chopsticks. It smelt delicious. Sitting at the tiny table heaving with cartons was so much more enjoyable than having a fillet steak in the hotel restaurant. Especially when his dining companion had such beautiful eyes.

'As I said, I have a Chinese every Friday,' said Bonnie, struggling with the chopsticks but not giving up. 'It's my weekly treat. I didn't have takeaways at all when I was married.' Stephen doubted the hygiene of places like the Great

Wall of China, which incidentally displayed on the walls all
the top awards it had won for cleanliness.

'Are those your parents in the photos, Bonnie?' asked
Lew, pointing his chopstick towards the mantelpiece.

'Yep,' replied Bonnie.

'You look like your mum.' Her mother had the same
large, bright eyes.

'That's what my dad used to say,' Bonnie smiled. 'I wish
I could remember her. Dad used to tell me loads of stories
about her so I'd have something of her, if not memories. He
wrote lots of things down in a notebook for me when she
died. He was full of sayings and apparently so was she.'

'Like what?' asked Lew, intrigued.

'Oh all sorts. Dad used to tell me to smile at rude people
and look after my pennies, that kind of thing. Mum told
him that the one thing she was going to make me grow up
believing was that I could do anything if I put my mind to
it, defy the odds, break the barriers.'

'She was right,' grinned Lew.

'She didn't mean you just had to wish for it and it would
be yours, though. Real life isn't Aladdin.' She had Lew
chuckling at that. 'She said that you had to back up your
wishes with action. If there was something you really
wanted, and if you could picture yourself doing it, then you
should pull out all the stops and go for it. There's skill
involved in proper wishing, and my mother was queen of
it, according to my dad. Long story but it was true, she was.'

'You've inherited her crown, then, Bonnie, because you
broke away from Stephen, didn't you?'

'I did.' Though she had many moments when she didn't
believe she'd actually done it and thought she must be
dreaming.

'You are my beacon that there is life after splitting up. I'll have to do some proper wishing now,' smiled Lew and Bonnie thought how very handsome he was. How could Charlotte Harley have slept with anyone else when she had this lovely man in her bed?

'It was the best thing I've ever done,' said Bonnie. And it was, even though it had kicked off the police enquiry. 'When I was still living with him and imagining what life would be like if I left, I didn't expect I'd end up with all this.' She looked from one side of the room to the other. 'I know it doesn't look much . . .'

'Your kingdom is lovely,' said Lew. And it was. He wished he could bottle the friendly essence of the little house and take it with him to the hotel.

Bonnie gave a soft chuckle at that. 'I love it. I can shut the door on the world and forget everyone outside it. I can breathe here.'

They ate in companionable silence for a few minutes, then Bonnie remembered something she had to tell him.

'There are some flats at the complex in the Town End. I know a lot of footballers rent them. They're furnished and there's secure parking and I know they have some vacant ones because they were advertising them in the *Chronicle* last week.'

'That would be ideal,' said Lew. 'Living in one room is driving me crazy. I'm hoping the house is sold sooner rather than later. I've priced it for a quick sale. Then I'll buy something for myself.'

'Old or new?' asked Bonnie.

'Old definitely.'

'How many bedrooms?'

'Three, four maybe.'

'Not big enough,' said Bonnie, wagging chopsticks loaded with lemon chicken. 'You could meet someone and have a house full of children, just like you wanted. You're only forty-four. Some rock-stars are having kids in their seventies. You've got time to have loads.'

A vision of The Beeches rose up in Lew's head. She was right. He could, couldn't he? There would be another woman for him, as surely as there would be another Beeches. The heart attack hadn't ended his life nor his hopes and dreams and neither would the divorce.

'Six bedrooms then,' said Lew. 'And enough land for two huge dogs and a playhouse and a man-cave so I can escape from all the noise.' He laughed and Bonnie's laughter joined his. That house sounded like heaven to her as much as it did him. The difference was that he would have it, she was sure. She wanted him to be happy with a nice lady. One who wanted children and loved the same things he did and who had never seen the inside of a prison cell.

\*

Stephen was just about to set off back home, presuming that Lewis Harley was staying the night when he saw him walking back to his car wearing what he supposed would be described as a 'soppy grin'. He wrote that in his book. It might or might not be relevant.

\*

Bonnie was also wearing a soppy grin. She thought that when Lew said he ought to get back to the hotel, he did so reluctantly. She hadn't offered him another coffee, even though she wanted to. She'd had the best-ever evening in his company but she had to be careful because the closer she got to him, the more it would hurt when she had to leave.

'Thank you for this evening, Bonnie,' he had said to her at the door. 'Thank you for letting me talk and for listening, thank you for your lovely coffee and making me feel so welcome in your wonderful home.'

'It's a pleasure, really,' said Bonnie, the last word lost in a quiet gasp as Lew's arms came around her and he crushed her to his chest and he placed a soft kiss on her cheek. Then he was quickly gone, but she could feel his lips upon her skin for much longer, and relished it until it faded.

# Chapter 68

The estate agent woke Lew up the next morning with the news that a couple wanted to view Woodlea that afternoon if possible. They had sold their house and weren't in a chain so they wanted a quick purchase. Lew texted Charlotte a perfunctory message to tell her that the agent would be escorting a couple around at two p.m. She didn't need to be present as Lew had given the agent a key, which he imagined Charlotte wouldn't be too happy about, but she hadn't resisted for obvious financial reasons. She sent back a very succinct OK. He neither wanted nor expected more.

That was a good start to the day, Lew thought, though he doubted he'd be that lucky to sell it so quickly. There was a house around the corner from Woodlea that had been on the market for over two years.

He had slept like a log. He put that down to the unburdening of his soul in Bonnie's little house. He could smell her perfume on his coat when he picked it up to go to the Pot of Gold. It was the scent of freesias and summer and he found himself wondering what her lips would taste like when placed against his own.

He walked into the shop and picked up the mail from the doormat: a brown envelope with no stamp and a handwritten address on it, some junk and a letter from the accountant. Then Bonnie walked in, and with her that beautiful scent that made him revisit the recent memory of holding her in his arms and wondering if he would be able to let go.

'Morning,' she called, her hair in a jaunty shiny ponytail today.

'Good morning,' he replied.

She tilted her head at the tone in his voice. 'Someone's in a good mood.'

'The magic of Chinese food,' he smiled. 'Do me a favour and put these in the back room for me when you go and put the kettle on. I'll open them later.'

Bonnie grinned and took the envelopes from him. In the back room, she sorted them into size order before putting them on his desk. That's when her smile died. The handwriting on the brown envelope was unmistakeable. She grabbed it and quickly stuffed it in her handbag.

Later he asked her if she'd seen a brown envelope that was in with the post that morning. She said that she hadn't but it would probably turn up sooner rather than later.

When Lew went out mid-morning to pick up some business cards from a local printer, Bonnie wasted no time in ripping into the brown envelope. It contained one unfolded A4 sheet of paper, a letter written in Stephen's hand.

To Lewis Harley

   I would like to thank you for taking MY WIFE BONITA MARY BROOKLAND off my hands. Although frankly I am very surprised that you have left your wife for a murderess about to go to prison for fourteen years. I do hope that she has not hidden the fact from you that she killed my terminally ill mother five years ago and is presently under police investigation. She was arrested last weekend and spent the night in a police cell. Perhaps you would like to ask her about that when you are carrying on. I think that it would be very harmful to your business if it got out that you are employing criminals. For this reason I would ask that you consider terminating her service before you ruin your credibility.

Yours sincerely
Stephen Brookland

Bonnie burst into angry tears. He wouldn't stop until he had totally destroyed her.

Then the doorbell tinkled and Bonnie pulled herself quickly together and checked her face in the mirror. She forced out her shop-smile, but it felt like a dead weight on her lips and she knew it would be a strain to keep it up today.

# Chapter 69

Three days later, Henderson was on his way to interview his witness in the Alma Brookland case when he received a call from Beth, the family liaison officer. Stephen was constantly ringing her or emailing or texting with remembered 'facts' that he thought might be relevant.

'He wants me to let you know that he'd forgotten to mention before that he had to tell his wife off a few times for being rough when shifting his mother's position in bed, and that she handled her as if she really resented her,' said Beth, coming through loud and clear on speakerphone. 'I've emailed you the details.'

'Okay, I'll add it to my notes.' He was convinced that Stephen Brookland's whole existence at the moment was concerned with raking up – or inventing – mud bombs to sling at his estranged wife. It didn't sit well with Henderson to have to include such deranged witterings, yet he had a duty to. Then again, Brookland was losing the plot so much, the more he said, the more he contradicted himself.

'I've had ten phone calls today from him,' said Beth. 'I'm going to persuade him to get some medical help. I really think he might have been better with a male FLO. He's very dismissive of women in general.'

That didn't surprise him one bit. In the interviews, Brookland had barely acknowledged Chloe Barrett's existence. Even when she asked him a question, more often than not, he would direct the answer at Henderson.

'He's bought himself a new car just so he can follow his wife without her knowledge, did you know? He's really not helping himself at all and I've tried to tell him as much but . . .' Beth didn't need to finish off the sentence.

'Thanks, Beth. We're just going in to interview a witness at her home so let me know if anything else crops up,' said Henderson.

'As it will,' came the resigned reply. 'Bye, Bill.'

'Doesn't say much about him as a son if he thought his wife was abusing his mother but allowed it to continue,' said Barrett, signalling left. 'Hardly a detail that you're likely to forget, either, is it?'

'Nope,' said Henderson. From all accounts, Alma Brookland was a large woman; tall and broad. Even accounting for her frailer frame at the end of her life, she still must have been a weight for the slender Bonnie Brookland to lift. 'Pull in here, Chloe. It says something if he's managing to wear Beth down,' he continued. 'She is one tough cookie.'

Mrs Katherine Ellison had agreed to be interviewed at her home, a substantial bungalow in the middle of an estate of equally large detached residences. All of them with neat lawns and herbaceous borders.

'There's some serious coin around here,' remarked Barrett.

'Wealthy retired,' replied Henderson. 'You could end up

here if you climb up the career ladder. Four bedrooms, summer house and a stone fountain.'

'And gnomes, don't forget the gnomes,' said Barrett, looking out at a colony of them peeping out from bushes and fishing in the ornamental pond of Mrs Ellison's neighbour.

They walked up the long path and Barrett rang the bell. Mrs Ellison appeared before the echoes of it had died; evidently she'd been watching out for them from the window.

'Mrs Ellison? Detective Sergeant Henderson and this is Detective Constable Barrett.'

'Come in,' said Mrs Ellison, moving out of the way so they could enter. It was definitely a 'shoes–off–at–the–door' place, so the detectives left them neatly on the doormat and followed the house–owner into a large square lounge with a very pale beige carpet on the floor and many framed family photographs on the walls.

Mrs Ellison had prepared a tray of tea. 'Help yourself to milk and sugar,' she said, handing Henderson a very fancy patterned saucer and cup with a tiny handle that he couldn't stick his large finger through. He took a couple of sips and then rested it on the nearby coffee table before opening his notebook and clicking on his biro.

'I apologise if this is upsetting for you,' said Henderson. 'It must be dredging up a lot of memories.'

'It's certainly a shock,' said Mrs Ellison. 'But I deliberately didn't say too much to Stephen when he came round to tell me what had happened.'

'Mr Brookland's been round to see you then?' asked Henderson, though he wasn't surprised.

'Yes, and I've never seen him so animated,' said Mrs Ellison with a frown.

'What exactly did he tell you?' asked Barrett, reaching for a Jam Ring from a plate of assorted biscuits. She was on a diet and hadn't had breakfast. The biscuits would offset the sugar deficiency currently making her limbs feel shaky. In other words, she told herself, they were essentially medicinal.

'He came to the house last Friday. About teatime. He said that new evidence had come to light that Alma hadn't died naturally and I should be prepared for a visit from the police because it appeared that Bonita might have murdered her. He was very dramatic. I couldn't talk for long as I had visitors, but I assured him that I would, of course, be available to you and would supply you with any information that you needed.'

'You weren't shocked by what he said?' asked Henderson, thinking what a top-class shit-stirrer Brookland was.

Katherine Ellison didn't miss a beat as she poured milk into her cup. 'Not at all. I've always presumed that Alma's death wasn't a natural one.'

Barrett's Jam Ring dropped into her tea.

*

'Mr Harley, I am delighted to tell you that Mr and Mrs Kruger have put in an offer,' said the estate agent with a tone in his voice that said he didn't believe it either. 'I think this has to be the quickest sale I've ever done.' It was the easiest commission he'd make all year. All decade, probably.

Despite the house being priced at below its market value, Mr and Mrs Kruger had still offered five thousand pounds less.

'Tell them I'll take it, but I'm not an idiot, nor am I

desperate and if they try to gazunder, the deal's off,' replied Lew.

'I will, of course. He's a solicitor so I'll be honest, I imagine things will run pretty smoothly.'

Lew could feel the estate agent's grin down the line. It was burning his ear. He texted Charlotte with the good news. She didn't reply.

# Chapter 70

'You've always presumed that Alma's death wasn't natural?' Henderson threw Katherine Ellison's words back at her in question form.

'Well, I wasn't there to personally witness her passing but ... oh goodness me –' she dropped her head and shook it slightly as if something distressing had just come to her '– poor Alma. She has rested in peace for five years and wouldn't want any of this.'

'Any of what, Mrs Ellison?'

'Her secret being exposed.' Her eyes suddenly widened in alarm. 'You're not going to dig her up, are you?'

'No, no, that's very unlikely,' said Henderson, careful not to dismiss the possibility entirely. 'What secret do you mean?'

'That she committed suicide. She wouldn't want anyone to know. She would have seen it as the most dreadful show of weakness and a complete betrayal of her values.'

Barrett reached for a custard cream. Her sugar-shakes were getting worse.

'What makes you think she committed suicide?'

'She told me she was going to,' said Mrs Ellison. 'She said that she'd sent off for a drug from abroad. Mexico, I think.'

'You knew about that?' Barrett said with a rogue squeak on the second word.

'I was her best friend, I knew everything,' said Mrs Ellison, lifting the cup to her lips and drinking from it delicately in a ladylike manner. 'I've known Alma Brookland since I was four years old. I loved her dearly, though sometimes I didn't like her very much, because she could be a horror, but we were ... what's that expression they use? ..."sisters from another mother", or something like that. I was always far closer to her than I was to my own sisters. She was my bridesmaid, I was hers. She is the godmother to my daughter, I am godmother to her son.'

Barrett noticed the little shudder of revulsion ripple her shoulders.

'You knew she was ill, then?' she said.

'Of course. She self-diagnosed when the symptoms started and she was right about what sort of disease she had. I don't think Stephen was aware that I knew though.'

Henderson and Barrett both had the same thought at the same moment: that they'd bet their lives that he didn't.

'I usually go to Spain for Christmas and stay there for three months,' Mrs Ellison continued, 'and I was going to cancel but Alma said I must go. She didn't want me to see her decompose daily; her words, not mine. We said our goodbyes before I left and that's why she gave me this.' She pulled a gold locket free of her blouse collar. 'That's the way she wanted it to be. Alma wasn't the sort of person to say things for effect and I had to respect her wishes.'

'Goodness,' said Barrett with a gulp. There were more secrets in this case than in Harry Potter's chamber.

'Don't get me wrong, it did upset me,' Mrs Ellison went on. 'That's why I was delighted when she rang me when I was in Spain. Her speech was very much altered but it was good to hear her.' Her lip trembled and she put her cup down on the coffee table, pulled a cotton handkerchief from out of her sleeve and dabbed her eyes. 'She could be a monster, but she was very dear to me.'

'I'm sorry this is upsetting you,' said Henderson gently.

'No matter,' said Mrs Ellison. 'Has to be done.'

'And what did you talk about when you rang her?'

'Bonita mainly. Her murderous daughter-in-law.' She gave a little laugh. 'Whatever Stephen has told you, I don't believe that myself. I always thought she seemed a thoroughly decent person. Alma of course hated her with a passion. No one would ever have been good enough for her Stephen.' She let out a telling deep breath. 'He was always an odd one. I never took to him. He thought he was above everyone, even as a child, rambled on about things he knew little about to appear more intelligent than he was. I think he moved in on that girl when she was very vulnerable and I told Alma as much but she wouldn't have it. Stephen was on far too high a pedestal. She blamed Bonita for all sorts of things because she couldn't bear to think Stephen might not be spending time with her of his own accord. Bonita was a whipping boy for Stephen; Alma was very jealous.'

This isn't what Stephen Brookland would have been expecting Mrs Ellison to say, thought Henderson.

'Sorry, you said she spoke about Bonita when she phoned you,' he said, pen moving fast on his notebook. A course in Teeline shorthand years ago had been one of the most useful things he'd ever done.

'Yes. I asked Alma how she was, obviously, and she was

very emotional – not like her at all. She told me how well Bonita was looking after her, how kind she was and how sorry she felt that she'd been so awful to her in the past. I think that was the main reason for her ringing me, actually: to put the record straight. She said that she'd misjudged her terribly. I said that I could have told her that. We didn't pussy-foot around one another, Alma and I. In all the years I'd known her, I'd never heard her admit she was wrong before, so I knew this was a very big climb down for her. Then I heard Stephen come in and ask what she was doing so we said our goodbyes – again – and that was the last I heard from her. Do you know Stephen didn't even tell me when she'd died? He didn't put a notice in the newspaper or anything. I would have flown back for the funeral if I'd known she'd passed. When I came back from Spain I went to see him and he told me that Alma had not wanted anyone at her funeral, which was nonsense, but it would have been wrong of me to make a fuss about it when I didn't know for sure. More tea? There's plenty in the pot.'

'Not for me, thank you, Mrs Ellison.'

'Nor me, thank you. What did he tell you about how his mother had died?' asked Barrett.

'Only that she had slipped away in the night and he'd been at her side holding her hand. But I didn't believe him, at least about the slipping away part. I *knew* in here' – her small fist pressed against her heart ' – that she'd been helped over the hurdle. Stephen would have known all about her having the drug, you know. Alma would never have kept that from him, especially not when he was the only person she could rely on to help her take it. And she would have wanted to make sure he was with her at the end. That's why

I refuse to buy his ridiculous pretence at being shocked about it. I'm just glad that Alma got her wish and he was there for her. He was her world.'

'Well, thank you very much for your cooperation,' said DS Henderson. He thought he had all he needed for now.

'He was there with her at the end, wasn't he?' pressed Mrs Ellison, hand clutching her locket. 'He didn't lie about that, did he?'

Barrett looked at Henderson for guidance.

'I believe Mrs Brookland was with her,' he answered diplomatically.

'Oh the lying brute, how could he?' said Mrs Ellison with feeling. Her voice was firm as she continued, 'Godson or not, I am done with him.'

Barrett refilled Mrs Ellison's cup from the pot and handed it to her.

'Thank you,' said Mrs Ellison, steadying herself with a deep breath. 'I wish they would just let her rest in peace. I probably shouldn't say this, but I'm going to: Stephen has a very strong reaction to rejection. His mother built him up so much that he never learned to take things on the chin. I only ever knew of him having one girlfriend before Bonita. A very quiet, shy girl, much younger than he was. He showered her with flowers and chocolates and attention in the beginning; in fact he wasn't recognisable as himself. It didn't take long for his façade to slip though and she broke with him. He couldn't accept it was over of course and he followed that girl everywhere, causing mischief for her, making her life an absolute misery. Her father threatened him in the end and made him stop. Like all bullies, he's a coward. I'm presuming Bonita has left him ... if so, you might want to think on what I've just told you about

Stephen Brookland and his past record with women who reject him.'

In the car Barrett raised her eyebrows. 'Brookland sounds a right weirdo, doesn't he?' she said, as they prepared to drive away from the curtain-twitching estate.

'Yes, but that doesn't mean he's not telling the truth,' replied Henderson.

'I wouldn't like to be the CPS with this one,' whistled Barrett. 'I mean, Bonnie Brookland knew that the old woman had that drug so she had a tailor-made opportunity to get rid of her, didn't she? And after all, what proof is there that the old lady bought it? She might have told Mrs Ellison she was going to but didn't. Who's to say that Bonnie Brookland didn't overhear her and buy it herself? That would explain why Stephen might be telling the truth and he really didn't know anything about it.'

'True,' said Henderson.

'Or if Mrs B did buy it herself, it might just have been a security blanket and she could have changed her mind about using it.'

'Yep.'

'Chances are she was gaga by the end and maybe couldn't have made the decision to kill herself,' Barrett went on. 'Jesus, what a conundrum. It's making my brain bleed.'

'The prosecution would use all those points if it went to court. Old lady, plenty of money, history of ill-will burden. Stephen Brookland's story fits the facts as much as Bonnie Brookland's does. It's only supposition that Brookland knew about his mother's plans to end her life. His word against hers. Then, of course, we have Bonnie Brookland unable to remember if she tilted the liquid into the old lady's mouth or not.'

'I'm beginning to think that she didn't but Stephen Brookland has managed to make her believe she did. Evil twat.' Barrett blew out two large lungfuls of air. 'Proper five million piece jigsaw this one, isn't it? Do you have to put everything into the report?'

'Everything, not only the choice morsels. It's not my job to be the judge, just to deliver all the evidence,' replied Henderson, a note of regret present in his voice.

'I think I'd pick prison before being married to Brookland.' Barrett shuddered as she clipped her seat belt into the socket. 'Do you think they will dig the mother up?'

'I doubt it,' replied Henderson. 'Even if that drug does show up in the remains, it still doesn't prove if it was self-administered or not. So what would be the point?'

'Based on the evidence so far, do you think the CPS are likely to prosecute? I mean, he could be telling the truth that his wife confessed to murder during a massive row.'

'He could,' nodded Henderson, non-committedly.

'And he could have been bluffing in that letter he sent her, just like he said he was, couldn't he?'

'Yep. That's what the prosecuting barrister will say.'

'And Mrs Brookland isn't helping herself by confessing everything. She's playing right into the prosecution's hands, surely?' She slipped the car into first and released the hand-brake. 'I mean, she could have pretended to know nothing about any of it and blamed his accusations on sour grapes because she left him. She's been sitting on it comfortably for five years, so why not carry on?'

Henderson didn't think she'd been sitting on it comfortably for five years at all. He would have bet that Bonnie Brookland would have been at the police station before now if it hadn't meant betraying her mother-in-law's 'secret' to the public. It must have been like living with a stomach full of burbling vomit for five whole years. No wonder she threw it all up so hard and so readily.

They pulled up at some traffic lights. 'So, back to my question, Bill, what would you predict the CPS will decide to do in this case?'

Henderson sighed. 'A very old terminally ill lady, a son with an axe to grind, an emotionally fragile woman spooning guilt on herself who is the only witness to what happened, plus five years to distort facts . . . is it really in the public interest to put this into a courtroom? On the other hand, a life is a life and if it's cut short by another person for whatever reason, that's a crime. Couple of cases recently have seen judges give out tough sentences, which is sending out a very clear message that the CPS are going hardline. I wouldn't be surprised if they did prosecute and she was found guilty and ended up with a custodial sentence. Not the full fourteen, but between five and eight.'

'Hard,' said Barrett, hitting the accelerator.

'Yep. This is the law, DC Barrett. Good things happen to bad people and bad things happen to good people. You're often only as innocent as the barrister you pay to make you look that way. Welcome to the justice system.'

# Chapter 71

For the next few days, Lew plunged himself into the taking apart of his marriage, piece by piece. When he wasn't on the shop floor in the Pot of Gold, he was liaising with his broker and accountant making a report of his financial situation to give to Adriana. He could understand why so many people who had put one foot on the road to divorce doubled back and took the easy option, but there was no way back for him. That door had been locked, bricked up and cemented over. He wanted out of this marriage as quickly and cleanly as possible, whatever it cost him. He couldn't think of Charlotte without also seeing the child they should have had, and he knew that his friendship with Gemma was over, too. He didn't want to know if she stayed with Jason or not; he wished her silently well, but if they passed in the street, he would say hello and move straight on.

Life at the hotel was driving him insane and he decided to check out one of the flats Bonnie had told him about, but when he rang Mike Bell, the estate agent dealing with the sale of Woodlea, he found Mike had an interesting proposition for him.

As Lew was locking up the shop on the Sunday night, an impulsive thought came to him.

'Bonnie, are you doing anything tomorrow? I know it's your day off, but I'm after a favour, just an hour max of your time.'

'What is it?' said Bonnie, intrigued.

'There's a house I want to look at and I'd value your opinion.'

'Yes, no worries,' replied Bonnie with a smile, but a much watered-down version of the one she usually wore. She had been constantly on edge for a week now, since she had intercepted the letter that Stephen had sent to Lew. Not even sleep gave her respite because Stephen followed her into her dreams. He had taken root in her brain like a parasite and if she thought she could have drilled a hole in her head and yanked him out, she would have done it.

'I'll pick you up at ten then?'

'I'll be ready. That'll be nice.'

Something was upsetting her, Lew knew. He'd asked if she was okay a couple of times over the past days, and she'd replied that she was – but she wasn't. Maybe she would tell him away from the work environment, the way he had spilled his situation to her over that Chinese meal. He was worried about her because he was fond of her. Very fond of her.

The *Daily Trumpet* apologises to Mrs Edna Harris for any distress caused in the article headed, 'Local Writer Pens Autobiography'. Mrs Harris has written a book entitled *Living with The Nuns of Barnsley: a First-Hand Guide*. Not, as reported, *Living with The Nonce of Barnsley: a First-Hand Guide*. Mrs Harris wishes it to be pointed out that she does not know any nonce in Barnsley or elsewhere and has never lived with one nor does she advocate any guide that might instruct one on how to live with a nonce.

# Chapter 72

David Charles rang Bonnie at nine the next morning. It had scared her to death. He'd told her that he didn't have a great deal of news; the file of collected evidence would be going to the CPS this week, but what she most remembered about the call was that the solicitor had told her it would be wise to prepare herself for a possible spell in prison. She was shell-shocked when she put the phone down. How did you prepare for something like that? She made a to-do list of various utility companies that she would need to contact, but she hadn't a clue what to say to them. And what would happen if she went straight to prison from court? Who would empty the little house of furniture and where would it all go? She was terrified, as much of being locked up as of what people she valued would think of her. Especially Lew.

He hadn't arrived by twenty past ten and the thought crossed her mind that he had found out. An anonymous letter – from Stephen – sent to the hotel this time so he would be sure of getting it. Her stomach churned with nerves. Then she heard the cheerful pips of a car horn out-side and she leapt to the window to see Lew's Audi and him waving at her. She was almost drowned by the relief that washed over her. She gave herself a quick check in the mirror hanging on the wall and picked up her key. Her hand was shaking as she locked the door.

'Bonnie, I'm so sorry I'm late. Some idiot rep for toilet rolls, of all things, blocked me in in the hotel car park.'

'It's fine, don't worry,' she returned.

'Everything all right?' he asked, noticing that her eyes looked slightly red.

'I've just had a sneezing fit,' she improvised. 'I think the pollen count must be high today.'

'Thank you for coming with me,' he smiled and her heart gave a tattoo of thumps in response.

'It's a change from making confetti,' she said, buckling herself in.

Lew chuckled. 'Is it a very lucrative sideline you have?'

'Put it this way . . . no. But the Rainbow Lady does buy my Chinese meal every week for me.'

*Rainbow Lady.* It fitted her perfectly, thought Lew, noticing the sundress she was wearing, spattered with dots of all colours. On her shoulders rested her yellow cardigan, bright as sunshine. She was bonny by name and nature and she never failed to lift his mood when he was in her presence.

'Where's the house?' asked Bonnie.

'Just outside Little Kipping,' replied Lew. 'The estate agent selling mine thought I might be interested. I should sensibly be renting one of those small flats you told me about, but since he told me about this, it's become stuck in my head so I thought what the hell. I figured that if it was awful then at least it would leave my brain alone.'

'Little Kipping is nice and very handy for Spring Hill.'

'Yep. All the planets are weirdly lining up for this one. It's a ridiculous size for a single man though.'

You won't be single for long, thought Bonnie. She wasn't sure she could bear to be around when he found another lady. The planets were also lining up for her leaving him, she knew.

'The name will have to go if I bought it. Coldred House. You just know that Colin and Mildred thought it would be a good idea.'

Bonnie giggled and it felt good because she hadn't been sure there was any laughter in her recently.

Lew took a left into Little Kipping, past the Black Sheep pub and a pretty row of cottages covered in purple wisteria. He took another left up a lane darkened by trees on either side conspiring together high above their heads.

'It's somewhere up here I beli— ah, there we go,' said Lew, 'just on the bend.' He took a right down an imposing drive, longer than he imagined, and there in front of them was Coldred House and a man in a slick suit, leaning against his car waiting for them.

'Wow,' said Bonnie, more of a sound than a word. How lovely it must be to have the money in the bank to buy somewhere like this. It was huge, double-fronted, square and solid with massive bay windows to the first elevation.

'Nice to see you again,' said the estate agent, walking over to shake Lew's hand and then Bonnie's, introducing himself to her as Mike Bell. She wondered if he thought she was Lew's bit of stuff and the reason why he had left his wife.

'As I said to you on the phone, Mr Harley, it's been on the market for four years so the owner has just dropped the price again. Quite considerably. It wasn't a bargain before but I'll be honest, I think you'll find it is now.'

Mike unlocked the huge door and pushed it open to reveal an enormous reception hall with the most beautiful ornate staircase. Bonnie would have bought it on this alone.

'Breathtaking, isn't it?' said Mike. 'I'll be honest and say I wish the person who'd decorated this had done the rest of the house.' He grimaced. 'Let's start with the worst.'

Bonnie didn't see the maroon walls in the lounge, she saw windows where sunlight would flood in every morning. She didn't see the broken, splintered wooden floorboards, but ones which were polished and glossy. She saw a crackling fire feasting on logs in the hungry mouth of the fireplace and a large red bear of a dog asleep on a thick rug in front of it, gently snoring and dreaming of bones.

'Horrendous, but it's only a paint job away from paradise,' guffawed Mike. 'Plus a total rewire and er . . . all the plumbing work. Let's go into the kitchen, you'll like this.' He clicked his tongue at Bonnie, as if this would be her domain.

'Mmm, MFI units,' chuckled Lew. 'Dozens of them. Nice.'

Bonnie saw a huge dining table in the centre of the room, herself standing at it folding cocoa into the contents of a bowl, a giggling child sneaking fingerfuls of the cake mix into her mouth. She saw a shiny green Aga pumping out heat and smells of stew and bread. She saw the door open to a garden full of nodding spring daffodils, and the cheery bubble of the brook beyond them.

'Be honest, what do you think so far?' asked Mike eagerly.

'It needs a lot of work,' said Lew, in a neutral tone, giving nothing away to him, though he turned to Bonnie and dropped a sly wink.

There was a study tucked next to a stately dining room, a cellar, a scullery and an orangery, as Mike called it. Lew called it a condemned conservatory, but he could see where Mike was coming from.

At the top of the magnificent staircase was a stained glass

window of a garden scene, rays of sunlight shining down on a green field of large yellow daffodils, their trumpets just a shade darker.

'It used to be called Daffodil House,' said Mike. 'And that's why. It's a tad cheesy, which is why I imagine the last owners changed it.'

'Yep, Colin and Mildred totally de-cheesed it,' Lew said for Bonnie's ears only and she snorted and then clamped her hands over her face in embarrassment.

'No ensuites but I'll be honest, the bedrooms are so large they could easily accommodate them,' said Mike, pushing open the door to the master bedroom. There was enough room for Bonnie's house to fit into, never mind an ensuite. Two massive windows afforded a view of the garden and the smoke-blue Pennines beyond. Bonnie saw herself leaning over a cot in the corner, checking that the baby was sleeping, then tiptoing back to bed where a Lew-shaped man was waiting for her to snuggle into. She turned away and found an awful built-in wardrobe temporarily interesting whilst the sudden blush faded from her cheeks. There were five more bedrooms on that floor, a gigantic house bathroom with a 1970s avocado suite and an attic, where once the servants had lived, split into four small rooms.

'It comes with three acres of land and a garage that is standing up on a wing and a prayer, I'll be honest,' said Mike. 'It's a house for someone with vision.'

'And a hell of a lot of money for renovations,' said Lew, shaking his head regretfully.

'The new price reflects that,' said Mike quickly, feeling this potential sale slip through his fingers like ultra-fine sand. 'I'll be honest, there haven't been any viewings for over a year. The owner will look at any reasonable offer.'

'Offer him seven grand less than he's asking,' said Lew. 'That'll make up for the knock I've had to take on mine plus interest.'

'You're going for it?' said Mike, with a strangled gulp. 'Really?'

'Really?' asked Bonnie also.

'Yes,' said Lew. 'Really.'

'That was a mad, impulsive, ridiculous, stupid decision, wasn't it? Thank God I didn't put anything in writing,' said Lew, pulling up outside her house half an hour later. 'I think Colin and Mildred must have cast a spell on me.'

'The house is beautiful, stunning,' said Bonnie. 'It's got everything you'd ever want a home to have. And it has that lovely happy feel in it.' Some houses had it; like the one she'd grown up in, which had borne all its best and happiest times like a watermark. 'If you can afford it, you should go for it.'

'My heart is leading my head on this,' admitted Lew. 'That's very scary for me.' Then he grinned his lopsided grin and added, 'I'll be honest.'

Bonnie burst into a peal of laughter. 'He was extraordinarily honest for an estate agent, wasn't he?'

Lew's laughter joined with hers and fed it, which in turn fired his and both of them thought that they couldn't remember when their bellies had last ached so much and so joyfully.

'I couldn't carry on calling it Coldred House though, could I? What do you think, Bonnie? Any suggestions?'

'I think Daffodil House is perfect,' she said, thinking that when the sun was in the right position behind the stained glass window, it would throw a warm golden light on the stairs. 'It's very yellow though. Do you like yellow?'

Lew mused for a moment. He pictured Bonnie standing

in front of that same window in her Bonita Banana mac. Yes he liked yellow very much.

'You might have to change the name of the orangery to the lemonery,' she smiled.

'I love it,' replied Lew. 'The lemonery. Yes, Daffodil House it is. Let's cut its marriage with Colin and Mildred out of its history and return it to its maiden name.'

If only it were that simple to erase history, thought Bonnie, unclipping her seat belt.

She didn't suggest he come in for a coffee. He was a man who could buy a mansion on a whim and she made confetti out of scraps of paper so that she could afford a Chinese takeaway once a week.

'Thank you for coming with me, Bonnie. Enjoy the rest of your day.'

Lew wanted to suggest lunch but something inside him held up a stop sign. He was developing strong feelings for Bonnie and she had enough on her emotional plate with that husband of hers. Moving in on her when she was vulnerable was Stephen's trick, not his.

As he drove away, his thoughts strayed to Daffodil House. Bonnie had not been the only one to see past the revolting paint and the peeling plasterwork. He saw logs spitting in the fireplace and a large dog asleep on a rug in front of it. He saw a grandfather clock at the bottom of the stairs made from the same dark wood as all the furniture in the house. He saw children playing hide and seek on every floor, and he saw them drawing at a huge wooden table in the centre of the kitchen. The door to the *lemonery* was open letting the heady scent of garden flowers drift in. In his imagination, it smelled just like Bonnie's perfume.

# Chapter 73

The cheque from Christie's arrived on the Thursday of that week. Bonnie rushed over to the door when she saw the postman's head appear in the glass of the door. She was always first to pick up the post at the moment, even if it meant excusing herself from talking to a customer. It was always a relief when she flicked through it and found nothing with Stephen's writing on it.

She knew that Stephen had been following her around because she'd spotted him in the Morrisons car park in the town centre the previous night. He was driving an Aygo now and she wondered if he had changed cars so he could tail her, and if so, how many times he had managed to do so before he gave himself away.

The lines between her life and her nightmares were starting to blur; more so with every day that took her closer to 5 July. The CPS would have her file; it would be in someone's workload pile waiting for them to study and assess whether or not to prosecute her. Stephen's account would be damning and no doubt Katherine Ellison would have told the police how she had witnessed the heated exchange when Bonnie told Alma that she hated her enough to kill her. No one could bear testimony to how her relationship with Stephen's mother had altered beyond all belief over those last three months, how their two hearts had reached out to each other, met on peaceful ground and embraced, and the quiet tender moments they'd shared. On her last morning, as Bonnie gently sponged her face, Alma had been agitated, frustrated by something inside her she had to get out. Then, as if she'd summoned every vestige of strength left inside her, she had grasped Bonnie's hand, held it as tightly as she could and said with slow, clear, laboured words, 'You're a good girl. Be happy. When I'm gone, promise me you'll leave him.' The effort had exhausted her and she'd fallen back against her pillow then and Bonnie had stroked the hair back from Alma's face and said, 'I will, I promise.' It had saddened Bonnie that she had failed to shield Alma from the truth that her son was a cold, unfeeling shit.

She had grown to love Alma a little over those last weeks, and she was worried now that the old lady's resting memory would be dragged awake, paraded, dissected, mocked. Her last days had been constantly on Bonnie's mind, replaying during idle moments, at night before she slept, in her dreams. And every time she revisited that defining moment of lifting the bottle to Alma's lips, not once could she see her hand tilting even a fraction. She knew now that whatever acid Stephen had tried to drip into her consciousness to corrode the facts, in no way could she have hastened Alma's chosen moment to die by a single second. But she had no proof of that.

Every day now, Bonnie expected to walk into work and find Lew reading a letter from Stephen telling him what she had done. He didn't know that she'd diverted his last letter but he might guess that was the case and try a more direct method of contact. She lived in dread of Stephen finding out Lew's email and writing to him that way, because she'd have no chance of intercepting it. She had almost crashed her car that morning, seeing a black Aygo following her up Spring Hill. She'd been looking in her rear view mirror more than through the front windscreen and had to brake hard to stop herself ramming into the back of a left-turner. It hadn't been Stephen but she was still shaking when she pulled into the car park and had to stay there for five minutes to compose herself.

But today the post contained no bad surprises, only good ones: a thank you card from someone who had safely received a much-desired clock which Bonnie had parcelled up and sent to Australia, and that big, fat, fabulous cheque from the auction house.

'Do you want me to take the cheque straight to the bank when I go to the dentist at lunchtime?' she asked.

'Yes, and as it is very unlikely to bounce, will you do me a favour and go around to Mrs Twist's house and give her a cheque of her own.'

'I'd like that,' said Bonnie.

'Don't rush back. Go have lunch outside somewhere.' *Let the sun work its magic on you and cheer you up, my lovely Bonnie.*

She was wearing a dress the colour of strawberry icing today, but even that bold shade couldn't brighten her. She was fading before his eyes and he knew that her divorce was far tougher on her than his was on him. She had no con-trolling rein on Stephen like the one he had on Charlotte.

Bonnie wasn't going to the dentist but had an

appointment with the doctor. She had fought against the stress long enough now and needed some medical help. She wasn't sleeping, her appetite had dwindled, she was on the verge of tears all the time.

The doctor prescribed her anti-depressants but, he warned, they would take six weeks to start working. In six weeks when they made an impact on her system, her life would have changed for ever. If the CPS prosecuted or didn't, Lew would know what she had been accused of because Stephen would make damned sure he did. Tablets wouldn't even make a dent in the resulting depression she'd have then.

*

Mrs Twist lived in a ground-floor maisonette just out of the town centre. The small estate was inhabited totally by pensioners who were engaged in an unspoken competition to have the best front garden. Mrs Twist's pansied borders were crammed with stone fairies, sitting on toadstools or reposing amongst the flowers.

Bonnie rang the doorbell and a rasping buzz sounded in the depths of the house. She knew that it would be answered because she'd seen two figures sitting on a sofa through the large picture window when she walked down the path. Sure enough, the door soon opened to a chain-length and Mrs Twist's face appeared. She surveyed the dark-haired lady wearing the bright pink dress suspiciously.

'Hello. What is it?'

'Mrs Twist . . .'

'If you're J'ovah's Witness, I'm Church of England. And I don't buy owt on my doorstep.' The door closed to a slit.

'Mrs Twist, I don't know if you remember me, but my

name is Bonnie and I used to work at Grimshaw's antiques centre,' said Bonnie, when she could get a word in. 'I was working there the day you brought in a box of things. The white Gulvase and other stuff and—'

'Yes, I do remember,' said Mrs Twist, cautiously. 'What about it?'

'There was a Chinese cup and saucer in the box. It was painted and held together with staples. You took it to the Pot of Gold and Mr Harley the owner bought it from you.'

'I'm not giving him his money back, if that's what you want. I sold it fair and—'

'Please don't worry, Mrs Twist, it's nothing like that. I appreciate this might seem odd, but I have some news about those two Chinese pieces.' She took a small step back from the door because she didn't want to frighten the old lady. 'I work there now, in Spring Hill Square, you see. That cup and the saucer turned out to be very valuable.'

Now she had Mrs Twist's full attention and the door opened again as far as the chain would let it.

'Oh aye?'

'Mr Harley would like you to accept this. It's a cheque for seven thousand pounds.'

Bonnie held the cheque up for Mrs Twist to see and the old lady squinted and stared at it, but didn't extend her hand.

'Just a minute.' Mrs Twist momentarily disappeared whilst she relayed the information to the other person in the house with her. Bonnie heard a woman's loud 'Never!' and stifled a chuckle.

Mrs Twist returned with her glasses on.

'Oh yes, I recognise you now. What's your name again?'

'Bonnie. Bonnie Brookland,' she replied, momentarily forgetting that she'd given her married name. Bonnie poked the cheque through the aperture. 'You just put that in your bank. Mr Harley didn't think it was fair not to let you have something from the sale.'

Mrs Twist took the cheque and her whole demeanour changed. 'Ooh, well that's lovely that. Very nice of him. Thank you. Thank you very much.'

'Goodbye, Mrs Twist. Buy yourself something nice. Enjoy it.'

Bonnie turned and the door closed and Mrs Twist walked into her lounge with the cheque. 'Look at this, Kitty,' she said and handed it to her sister, who picked up her glasses in order to scrutinise it thoroughly.

'What did she say she was called?' asked her sister.

'Bonnie Brookland, she said. If she hadn't told me to go somewhere else I wouldn't have my spending money for our Italian caper. I thought I'd got a good deal with that hundred and fifty. And I felt rotten afterwards, Kitty, because I think I dropped her in it with my big gob. I told that Grimshaw fella that she'd said to go try another shop. I've felt bad about that ever since.'

Her sister rushed over to the window and knocked hard on it. Bonnie, about to get back into her car, turned around.

'What's up, Kitty?' asked Pauline Twist.

'I want to talk to her.'

Katherine Ellison, or Kitty as her younger sister had always called her, hurried to the door and trotted down the path towards Bonnie, who recognised her instantly.

'Hey, I want a word with you,' called Katherine.

Bonnie prepared herself for an onslaught. She felt tension prickling her skull.

'You remember me, don't you?' said Katherine.

'Yes, yes, I do,' said Bonnie.

'Come here, I want to talk to you.' She beckoned Bonnie forwards. Bonnie kept a safe distance because she half-expected the older woman to try and slap her.

'I've had the police round, you know.'

'Yes, I expected that,' replied Bonnie.

'Did you help her?' Bonnie noticed that Katherine was wearing the locket which used to be Alma's. Her voice had a tremble in it, an appeal. 'Please, Bonita, will you tell me honestly what happened to Alma? I know she'd bought something to end her suffering.'

Bonnie's heart jumped in her chest. 'You knew?' She couldn't think straight or what that might mean for her.

'Yes I knew. It was something that would make it look as if she had died in her sleep so that no one would know what she'd done. She told me.'

Bonnie's mind started spinning; her stomach felt heavy, flooded with a sick feeling.

'I told the police I knew,' said Mrs Ellison.

Bonnie hiccuped a huge sob that came from the deepest part of her, as if it had been pressed down like a jack-in-a-box and suddenly released. It was the first glint of hope she had seen in her dark sky. It meant everything to her.

'Please tell me you were with her at the end, that she wasn't alone?' Katherine Ellison's voice was full of a desperate need to be told what she wanted to hear, truth or not and she repeated the word. 'Please.'

'I was with her,' said Bonnie. 'She drank the drug and I held her and she fell to sleep, just drifted off, I promise you. It was so gentle that I don't know when she took her last breath. And I sat with her afterwards until Stephen came back.'

'Poor Alma. My poor darling friend.' Katherine Ellison shook her head, holding back a huge weight of emotion. So it was true then, Stephen had failed his mother when she needed him. It would have broken her heart.

'Mrs Ellison, I know she didn't like me very much for many years and I won't lie, I wasn't fond of her either, but I swear to you that I did everything, *everything* I could to make her comfortable and we made our peace in the end. I was very sad when she went.'

'Thank you,' Mrs Ellison replied. 'I would have liked to have been at her funeral.'

Bonnie frowned in puzzlement. 'Stephen said that he had rung you and told you about the arrangements but you'd decided not to come.'

Mrs Ellison's top lip tightened but it was not worth airing what she thought of him again. There was no end to his callousness.

'I'm so sorry,' said Bonnie. She knew from the expression on the older lady's face that yet another of Stephen's lies had just come to light.

Katherine sighed. 'It can't be helped now. I went to her grave and paid my respects when I came home. I didn't want her thinking I didn't care enough to show up.'

'I don't think she'd have thought anything negative about you, Mrs Ellison, from the way she spoke about you.'

Katherine Ellison's eyes lit up. 'Really?' she said, interest sparked.

'When she could speak she told me all about you and her as girls,' said Bonnie. 'About ice skating when Tinker's Lake froze and about you both trying to get pink hair by dyeing it with your mother's food colouring. All sorts of stories: when you went dancing, her wedding when she dropped her bouquet just before the car came and you mended it with pins for her. She loved you very much.'

Katherine groped for Bonnie's hand, sudden tears half-blinding her. For Alma to have shared things like that with Bonnie proved beyond measure how much she had come to mean to her. Alma didn't give herself away easily.

'We said our goodbyes before I went to Spain but she rang me there, you know. She told me how kind you were to her and how she'd misjudged you. I told the police about that phone call too.' Katherine Ellison's cheeks were damp but she was smiling. 'Thank you for being with my friend at her end. Thank you for telling me the truth. I wish you well, Bonnie. I hope I've helped you.'

And with that, Katherine Ellison turned and walked back into the house.

# Chapter 74

Stephen had plenty of time to spy now that he was on extended sick leave for stress. He'd confided in his HR officer at work that he had discovered his mother might have been murdered by his wife and hoped that she'd spread it around because she was a renowned gossip. Ironically, she'd felt sorry for him and respected his privacy.

He had seen Bonnie leave and he knew that there were only two customers in the shop, accompanied by a guide dog. He walked in, setting the doorbell tinkling. Lewis Harley had just finished wrapping something up for them and was saying that he would see them again soon he hoped. Stephen pretended to browse and only when the couple left did he turn to face Lew and saw that he was instantly recognised.

'Mr Harley,' he said with a sly grin, under the impression that he was talking to the enlightened. 'I can't believe you're still employing my wife.'

'I would like you to leave,' said Lew. He would remove him forcibly if he had to.

'Have you no shame?' Stephen's smile dropped.

'I won't tell you again.' Lew stepped forward and Stephen scuttled backwards towards the door.

'After what she did you'll still . . .? I'm going, I'm going,' he cowered as Lew strode right up to him.

Lew reached behind Stephen and pulled open the door. 'Get out please,' he wanted to shout, though he kept his voice level.

'A fine way to conduct business,' Stephen huffed. 'Well, I did try to warn you.'

'What are you talking about?' growled Lew, losing the last vestiges of his patience.

'My letter to you explained everything,' said Stephen.

'I have no idea what you mean,' returned Lew and Stephen knew from his reaction that he really didn't. He'd posted that letter through the door of the Pot of Gold himself. If Lewis Harley hadn't seen it, Bonita must have intercepted it.

'Ask Bonita what she did,' he said, with a salacious twist to his mouth. Then, grenade dropped, he turned from an irate but puzzled Lewis Harley and walked back to his car with a self-satisfied swagger in his step.

Lew didn't know whether to tell Bonnie about his visitor that lunchtime, spitting out his cryptic clues: *After what she did. Ask Bonita what she did.* What did he mean? Nothing, probably; he was stirring. And what letter? Something was bobbing around in his brain about a missing brown envelope that never turned up but it flittered away when he tried to pin it down.

He weighed it up in his mind and by the time Bonnie returned, he decided he should mention it to her: forewarned was forearmed. He asked her first about Mrs Twist but there was no easy bending of the conversation around to Brookland. He might as well just come out with it.

'Bonnie, Stephen was here today. I think he was looking for you. I threw him out. Not quite as dramatically as you can throw people out but I told him not to come back.' He smiled, hoping to put her at ease but she was blanching before his eyes.

'Did he say anything?' she asked.

'Not a lot. That he'd explained it all in a letter. And that I had to ask you what you'd done.' He gave her a puzzled look. 'I have no idea what he means, nor am I going to give it headspace. And neither should you.' But he saw worry cross her face like clouds cross the sun and he knew that there was something she wasn't telling him. *That bloody man*, he thought. 'Look, forget I said anything. Put the kettle on, Bonnie,' he said extra cheerfully, 'and break out the biscuits.'

Bonnie went into the back room to take off her coat and once she was out of his sight she bit her hand hard in an effort to stop the sob escaping her. The time had finally come. She had to leave the Pot of Gold before she too was thrown out.

She had walked back into the Pot of Gold after speaking to Katherine Ellison with hope in her heart that someone was on her side; that, at last, there was weight to the testament of her honesty; and it brought a pinprick of light to the end of the very dark tunnel in which she was crawling. But really, it meant nothing. Whether or not a jury believed what Mrs Ellison had to say above Stephen's spurious account, she, Bonnie Sherman, *had* committed a criminal act in assisting a suicide and she had no intention of not admitting to it. And Lew Harley did not associate with people like that; he was a highly regarded businessman, respected, honourable. She would not put him in the uncomfortable position of having to let her go once Stephen had exposed her, because she knew he was a good person and it would not be a duty he would relish.

She turned the sign in the door from open to closed as normal, sadly aware that she would not be back tomorrow. This would be the last time she closed the blinds, washed up their coffee mugs in the sink, shut down the PC, did a final circuit around the shop to check that all the lights were off. She would not see Lew Harley again. It was for the best. She was in love with him and it could go nowhere, they were from different worlds. She said goodnight to him, savouring the smile in his lovely deep blue eyes, knowing that she could not bear to risk another day and find those eyes unable to meet with hers; she would crumble from the pain and the shame. Once she reached home she wrote him a note, sealed it and drove straight back to the Pot of Gold to push it through the letter box for Lew to find in the morning. She noticed the black car tailing her and knew from the registration plate that it was Stephen. It didn't matter. It was over. He had won.

# Chapter 75

Lew walked in the next morning humming. His ridiculous offer on Daffodil House had been accepted and the Krugers wanted to move into Woodlea as soon as possible because they were presently renting a barn conversion out in Ingbirchworth which was costing them a small fortune. The sun was shining; he felt excited by the changes in his life but also that he was securely anchored to the lovely Pot of Gold. And The Rainbow Lady. He had decided that today he would throw caution to the wind and ask Bonnie if she would like to go out for dinner. He didn't have to make a big thing about it, just an informal 'works outing' he'd call it, to celebrate receiving the Christie's cheque. He wanted to know if there was the faintest chance that she might like him as more than just as a boss.

He picked up the blue envelope resting on the doormat. It had 'Lew' on the front. He slit it open using his finger and pulled out the folded sheet inside. He read it and then read it again because it didn't sink in properly the first time.

*Dear Lew*

*I am so sorry to have to tell you this way but I have found another job. I didn't want to let you know like this but they want me to start straightaway and I really do need a totally new beginning.*

*I have loved working for you. The Pot of Gold is the nicest place on earth and you are the best boss. I hope your divorce goes smoothly and that you are very happy in Daffodil House as you deserve to be. I hope you find a lady who makes you smile and likes all the same things that you do and gives you everything you want in life.*

*Be happy – and thank you.*

*My very best wishes*
*Bonnie*

He didn't buy it one bit that she had another job. She wouldn't have let him down like this, he knew that much of her. Then again, Stephen coming to the shop yesterday had totally freaked her and he understood completely why she might need to get away. He would give her space and time. She'd been putting on a brave face, a glass one and Stephen had smashed it. He crossed to the desk and wrote her a letter of his own.

*Dear Bonnie*

*I understand totally your need for a fresh start. The strain of your divorce must be terrible.*

*Enclosed are your wages to date, plus a bonus. The Pot of Gold will be a poorer place for your not being in it.*

*Your job is here waiting for you. No one else fits.*

*Lew x*

He would post it on the way home. Even if her car was there, he wouldn't put her under any pressure to open her front door, but just shove it through her letter box and leave. And he would hope that she'd read the words and believe him because they were true.

# Chapter 76

It was the oddest sensation sitting opposite a woman to whom he had been married for fourteen years, been intimate with, trusted, loved, honoured his vows for . . . and yet be looking into the eyes of someone he had no feelings about at all. They hadn't even cheek-kissed when she arrived at the table. Lew had directed that one. In retrospect he thought maybe he should have, out of courtesy, but the moment had passed.

Adriana de Lacey had thought that it would be a good idea now the divorce was in full swing for Lew to meet with his wife and converse civilly, if that were possible. The more a couple argued over the nitty-gritty, the richer it made her, but she was of the school that believed that the more a couple sorted things out between themselves, the easier it made her job – and life for all concerned.

Charlotte was in full designer offensive: the Roland Mouret dress and jacket which Lew always said he liked her in the best, the Tiffany jewellery which Lew had bought for her, and she was carrying the red Lulu Guinness handbag, the present that Lew had left on her pillow the night of

'Cakefacegate' so she would have something nice to come back to if the evening hadn't been quite up to standard. He could have laughed about that, had it not been so tragic. She had lost even more weight, he noticed. He wasn't sure if that was by design or stress, but either way it didn't interest him enough to ask.

'I have to say it was a surprise to hear you wanted this face to face meeting,' said Charlotte, blue eyes sparkling, red lips glossy and smiling. She picked up her glass of white wine and sipped it delicately. She crossed her long legs and he knew that every movement she was making was especially deliberate and chosen to show her off at her finest.

'I thought it was best that we were civil. We have a lot to sort out. We could make it relatively painless or throw all our money at the solicitors,' he said, then lifted his half-pint of diet cola to his lips; a drink that said both *this is not a cosy social meeting* and *I don't intend for it to last very long.*

'I agree,' said Charlotte.

'Have you found somewhere else to live?' The Krugers wanted to be in by mid-July.

'I'm going to move in with a friend for a while and then look for something when I get my settlement.'

He wondered which friend. He guessed it wasn't Gemma, which would only leave Regina. Surely not.

'I think a full and final settlement would be best, don't you?'

Charlotte tilted her head at him and then she laughed. 'Do you now?' Regina had warned her not to accept this. Lew expected that answer and had prepared for it.

'This is what I propose.' He reached in his jacket pocket, pulled out two sheets of folded paper and pushed the top one across the table at her. 'I've been generous.' And he had, but not stupid. Charlotte picked the sheet up, opened it and read it, long chocolate fingernails showing at either side, like bear talons. 'It's a one-time offer. I don't want any financial association with you, Charlotte. I want a clean break. This, however,' and he put the second sheet down on the bar table, 'is what you are entitled to and the most your solicitor will get for you. You can stick your claws into my pensions if you wish, but you'll be much worse off for it. Your call.'

He saw her throat rise and fall with a small swallow. She flashed a smile at him then, a hurt, brave one. A little part of her had been clinging to the hope that he'd called the meeting to stop the divorce, not accelerate it. Regina had told her to stick her crampons in until he bled, milk Lew for all he was worth, haunt him and make her presence felt every day for the rest of his life. Charlotte thought she would find a little love still left for her in his eyes, but there was nothing. He was looking at her as if she was a client and they were conducting some business. And he would forget about her as soon as the dotted line was signed.

Charlotte had done a lot of thinking in the four weeks since Lew had walked out on her. She missed him terribly, but with her hand on her heart, she didn't know if she loved him. It wounded her that he didn't want her any more, but that wasn't the same thing. She missed the attention he gave her, his company, the chivalrous way he treated her and the lifestyle they had much more than she missed his arms around her. She had been at her wits end when he had his heart attack, but on more than one occasion, she had sat by his hospital bed and mulled over how she would spend the enormous amount of money she'd receive if he didn't make it and she had to claim on his life insurance policies. She'd had the decency to hate herself for those thoughts.

She hadn't lied to Lew about sleeping with Jason because she could. She'd been to see him in all honesty about a car problem. He looked like the cock of the walk in his showroom, and she'd been unsure if she was imagining the little flirtations when he asked her into his office for a coffee. So she went back the week after to ask something else, and realised that her intuition was spot on. He'd taken her on his office desk and it had been dirty and raw, dangerous and thrilling and she hadn't once thought about the gold band on her finger. She didn't fancy him at all, but he made her feel powerful, sexy, desired, and a little bit evil because she'd got one over on his Miss Goody Two-Shoes wife whom she had never – and would never – be as virtuous as. Just as Jason would never be as fine a man as Lew. He was the best she could have ever had.

Charlotte had also learned that there wasn't that much in Regina's life to envy, apart from her money; and Charlotte could have enough of that without having to tear out Lew's innards and have him think of her often, but with nothing but spitting hatred, which would have been a result for Regina. As soon as she had bought another house, Charlotte had decided that she would never see Regina again.

She looked at the figures on the first sheet once more. He *had* been more than generous.

'Okay, I'll agree to this. I'll take it in to my solicitor.' She smiled, desperate to see a little of the old Lew, the one who looked at her with eyes full of love. But he didn't exist any more. This was another Lew, one that had grown from the ashes of the man she had destroyed. She had no place in this Lew's life.

'I thought you would.' Charlotte heard it as, *I thought you would because you're a greedy cow.* He might as well have slapped her.

'It wasn't all bad, was it?' said Charlotte, gulping back a throatful of tears with the last of her wine. 'We had some lovely times.'

'We did,' agreed Lew, but he wasn't sure any more. He had loved Charlotte very much, but when he stopped to think about it, he couldn't honestly say he *felt* loved by her. So many memories were tainted with the stain of the lies bleeding through them now. Moving into The Beeches because they both wanted a large family, the perfect holiday in Bali – he had taken her there to recover from the 'miscarriage' . . . he couldn't unpick the nice memories from the needles, the hidden barbs, the thorns. And he had no intention of even trying.

When Lew got back to the Pot of Gold, the couple with the guide dog were hovering by the entrance. He'd had to shut up shop when he went to meet Charlotte because there was no one to man it whilst he was away.

'Sorry about that, hope you weren't waiting long,' he said, unlocking the door, switching off the alarm, turning the sign around from closed.

He needed an assistant but he'd kept holding off from advertising for one because he hoped Bonnie would come back. Come home. Much as he loved the Pot of Gold, there was something missing because she wasn't there busying around, making coffees, dusting, arranging, just being there with her coloured dresses and her sunshiney smile. The Pot of Gold had reduced charm when there was no Rainbow Lady there. He had posted the letter through her door only eleven days ago, and yet it felt like forever. He hadn't lied when he'd said that no one else fitted. Not in the shop, not in his heart. They both had a Bonnie-shaped hole in them.

'Where's that lovely woman that works here gone?' asked the couple.

'She's having some well-needed time off,' said Lew. He said more or less the same thing to Stickalampinit, Long John, Stantiques, Clock Robin, Butterfly Barry, all the traders and dealers who were her friends and wanted to know why she wasn't there because they were worried about her. They'd asked him to pass on the message that if there was anything she needed help with, she only had to ask. Every time they came through the doors, they'd enquire when she'd be back. Tell her to hurry up, they said. Tell her the place isn't the same without her. He'd told them all that she was having a couple of weeks away to 'sort things out'. He left the reason vague. He didn't want to admit that she'd gone for good because saying it aloud would make it real.

# Chapter 77

Bonnie read the letter for the hundredth time. *No one else fits*, he had written. She had been in the house when he posted it eleven days ago. She had spotted him walking past the window and she had frozen. She had heard the letter box flap open and shut and watched the envelope drop to the floor. And that was the last of him that she would ever see, she knew that. It was a small consolation that she would never have to look into his beautiful twilight-blue eyes and find revulsion there.

She boiled the kettle and put a teabag in a cup. She was out of coffee but found it hard to go out to the shop these days. She felt as if that sun in the sky was picking her out like a giant searchlight intent on highlighting to everyone the criminal in their midst. She had too much time to think, sitting alone in the house all day, every day. By now she had enough bags of confetti made to stock an aircraft hangar. She needed a job, but her police bail date was in three days time and she had no idea how long after that her court date would be. She had a meeting with David Charles at two-thirty that afternoon and she was scared stiff about what he was going to tell her. She knew without a doubt that she was going to prison. How could she not? She was guilty of assisting a suicide at best; at worst they would level the charge of murder at her. It wouldn't be hard to plant seeds in a jury's mind that she had acted to rid herself of a burden she resented. Stephen was both eloquent and believable, and his barrister would have her saying all the wrong things and twist her words. And at the heart of it all, the truth was that if she could rewind time, she would have acted just the same and helped Alma take the little control she had left. Oh yes, she was going to prison all right, and no amount of wishful thinking was going to change that.

# Chapter 78

David Charles gestured towards the chair. 'Please take a seat, Bonnie.' He thought that the woman in front of him was so much more fragile than the one he had seen the morning after her arrest. She was wisp-thin, pale and there were dark rings around her eyes that told of sleepless nights, even though she was taking tablets designed to alleviate that. This was a woman crushed under a press of mental torture and yet he noted that she held her head high when she walked into his office. She might have been terrified of this tough world of police and cells and authority, but she had never once kicked against accepting the punishment for the part she had played in Alma Brookland's death.

'I asked you to come in for an update because I thought it might help you if you had any questions to talk through with me. Any trouble from your husband?' said David Charles.

'He's left me alone since I quit my job,' said Bonnie. He couldn't follow her in the car, because she didn't go anywhere. 'David, can you tell me what will happen on Friday? I can't remember. Do I need to take anything with me when

I turn up at the station? Will I have to stay in . . .' She was gabbling fretfully. David held up his hand and stopped her flow.

'Look, Bonnie, since my secretary rang you yesterday to make an appointment with me, there's been a proper update. I won't beat about the bush . . .'

*I won't soften the blow, I'll tell you it as it is, plain and simple, let's call a spade a spade;* her whole body scrunched up, her jaw tightened, she prepared herself.

'. . . in the last hour I have been told formally by the police that the CPS have knocked it back. They aren't prosecuting you. There's insufficient evidence and it is not in the public interest to take you to court, so it's over. And the police agree.'

He didn't expect her to react. People who were told this sort of news often didn't. 'Kicking bricks into treacle' was the phrase he likened it to. They were numb, thrown into shock, their brains would not accept what they'd just been told because they'd built a protective fence around themselves to guard against false hope and it would not be demolished by the impact of a few words. Sometimes he'd see the sun dawning on their faces as bit by digestible bit the information started to sink in, but he wasn't seeing this now with Bonnie.

'Bonnie, you can go home and carry on with your life,' he said gently, slowly.

'What about the police station on Friday?'

'There are no charges to answer, you are free. You do not have to turn up at the station. The police will send a letter to confirm all this but that's it, the end.' He buzzed on his intercom for his secretary to get a glass of water for Bonnie. He was a little worried she was going to faint.

'Please tell me you aren't in your car. I would not advise you to get behind a wheel,' said David.

'I had to get a taxi here because my car's got a puncture.' She'd had it a week but didn't want to go out of the house to get it fixed in case she saw Stephen framed in her rear view mirror. *Stephen*. She hadn't realised she'd groaned aloud until David asked if she was all right.

'Stephen. He'll go into overdrive . . .' The water was jiggling in the glass because her hand was shaking so much.

'Bonnie, he will be in big trouble if he does. He will have to forget it.'

'He won't though.'

'I think we both know that he wasn't primarily trying to get justice for his mother,' said David with conviction. 'If Stephen contacts you again, you must report him to the police for harassment, you won't have any problem with them believing you. He'll find that he's the one being arrested and investigated if he's not careful. He's told quite a few lies, has old Mr Brookland.' DS Bill Henderson had even told the solicitor that the police would be only too happy to review those statements Stephen had made. 'Once the law has told him to stop harassing you and he doesn't, he's flipping the bird at the law more than he is at you and the law doesn't like that, Bonnie. It makes the law very angry. Do you understand what I am saying?'

'Yes, I do. There's no . . . no chance you could have misheard what the police said?'

Maybe with other clients, David might have been slightly insulted by that, but now his face broke into a smile.

'None.'

'I'm sorry if that sounded rude. I . . .'

'Bonnie, you've been through a lot. But you can trust me

in this, it's over. Forget it and pick up your life where you left it. One of the receptionists downstairs will ring a taxi for you.' David Charles held out his hand. 'I wish you well, Ms Sherman. And I hope I don't see you again for the very best of reasons.'

Bonnie stood up. David Charles had a warm, firm, genuinely happy-for-her handshake.

'What about money? I must owe you some ...'

'You didn't incur any charges.' It was a small lie but a right one. The bill was minimal as most of it had been paid by Her Majesty's government. As a partner of the firm, he could and would write it off.

'Thank you, David. Thank you so much.'

She turned at the door. 'I was very fond of Alma by the end, you know. And she was fond of me.'

'I don't doubt it, Bonnie.' And he didn't.

Bonnie waited in reception with the glass of water, the words tumbling round and round in her head. *It was over. It was over. It was over.*

# Chapter 79

Just as the taxi was depositing Bonnie back home, Stephen Brookland received the news via Beth his FLO that the CPS were not going to prosecute and he was livid. She couldn't pacify him and listened patiently to his ranting about all the people he was going to contact: the newspapers, the TV, his MP, the Pope. She tried to warn him, yet again, that he could get himself into serious trouble and he should forget it and treasure his memories of his mother, but he hung up on her with blatant contempt. Then he rang David Charles, whose name was recorded in his thick file of evidence. David was only too happy to take the call when his secretary rang through to tell him there was a rabid gentleman who wished to speak to him about the murder his wife committed.

'Mr Brookland,' David greeted him cheerfully. 'How can I help you?'

'Do you realise what you've done in letting that woman free to roam the streets?' Stephen bellowed.

'I think you'll find the CPS are responsible for the outcome of the investigation, Mr Brookland, not me.' David was as calm as Stephen was manic.

'I won't let her get away with this. I'll make sure everyone knows what a murdering bitch she is. I've got an appointment with the editor of the *Daily Trumpet* later today, in fact.'

He was bluffing. David knew the new editor well and there was no way he'd touch this story with the longest bargepole in history. At least not from Brookland's angle. There would be mileage in a human interest story from his wife's perspective, but David would have bet his bottom dollar that Bonnie Sherman would just want it all to go away.

'I'd be very careful if I were you, Mr Brookland,' warned David. 'Unless you want this case to come back and haunt you in the worst possible way. The police just might want to revisit all the evidence you gave and gather up all those inconsistencies. You could find them building a case against you. Perverting the course of justice carries a stiff penalty these days.'

'What?'

'Reap what you sow, Mr Brookland. There is no case to answer against your wife, deal with that and move on would be my free advice.'

'Go to hell,' said Stephen and slammed down the phone.

Bonnie sat in her front room surrounded by all the lovely hotch-potch furniture with a cup of coffee in her hand. David Charles's voice was playing in a continual loop in her head telling her that there were no charges to answer, she didn't have to go to the police station and she wouldn't end up in court, but she couldn't believe it. Deep down she knew he wouldn't have told her if it wasn't true. But even if they had let the case drop, Stephen wouldn't.

The coffee had gone cold and she hadn't even sipped it.

*What now*? asked a voice within. *What do we do?* She had been so sure she would have to face trial, have her picture plastered all over the newspapers and the internet, end up in prison, that she hadn't planned for this outcome.

Now there was no longer a reason for Stephen to keep his mouth shut because there was no case to damage, so he would tell everyone what she had done. Once heard, it couldn't be unheard: *mud sticks*. Stephen would flout the law, whatever David Charles said might happen to him if he did.

She would have to leave and go to a place where no one knew her, where Stephen couldn't find her. She'd have to give up this lovely little house where she felt protected and cosy.

An urgent rapping on the door shocked her so much she dropped the cup of coffee and saturated her sober black solicitor-visiting skirt. It was a demanding, impatient Stephen kind of knock.

Bonnie heard the flap on the letter box spring open and a voice call through it.

'Bonnie, it's Valerie. I know you're in so open this damned door. What's going on?'

# Chapter 80

Bonnie opened the door and there stood her lovely friend, tall and tanned and long and lovely, like an older version of the Girl from Ipanema.

'So you are alive?' Valerie said, marching straight into the lounge and taking a seat at the table. 'I hear from Lew that you're on leave to "sort yourself out". I knew he was lying, of course, the man's an idiot if he thought I'd buy that. I'll have a black coffee please, and the truth.'

Bonnie obediently and silently walked into the kitchen and reappeared with two mugs. She sat down opposite Valerie and as soon as she raised her head and made eye contact with the older woman she burst into tears.

Valerie leaned across and gripped Bonnie's hand. 'You're going to talk to me,' she said in her no-nonsense tone. 'You're going to tell me what's going on.'

'When did you get back?' asked Bonnie.

'Sunday evening. I went into the Pot of Gold this morning to replenish my stock and see you, and then Lew tells me that load of rot.'

'I've still got your iron and your—'

'Oh bugger the iron. What's wrong?' Her voice softened. 'Dear Bonnie, what's happened?'

Inside an exhausted, bewildered Bonnie, the dam wall crumbled and out it all gushed. Every last detail about Alma and Stephen and the police. And Valerie listened and digested without one atom of judgement or repugnance present in her eyes, her voice or her manner.

If Valerie had owned a mobile she would have rung as soon as she left Bonnie's house, but as she had managed all her life quite adequately without one, she had to wait until she got home to use her landline. She called Clock Robin before she had even taken her coat off.

'Valerie, what can I do you for?'

'Are your lock-picking skills still intact?'

'Apart from when the arthritis in my thumb flares up. Why?'

'A dear friend of mine . . . of ours is in need and I think your services may be required to help.'

'Say no more. At least not on the phone, Valerie,' said Robin, who had once been more infamous for his silky catburgling skills than famous for his knowledge of timepieces.

# Chapter 81

'You don't think we're going too far, do you?' asked Mart Deco, watching Valerie pull the balaclava over her head. 'I mean, what if there are security cameras and they've picked us all up.'

'There are no security cameras aimed at the house,' replied Clock Robin. 'I had a good look round earlier on. I did a little leaflet dropping and cased the joint. Trust me, I can smell CCTV cameras from a thirty-yard range. We're fine.'

'What if laddo rings the police?'

'He won't ring the police,' said Valerie, pulling on enormous black padded gloves that gave the impression her hands were like bunches of overripe bananas. 'He'll be too scared to watch re-runs of *The Bill* when we've finished with him.'

'We aren't actually going to do anything to him though, are we?' asked Mart, looking concerned.

Valerie's hands went to her waist, which looked anything but slender now in the oversized donkey jacket.

'What do you think we are, Mart? Animals?'

'No, don't be daft. It's just that we all look really ...

serious,' he replied. Despite being the size of a brick shithouse with a Grant Mitchell haircut and having a face that looked as if someone had been chopping wood on it, Mrs Deco had drawn some teardrop 'prison tatts' on his cheek and a 'cut-here' line round his neck with a Sharpie to make him look hard. 'Even you, Valerie.' And that was before Long John handed her the two-foot-long bolt cutters.

'Well, Stephen Brookland isn't going to be intimidated by a woman,' she laughed by way of a reply. 'But he will be by someone in a balaclava holding something that could have him singing soprano with a single clip.' She opened the cutters and snapped them shut again in Mart's face. He and the other four men at his side all closed their legs simultaneously.

'We aren't going to stop him making Bonnie's life an absolute misery if we turn up and wag our fingers at him, darling. Do you want Bonnie looking over her shoulder for the rest of her life? She needs us, Mart. Some people will not see reason and the only way to deal with the Stephen Brooklands of this world is to give them a short sharp shock that they won't forget in a hurry.'

'We have to make it look convincing, Mart,' added Long John. He knew that his friend was a sensitive soul and he'd had a rough year and even though he had been the first to stick up his hand and volunteer his services, he was a law-abiding citizen at heart. 'Stephen Brookland is a bully and like all bullies, he will be a chuffing big coward as well. Valerie is right. This is the only kind of thing that sort listen to.'

'If you want to stay in the van, Mart, none of us will hold it against you,' said Valerie softly. Her voice and sadistic appearance were wildly at odds with each other.

Mart pursed his lips and nodded decisively. 'No, I'm doing it for Bonnie as I said I would. And for Brian.' He looked up at the starry sky. 'I owe Bonnie's dad more favours than I can count.' He smashed his gloves together like a superhero. 'Come on, guys. Let's do this thing.'

*

Stephen Brookland had taken some Night Nurse. He didn't have a cold but it was guaranteed to knock him out because he'd hardly had any sleep at all in the three nights since he was told the CPS had dropped the case against his wife. His stupid family liaison officer had been as much use as a damp match, telling him to forget it and move on. And that idiot solicitor who had been looking after his wife had more or less threatened him with police action. *Him* – the innocent party in all this. He had felt sure the newspapers would be interested in the story of his mother's murder, but no one had replied to his emails. The world had gone mad, no wonder he was suffering from insomnia.

He had drifted off to his medically-induced slumber that night weaving plans: *Murderer* written in red paint across the front of the house where his wife lived in Rainbow Lane. He'd find out how Facebook and Twitter worked and feed her name onto the internet and watch her infamy spread worldwide. How dare she have the effrontery to leave him? His mother's demise was the perfect evocative vehicle to ride in order to punish his perfidious wife for her abandonment of him.

An urgent ting-a-ling-a-ling-a-ling sound drew him slowly up through the depths of sleep to the surface of consciousness, though confusingly his brain discerned a different pitch to the alert on his alarm clock. He opened his eyes to find a crescent of six people standing around his bed, all carrying torches trained up at their faces to distort their features. In the middle of them all stood a very tall figure, dressed like the others in black clothing, but this one had on a balaclava with three small circles cut out for the eyes and mouth. He, he presumed, was carrying something in his gloved hands, but Stephen couldn't make out what. The word 'enforcer' drifted into his mind and made his eyebrows shoot up his forehead. He turned to the clock on his bedside cabinet. It read two-fifteen.

'No, you're not dreaming, Stephen,' said the figure nearest to him on his left, a very short man who was vaguely familiar.

Stephen's back snapped upright; he was now certain this was not some sort of hallucination.

'What the—'

'Shhh. It's nighttime,' said the enormous man on the right. His finger was resting against his lips. The torchlight picked out the tattoos on his face and neck.

'Who are you?' said Stephen, in a panic. 'I haven't much money. My wallet is in that drawer.' He pointed to his dressing table. 'I have a computer on the table over there. I don't have any iThings or a mobile or expensive equipment such as—'

'Shuttup a minute, for God's sake. You're making my ears bleed,' said the short man. 'And you can stop lying as well because we know you're absolutely minted. I've heard you make Richard Branson look like a church mouse.'

'I . . . I'm not, I . . .'

Stephen's eyes swept over the forbidding figures and it dawned on him then where he knew these people from.

He'd seen them go in and out of the Pot of Gold when he was spying on Bonita. They were antique dealers. Just common antique dealers.

'He's worked out who we are,' said Long John, watching the changes on Stephen's features slide from panic to confusion and then enlightenment.

'Get out,' ground Stephen through his teeth. 'All of you. Before I call the police.'

'I don't think so, Sunshine,' said Robin, taking one step forward in perfect synch with Valerie. She lifted up the bolt cutters so Stephen could see them clearly.

Stephen's eyes widened to the size of spaceships.

'Wha . . . what . . .'

'You see, Stephen,' began Long John with calm menace, 'we don't like what you've been doing to Bonnie.'

'Bonita?' said Stephen, his eyebrows dipping in puzzlement. 'You're here because of her? Do you know what she did? Well, let me tell—'

'We all know,' said Mart. 'She helped your mum when she needed someone. Unlike you, you gutless bas—'

Stan put his hand on Mart's arm to quell his rising anger. Mart's mum had died in February and he was still raw from the pain he'd had to watch her endure.

'Now, what we can't understand, Stephen, is why you aren't getting on with your own life and leaving her be. Because we're her friends and we care about her,' said Long John, smiling in the way a crocodile might smile at an antelope before dragging it into the water. 'So—'

He was interrupted by Stickalampinit talking as if he had cotton wool stuffed in his cheeks and had just got off a plane from New York.

'We're here to make you an offer you key-ant refuse.'

The others turned to look at his oddly swollen jawline and realized that he *had* stuffed cotton wool into his cheeks.

'It's less painful if you go with it rather than try to pull back,' Long John advised.

'The only poi–sens you'll be able to talk to are gonna be de fishes,' said Stickalampinit, obviously enjoying being a mob godfather for the day.

The dealers started to roll up their sleeves in preparation. The tall figure snapped the bolt cutters ominously.

'Wait a minute,' said Stantiques, with a contemplative finger placed artfully on his cheek. 'If we cut off his tongue, he can still write things down, can't he?' He made a chopping motion with his right hand against his left wrist.

Stephen squeaked.

'Good point,' said Long John. He addressed Stephen. 'You left or right-handed?'

Before Stephen could answer, Sticka-'Don Corleone'-lampinit spoke. 'It don't make no diff'rence. Take off da left, he's gonna be able to type with da right. Take off both of da hee-ands and he's gonna learn how to type wid his feet.' He pointed at Valerie. 'Hannibal's gonna have to take everything aw–f.'

Stephen repeated the tall man's apparent name at a pitch only sheepdogs could hear properly and Long John bit his lip to stop himself giggling.

'It's not his real name, but Hannibal fits him much better if you know what I mean,' Robin explained to Stephen. 'He's been looking forward to a nice tongue sandwich with his Chianti. And now, it seems, he's going to have a finger buffet too.'

Stephen farted in fear and Mart wafted his hand in front

of his face. Long John sat down on the edge of the bed at Stephen's side and rubbed his chin thoughtfully.

'Oh Mr Brookland, this is turning out to be a much bigger job than I thought. We've only brought bolt-cutters, you see. Would you mind staying here quietly whilst I go and get my full tool kit from the van?' He smiled a dangerous, humourless smile, his front gold tooth twinkling in the torchlight. Stan and Robin shivered at the sight of it. It would be too easy to believe that Long John wasn't acting.

'Please don't hurt me. I haven't done anything. I won't tell anyone. Just take my money and my cufflinks,' Stephen begged, panicking now and scrabbling around in his brain for bargaining tools. 'I've got some foreign coins in the same drawer . . . and a signed photo of Conway Twitty.'

Stan gave a snort of laughter and tried to make it look like a sneeze. Everyone thought it was a good job Starstruck wasn't with them.

'That's very kind of you, but no thanks,' said Long John. 'You see, you can't buy loyalty to friends, Stephen. Not even with a million pesetas and a scribble from a country and western great.' He looked at his watch and stood up. 'I'll be back in fifteen minutes, boys.'

'Wait,' called Stephen, but Long John was gone.

No one spoke for what seemed like ages, then Valerie started tapping the bolt-cutters against her cupped hand with obvious impatience.

'Once he smells fear, he don't like waitin' none,' Stickalampinit explained Valerie's actions to Stephen who started wildly shaking his head from side to side like a little boy protesting that it wasn't he who had drawn on the wallpaper with felt tips.

'If you go, I won't call the police, I promise,' Stephen wailed.

Stan leaned in close to him.

'Why don't I believe you, Stephen?'

'I'll swear on a Bible. There's one in my wardrobe. It was my mother's.'

'You would ha' sworn on da Bible in coor-t, Mr Brooklyn, and lied your freakin' head orf,' said Stickalampinit, so stuck in Americanisms, they even transferred to Stephen's name. 'So maybe you can see why we ain't taking dat as no reek-o-mendation.'

A moment of silence ensued so still that they all heard Stephen's gulp.

'Do you know what a hydra is, Stephen?' asked Stan, not waiting for an answer before continuing. 'It's a mythical being and as soon as you cut off one of its heads, two more grew back in its place.'

Stephen looked totally confused and unsure why the conversation had shifted to Greek mythology.

'We are the hydra,' said Stantiques, spreading his arms wide. 'You can have us all arrested, but for every one of us you report, two more dealers will come and pay you a visit.'

'And we are de nice guys,' added Stickalampinit. 'The others –' he lifted and dropped his shoulders regretfully '– they're da ones that make us look like liddle pussy-kets. Even Hannibal don't like to hang around wid dem.'

'I promise, I won't ring the police. You have my word.' Stephen smiled hopefully just as Mart's mobile rang in his pocket. He got it out and spoke into it. 'Yes, everything's fine. Oh you've got the tool-box and you're on your way back, that was quick. Okay, see you in five minutes, *Killer.*' Mart was rather proud of thinking up that little touch. He clicked off his phone, slipped it back in his pocket and addressed the 'hydra'. 'He's got the tool-box, he's on his way back and he'll be here in five minutes.'

'I won't say a word,' Stephen said again. His voice had more vibrato than Paul Potts singing 'Nessun Dorma'.

'I know you won't,' Stan said, suddenly serious. 'And I know you won't because we will hear about it if you do. The antiques world is a close-knit community, Stephen, and we look after our own. We have eyes and ears everywhere.' He nodded a signal to Mart, who crossed to the window and snatched open the curtains. Something small was hovering outside with a light on the front. 'We've had drones tailing you for weeks. We've been watching you watching Bonnie. We know what shopping you buy, where you have your hair cut, even what top-shelf magazines you buy from the newsagent.'

'I beg your pardon,' protested Stephen. 'I do not buy—'

'Thing is, as you know, if you throw a bit of mud around, it sticks. Lots of people believe lies, Stephen. That's what you are relying on, isn't it? You can't get your day in court, so you're going to punish Bonnie by painting her as black as your soul, aren't you?'

From what Bonnie had told Valerie about Stephen, she suspected what his modus operandi might be. From the speed at which the blood drained from Stephen's face, she'd hit that nail squarely on the head.

Mart pulled the curtains shut again.

'So if you want to keep everything intact, Stephen, I think it would be wise of you to stay right away from Bonnie, give her what she's due in the divorce and let your mam lie in peace, don't you?' Stephen stared at him, frozen, so Stan repeated the two words at volume. 'DON'T YOU?'

Stephen wagged his head.

'For the benefit of the recording, can you please answer that verbally.'

'Recording?' asked Stephen.

'Just ian-ser the question,' said Marlon Brando, holding his hands out in exasperation.

There was an audible knock on the back door. Stephen jerked.

'It's Killer with the tool-box,' said Stan, running with Mart's brainwave. 'Let him in will you, someone?'

'Yes, I promise. I swear,' gasped Stephen. 'I really do, I swear on everything.'

'That's the spirit,' said Stan. He raised two fingers, pointed them at his own eyes and then at Stephen. 'As Sting once said, "I'll be watching you".'

'Every move you make,' added Stickalampinit for good measure.

As they filed silently out of the door the tall figure in black snapped the bolt cutters one last time and Stephen knew he'd have to get up and change his fitted sheet.

The troupe of six silently and sleekly walked down Stephen's back garden, strode over the low fence and traversed the farmer's field. It was a moonless, pitch-black night but guided by their downward angled torches and holding on to each other they quickly reached the darkened street where they had parked Stan's van. They all piled in the back of it, except Valerie who climbed into the front passenger seat. She stripped off the black balaclava and shook out her steel-grey long hair.

'I think we can safely assume that Bonnie won't be getting any more trouble from that awful man,' she said.

Stickalampinit pulled the cotton wool out of his cheeks but strangely his voice remained the same. 'He ain't gonna give no one no shit never.'

'I'll fly the drone a few times up to his window when I know he's in,' said Long John, lifting up his son's remote control helicopter with a battery-operated LED light duct-taped on the front. 'Just to make sure he knows the hydra wasn't making idle threats.'

They laughed and the joyful sound bounced around the van. They felt that, wherever he was now, Brian Sherman would be chuckling with them, touched that his past kindnesses to them all hadn't been forgotten.

# Chapter 82

Long John was taking an age to polish an Asprey silver pill box, Stickalampinit was arranging his latest creation in his unit — a stuffed scraggy ancient fox with a lightbulb sticking out between its ears — and he and Mart Deco were giggling like schoolboys about something that had happened last night, or so Lew picked up in a snatch of conversation. Starstruck was telling the story of how he met Frank Sinatra to Butterfly Barry who was pleased as punch with the Painted Lady stained glass panel he'd just bought. The old couple with the guide dog were back in yet again looking through Vintage Valerie's clothes. They were all jigsaw pieces that made up a wonderful picture of familiarity. But it was not complete because there was a piece missing, in the shape of The Rainbow Lady, and the sense of loss hadn't faded at all with the days that passed.

He missed her bringing the sunshine in with her when she opened the door each morning, he missed her bright colours, her smile, her lovely hazel eyes. He just missed being with her, in her orbit. And he had no idea what to do about it because he wasn't even sure she thought about him in the same way he thought about her . . . but he wanted to find out. Even when he had been walking around Daffodil House with her, she was the one he pictured drawing the curtains in the evenings, planting flowers into tubs in the garden, sitting at the table with and eating Chinese food out of cartons.

The door opened and in walked a group of four old ladies.

'This is the place I was telling you about,' one of them was saying.

'Oooh, I love places like this,' said another.

'We'll have a poke around and then go for tea next door. They do a lovely cake.'

Two of the old ladies made a beeline for Uncle Funky's toys and teddies, the other two came up to Lew at the counter. One of them knocked on it to attract his attention.

'Hello,' she said. It took him a couple of seconds to register who she was.

'Mrs Twist. How lovely to see you again.'

Pauline Twist patted her hair at the back, flattered that she'd been remembered.

'I came in to say thank you for that cheque you sent. It was very nice of you, very unexpected, very decent. I can't imagine anyone else would do it.'

'It's a pleasure,' smiled Lew. 'Though I can't take all the credit as it was Bonnie's idea as well. The lady who took it to you.'

'Where is she?' asked the other lady, who Lew guessed was her sister. They were very alike in their facial features.

'She's having a . . . little bit of time off,' said Lew, rolling the same line out yet again.

'I'm not surprised, are you, Kitty?' said Pauline, turning to her sister.

'Is she all right?' asked Katherine Ellison.

'You were so happy for her, weren't you, Kitty?' Pauline Twist leaned forwards to Lew and thumbed back at her sister. 'She spoke up for her, you know.'

'Pauline,' Katherine cautioned her sister with a tug on the arm.

Lew had no idea what she was talking about, but he wanted to find out. He jumped on the moment and bluffed.

Looking around to make sure he wasn't in danger of being overheard, he whispered, 'It's all right, I know *all* about it.' He felt his heart rate quicken with tension. 'Bonnie's told me *everything*. That's why she's off work.'

The ladies bought the lie. 'Stephen came to see me again,' said Katherine. 'He should let Alma lie in peace. He doesn't care half as much about her as he pretends to. He's using his poor dead mother to try and control his wife. And I told him as much and not to come back. I'm just glad it's all over. Bonnie must be so relieved.'

Now Lew was totally confused. He didn't understand what Stephen's late mother had to do with anything.

He heard the front doorbell jangle and saw, out of the corner of his eye, Valerie walk in. She waved to attract his attention and he gestured that he'd be with her soon. But he wasn't about to break off this conversation for anyone.

'Look, I have no right to ask this,' said Lew, 'but I think the world of Bonnie and I know Stephen has been trying to cause trouble for her. Will you tell me the whole story so I can help?'

'I thought you knew.' Katherine Ellison's spine stiffened.

'I lied,' said Lew. 'I'm sorry. But I'm worried about her. Really worried. Please.'

'I'm afraid it isn't my place . . .' Katherine Ellison edged backwards.

'Please. I've been so concerned. Help me to help her.'

Katherine looked at her sister for guidance.

'The only other person who can tell me what's going on is Stephen,' Lew tried.

That worked. 'You'd better tell him, Kitty,' said Pauline. 'At least he'll get it straight from you.'

Katherine Ellison gave a long sigh of resignation. 'Do you have somewhere we can talk in private?' she said to Lew.

# Chapter 83

Bonnie could hear the man talking from around the corner, as she walked back home with her bag of shopping from the supermarket on the High Street.

'I know you're in there. I'm staying here until you speak to me. Enough of this nonsense. Bonnie Sherman, come out unless you want me camping on your doorstep and upsetting the neighbours.'

She peeped around the corner to see Lew speaking into her letter box. He'd been there some time from the way his hair was plastered flat with the rain.

'I'm not joking,' he said.

'Lew.'

He straightened up and turned to see Bonnie there standing in her Bonita Banana yellow mac and under it, her dress with the coloured splashes on it. The one she had worn when they went to see Daffodil House. He wanted her to see it again. He wanted her to help him pick the carpets and the wallpaper and the plants for the garden: rainbow colours and daffodils, millions of them.

'Oh, you weren't in after all. I saw the car and presumed—'

'I've just been to the Co-op. It's only round the corner. For coffee and milk and stuff,' she said, not knowing why she was going into detail. The sight of him was doing all sorts of weird things to her. She felt hot but she was shivering. She felt anchored to the ground, but light enough to blow away. She felt as if someone had just injected a giant syringe full of joy into her heart, but it was racing with fear too. Her whole body had no idea how to behave.

'I've been here for ages.' His voice was a croak. It was so good to see her, but she looked so thin and crushable. He wanted to clear the space between them and wrap his arms around her but he was scared she would break.

'Have you?'

'So, you have coffee and milk.' He pointed to the bag of shopping.

'Yes, I have coffee and milk.'

They both wondered at the same time why they were talking like a Janet and John book.

'Can I come in?' asked Lew.

She nodded shyly and unlocked the door and Lew walked into the sweet little lounge that smelt of beeswax polish and summer flowers. He took the bag of shopping from her, put it down on the carpet and then hadn't a clue what to do. The air between them seemed to vibrate from the emotion crowding the room: disbelief, uncertainty, tenderness but above all hope.

'Bonnie, I . . .'

Nothing could have held her back: she threw herself at him and he pulled her so close his body began to mould itself to hers.

'I have missed you so much,' he said. 'We have all missed you.'

And Bonnie Sherman, 'as in the tank', let herself savour the sensation of being pressed against him, feeling his heart say hello to hers through their skin. She had wished for this moment so many times, pictured how it would be to have Lew Harley's mouth move in her hair, the touch of his hands, the strength of his arms around her but she had never thought it would happen. He was a wish too far, a star too high, yet here she was breathing him in, hearing him say her name as a lover would.

'I know all about Stephen's mother and what you did for her. Katherine Ellison came to see me. And so did Valerie. Oh, Bonnie, you should have told me, I would have been there for you. How could you ever think I wouldn't understand?'

He could feel her tears through his shirt as he held her in the circle of his embrace.

'It hasn't been the same without you, Bon,' said Lew. 'Come back to the Pot of Gold. Come back to us: Stickalampinit, Mart and Valerie, Long John, Clock Robin ... come back to me. They love you, I love you. Bonita Banana Sherman, I bloody love you.'

She lifted her head and when she looked up at his handsome, beloved face and into his indigo-blue eyes, she knew this was the sort of love she'd only dreamed of ... and wished for. A feeling only bettered, seconds later, by Lew Harley's gorgeous lips cautiously, softly, fabulously meeting with hers and sending the brightest colours in the universe flooding forever into that infamous grey Sherman rainbow.

# Epilogue

It is summer and in the park a man is pushing a pram in the sunshine. He and the woman linking his arm are only taking a short walk because the second baby due in two months is a whopper. The red fluff of puppy chasing the ball will have to make do with that, but he'll survive. Both children will be in the same year at school because the parents didn't want to waste much time.

There is still a lot of work to do in Daffodil House, which has reverted back to its old name. But the lounge is bright and the sun streams in through the huge windows during the day and the kitchen, despite its size, still manages to remain cosy and a place where people want to linger. One Friday every month, the couple who own the house sit at the table in there and eat Chinese food from the cartons and they never lose sight of simple pleasures such as that.

The house is filled with beautiful old furniture, except for the nursery which has some new pieces in it and rainbows painted all over the walls. There is a mobile hanging over the cot with bananas dangling from it.

The man wants to tell the world that when life offers you

a second chance, you take it and hold it and run with it and you cherish it. And that pots of gold really do exist at the end of rainbows, because he's found his.

The woman wants to tell everyone that if you wish for something, then picture yourself doing it, then you go for it with all your heart, you really can make your dreams come true, just as she has. Because Bonita Banana Harley is her mother's daughter. She is the Queen of Wishful Thinking.

*The greater your storm,*
*The brighter your rainbow.*

# Acknowledgements

It's always a delight to thank people who have helped me whilst writing a book. With this one, I had to work again with two wonderful gentlemen who have to be top of my list for credit.

Firstly my ex-solicitor, and now super-savvy business consultant, David Gordon at dcgbusinessplus.co.uk. I'm so glad that the course of events in the 'noughties' brought me into contact with such a great bloke. It was a pleasure to be his client then and no hardship to liaise with him to make sure I have all my legal 'I's dotted and my 'T's crossed now. And it's slightly cheaper to talk to him as a friend. Is the competent, brilliant, razor-sharp David Charles based on him? Of blooming course he is!

Equal top billing is my 'go-to' policeman who at heart is still the dear, daft kid who shared my passion for Steeleye Span many moons ago; I remain a superfan. Superintendent Pat Casserly is a fount of knowledge, a blessing for a writer and is never too busy to shut an old pal in a cell. For research purposes only, you understand. West Yorkshire Police have been incredibly helpful to me on many occasions – thank you all. Pat, I adhere to our deal on payment for information supplied and if ever one of my books is made into a film, I will do my utmost to fulfil my promise to you.

Thank you to my agent Lizzy Kremer, who always makes her writers feel as if they are her only client. Lizzy, you are the BEST. I hope you never get sick of people telling you that.

Thank you to my publishers Simon & Schuster and the team: God, Suzanne, SJ, Laura, Emma, Dawn, Dom, Joe, Jess, Rich, Sally and Sian. Apologies to anyone I've missed! And my gorgeous ex-editor Clare Hey, whom I shall miss terribly, but I know that I am in the safest hands with the fabulous Jo Dickinson.

Thank you to my amazing copyeditor Sally Partington who I love working with, one of my favourite parts of the whole process. She makes me look like a real writer who knows where to put a semi-colon.

Thanks to all my friends at the *Barnsley Chronicle*. I reiterate, the *Daily Trumpet* is not based on them. I'd love to tell you which newspaper really inspired it though.

Special thanks to the Team Milly ladies who are a joy to know and to Mike Bowkett at Gardeners who has backed my horse from the off.

Thanks also to the Higgs family. Yes, there really was a scrapyard in Barnsley patrolled by a lion – Ben. Ben's owner, Dennis, really did used to freeze sheep's heads for him to lick in summer and he did ride with Dennis in the truck. And he liked to lie on the rug and watch the telly. The family have given me some lovely material over the years. Our town is crackers and I love it.

Huge thanks to my beloved sons Tez and George who keep me topped up with coffee and don't moan too much when I'm on an edit and the laundry is piled high as Everest. Massive big sloppy-kiss type thanks to my fiancé Pete who is an antiques dealer and has supplied me with loads of details of the antiques world, including all those marvellous nicknames. There really is a Boombox and an Uncle Funky, amongst others. And all my mates because lovely people are the most important thing in this world. And Starbars.

And thank you, dear readers, because without you I wouldn't have a job. I'd still be doing this for a hobby but I wouldn't get any of the touching letters and the emails that say that my creations have found their way into your hearts. There are few greater compliments that you can give a writer.

If you loved reading

## The Queen of Wishful Thinking

turn the page for the first chapter of

## Sunshine over Wildflower Cottage

Available now in paperback and eBook

# Chapter 1

A person could have been forgiven for thinking that by driving to the hamlet of Ironmist, they were crossing the boundaries of time as well as county divisions. Viv Blackbird half expected to see King Arthur and the knights of his Round Table in her rear-view mirror when she had passed the grey stone castle on the crest of the hill. The castle was the seat of the Leighton family, she knew. They owned most of the land around here and had done since before the Big Bang. The area from the hilltop down to the hamlet below had once been called *High-on-the-Mist,* though the name had long since been contracted to Ironmist, or so the internet told her. Viv was headed for the bottom of the dell where the Wildflower Cottage Sanctuary for Animals was situated. As the road turned sharply away from the castle and began to dip, she could see how the old name had suited it perfectly. A low mist had settled in the bowl of the valley. It was as if the ground were made of smoke. It looked both beautiful and weird; but then weird was good sometimes.

A black horse was trotting along the road. Its rider was a

woman who was wearing her long hair loose and it was as black as the horse's mane. Viv dabbed her foot on the brake, even though she was hardly speeding anyway, and swung out to the other side of the road. The woman didn't even acknowledge the consideration. In fact, if anything, she gave Viv a look that said *what is your car doing on the road anyway?* Viv hoped she wasn't representative of the welcome she was going to receive. She'd never lived in a place as small as this but knew they had the reputation of being cliquish. She also hoped there weren't any horses in the sanctuary. She didn't like the unpredictable massive things and couldn't understand how anyone would want to climb up onto their backs and give them free licence to throw you off and then trample all over you.

Viv turned down what she presumed was the main street through Ironmist, passing a pretty row of cottages, a barber on one side of the road, a pub called The Lady of the Lake on the other. A woman was washing her front step with a bucket of water and a scrubbing brush. An A frame stood outside the Ironmist Stores and Post Office holding a hand-written sign which read: *MR WAYNE HAS HAD HIS OP AND HE'S FINE.* Viv smiled. That notice gave her better hope that she was about to join a friendly community.

*Jesus.* She slammed on her brakes as a dog wandered into the road. A huge beast of a thing. It was larger than the dog that had played the title role in the TV adaptation of *The Hound of the Baskervilles.* A tall, squarely-built young man approached the car, holding up his hands apologetically. Viv lowered her window as he indicated that he wanted to speak to her.

'I am so sorry,' he said. 'My fault. I let go of his lead. Are you all right? You're shaking like a jelly.'

Viv looked at her hands clamped onto the steering wheel and noticed that her little finger was vibrating.

'I'm okay, thank you,' she replied, though she didn't entirely feel it. Thank goodness she hadn't been going any faster.

The man stroked the big dog's head. 'He's called Pilot,' he said. 'He's twelve. I love Pilot.'

The man's size had deceived Viv. Up close, she could see he must only have been about eighteen or nineteen and mentally, he seemed to be much younger.

'Well, you make sure you hold on to his lead properly next time,' Viv said softly.

'I will,' he replied. 'Where are you going, lady?'

'To Wildflower Cottage, the animal sanctuary,' replied Viv. 'Am I heading in the right direction?'

The young man brightened. 'Oh yes. That's where Pilot lives. Don't tell them, will you? They won't let me walk him again.'

'I promise I won't.'

'You need to turn right just after the café. It's on the corner. It's called the Corner Caff.'

'Thank you. That's very kind of you.'

'My name's Armstrong. If they ask, will you tell them that I'm doing a good job? I'm going to take Pilot for a biscuit at the bakery up the road. They make biscuits with liver in them especially for dogs. Pilot loves those.'

'I will,' smiled Viv.

'See you. Come on, Pilot.' And with that, Armstrong tugged on the lead and he and the giant shaggy dog began to lumber up the hill.

Viv set off slowly in case anything else should run into her path. She didn't want to start off her new job in an animal sanctuary by killing something. The café on the corner was painted bright yellow and hard to miss. She swung a right there and was faced with a stunning view of the bottom of the valley. In the centre of it sat a long cottage couched in a bed of fairy-tale swirls of low mist and to its left was a tall tower with a crenellated top. Viv's jaw tightened with nervousness as the car ate the distance towards it.

She parked as directed by a crooked wooden sign saying 'Visitors', at the side of a battered black pick-up truck. As she got out of the car, she noticed sprinkles of flowers in the mist, their violet-blue heads dotted everywhere she looked. The second thing she noticed was the biggest cat she had ever seen in her life walking towards her, muscles rippling under his velvet black fur. She'd thought her family cat Basil was huge but this guy was like a panther. The cat rose onto his back legs in order to brush his face against her thigh. As Viv's hand came out to stroke his head, a voice shrieked from the cottage doorway.

'For goodness sake don't touch him. He'll savage you.'

A tall, slim woman had appeared there. She was wearing a long flowery hippy dress and had a mad frizz of brown hair. 'He's called Beelzebub for a reason. Bub for short.' She walked towards Viv with her hand extended in greeting. 'Viv, I presume,' she said. 'I'm Geraldine Hartley. We spoke on the phone.'

Viv had rung the sanctuary as soon as she spotted the advertisement in the *Pennine Times* and after a surprisingly brief conversation, Geraldine had offered her the job right there and then, subject to a personal reference and an assurance that Viv had no criminal history or accusation of animal cruelty. The wage was basic, cash in hand, although meals were included as was a small grace and favour house.

Her friend Hugo, who now had a scientific research job down south in London had supplied a glowing appraisal of her abilities and character. She'd taken the risk of giving a false address in Sheffield and so far there had been no comeback. It wasn't the most professional organisation she'd come across.

Viv shook her hand. Geraldine had a very strong grip. She also had the most beautiful perfume. Viv instinctively breathed it up into her nose and her brain began to dissect the scent: *rose – definitely. Violet – probably. Orris . . . maybe.* It was floral, but with a hint of something else that she couldn't quite pin down. Complex, but there wasn't a scent yet that she couldn't separate into its basic elements, given time. Her olfactory senses judged it to be delightful and something that her mother would love.

'Welcome to Wildflower Cottage.' Geraldine brought her back into the here and now by lifting her arms and spreading her hands out towards the sky as if she were an evangelist about to address her congregation.

'It's so pretty here,' replied Viv, opening up her boot and taking out her luggage. 'The mist is very unusual.'

'We get a lot of it,' said Geraldine, lifting up one of Viv's suitcases. 'Come on in. I expect you're dying for a cup of tea. Or are you a coffee girl?'

'A tea would be lovely, please,' replied Viv. She didn't say that she was already full of tea having stopped off at a service station halfway through the journey and had two pots of the stuff whilst soul-searching at the table. *What are you doing?* her brain threw at her. *Have you really thought this through?* She had texted her mum and told her that she was stuck in traffic, because she knew she would be worrying why she hadn't been in contact to say she had arrived. She didn't ring because she thought that hearing her mother's voice might have had her abandoning her plans and running back home.

Viv followed Geraldine into a spacious, rustic kitchen-lounge with a heavy beamed ceiling, thick stone walls and a Yorkshire range fireplace. There was a massive furry dog bed at one side of a bright red Aga and a cushioned cat bed between a long oxblood Chesterfield sofa and an old-fashioned Welsh dresser. A bird with round angry eyes was hopping about on the stripped pine table in the centre of the room. Suddenly it took flight and swooped towards Viv, who ducked and screamed.

'Viv, meet Piccolo,' said Geraldine. 'He gets excited, bless him. We've had him from an egg which his sneaky mum hid from us. There's nothing wrong with him but he's imprinted on us. He thinks he's a cat with wings.' She called him and Piccolo flew towards her, landing on her hair. 'It doesn't hurt me,' she said, seeing Viv's look of horror. 'Unless I move too fast and he feels the need to grip on.'

She crossed to the Aga and put a large kettle of water on it to boil, still wearing her living breathing owl hat. 'You'll find that this is not your typical animal sanctuary.'

Bub swaggered in and over to Viv, butting her leg with his large head and making friendly chirrupy noises. She bent down to stroke him, remembering just in time to pull her hand back as his paw came out to strike her, claws extended.

'Told you,' laughed Geraldine. 'He's a duplicitous bugger, that one.'

'I met one of your helpers up the road,' said Viv, attempting to be friendly. 'Armstrong, I think he said he was called.'

'Armstrong Baslow, yes. Did he have a rather large dog with him? Please say yes.'

'Yes.'

'It's the first time I've let him take Pilot out. The old lad needed a walk and with being by myself at the moment, I haven't had time.'

'Pilot – that's Mr Rochester's dog in *Jane Eyre*, isn't it?'

'It most certainly is. You can blame me for that. But as a rule of thumb, if the name is ridiculous, it'll be something Armstrong has thought of. When Pilot first came to us, I thought he looked exactly as I'd imagined the Pilot in the book to be. Poor soul had been wandering around the moors for God knows how long. Someone had obviously dumped him. But he took to the name straightaway, bless him.'

She laughed and Viv warmed to the sound. Geraldine must be a nice person to have such a lovely, tinkly laugh, she decided.

'As for Armstrong's name, in case you're wondering, his father was a space enthusiast,' Geraldine continued. 'He died last year and they sent his ashes up to heaven in a firework, can you believe?'

Viv was hypnotised by the owl's antics. He was on the edge of the table now and seemed to be reprimanding the cat with angry flaps of his wings and squawks. Then he jumped down onto the floor beside him.

'Oh my God . . .' Viv shooed at the predatory Bub by her feet. She was sure she was about to witness the last few seconds of the bird's life.

Geraldine laughed as she watched Viv in full panic mode whilst Bub flashed her the sort of look he reserved for viewing things he'd done in his litter tray.

'Piccolo is safer than the rest of us with Bub. They have what Heath always calls "an affinity".'

'Heath?'

'Heath Merlo, the boss,' explained Geraldine. 'I thought

it was serendipitous that his name means "blackbird" in Italian. It was like a sign that you were the one we should take on. Mind you, we were hardly overrun with applicants.'

It was the first time Viv had heard mention of 'Heath'. She'd presumed that Geraldine was the one in charge.

'Heath is away with Wonk at the moment.' Geraldine went into further explanations. 'Wonk is our three-legged donkey. She's having a new prosthetic limb fitted because she's outgrown the other one.'

'You have a three-legged donkey here?'

'Yes. She had a rich owner who left us Wonk when she died on the proviso that we would look after her. Her legacy goes a long way to supporting us. Come on, I'll give you a very quick tour whilst the kettle is boiling. It takes an age and I don't help matters by always over-filling it.'

Geraldine beckoned her to follow and they left the owl cawing an angry protest at being left by himself with no one to entertain, stomping up and down the table on legs that looked too long for his small body. Viv was sure the low mist had thickened since she had arrived. Walking behind Geraldine, even at a close distance, Viv couldn't see her feet and it was as if she was floating.

'I've never seen mist like this before,' said Viv.

'It is unusual,' replied Geraldine. 'Legend has it that years ago the valley was a sacred lake inhabited by a water nymph called Isme who was trusted to look after all the creatures who lived in it, but she fell in love with the local bad boy – the Lord of the Manor's son. One day he stripped the lake of all of the fish and Isme's furious father forced his daughter to take revenge by dragging the young man into the lake and drowning him. Heartbroken, Isme withered away and the lake dried up with her until all that was left was a lingering mist and the wildflowers which had taken seed in the places where her tears had fallen.'

Viv bent down to a vibrant blue patch of them. 'Love-in-a-Mist. How beautiful.' She had recognised them immediately.

'I see you know your plants,' smiled Geraldine. 'They flower continually.' She picked out a plump purple seed case hidden inside its lacy netting. 'I think they're as pretty when they pod, don't you?'

They carried the faintest scent of strawberries tinged with smoke. Viv could pick it up, just, but it was almost missable, even to her.

'We'll start from furthest away and work our way in,' decided Geraldine. 'Our birds.' She lifted a large stiff leather glove from a hook outside the door and Viv wondered why she'd need that.

'At the back of the house, there, is our food preparation area,' said Geraldine, pointing to an outbuilding with an arched barn door. 'Do you want to see inside?'

'Not really,' said Viv. She guessed it wouldn't be full of packaged ready meals.

'Thought not,' grinned Geraldine. They walked down the dirt-track road. Viv didn't really need to see the birds – she'd hardly be interacting with them. And she didn't like birds even more than she didn't like other animals. The Alfred Hitchcock film *The Birds* encapsulated all her worst nightmares: their capriciousness, their flapping wings, their ability to peck out your eyes. She shivered at the thought and hoped they were all locked away.

They arrived at the aviaries clustered around a central grassy area where perches were studded into the ground.

'This is our flying arena,' explained Geraldine. 'And there are our birds. None of them would survive in the wild. They're all damaged in some way, poor dears.' She sighed. 'Come on, Vivienne, let me introduce you to our family.' Geraldine walked to the first cage.

Staring at Viv was a large tawny owl with the most beautiful feathery face.

'That's Melvin. He was found with terribly broken wings. He can fly after a fashion now but it's not a very good fashion. His partner in crime is Tink there.' Sharing the same shelter was a much smaller owl with eyes that seemed to take up half her head. 'They used to talk to each other through the wire, so Heath decided to test them in the same aviary and they bonded. It's very sweet to watch them when they are perched together. They lean on each other.'

Tink was tongue-clicking at Viv as if she was warning her off looking at her fella. Viv sent a silent psychic message that Tink had nothing to worry about – she would be staying as far away from them as possible.

They moved on. 'In here is Beatrice, our eagle owl. Rescued from a wardrobe – I kid you not – where a stupid prat was keeping her as a pet.' Geraldine shook her head in dismay.

Beatrice's orange-ringed eyes swung over Viv as if she were of no value.

'Come on in,' said Geraldine. 'Beatrice is a love.' She pulled the latch back.

'Are you kidding?' said Viv.

'No, not at all.' Geraldine opened the door.

'I . . . I can't,' said Viv.

Geraldine put her left hand into the glove.

'You'll be doing this in no time if you choose to. Beatrice

is a good one to start off with because she gets on with everyone.'

Viv would rather have eaten her own head than interact with birds. Especially large terrifying things like this one.

Beatrice started making a 'yarp' sound.

'That noise tells you that she's happy I'm around,' said Geraldine. 'She's bonded to me. And I've bonded to her, haven't I, girl?'

The bird lifted up its wings and seemed to rise up as if on a heat thermal, coming to perch on Geraldine's outstretched glove.

'I have arm muscles like you wouldn't believe,' chuckled Geraldine. 'She's quite a weight, I can tell you.' Geraldine gave the owl a scratch on her head as she addressed her. 'And you've just had your twentieth birthday, haven't you, my love? Okay, off you pop.' She jiggled her arm up and down but the owl gripped on.

'She's spoiled,' laughed Geraldine. 'Go on with you. I'm showing a guest around.'

In the next cage was a large white owl that started flapping her pepper-speckled wings as soon as they neared.

'Just as Beatrice loves everyone, Ursula hates everyone, even Heath.' Geraldine clucked at the bird in greeting. 'We keep trying to get her to trust us, but we haven't made a lot of progress, I'm afraid.'

The large white owl stared at Viv with 'I want to kill you' eyes and started bobbing her head up and down.

'Why is she doing that at me?' said Viv, feeling ridiculously intimidated.

'Well I never,' Geraldine said, raising her eyebrows.

'What?' asked Viv.

'That's very interesting. She's interacting with you.'

'Is she?' asked Viv.

'Yes, she most certainly is. She's taken her eyes off you to bend her head. That's a sign of trust.'

'Oh.' That bird was a rotten judge of character, thought Viv.

Geraldine grinned. 'There is no rhyme or reason why birds love you or hate you. They just do.' She pointed across to a cage. 'There's a red-tail hawk over there called Sistine that I found entangled in thorns and I nursed her back to health. But is it me she's grateful to? Oh no. She's Heath's girl.'

There were hawks and eagles and owls and the ugliest bird Viv had ever seen in her life: a white-headed vulture. The inside of his aviary looked like a Toys R Us for birds. He had a tyre on a rope, a ladder, a huge rubber Kong, a climbing frame.

'Frank turned up in a Manchester scrapyard. He can't see very well but he likes to play,' smiled Geraldine. 'He's likely to run off with the hosepipe when you clean him out.'

Viv hoped that Geraldine meant a general 'you' and not a specific one. She wouldn't be cleaning Frank out. Ever.

'Like fresh eggs for breakfast?' asked Geraldine as they made a slow walk back towards the cottage. 'We've taken in some ex-battery hens. They're just getting used to being outside and having room to move. They're learning to scratch for worms and insects and their egg yolks are lovely and golden as a result.'

That nearly put Viv right off eggs for life. She had always been quite squeamish and once hadn't eaten cod from the chippy for over a year after hearing that it ate any old rubbish it could get its jaws on, unlike the more discerning haddock.

The sanctuary was also home to three limping geese, all with deformed feet, who still managed to swagger around like drunken John Waynes; and a blind baby goat called Ray who was glued to the side of his sighted twin Roy. In a run with a wooden shelter in the shape of a giant Toblerone were two hedgehogs – a strange albino one who looked as if she would glow in the dark and another with incredibly short prickles, as if he'd had a tough-guy crew cut: they were introduced to Viv as Angel and Bruce Willis. They wouldn't survive in the wild, Geraldine explained. They'd taken in lots of hedgehogs over the years, and patched them up and sent them out again – but only if they knew they'd be safe. There was a huge black hairy pig called Bertie who had formed an attachment to a beautiful pair of shire horses who looked as if they were wearing shaggy fur boots. As soon as they spotted Geraldine, they started walking across their field towards her.

Even though there was a sturdy barrier between them, Viv instinctively took a few steps back.

'You don't have to be scared of Roger and Keith, duck,' said Geraldine. 'They're as gentle as spring lambs.'

'They're huge.' The hairs on the back of Viv's neck stood up as two tonnes of horse approached the fence. They could cause a lot of damage if they were suddenly spooked: flatten her like a pancake, kick her into Kingdom Come. She'd err on the side of caution, thank you, and not get too close.

'Roger and Keith have been at Wildflower Cottage for ten years,' explained Geraldine. 'Heath's father took in four shires from a disgusting farm near Saddleworth, but Pete didn't make it through the first night and we lost John only a few weeks ago.' She sighed. 'He was such a dear fellow. I'm only glad that he had a few safe, happy years with us.

He's buried in our graveyard with all his sanctuary brothers and sisters behind the house. I can't bear the thought if we have to—' She pulled herself up short and shook her head. 'Anyway,' she said then, as if she was forcing herself to move on. She extracted a tube of Polo mints from her pocket. 'Want to give one to the horses?'

Viv declined hurriedly.

Geraldine tilted her head and looked down into the eyes of the much shorter Viv. 'I must say, you're not at all what I expected.'

'Oh?'

'In a nice way, I mean,' Geraldine said. 'Some people have sounded perfect on the phone and when they arrive . . . well, I've known I've made a huge mistake. But I don't get that feeling with you. Though you're not at all confident around animals, are you?'

'I wouldn't do them any harm,' Viv replied quickly, to dispel any fears Geraldine might have on that score. 'But admin is more my thing.'

'Well, that's what we need really. Someone efficient. Heath has let things slide and hasn't got the time to sort out the backlog and I'm not very good at that sort of thing. I can't use computers and I don't like being on the telephone, as you might have been able to tell. I much prefer to roll up my sleeves and pull a pair of wellies on.'

'I passed a lady on a black horse when I drove down the hill. Is that one of your animals too?' asked Viv. Did she see Geraldine bristle slightly?

'No. That'll be Antonia Leighton. She lives up in the castle at the top of the hill. Let's go and get that cuppa,' said Geraldine. 'Are you hungry? That's one good thing about working here; everyone in Ironmist thinks we're starving, so they're always sending us cakes and bread from the bakery and pies, butter, vegetables, you name it. It's a very kind place.'

*So that was Antonia Leighton*, thought Viv. She hadn't recognised her because she looked very different from the smiling picture she had seen in the glossy magazine. She was the daughter of Nicholas Leighton, the man that her friend Hugo had said would be a very useful person to get to know. And he was the real reason why Viv was here.

# Milly Johnson
# AFTERNOON TEA AT THE SUNFLOWER CAFÉ

**Love and friendship bloom at the Sunflower Café ...**

When Connie discovers that Jimmy Diamond, her husband of more than twenty years, is planning to leave her for his office junior, her world is turned upside down.

Determined to salvage her pride, she resolves to get her own back. Along with Della, Jimmy's right-hand woman at his cleaning firm, Diamond Shine, and the cleaners who meet at the Sunflower Café, she'll make him wish he had never underestimated her.

Then Connie meets the charming Brandon Locke, a master chocolatier, whose kindness starts to melt her soul. Could he be her second chance at happiness?

Can the ladies of the Sunflower Café help Connie scrub away the hurt? And can Brandon make her trust again?

**Paperback ISBN 978-1-4711-4046-4**
**Ebook ISBN 978-1-4711-4047-1**

# Milly Johnson
# THE TEASHOP
# ON THE CORNER

Spring Hill Square is a pretty sanctuary away from the bustle of everyday life. And at its centre is Leni Merryman's Teashop on the Corner, specialising in cake, bookish stationery and compassion. And for three people, all in need of a little TLC, it is somewhere to find a friend to lean on.

Carla Pride has just discovered that her late husband Martin was not who she thought he was. And now she must learn to put her marriage behind her and move forward.

Molly Jones's ex-husband Harvey has reappeared in her life after many years, wanting to put right the wrongs of the past before it is too late.

And Will Linton's business has gone bust and his wife has left him to pick up the pieces. Now he needs to gather the strength to start again.

Can all three find the comfort they are looking for in The Teashop on the Corner? And as their hearts are slowly mended by Leni, can they return the favour when she needs it most . . .?

Paperback ISBN 978-1-4711-1464-9
Ebook ISBN 978-1-4711-1465-6

# Milly Johnson
# IT'S RAINING MEN

**A summer getaway to remember. But is a holiday romance on the cards . . .?**

Best friends from work May, Lara and Clare are desperate for some time away. They have each had a rough time of it lately and need some serious R & R. So they set off to a luxurious spa for ten glorious days, but when they arrive at their destination, it seems it is not the place they thought it was. In fact, they appear to have come to entirely the wrong village . . .

Here in Ren Dullem nothing is quite what it seems; the lovely cobbled streets and picturesque cottages hide a secret that the villagers have been keeping hidden for years. Why is everyone so unfriendly and suspicious? Why does the landlord of their holiday rental seem so rude? And why are there so few women in the village?

Despite the strange atmosphere, the three friends are determined to make the best of it and have a holiday to remember. But will this be the break they all need? Or will the odd little village with all its secrets bring them all to breaking point . . .?

**Paperback ISBN 978-1-4711-1461-8**
**Ebook ISBN 978-1-4711-1462-5**

## BANYAN TREE
~VABBINFARU~

# WIN A HOLIDAY OF A LIFETIME AT
# BANYAN TREE VABBINFARU IN THE MALDIVES!

### Included in the prize:

- A seven night stay at Banyan Tree Vabbinfaru in a Beachfront Pool villa for two people
- Full board basis, incl. soft drinks, excl. alcohol
- Return transfers from Male to Banyan Tree Vabbinfaru
- Two × return economy flights from London to Male up to a value of £700 per person
- Trip to be taken between 1 November 2017 and 30 April 2018 Blackout dates include 27 December 2017 – 5 January 2018

**To enter the competition visit the website**
**www.simonandschuster.co.uk**

Entrants must be resident in the UK only